EVERYTHING I WANT

K. L. SHANDWICK

THE EVERYTHING TRILOGY

Enough Isn't Everything

Everything She Needs

Everything I Want

Love With Every Beat

Just Jack

Everything Is Yours

ACKNOWLEDGMENTS

Cover design by Sofie at Hart and Bailey
Edited by Andie M Long Editing and proofreading services

Thank you to Kris, Julie, Russ, Tracy, Vicky, Carole my Beta readers and for giving me their support by encouraging me to keep going.

It takes courage to face the past and not allow it to affect the future, no matter how difficult that may seem. Traumatic events and tragic circumstances mar the lives of many people, but the scars remain largely internal.

Moving forward takes great courage and requires the right support. In this book Lily's friends demonstrate the skills needed to help her, but ultimately Lily herself, has to take responsibility, too. Life is about tough choices and staying true to your own feelings.

This book is encouragement to dig deep and test your boundaries in a positive way, and is written for all those who choose to meet those challenges head on.

Pete: My husband and best friend. Thank you for allowing me to neglect you to put this together, for feeding me, supporting me, being my sounding board and crash dummy for listening to the scenes! (I love you very much)

Chapter One

REMINISCING

"*J*eez, Lily, will you sit still for goodness sake? I won't be responsible if I injure you," Holly huffed as she used the flat iron on my hair. I grinned into the mirror at my gorgeous, tall, blond friend. "Sorry, force of habit, you know I'm not great at this stuff."

Holly twisted her lips and flicked her long, platinum blond hair, her big brown eyes smiling at me, as she wagged the straightener. "Well, that's because you don't like pampering. I don't know why I'm bothering, you're as cute as a button, and the men go ape shit for you, anyway," she teased.

Holly was a beautiful, straight-talking Texas girl. She had proven herself to be a great friend to me during the past two years that I had shared an apartment with her and Saffy—a friend from Oklahoma City. She had been Saffy's friend first, but when Saffy had abandoned us to move back to Oklahoma, Holly chose to stay with me in Florida.

Saffy had been a long-time friend of mine and I was so disappointed when she ran out on me after all the plans we'd made. None of them worked out. This was mainly due to my music studies and performing taking up almost every waking moment. Saffy had fallen into a relationship with Will, who I'd performed with. She'd begun dating him almost immediately after we had met him. However, she had some unresolved issues from a previous relationship, which led to a mistrust in men.

Neither Holly nor I knew about James, her previous boyfriend, or that she had even been in a relationship. Imagine how surprised we were to find out that this guy she secretly loved existed, and he had finally decided he loved her back. Apparently she couldn't live without him and transferred back to her home state to be with him.

And that happened just three months after I had moved halfway around the world to fulfil my part of the bargain between us.

After I had gone home for Christmas, Saffy had upped and left 'The Sunshine State' to move back to Oklahoma City leaving Holly and me high and dry. She never even discussed it with me, and she hadn't spoken to me since. I figured she probably couldn't face me now.

There was another added complication to all of this though. I'd had oral sex with Will one night, when he was still with Saffy. If I said it happened by accident, well the start of it anyway, I didn't think there was a person on earth who would agree with me.

So, although she never found out about it, I really couldn't judge her for anything that she did. In hindsight, I didn't hold her leaving against her. Being in a complex relationship with my ex-Alfie had blown my theories clean out of the water about what I was willing to do for love.

When I had swapped London for Florida at twenty-one years old, I was naïve and innocent. Though I'd never believed it at the time.

During the early months after my move I had made some incredible mistakes regarding my relationships with men.

Life had been simple before Alfie Black's proposition and the subsequent mistakes I'd made with Will and Saffy's brother, Matt. For quite a while my life had felt as if it were in a downward spiral. That was before I woke up to how depressed I was about how Alfie had treated me. He was my nemesis and it took long time for me to finally break free of him.

My mind flitted back to the chance meeting we had during my registration day at college. Even though we weren't together anymore it was the one day that would stay with me. When he made me that proposition I should have run a mile.

I was stupid to think I could do a no strings, sexual relationship. There was no way I could have handled something like that. But it appeared to be a solution to my curiosity about sexual desires. Alfie and I both lived and breathed music, and I was in a place where I didn't want the complication of a boyfriend...I mean, what in the Hell was I thinking?

It was probably the worst decision of my life to date, because I fell for him like a stone falling from a great height. I was so smitten with love for him, I struggled for a long time to go forward with my life after we split up.

These turbulent times during the first year of college were horrible for me. The highs and the lows I endured in the following months, when I was learning to live without him, were excruciating.

Alfie kept telling me for most of our relationship that he couldn't love me, but I fell for him anyway. The other thing about our complex relationship was, although he kept reiterating it to me, Alfie wouldn't or couldn't leave me alone.

It was as if he kept playing with, and plucking at, my heart even after he knew what my feelings were for him. Falling for Alfie was too easy. I couldn't believe how quickly I fell under his spell. But I was drawn to him before I even saw him.

I think I fell in love with his voice first, and when I saw

who it belonged to, I guess I just kept on falling for the rest of him as well. I couldn't take my eyes off of him. I still thought he was definitely the sexiest man alive.

Alfie was drop dead gorgeous. I'd never been so drawn to a man in my life like I was him. All I had to do was think of his name and he was instantly in my mind's eye. The image in there was not how he looked at the present time, but rather the man that was with me the night before he left me.

Tall, lean, and muscular, but not bulky, Alfie had a strong, athletic build. His beautiful, even features, and gorgeous, full lips were to die for. And apart from his amazing good looks he could wear just about anything and still ooze sex appeal. He was definitely a magnet for women.

When I thought about how his dark blond hair with sun kissed tips felt when my fingers sifted through it my heart ached. I knew I would never how soft it felt or the feel of his satiny, smooth, silky skin when the palms of my hands skimmed over his hard body.

Most of all, I missed his touch and the scent of him; his big strong arms always felt protective when they wrapped around me, and the way he I fitted into the contours of his frame when he pulled me against him.

Before Alfie I had been so single-minded about studying in Miami that I had never allowed myself to get involved with any boys at home, for fear of someone capturing my heart and putting an end to my plans with Saffy, but I never realized how much heartache would await me in my new venture.

Holly laid the straightener down on the countertop and met my gaze in the mirror. "Perfect." She smiled affectionately, before leaning in to hug me.

"I'm so proud of you, Lily. This is going to be a fabulous

day. We need to start getting dressed; it's nearly time
to leave."

She handed me a Buck's Fizz. "Only the one. I don't want
you staggering and slurring during your graduation. You know
how you get." She winked, and I chuckled at her playful
comment.

I stood and walked over to her as she began winding the
wire of the hair straighteners as she tidied them away, and
hugged her. "You have no idea what you did for my sanity,
Holly. I will never know how to thank you properly for all
that you've done for me during these past two years."

She flashed her gorgeous smile. "Oh, I have a few ideas on
that, don't you worry. I've been quietly making a list," she
teased.

I held her hand. "Seriously Holly, I could never repay you
for all the support you have given me. You pulled me back
from the depths of despair and put me back together again,
more than once."

I felt tears begin to well in my eyes.

"Yeah, I'm great like that. But like I said sweetheart, I
have a list, you'll pay alright." She teased again, trying to
make light of my genuine heartfelt thanks for her love and
guidance during some really horrible times. This was especially true during the previous eighteen months.

"Now then, Lily, we're not going to get all maudlin about
things today. This is a very happy day for you, honey. Let's get
you fixed so that you sparkle in that drab graduation gown
of yours."

With that, she bustled herself out of the bathroom and
into my bedroom before opening my closet door to find the
outfit we had shopped for together.

I pulled myself out of my funk and stepped into the black
and white, silk, figure-hugging dress that we had chosen. It

felt luxurious next to my skin. My golden tan made my blue eyes sparkle and the white of my eyes shine brighter.

Looking like any other girl from Florida now, my appearance was completely different compared to when I moved overseas with my creamy, pale skin and contrasting long, dark hair.

My hair had been cut and styled from the long, dark brown, curly hair I used to have. It was still long, but now cut into a style with long layers and fell midway down my back.

I always wore it straightened now, and it framed my face, seeming to make my blue eyes appear bigger. Holly loved it and said it was a 'grown-up's' haircut.

Holly turned the radio up. "I love this song. It makes me feel great when I hear it, but it also reminds me of you." She was referring to Bruno Mars 'Just the Way You Are'.

I smiled. It reminded me of her as well. The song was one of my favorites too. We had played this song in the car several times on the way to the Florida Keys, when we had a 'girlie' weekend last fall.

We both began to sing and dance around the room to the music, each of us trying to outdo the other as to who could sing it the loudest.

Holly grinned at me, and we burst out laughing after the song finished playing, and I turned to face the mirror. I began to put some mascara on, and my mind flitted to the boys who were coming to see me this afternoon.

My band, XrAid, consisted of four hot men plus me. They were guys who'd been my world for the last eighteen months. Cody, Lennon, Digs, and Shawn had shown me loyalty and had protected me from day one, and I loved all of them dearly. To be honest, I didn't know what I would have done if it hadn't been for them.

I think if they hadn't come into my life when they did, I

would probably be at home in London now, working in some dingy nightclub.

As if on cue, my cell buzzed. I swiped the screen, and Cody's ID flashed with a text message.

Cody: Good luck today babe. I hope you're wearing something that isn't too distracting up there. : wink.

I smirked at his text. My bandmates had a standing joke about how I looked. They were always ragging on me about what I was wearing and telling me I was too distracting if I wore something a little risqué.

It was obvious they were afraid I would meet someone and leave the band. I couldn't blame them; that was at the heart of how I had gotten my start with them. The original female in the band had met someone and left with him to follow his career.

They should know me better than that. I split up with Alfie for that exact reason. I couldn't give up everything I had worked for to follow his career, no matter how much I loved him. I knew I would have ended up resenting him further down the line if I did.

In another life, Alfie would have been, without a doubt, the perfect man for me. His appearance, the way we connected, and how he made me feel, were the things I still missed about him every day.

The way those hazel eyes took on that green hue when he looked at me, showing his desire for me. And how those same eyes had worshipped me with an intense stare, especially after he'd told me he was in love with me. How they looked as we locked eyes with each other.

Those same eyes, searching my soul when we made love, still made my throat constrict. A lump formed there, making it difficult to swallow, whenever that particular memory flashed back to our time together.

His eyes were a hazel color but they changed like mood

stones, and were mostly green when he was with me. They took on that green hue when he was turned on, excited, or angry.

When I thought of his eyes, memories flooded me of the times he hovered above me on the bed giving me his sexy, lopsided smile.

It always took my breath away and never failed to thrill me. When he smiled wide enough, the one dimple in his left cheek would appear and it melted my heart every time.

Alfie was a case of the right guy for me, at the wrong time, and in the wrong circumstances too. My heart had beat to his tune far too much at the time, and it had taken me a long time to feel okay about what had happened between us.

I always sighed when I thought of him. Apart from his looks, he was super talented as a musician, too. In private, he had turned me on with his passionate, lusty, intense stares, and drove me wild with desire. He'd seemed to be completely wrapped up in me behind closed doors yet treated me like dirt in public.

I just couldn't separate my emotions from a sexual relationship, so I tried to resist Alfie on multiple occasions during that first year. He was quite relentless in pursuing me, though.

He would turn up at my gigs or catch me on my own, playing his mind games and plucking at my heart strings. He even found me in London.

Every time I tried to resist him, he would tell me he 'needed to be with me', and that '"he wanted me'. Not enough to put me first though. I had never come first in Alfie's list of priorities, yet he still managed to break down my resistance to him.

Maybe if we had started out differently, with him being more honest with me, I would have felt more secure in the relationship. Who knows, I might have given everything up for him. Deep down, though, I knew that would just have made me bitter in the end.

I could analyze how things were and what might or might not have happened between us some time down the line, but it wouldn't change my reality.

Alfie was on the verge of being discovered when I met him two years ago. His band, Crakt Soundzz, had been signed, and he was going places. When it finally looked as though we could be together, and he had declared how much he loved me, I realized I couldn't be what he wanted from me. I had my own band and dreams.

Chapter Two

END OF AN ERA

*A*s painful as it was, I had ended things between us for the second time with a phone call. We had made love all night, the night before, then he'd left me without telling me, because he, "could never say goodbye to me."

I hadn't seen him face-to-face or spoken to him since. Although it almost broke my heart, it was the right thing for me. If I had given up my music to follow Alfie's dream, I just knew I would have lived to regret it.

Now Alfie was a global superstar, he'd gone from zero to millions of followers, idolized by women the world over. I felt hurt and a little sad every time I saw his name linked to various models and movie stars. I didn't actively follow how he was doing, it was just... unavoidable.

His beautiful image or voice seemed to be everywhere I went, like he was haunting me. His eyes always drew me to his image on posters or on web pages. They were a constant reminder of the way he used to stare at me intensely, unblinking, except for the hazel color staring back at me.

Apart from the pictures, live images on TV, chat shows and of course the unmistakable rich, deep timbre of his voice during radio interviews or when singing his music—which played on a loop on the radio stations and in stores—I didn't think about him at all. That's a lie, as well.

I coped okay with these constant reminders of him, but I had to admit, my heartbeat accelerated or sank depending on my mood, when I heard 'our song'.

As for me. I was tremendously busy with XrAid and loving every minute of it. My heart had mended to some degree, but I was too busy with the band to be in a relationship with anyone. I had gone out with guys for dinner and even kissed a few. However, that was the extent of my contact with the opposite sex.

Mostly, I spent time with my four bandmates; Holly and her fiancée, Brett; and my friends in London, Jack and Elle. Jack and Elle were still the two most important people to me, apart from my parents, and had stuck with me through thick and thin.

Jack was more than my friend though, he was my platonic soulmate, and we had been in each other's pockets emotionally since we were four years old. I'd like to think I never took Jack for granted, because he was the single most important person in my life. He was the family I chose.

Elle, on the other hand, was a free spirit. She happened to be engaged to Drew, the lead guitarist of Crakt Soundzz and one of Alfie's closest friends. If I were Elle, I would have felt weird being around Drew and Cody together; Elle had a 'thing' with Cody once too, but they all seemed fine together.

She met Drew for the first time when Crakt Soundzz played in London a couple of years ago, then met him again when she came to see me in Florida. Being with Drew had added a bit of a complication in our friendship, but we made it work.

Elle and I saw each other when Drew was over in the USA, or if we happened to meet up in London. Unlike me,

Elle gave up her career to follow her man and had spent the last eight months on a world tour with Crakt Soundzz. Being a dancer, Elle knew her career as a performer would have a limited shelf life.

We had an agreement that we wouldn't talk about the band. She could talk about Drew, but I didn't want her to tell me what was going on in Alfie's life.

"You all ready and set to go?" Holly's voice broke into my thoughts. I looked wistfully at her. "What?" She stared at me with bunched brows.

"Just thinking…"

She cut in, "Well, don't. Let's go." She tugged at my wrist. "Think of all the people that love and are waiting for you, honey." I smiled at her and nodded. "You're right. Come on, we don't want to keep them waiting in the sunshine."

Holly turned on the radio in the car as we headed to campus. The Fray 'How to Save a Life' was playing. We sat through it silently. To be fair, it was a great song.

Afterwards, the DJ said, "Now for one from one of my favorite bands, this is Crakt Soundzz, 'Insatiable'."

My eyes darted to look at Holly. This was the song that Alfie was writing the day we met. I had helped him with a line when he had hit a sticking point. That line? 'Music is the sound of feelings, and she listened to what he felt'.

The timing of the song, and hearing his voice, couldn't have been worse for me. It had been there at the beginning of my college time, and now there it was again, at the end. Holly quickly switched channels on the radio, and Kelly Clarkson's 'What Doesn't Kill Us Makes Us Stronger' filled the car.

My eyes had been welling up with tears, but we both burst out laughing. "Now Lily, listen to Kelly, that's definitely a sign your college days are over." She chuckled and leaned over to squeeze my hand. Sucking back the tears, I forced myself to smile.

We arrived in the college parking lot just in time to stop my mood sinking beyond the point of no return. I dug deep and struggled not to cry, it was hard hearing his voice singing that song and I felt a desperate feeling of loss for a moment.

Waiting for me was Will, Mandy, Neil, and Nick and they were the perfect distraction from Alfie. Will strode over and hugged me tightly. I was happy to see him. We went through a lot in the early days of college. Despite everything that happened between us Will had taken me under his wing when I first arrived. Musically, Will, was an amazing saxophone player and we had been good together, until one night of insanity between the both of us nearly ruined our friendship.

I didn't know how, but we managed to recover from it. Maybe it was because we were both playing music in bands now, and not working together. Anyway, I was so happy that we were able to remain friends; he meant a lot to me.

Mandy and Neil were with Will the first day we met, and it was actually Mandy's invite to watch them perform that began the friendship between all of us.

I remember envying Mandy's sense of identity back then; she looked fabulous with her petite frame and dark, almost black, edgy, bobbed hair. She seemed so self-confident then and was a brilliant singer.

Who would have thought I would progress to be more successful than she was, with my career to date? Strange how fate took that turn with me.

There had been a few ups and downs between Mandy and me. She was still in contact with Alfie, but we had the same arrangement as I did with Elle. I didn't want to know about Alfie's life, and I didn't even suppose he'd be that interested in mine these days.

Nick was Neil's friend first, but was now also one of mine. If he hadn't invited me to an 'Open Mic' when I was at a low point after Alfie, I would never have met Louie Dyer or been invited to audition for XrAid.

Nick always had a soft spot for me. He was a great-looking guy, tall and muscular with dark brown cropped hair, chiseled sharp features, and almost black eyes. He had olive skin, and the way he seemed to always have a five o'clock shadow of hair growth to his jawline made him very appealing.

Although he was very attractive we'd never been anything but friends. I was really glad about that. He was the kind of guy that didn't let girls get close. I'd lost count as to how many girls I'd been introduced to by him in the past two years.

Although Nick was instrumental in Louie discovering me, I liked to think that fate had more to do with my life than I had given it credit for. I had always thought we made our own luck in this world.

All of us stood in line to collect our graduation cap and gown. We had opted for a rental company who provided them. None of us wanted dusty old graduation gowns hanging around for the next forty years.

"Sexy!" Nick chuckled at the strange cap and gown with my killer heels. "Do you have any black rimmed spectacles you could put on, Lily. I feel a fantasy coming on."

Will let out a loud, rumbly, belly laugh, and Neil snickered, but his eyes flicked to Mandy, checking to make sure he hadn't been caught getting involved in their banter.

We took our places in the rows of seating at the front of the auditorium. I knew that there were a lot of people rooting for me back there in the 'spectator' section.

I had seen my mother, father, and Jack, when they arrived last night. Jack had brought his girlfriend, Rosie, with him. He joked that she might be a keeper, because she was named after a flower just like me. It felt weird to have him here in Miami, but not with me at the apartment.

I was very fortunate that Will's surname was Patterson. We were placed in alphabetical order, and because I was Parnell, it meant that he was sitting next to me.

Will clutched my hand and squeezed tightly. "You look wonderful." A wide smile spread over his face when he glanced affectionately at me. "Life friends, Lily, right?"

I smiled back at him. "Absolutely."

We all sat patiently, if a bit bored, while Dean Hockney droned on about how well this year's group had done and how proud he was of each and every one of us. Then we had to file row after row up toward the stage to collect our pretend parchment paper with a red ribbon tied around it. The real diplomas were being sent to us through the mail. It was all about the ceremony and what it symbolized.

There were a few people that had gotten loud cheers, and the rest of us instinctively knew they were either the 'bad boys', or there was some kind of special story behind them being up there today.

When the ceremony was over, we went to find our visitors. Jack gave me his usual greeting, running toward me with his legs slightly bent and his arms wide to receive me. "Oh. My. God. You look absolutely ravishing in that, you don't have any eye glasses do you?"

I snickered and looked past him to my parents. My eyes caught the look on Rosie's face, and boy, she looked pissed over Jack's comments. I made a mental note to have a word with him about toning his flirting down.

"Thank you for coming," I said, making a special effort with her to appease Jack's behavior. She nodded, but I didn't miss her pursed lips and narrowed eyes as she regarded me. My immediately thought she was going to be hard work.

My mother pushed past her. "Lily, darling, I am so proud

of you. I can't believe how much you have grown as a person since you came here. I'm glad I talked your dad into accepting your choice to study here." I grinned at my dad. My mom never missed a chance to get back at him if he was wrong about something.

When my mom released me, I moved over to my dad and cuddled him tightly. He whispered in my ear, "My beautiful little girl's all grown up now, huh?"

Tears pricked my eyes and I squinted up at him; the sun was behind his shoulder and made his face difficult to see. "I guess...since I'm almost in my mid-twenties," I answered, smiling, and he kissed the top of my head.

Suddenly I heard a loud whistle behind me. Turning to look I saw my bandmates standing grinning at me. Lennon asked, "Anyone comment on that hot outfit you're wearing yet?"

Jack smirked. "Beat you to it, mate." He grinned, looking smug.

I smirked and shook my head. "Actually, Nick beat all of you, even down to your spectacles comment, Jack."

He muttered, "Jesus, the guys here are predatory. I hope you're taking precautions, beautiful."

Rosie shifted from one leg to another.

"Don't mind the silly talk, Rosie, these guys are all hot air." I smiled, trying to include her, but she threw me a dagger-look back. Somehow, I knew we'd be having words at some point but definitely not today.

Louie—our band manager and owner of three of the best nightclubs in Miami—had arranged for my friends and me to have our graduation party at D'mond, one of his clubs.

We were due to play the day of our graduation and I asked him to keep us on the usual schedule. My parents had never been to one of our gigs yet, and I wanted them to see the progress I'd made.

Afternoon drinks were arranged on one of the balconies at D'mond, and the setting was lovely. Will's dad came, and I met all my friends' parents in one hit. Everyone got along well, and I was so happy to see that they mingled easily with each other. Cody signaled to me when it was time for my sound check. I slipped out and went through it with the sound guys, then headed back to let them know I would see them after our performance.

Lennon wandered over and put his arms around my shoulders from behind. "So... you're ours now." He smirked. "Now, we can really get to grips with our music!" He grinned again then scooped me up in a hug.

As a band, we had collectively been writing like mad which had resulted in some great songs for our album. Louie had introduced me to Barney Sherman, a producer, who was showing more interest in us as recording artists.

Barney had told me that when I finished college he'd set up a meeting for the guys in XrAid to discuss our development as a band. I was fully on board and mentioned this to Louie. As far as our club manager was concerned, we were bound to get signed, and he had no intentions of interfering with any chance we might have in the bigger scheme of things.

Once I had changed into my outfit for the gig, in the bathroom, I wandered into the dressing room wearing some leather hot pants and a baggy, green, silk top that hung off one of my shoulders. It exposed part of my black lacy bra on underneath and I rounded the ensemble off with my signature stilettos. "Fuck," Lennon grunted when he looked at me. "You're just determined to try my patience now. I don't want guys leering at you, Lily. Put something else on."

Grinning at him, I shook my head. "Get a life, Lennon." Digs and Shawn erupted in a bout of raucous laughter, instantly remembering something Cody had said at my audition for the band. Cody had commented on my appearance that day, saying something like, with the way I looked he would have to learn to bounce around on stage with a permanent hard on. I had flushed, but stood my ground.

"Fine! Wear it, don't mind me," he snickered.

"I think Lennon needs a girlfriend," I quipped. Shawn spurted out his soda drink and nodded exaggeratedly.

"Stop it, you're killing me. What happened to the innocent little English girl we used to know?"

I smirked. "Guess she grew up fast being around you guys. So watch out... all of you."

Digs high-fived me and smirked knowingly back at me. "Yeah baby, you're one of the guys now, huh?" It was more of a statement than a question, so I just smiled back at him and winked. To think, I was afraid of him in the beginning because of his tattoos and Mohawk. But he was actually a really hot guy and one of my best allies.

Chapter Three

TOUGH DECISIONS

*A*lthough I had been playing in Louie's clubs for almost two years, it never got old. I still got nervous stepping out in front of everyone. That didn't mean I wasn't confident though.

I was a far cry from the meek girl that crept out on stage for my first gig with XrAid. I was pretty recognizable in stores too these days.

The occasional club goer would approach me to tell me they loved the gig they had seen at one of the clubs. It was cute when that happened.

It seemed strange to see my parents standing in front of me tonight. We were used to people in their teens, twenties, and occasionally their thirties, as our audience.

I played well, and as usual, Cody and I had a real rapport going with the crowd up there. The best part was seeing the look on my dad's face when he saw me rock out with Lennon on our guitars. I almost burst out laughing as he began to get carried away by our music.

We finished our set, and everyone got together again out

at the front of the bar. Before I could speak, Jack pushed in front of everyone. "Mine! First dibs on the dancing," he called out.

My eyes flicked to Rosie, and I pulled on the hem of Jack's t-shirt. He leaned into me, and I spoke into his ear. "You need to tone it down, Jack. You're making your girl uncomfortable."

Jack turned his head in her direction and sure enough, Rosie's face was like thunder. Her eyebrows were knitted tight, and if her mouth pursed any more it would have looked like a butt hole.

Jack looked back and chuckled. "Damn, she does look pissed, huh?" I nodded and gave what I hoped was a sympathetic smile in Rosie's direction. "Hmm, this is a difficult dilemma," Jack said. "Do I wait until tomorrow and piss her off by telling her we're not changing or do I do it now? The thing is if I make her deal with us now, I'll need to accept that I won't get laid tonight." He looked confused by the choices he had given himself.

Jack's eyes flicked to Rosie then back to me. "I'll be right back, bathroom break." He walked off in the direction of the men's restrooms.

Cody leaned in. "What was that about?" I told him, and Cody mumbled, "Poor Rosie, she's going home alone tonight, huh?"

I scowled at Cody. "What makes you say that?"

Cody chuckled. "Seriously, Lily? He's never going to put anyone before you, even if they have a vagina that does tricks." I couldn't help but giggle at Cody's comment.

"Ask her to dance Cody, please... for me?" Cody's eyes flicked across at her, and he smiled. Her face froze, and then she cracked him a forced smile.

He looked back at me and sighed. "Poor girl, next you'll

be asking me to fuck her so that Jack can go home and spoon with you."

I smirked, and I fought for it not to turn into a wicked grin. "Damn, you're thinking about that now, jeez, Lily." He walked up to Rosie and bent his head close to her ear. Cody was used to getting his way with women. He could be charming and attentive, and he was extremely hot looking, too.

He took Rosie by the hand, his other hand gently placed at the small of her back as he led her toward the bar. I saw his hand go up from her back as he signaled with two fingers. The bartender placed two shot glasses and a bottle of tequila on the bar.

Good boy. Cody had taken her to loosen her up a little before heading to the dance floor. Maybe he'd tell her that she had nothing to fear with our relationship, but if he did that, I knew he'd also tell her not to mess with it because she'd only get hurt.

By the time Jack came back, he looked way more relaxed than when he went to the men's room. "Okay, Lily, dance time."

I looked puzzled. "What about Rosie?" I wondered what he was doing and raised one eyebrow.

He looked over at the bar where she was standing. "What about her? If she can't deal with us, then it's best we figure that out now, don't you think?"

I shook my head. "Jack, that isn't fair to her; you need to consider her feelings too."

Jack twisted his mouth, and sighed heavily. "Well, I was thinking about that." He stared into my eyes. "What do we do? Do we hide how we feel about each other, so that someone else can be happy? What if that made *me* unhappy? What if I couldn't ever be spontaneous around you? Or you, with me? Would you be happy with that?" I thought about what he was saying and realized that I had been upfront with Alfie about Jack.

My thoughts were that Alfie had to deal with our friend-ship. It wasn't even an option that I would cut *my* affection for Jack out of the equation.

I understood how he felt, but it had to be Jack's choice. I wasn't going to ruin his happiness so that we could continue to flirt and cuddle. "Let's put our other flower to the test. Either way, we'll both know where we stand," Jack said. It didn't feel right to me to put Rosie in this situation, but Jack wasn't giving me a way past this.

He pulled me onto the dance floor and began dancing with me, his hands on my hips as we swayed to the music. His eyes flicked over to her. "Good sign, she's not got her gun out yet." He winked.

I giggled. "You're a bad man, Jack."

He snickered. "Not bad ass enough for you though, eh? I mean, I don't have a bejeweled dick or anything like that."

His smile froze on his lips. "Sorry, that was out before I thought about what I was saying. Don't let it ruin the night." I knew that Jack was joking, but he had made reference to Alfie's genital piercing. It was an innocent flirty joke from Jack, but his choice of humor left me feeling more than a little off balance.

"C'mere." He grabbed me and tugged me into his chest, his big strong arms wrapping around my waist. I inhaled Jack's familiar scent. It was comforting, and his breath smelled of tequila and limes, as his mouth passed over my face.

He kissed my forehead as we swayed to the slow music. "I wish I could wipe him out of your memory."

I swallowed hard before answering. "Me too, Jack, but I'm doing fine now." I smiled up at him.

"Sorry for the..." I shook my head. "No need, Jack, I know

it was a slip." We finished dancing, and I excused myself to go to the bathroom.

Rosie and Mandy were nowhere in sight. As I went to push the restroom door, I overheard Mandy talking.

"You have no idea. If you love Jack, then you'll accept Lily. She is no threat to you, except if you try to come between them. Jack loves Lily like he would love his own child, with a whole layer of his heart. If you want a layer of Jack's heart, you'll love her, too. There will be no compromise on that."

I heard her use the toilet. "Those two would never cross the line into a sexual relationship. It's complex, but beautiful, what they have. Accept it, or walk away, Rosie. Sooner or later you'll realize that's the choice you'll have to face."

I pushed the door open and smiled when my eyes met Mandy's. "Hey guys, what's happening? Did you enjoy the gig, Rosie?" I could see that she was struggling, so I quickly added, "You don't know what it means for Jack to invite a girl. You must be very special, Rosie." She smiled, and I knew we were alright—for now.

Holly and Brett showed up late to the club; she had gone straight to work after my graduation ceremony. Brett kissed my cheek. "Hiya beautiful, congratulations."

I hugged Brett, and he signaled to the waitress, circling his arm around the drinks on our table. He made a small movement with his thumb and forefinger like he was holding a shot glass.

She nodded and went to get shots for everyone. She brought back a bottle of tequila, some salt and limes, and a bottle of Jack Daniel's.

It was comical watching my mother take a shot of tequila. Jack quipped, "Way to go Roslyn, my turn for some of that dirty dancing next."

He winked, and my mother nearly choked at the thought.

My dad smirked and muttered, "Yeah, and I get to swap with Rosie."

Lennon's eyes went wide with surprise. "Jesus, you are all incestuous, and they say that some parts of America are full of inbred folks." Everyone chuckled, staring at Lennon and his attempt at making a joke.

Digs chuckled and his eyes flew over to the far side of the bar, narrowed then flicked back to Jack. His head nodded in the direction he wanted Jack to look at. I followed Jack's gaze and froze.

Elle was walking toward me with a grin on her face, looking pleased with herself. "Hey!" She smirked at me and the surprised look I must have been sporting. "Well, well, and what do we have here?" She glanced at my half-drunk parents, smirked, and rolled her eyes then nodded briefly at Jack, before sweeping in towards me for a tight hug.

"You didn't really think I was going to miss your big day, did you?" Tears sprung to my eyes, but I was completely stoked that she had come to see me.

Drew stood behind her, his hand on her shoulder, smiling at me nervously. He looked affluent, and well-groomed. When Elle moved aside, Drew and I had a hesitant moment before he rushed forward.

"Come here, you," he cooed, his large arms wrapping around me as he tugged me in tightly against his chest.

Drew kissed the top of my head. "I hear you've been doing great things, Lily." He rubbed the back of my shoulder while he spoke to me. It was great to see him, but painful at the same time.

This was the first time I'd seen anyone from Alfie's band since the last time we were here in the club well over a year ago.

I'd promised myself a happy day, and I wasn't going to let anything upset me. "Yeah, well, Elle tells me that you've been busy too. She seems to be somewhere different every time I try to meet up with her."

It was the best I could do. I didn't want to talk about his band. I hated that our conversation was strained, but everything else I'd done was the same as when he left.

Louie sent my parents, Jack, and Rosie, back to their hotel in his car. The driver came back for me and the guys afterwards and drove us all to Lennon's place. We had all arranged to stay at his house tonight, so that we'd be able to organize the food for a cookout for all of our friends and my parents tomorrow.

Lennon was lucky enough to have a pool, and I was really looking forward to sitting around it and spending some quality downtime with Jack, and my parents.

When we all got to Lennon's, Digs crashed on a large metal hammock that looked really comfortable, but sat randomly in the corner of the large sitting room.

He was out like a light. Shawn stretched up with his hands above his head, his t-shirt riding up out of his dark blue jeans. He let out a loud grunt. "I guess I'll go upstairs and get naked, no bathrooms down here for me to wander in and out of anyway." He winked then flashed us a cheeky grin.

Cody punched him in the side of the arm. "Dang, Shawn you mean we'll miss out on that cute way you scratch your nuts when you're looking for something?" I snickered, but kept my mouth shut.

Lennon, Cody, and I flopped down on his large sectional after he found some sodas and water for us to drink. "Great night, Lily. Your folks are a hoot. I'm just a teeny bit jealous of you and everyone that you have around you."

I knew that Lennon's dad had skipped out on his mom and him when he was little. "You don't have to be jealous Lennon, they're your folks as well now; we're family."

I got up and sat on his knee, planting a kiss on his forehead. I heard him swallow audibly at my gesture, before his eyes met mine. A slow smile curved his lips. "You have no idea what that means to me."

We sat around talking about how the band could be better. We discussed how we should deal with the loads of song material we had, and I agreed to call Barney next week. This should give us time to select and record a demo tape of the best of what we had, to showcase XrAid at Barney's label.

We talked about what we could do to raise the profile of the band. Cody muttered, "Pity about the festival."

Lennon shot him a look, and Cody winced briefly, then his face went passive. Lennon sat forward on the couch. He placed his hands between his open knees then rubbed his hands together. "Festival? What festival?" I looked puzzled at both of them and wondered what in the Hell they were talking about.

Lennon's eyes flicked to Cody, and he scowled, "It's nothing, it didn't come to anything." Cody shifted uncomfortably, and Lennon shook his head at him when he thought I wasn't looking. I could see they were lying.

"Okay, what am I missing here?" I stood up and slapped my hands on my hips, walking around the sectional. Lennon's eyes followed me, running his hands over his head nervously. "We were invited to play at the 'On the Verge of Fame' Festival."

I knew all about music festivals and what they could do for a band. This one in particular was a huge deal. This was a music promoters' gig that was seen as a huge stepping stone into wider recognition for bands. It was by invitation only.

Some of the best bands in the world had started at this particular event, and I knew that 'music suits' used these gigs in search of the next big thing.

"Wow! And we're not going, why?" Cody stood up and wandered over beside me, placing his hands on my shoulders.

We stood eye to eye with him gazing at me sympathetically. "They always have a big band to headline. The headliner this year is Crakt Soundzz. We're not going, Lily." I took a minute to digest what he was saying to me. These guys were willing to sacrifice everything because of my previous relationship with Alfie?

I looked between them, and Lennon gave me a small smile. "It's okay, Lily, we discussed it between us, we all feel the same." I was angry and hurt, they had been talking behind my back and discussing what was best for me without discussing it *with* me.

"Am I even part of this band or just window dressing? No one fucking discussed it with me," I spat, annoyed at their efforts to keep something this important from me.

Lennon sat looking up at me with his elbows balanced on his knees, his hands spread out at me, palms up. "We don't want to put you through that, Lily. We know what splitting from that guy did to you."

I shook my head, trying to be measured in my response. "So... you'd put my personal life before what's best for the band? You're all unbelievable. Touched as I am, this is about our careers here. Not my love life, or the lack of it. If this had been Cody or any of the others and a girl, would you have considered not going?"

Cody grimaced at Lennon. "She has a point, Dude; we would still have played regardless."

I smirked, exhaled loudly, and threw my hand out at Cody. "See? We still have time right? You didn't tell them we wouldn't be going did you?"

Lennon began to protest, "But it means..."

I cut in. "Damn, Lennon, I know exactly what it means, and I'm fine with it."

"It's in two weeks, Lily. You can face him again without going to pieces like before?" Lennon asked, clearly worried. I twisted my mouth. I was angry with Lennon, but my heart burst with the consideration he was trying to show me about potentially having to face Alfie again.

"It's been over a year, Lennon. I pretty much doubt we'd run into them during the event anyway. We're small fry compared to them."

I huffed, and Cody walked over and sat back down. I squeezed between them and took their hands in mine. "Look, they'll be somewhere separate from us. Besides, there isn't any rule that says I have to stay there after we've performed. Crakt Soundzz is the headline act, so chances are we'll have played and gone by the time they even get there." I smiled, trying to reassure them that it would be okay to accept the offer.

Lennon still looked worried. "If you're sure... I'll call them later."

I smirked, feeling smug that I had won the argument. "You do that, Lennon; there's nothing and no one that is going stop us as a band. Do you hear me? I gave Alfie up to do this, Lennon. Don't you get it? I walked away from his life to follow my own dreams."

Cody pulled me against him and kissed my cheek, offering me support for my admission. I glanced up smiling at him. "We're playing at 'On the Verge of Fame' OMG!" He chuckled.

It took some convincing for Shawn and Digs to get that I really wanted to go perform at the festival, but once I had them on board, we had intense rehearsals during the following two weeks.

We knew we had an hour slot at the event. Some of the bands were only given half an hour, because they didn't have sufficient material the sponsors felt they wanted to hear. We must have impressed somebody, somewhere.

On the day of the festival itself, I was getting dressed, and

I had some killer heels that I wanted to wear with my outfit. I was having difficulty locating exactly where I had put them and was rummaging through my closet.

I crouched down low, pulling out boxes, trying to find the shoebox containing the navy blue Jimmy Choo shoes. I had almost forgotten I had them. It had been so long since I'd worn them.

I knew I bought far too many shoes when I could almost forget I had these! As I stood up, I bumped into the pole I used to hook on to things when I needed to retrieve items from the top shelf.

It accidently knocked against my memory keepsake box and sent it tumbling to the floor spilling the contents. A picture of Alfie and me wrapped in each other's arms lay on the floor, taunting me from where it had landed. There we were; Alfie and me, the once briefly happy couple. The smiles and mutual looks of adoration between us, as we looked at each other, had been captured in the photograph perfectly.

My eyes immediately filled with tears at the sight of this picture. It reminded me of a day we had spent on the beach. We had spent the whole afternoon lying there, in a romantic embrace, until the sunset.

I gathered up my keepsakes from the floor and scooped them back into the box. My eyes fell on the letter Alfie had written to me. My heart skipped a beat at the sight of it. He'd written it a couple of weeks before I ended things.

My fingers were shaking as they unfolded the paper. I sat quietly reading; remembering the effect the letter had on me at the time. I was delighted with it back then and couldn't have been happier to get it. Seeing it again, it still had the same effect on me. It was like a punch to my heart.

To my beautiful, incredible, amazing girl who holds my heart.

Today my life is perfect. Thank you, darling, for giving me another chance. I won't squander it, I promise. I love you too much to ever let you go again. I will try with all of my heart never to let you down again. You make the sun shine brighter, music sound sweeter, and my heart feel fuller. I could never do justice to how I feel about you, or the love I have for you, by trying to express those feelings in words. I need you to breathe. You are like pure oxygen to me. When I touch you, we are amazingly connected. I think somehow my feelings radiate throughout your body. Your feelings ignite mine. You once gave me the perfect lyric for my favorite song, 'Listen', and I hope when I next play for you, you'll listen to my feelings for you. Until then, know that you have my heart, my body, my soul, and all that I am. I am yours and you are mine, always and forever. I love you. These words are hollow and nowhere near what I want to convey to you, Lily, but I will do whatever it takes to be everything you need.

Alfie x

My heart cracked in two, and I began to cry. I still loved him so much, but I knew I had to stay strong. I shook my head as if to try to shake the memories from my brain and stuffed everything back in the box.

I didn't even know why I kept those trinkets. We had been over for a long time now. I pushed the box to the side and placed others on top of it. I trembled when I thought about the potential reality that I faced.

It was a distinct possibility that I might just bump into him at the festival, if I was unlucky. Before the timely appearance of the memory box, I had been mentally preparing myself just in case I saw Alfie.

My confidence had begun to wane and I wondered if I'd be able to keep it together. I had to find the confidence for XrAid, as well as myself, no question about it.

I kept telling myself if I came into contact with him I was going to keep it light and professional. I really didn't believe it would happen though.

There were eight stages, and Crakt Soundzz was playing on the biggest one at the end. Never for a moment did I think we'd end up playing on the same stage, but that's exactly what the running order said when it was emailed to us.

All the bands on our stage had an hour slot. XrAid was fourth in the running order. So, there was a three hour gap until Crakt Soundzz took the stage. I figured we'd be long gone by then.

Holly stared past me into the mirror, where I was applying kohl to my eyes. "Are you sure about this, honey?"

I smiled softly and turned to face her. "Honestly, Holly, Alfie's long over. I purposely didn't put myself in situations where he was, because I didn't want any more angst about our situation. I think I can safely say we're both over it now."

She hugged me tightly. "Well, if you're sure."

I smirked and tried to sound convincing. "Positive," I concluded with what I hoped was a finality to my voice, even if it wasn't what I was feeling.

Lennon came over and picked me up with the rest of the guys apart from Digs. Lennon told me that Digs was coming under his own steam, since he was bringing his sister.

The radio was blaring, and Shawn was already getting into the zone, tapping out the percussions in time to a song I had never heard before.

"Damn, wish we'd written this. I could have done so much better with it." He sounded frustrated about the percussions. I smirked at him, and he held his hands up. "What... I definitely could have." He grinned, and his eyebrows rose up into his hairline.

We arrived at our stage area to check out the running order. Lennon's eyes scrolled down the list, and his head spun to stare wide-eyed at me. His face had gone pale, and I just knew there had been a last minute change that would affect me.

"We've been moved up to sixth now. "Cody looked at me,

and I tried hard to appear unaffected. Damn, it was too close to Alfie's slot for comfort.

I schooled my face, smiled, and put on a brave face. "It's fine, guys, I'll do my bit, but I'd appreciate if you would grab my stuff afterwards. I'll just head out as soon as we've finished playing."

Lennon nodded. "Sure thing, sweetheart."

Chapter Four

BUMPING CHESTS

The festival itself had a fantastic buzz. There were all kinds of people, young and old, and the music was extremely loud. We walked around, checking out the competition, and I actually began to enjoy myself.

Maybe I was relaxed, because in the back of my mind, I knew Alfie would never be out here among the crowds of people. He was far too famous to do that. He would get mobbed.

Lennon and the others were happy to hang out there with me until we had to check in backstage. We made arrangements with the production team to be in our dressing room thirty minutes before our set. They knew we were there, and what we were doing.

In my mind, it was less likely I'd have any awkward moments coming face to face with Alfie, Drew, or any other Crakt Soundzz band members.

I stood out front watching the band before us. They had an hour set as well. The daylight had faded, and it was dusk by the time they had started.

I was pleased we were getting to perform outside in the

dark. I had only ever done that once before at a beach party
—when I performed with Will when I first came to Miami.

I had loved the atmosphere that night. I smiled to myself,
thinking I had come a long way from the innocent little girl I
was then.

Glancing at my phone, I saw it was almost thirty minutes
until we were up for our set. The guys left me ten minutes
ago and headed back there to give me a buffer before I joined
them.

I headed to the side of the stage and wiggled the backstage pass on my lanyard at the security guy. He was standing
guard at the barriers, which separated the public from a huge
set of black curtains. They provided a screen to protect the
artists from the crowd.

He moved the metal barrier and smiled as he waved me
inside. I asked where the XrAid dressing room was, and he
pointed to an area with makeshift dressing rooms that were
painted mainly black, like plywood encased, porta-cabins.

On the door was a laminated name tag, which bore our
familiar logo in black, white, and silver: XrAid.

I pushed the door open and saw Shawn pulling up his
pants. He'd obviously just been changing into them. "Argh,
quick get me some bleach for my eyes," I shouted, pretending
to be blinded.

"Didn't someone tell you that it isn't the army you signed
up for? It's a band, Shawn. You're not a commando. It *is* okay
to wear briefs now and again you know." I smirked and
pretended to look disgusted.

Cody and Digs chuckled and quipped in unison, "And,
she's back!"

I had long ago forgotten about modesty when I was
dressing in front of the guys. I pulled my t-shirt over my head
as I walked over to the suit bag in the corner.

Pulling out a little jade green, leather, thigh length dress from it, I pulled it over my head and smoothed it down the front of me.

"Fuck," Lennon grunted.

My eyes flicked to his. "Do we really need to go there with my outfit again? Now? Today?"

He shook his head, and I took my black patent six-inch stiletto heels out of my bag. "Fuck, I know you've heard this before, but damn you have hot legs in those," Digs muttered.

"Digs, shoes don't keep your legs warm... they keep your feet warm, honey." I smirked and continued to slip the second shoe on. Cody snickered but said nothing, and I turned my head to Shawn. "Comments?"

He shook his head. "I'm quitting while I'm ahead... I *am* ahead, right?"

I chuckled and pulled on the door handle, just as the five minute knock came. "If you say so, Shawn."

When I opened the door, and began to stride out, I walked straight into a solid wall of muscle. His body heat instantly radiated toward mine as soon as our chests collided.

His smell instantly drew me in, and I had a tingling sensation inside of me, which coursed through my veins, as his hands gripped the bare flesh on my arms. His touch ignited a rash of goosebumps over my flesh and a pool of moist, wet, slick juice trickled into the thin material between my legs.

Outwardly, the effect of him being there almost paralyzed me. Even after a year or more, the sight and smell of him affected me so much. It was truly a heart-stopping moment as I stood there feeling dizzy, my throat constricting, and I found swallowing impossible. I looked up slowly. Just seeing the silky skin of his neck made me want to press my lips to it.

Alfie was standing right in front of me. A ghost from my past. He looked perfect. His tongue darted out, making his plump lips look positively edible. "Hey," he cooed, his eyes lighting up as he saw me. I froze completely, stopped in my tracks, and my eyes were instantly locked into his.

"Two minutes, guys, you need to be up front right now," the stagehand called. I couldn't move. I just stared at his face until a hand slipped into mine, gripping it tightly. It was Cody.

He pulled me past Alfie and began tugging me along. "Keep it together, Lily, you can do this," he whispered into my ear as he hauled me in the direction of the stage. "We're on. You need to let it go for now."

I shook my head as I rushed along the dark passage and up the stairs leading to the stage. "Please give it up for XrAid," the emcee announced. There was no time to dwell on anything. I had a job to do.

The crowds at the festival were insane. The noise and buzz were like food to us, and it helped me push past what happened right before we had gotten up on stage. We couldn't have wished for a more rowdy and enthusiastic bunch of people. They were so supportive.

As bands go, we were great in front of the crowd. We played flawlessly. I had found myself playing my guitar aggressively which worked out fantastic for the band, but only made me feel more frustrated with myself for allowing Alfie to affect me this way again.

Despite Alfie's presence, everything was going great with our performance, and I coped much better after seeing him than I thought I would.

We only had three more numbers left of our set, and I would be able to get the Hell out of there. Far away from Alfie. I wasn't relishing the thought of making small talk and acting like we were okay. I just knew I couldn't have stood around pretending like that.

Just being so close to him, even for a few seconds, had made my body hum. When my eyes had connected with his—

after the initial shock—my heart had begun to race and my body spontaneously reacted to the chemistry we had as a current of electricity passed through me.

From the brief, close-up glimpse I'd caught, he was even more handsome than he had when we were together. His scent was like a warm blanket that I wanted to snuggle into. Alfie was still both dangerous and irresistible. Hence, my emotional conflict as far as he was concerned.

His wealth and fame suited him. He appeared a little more mature but even better looking. Just thinking about him again gave me an instant feeling of heartache. I missed him desperately. After more than a year apart, then seeing him again, I realized the despair for my loss of him was as strong as the day we parted.

The next number was one that Lennon and I sang together. Cody played keyboard for us. It was a slower rock ballad, and one of my favorites. Lennon wrote it, and it was about a guy who caught his girlfriend cheating. The words were pretty dark, but it was full of emotion. I had a hunch that it was a personal experience of Lennon's. He always connected instantly with this song and had a troubled, faraway look in his eyes whenever he sang it.

Lennon also had a lot of issues with women. He was a stunningly handsome, tall, slender guy, with mussy, sandy-brown hair. His deep brown eyes and sun-kissed bronze skin caught the eye of every women he encountered. Alfie was a master flirt, getting girls to hook up was easy, but he never let them get close. I wondered if he'd been burned by a girl in his past. He was polite and respectful but never allowed any girl to get close to him.

During my performance, I turned to walk to the edge of stage left. Alfie was standing right there in the wings, watching me intently, his arms folded across his chest. His confident stance added the 'bad boy' vibe to his aura.

Unsmiling he wore a serious expression and I knew couldn't allow my eyes to linger on him. Just the briefest glimpse left an ache in my heart.

My feelings for him were dangerous and felt too painful to deal with. I changed direction and walked over to the right, getting as far away from him as possible. I usually walked back and forth across the stage this way, during this song, but I found myself hanging out over the other side of the stage from where I usually stood for the remaining time I was up there.

Cody squeezed my hand before the last number. "Are you holding up okay, babe?" His voice was full of concern of how Alfie being there was affecting me. Cody's eyes flicked to the left, where Alfie was still standing, as he spoke.

"Yeah, no sweat, don't worry." I forced a smile and hoped it appeared genuine.

As we finished the last number I waved to the crowd, and they cheered appreciatively, but as soon as Cody had secured my guitar in his hand, I left the stage to the right. Running down the dark passageway, I passed by a constant stream of people. There were technicians and roadies, wardrobe people, and musicians. I dodged them and the equipment as I headed out of the private area.

When I reached the security guys near the exit, I remembered my purse was in the dressing room. I asked one of them to go back and grab it for me, explaining that there was someone I needed to get away from. Without it, I didn't have any money to get home.

This was the flaw in my plan to escape without running into Alfie. I knew I couldn't face going back there. So, I stood for about five minutes and realized that the big bearded guy I had asked to help me probably wasn't coming back.

I felt sick at the thought of going back in there, but was more confident enough time had passed that Alfie had probably figured I'd left. Besides, I thought his band would be preparing to go on stage by now.

I walked back, slowly retracing my steps in the direction of the dressing room assigned to us.

As I neared the door, I heard Cody's voice sounding slightly raised. "Leave her the fuck alone, Dude. She's been doing just great without you."

Lennon's voice interjected. "Alfie, she's gone. Doesn't that tell you everything you need to know? She didn't want to see you."

Someone cleared their throat, and I heard Digs add, "Sorry, Buddy, you're too late to want to talk to our girl."

Alfie chuckled. "Will you listen to yourselves. 'Our girl?' She collectively belongs to y'all now? All I want is to talk to her, make things okay between us."

Cody's voice sounded impatient with him. "She. Doesn't. Want. To. Know. Besides, dude, it isn't all about you. This is about Lily, and she's doing what's best for her now. The fact she's left already, makes me think her not talking to you makes things okay with you both in her world."

XrAid's dressing room door opened, and I ducked between two roadies and several groupies that were milling around. I swallowed noisily as I hid myself while Alfie stormed past them.

I quickly scooted across to the dressing room and rushed inside, banging the door behind me, and leaning against it. "Lily!" Shawn's eyes were wide, and Lennon's head snapped around, his eyes connecting with mine.

"What the fu..."

"I forgot my purse, and my money is in it."

Cody jumped to his feet and tugged me in for a hug. "He was here looking for you, just now."

I nodded, and the look on my face told him I already knew this. "Yeah, I know, I almost walked in on you all. He's gone back to his dressing room now, quick give me my purse, and I'm gone." Digs swiped it off the table and tossed it at me. I caught it, and Lennon came alongside.

"You want me to walk you out?"

I shook my head. "He'll be busy now. I'll just sneak past, and I'll be gone in a few minutes. Don't worry. I'm fine. I just need to get out of here."

I pulled the door open and ran past Alfie's dressing room with my heartbeat pulsating rapidly in my neck. I headed for the dark passage again that would connect me with the general public.

The corridor was nothing more than some chipboard painted black, but it separated me from the backstage army working on the other side of it.

The jungle of metal poles, holding up the makeshift stage, made the space under the stage as big as it was above. There was a network of people weaving in and out of the scaffolding poles as they laid cables or moved equipment.

The backstage and technical crews worked with a sense of urgency to support the acts. Although the talent of the artists was what the crowds came to see, without the crew's support, the magic above there on stage wouldn't happen.

Adrenaline pumped through my system. My senses were finely tuned. My nerves jangled and my senses were on high alert as I fled the backstage area. My heart was pounding in my chest and restricting my breathing at the same time. I felt slightly dizzy with the fear of being caught by Alfie. I really didn't want to face him again.

I was almost at the end of the passage and could see the security detail when someone swung around one of the scaffolding poles holding the stage structure up. He came out of nowhere, swinging into my pathway, and slammed straight into me. He knocked me on my ass and totally took the wind out of me. A strong arm swept under my shoulders, while his other hand snaked around my waist, pulling me off the ground.

A familiar electrical current ran through my body from his touch and his scent was so...him. My mouth went dry, and I swallowed hard. "Sorry, darlin', I didn't know anyone was there."

His voice was overwhelming and melodic. Tears pricked in my eyes and I fought with myself in the dark to not to allow him to affect me, not to let him fill me with sad feelings again.

"I'm fine. Let me go. I'm in a hurry. I need to be somewhere."

I heard Alfie exhale heavily. "Lily? Is that you? God. Are you okay?"

His hand tensed on my waist. I tried to take a step back. Pressure gripped at my shoulder and he tugged me closer into him. I nodded in the dark. "Yeah, sure I am. I need to go, Alfie."

His voice came back sounding agitated and abrupt. "You can't even speak to me? After all this time, we're just going to be what... strangers now, Lily?"

I sighed heavily, and his grip landed on my wrist. He still knew me well. He was preventing me from running away from him. "Of course, we can talk, but I'm late. I need to run," I lied.

His presence totally unnerved me. My heart was beating erratically as I fought for control of my emotions under his touch. Alfie drew a deep breath and grabbed my other hand. He began pulling me back in the direction of his dressing room.

"That's a crock of shit, Lily. You can spare me five minutes at the very least." Still holding my hand, he flung the dressing room door open. It bounced off the wall, and he stopped it by slamming the palm of his other hand against it.

All the guys' heads turned, their eyes flew over in the direction of the noise and settled on me. Des' eyes widened. "Shit." The word was forced out.

"Get out! We need privacy," Alfie barked at Drew, Des, and Andy.

Drew stood up and glanced at me with concern. "You okay with this, Lily?"

I didn't get to answer. "Mind your own fucking business, Drew. Out."

Alfie sounded major-league pissed. His mood wasn't lost on his bandmates either. The whole time he was talking to them, his eyes never wavered from mine.

Des walked across and put his hand on Alfie's shoulder. "Come on, Dude. Don't do this now. We're on in twenty minutes," he warned him.

Alfie broke his gaze to glare at Des. It stopped Des from commenting further. Des threw his hands up. "Fine. Ten minutes, Alfie. Then whatever the fuck is going on is forgotten. We've got a gig to do."

Des walked out the door, banging it hard behind him. Andy picked up a towel. He draped it over the back of his neck and opened the door, shaking his head.

Staring Drew sighed, "Why can't you just leave her alone, Alfie? Can't you see what this is doing to her?" Drew gestured him to look at me and shook his head. He gave me a sympathetic look. "I'm outside if you need me, Lily."

I could see Drew understood how difficult this was for me. I had always suspected Elle had probably spoken to him about how I was feeling back at the time when Alfie and I split up.

Chapter Five

COINCIDENCES

Once we were alone, his breathing seemed ragged as he continued to stare into my eyes. I was as nervous as Hell, and the ache I had inside from missing him was back in full force.

It was torturous for me to be near him and look at him so closely again. The fleeting encounters I had with him had attacked my senses and brought back so many memories of our time together.

Reaching forward, Alfie clung to me. His strong arms held me tightly, like he might never get the chance to do this again. The front of his hard body came flush with mine. I could feel he was aroused as he tilted his hips into mine. My body went stiff, and I fought with everything I had inside me to resist him, even though I still craved this closeness with him.

A shuddery breath left Alfie's mouth and kissed the skin on my neck before he trailed his nose the length of it and let me go. In my head, I was telling myself to get out of there before something happened between us. Because if it did, I knew I'd be lost to him all over again.

Protecting myself, my arms came across my chest. I was afraid if he touched me again, I wouldn't be able to remain strong. I couldn't think of anything at all, except to wonder what was going through his mind. What was he thinking, after seeing me again? When he eventually spoke, his low, rich voice was so soft and tender.

"The last time I saw you, Lily, I never thought you could look more beautiful than you did that morning." He sighed heavily. He was taking shuddery breaths, as his dark, sensual eyes ticked over my body. He shook his head from left to right. I wasn't sure if he was doing this absentmindedly, or because I was really in front of him. I could relate to that, I couldn't believe it either.

"You were lying on your stomach, so peacefully asleep. I watched you for the longest time. Your beautiful, long, dark hair was cascading across the smooth, silky skin on your back. And the contrast of it ending just above the sun kissed dimples at the base of your spine was incredible."

His eyes shone with love at the memory. It made me want to cry. He tentatively took a strand of my hair between his thumb and forefinger. "Some loose strands of hair were spilled over onto my pillow. The sheet draped across you was barely hiding your butt. Tantalizing me. The crack of your butt was just visible. You think I really wanted to leave you like that?"

He chuckled softly. "You had a slight smile on your face, lips slightly parted. You looked so peaceful and content. The breaking dawn light made you look so serene, absolutely perfect." He swallowed hard, and I heard a noisy click in his throat before he closed his eyes.

From his description of the moment, the scene might as well have been running on playback in his mind. He exhaled very slowly, and his gruff voice was charged with emotion. It almost cracked when he spoke as he began shaking his head again, staring at me eye to eye. "I was so very wrong about that, Lily."

His eyes twinkled as a smile reached up into them. "You're even more beautiful now," he whispered huskily. His smile grew wider and flashed the dimple in his left cheek. As Alfie's eyes stared into mine, they were sparkling with vivid flecks of green. The memory he was relaying gave him pleasure.

Before I knew what was happening, I was being drawn to him, my body tilting toward him, like a magnet being teased toward steel. I caught myself just as I was becoming caught up in the moment. "Don't!" I stepped to the side and swallowed hard; my mouth was dry.

My hands automatically rose to his chest to create a barrier between us, but I instantly regretted my action, as I could feel his warm, hard chest and his strong, rapidly beating heart beneath my palms.

The band on stage was playing a cover of 'It's Not Over,' by Daughtry. Alfie heard this, nodded his head towards the stage to bring it to my attention and gave me his signature lopsided smile. The smile I always had problems resisting.

Fighting against this love wasn't easy, but I dug deep and stood firm. "I made a decision about us, Alfie, and we moved on. Our lives are very different now."

Wrapping his fingers around mine on his chest, I felt an instant buzz and for a second, we connected. I pulled my hand away as if I'd been bitten. The feel of his skin touching mine gave me goose-bumps, and I was swamped by all the familiar feelings of desire along with grief at the same time. Feelings I'd been suppressing since I ran into him before I went on stage. The connection seemed even stronger than I had remembered it.

"Stop it, Alfie. It just wouldn't work, we'd only hurt each

other more in the long term. I'm at a crossroads with the band, and you have a fabulous life living *your* dream."

I threw my arms wide. "Don't do this. Let me walk away. Please don't make me cry. You're a great musician. You have fame, and everyone loves you, Alfie. I'm contented with where I am at." I tried to smile even though it was killing me. "I wish you all the best in life, Alfie, truly, I do."

I saw what I was said didn't have much impact on him. So, I made the decision to talk about his girlfriend. He had been splattered all over the press with a pretty blonde-haired girl a few days before.

"Why are you even doing this to me again? You're in a relationship, Alfie. I'm glad you found someone that makes you happy, I think it's great." I really hoped she would drop dead, but I couldn't tell him that.

"I'm happy for you," I lied. I tried for a warm smile and to make my voice sound sincere. "I really don't want to be dragged back to our past. So, please just...let me go."

Alfie raked his hand through his hair and shook his head. "What if I'm not happy? What if my dream isn't my dream without you? I love you, Lily. It broke my heart to leave you that morning. Just so we're both clear on those two points." He wagged his finger between us.

"My feelings for you are even stronger than at the height of what we had. You are the first thing I think about every single day, Lily." Alfie shook his head vigorously from left to right, his intense look never breaking his stare. He left me feeling paralyzed again.

I tried to swallow past my parched throat. It made a noisy, forced sound as I still stared back at him. I couldn't go through all the horrible feelings and insecurities again with him. So, I did my best not to show any emotion.

Eventually, he broke his gaze and inhaled deeply. Before he could say anything else, I tried to shut down the conversation. "I need to go now." My voice sounded slightly harsher than I'd intended.

When I was speaking; as if on cue, a knock on the door signaled ten minutes until his band had to perform on stage. Alfie flexed his neck both ways and cleared his throat. "I need to warm up before I go on."

I smiled slowly, how could I not, when I was looking at the man I loved?

"It really was...great to see you, Alfie." I said this sounding torn. Apart from all the horrible conflicting feelings I had, he still had my heart, and I was still *in* love with him. The complex situation of our lives and a relationship with Alfie was the only reason we couldn't be together.

I stood up straight, and he broke the stare, preparing to leave. Alfie blew out a forced breath and shoved his hands into his jean pockets, his arms stiffening. Then he relaxed them, but left his hands in the pockets. His stance and attitude changed, and he became almost arrogant.

"Sure, I only wanted to say hi. I've done that. And to tell you that you're going to be a star, sweetheart. You and your band were great out there today. You've come a long way from the shy, little girl I had sitting beside me on the campus lawn, blushing."

I smirked and when I looked up at him, his face softened again. "I guess I have, but as for the star part, I have never been interested in fame and fortune, Alfie. I'm already wealthy, and I'm not really one that relishes being in the limelight. It has always been about the music for me, that's why we would have never worked. I have dreams, too, but in another life...who knows what we could have had together."

I turned and pulled the dressing room door open and as I was walking through the door, Alfie's voice was barely audible, but I heard him say, "I'm never going to give up on you, Lily Parnell."

I managed a weak smile at Drew, dropped my head and hurried back down the dark passage to the exit, sucking up the emotions that were threatening to engulf me. Fighting with every ounce of strength I had in me not to turn back and run into his arms.

I was physically shaking from the exchange between us, and my body was aching to experience everything he used to make me feel. I was not going to allow myself to do that though. Not when I'd come so far again.

I headed toward the security barrier to take me outside, and Lennon's long fingers wrapped around my wrist. "Drew told me where you were so I waited out here for you. I thought maybe you could use a friend. Digs already left and took the others home."

I smiled affectionately at Lennon. Touched. He was still looking out for me. He always seemed to be one step ahead and in tune to just what support I needed and when I needed it the most.

"Thanks, you're too good to me, Lennon, what did I ever do to deserve you?" I mumbled as he wrapped his arm around my shoulders and pulled me into his side.

We headed over to his car over in the field parking lot. A couple of high school boys came toward us, and one started bouncing on his toes.

"Lennon, Lily, can we get your autographs, please?" I raked around in my purse and found a pen. I had some post-it notes in my bag as well. "Is this okay?" I gestured at the small lime green pad.

The taller of the boys grinned. "Sure, anything Lily, I think you're incredible," he swooned and wiped his sweaty palms down the thighs of his jeans.

"What's your name, honey?"

I could see he was a little star struck. It reminded me of when I first met Rick Fars, the lead singer of Cobham

Street. His friend nudged him. "Bradley," he squeaked out, his voice getting caught in his throat. He cleared it and tried again, "Bradley." He managed to make it sound lower this time.

His friend was much more self-assured and cocky. He was smirking. "Bradley here has a 'thing' for you, don't ya, Brad?" he teased making quotations with his fingers on the word thing.

Bradley blushed and held his body awkwardly. "Jeez, Denver, thanks," he huffed. My eyes glanced at Lennon, who was graciously trying to remain passive about Denver's admission.

I smiled warmly at him. "Well, you know, Bradley, if I was like about eight years younger, you'd have definitely had a shot with me." I winked. I handed the note I'd been writing for him.

Bradley's eyes flicked to Denver, a smug look crossing his face as he looked down at the post-it I'd given him.

To Bradley, you're going to break someone's heart with those good looks of yours one day. Thank you for coming to see us play at 'On the Verge of Fame'.

With love

Lily Parnell xx XrAid.

A wide grin spread across his face, which was slightly flushed now. "Thanks, Lily." I leaned forward and kissed his cheek. His hand flew up and caressed where my mouth had been.

Lennon finished signing his post-it and handed one to each of the boys. "I'll skip on the kiss if that's okay with you dudes," he teased.

For Denver, my note was more generic. I just signed my name and 'watch this space'...He seemed just as impressed with that as Bradley did with his note. Lennon excused us, and we resumed our walk to his car.

He began to chuckle and nudged me. "What? What's so funny?" I asked.

Lennon smirked. "You do realize that kid almost creamed his pants back there with the way you handled him?"

I bunched my brows. "What do you mean? I thought I was cool."

He chuckled harder. "Oh, you were cool alright. Don't think that's quite how Brad was feeling. He's a horny teenager, and you're a hot rock chick. The little dude will probably be tugging himself off to that post-it note. It'll be stuck on his headboard for months after that little display."

I smirked. "You're horrible, Lennon."

He nudged my shoulder. "Yeah, but honest, right?" I giggled, and he nudged my shoulder with his. "Feeling better?" he asked, looking me in the eye. I had managed to walk away from Alfie this time without shedding a tear.

"Yeah, it's all good, Lenny. I have made my choices, and I'm definitely not looking back. Maybe seeing him today will give me closure now. We broke up over the phone, and it's a long time ago now. It wasn't as scary seeing him as I thought it would be, but then again, I've grown in many ways since then."

Lennon nodded and smiled. "You sure have."

Chapter Six

DILEMMA

*I*n the days following my encounter with Alfie, I kept myself busy. It helped push the thoughts of him further from my mind. After a week, my feelings about meeting with him were under control. I wasn't allowing them to consume me the way I had in the past.

I had a distraction, which helped tremendously, in the form of a hot guy named Luca. He was a friend of my manager, Louie. Luca was Italian, but had lived in the USA for the past two years. Louie introduced us the day after the festival, and we'd hit it off right away.

There was something that really attracted me to him, and he was fun to be around. When he asked me to dinner on my day off, I didn't know why, but I had no hesitation in saying yes.

Lennon and Cody were flummoxed when I agreed. They had been ready to do their usual routine of putting him off when I smiled and accepted.

When I told Holly about my date, she freaked out. She couldn't believe I actually wanted to date him.

Holly suggested we double date at first. It made sense,

because I didn't know him very well. Although he was Louie's friend, none of us knew much about him, outside of what Louie knew of him since he'd been in the USA.

Luca drove us to Fort Lauderdale, and we had dinner in a small, family run, Italian restaurant owned by his uncle, Giovanni. His family was so warm and welcoming, and I felt relaxed in their friendly company.

His uncle was very complimentary when he spoke about me to Luca. The authentic Italian food, and the rustic presentation, was absolutely to die for and all completely organic.

When Luca disappeared into the kitchen to thank his cousin Marco personally, Holly squeezed my hand under the table. "Damn girl, when you get back on that horse you do it in style. He's freaking gorgeous," she whispered.

I nodded in agreement and gave her a smug smirk, feeling pleased she approved. What she said was true. Luca was a gorgeous looking man. The added bonus being, he looked the opposite of Alfie.

Luca's dark brown hair, beautiful almond shaped eyes, and kissable mouth were only a few of the finer attributes of his appearance. It was his mouth that my eyes had initially honed in on.

Alfie's smile was lethal. He had a very sexy smile. And the way his tongue kept flicking back and forth between his lips each time he took a drink from the wine glass he held was mesmerizing. Watching him turned me on. I couldn't drag my eyes away. That feature along with his chocolate brown eyes just did it for me.

Luca was almost as tall as Alfie, but his gentlemanly physique and the way he presented himself could not have been more different. I liked that about him. Anything that reminded me of Alfie made me feel depressed.

After dinner, Luca took us to another friend's club,

'Clouds'. He strode straight past the long line of club goers, who were waiting patiently to gain entry. He fist-bumped a massive, muscle-stacked, security guy, who stood in a black suit and bowtie.

"Jonnie, how are you doing?"

Jonnie, the door guy, had a menacing look as we approached but it transformed to a pleasant expression. "Luca, welcome back, great to see you, Dude." He stepped aside and nodded at us as we walked past him and entered the club.

Like Louie's clubs, the nightclub he took us to was a mega-club. The venue was massive with five different rooms, each catering to different genres of music. The place was full to capacity. The throng of party goers had the place jumping.

Luca told us that they had some amazing acts perform there. Lady Gaga had performed there in recent weeks.

As we entered the foyer, a very elegant looking woman in her late twenties approached us. She was exceptionally beautiful and carried herself with such grace.

Tall, slender, and leggy, she was dressed impeccably in a white, figure-hugging dress. She sashayed toward us, her long sleek brunette ponytail swishing from side to side behind her.

"Well, Well! If it isn't sexy Luca!"

A humorous grin spread across his face, as he stooped to kiss her cheek. "Louisa, these are my friends, Holly and Brett, and my date, Lily."

Louisa eyed me up and down and extended her hand to me. "You're a very beautiful girl, Lily. Luca's a lucky man. Make sure you take care of her." Her voice had a slight accent, and she scowled at Luca.

He huffed and shook his head, a smile on his lips. "Lily, I didn't plan this, and I know it is way too early for you to meet *all* of my family, but this is my sister. I didn't know she was working tonight."

I snickered at how awkward Luca seemed, as Louisa pulled me toward her and hugged me warmly.

She showed us to a VIP section. The seating was brilliant white, plush, padded leather and was arranged on three sides around a huge low square table.

There were black drapes on either side, which could be drawn for privacy from the other VIP areas, but with the ability to mingle with the others if we, and the other sections, decided to do that.

As we were being seated, I noticed that the drapes to the next section were already drawn, indicating that someone important was next to us.

Each sectioned off area had a view of the main dance floor downstairs as well. There was a central pathway, shared by all the VIP sections, leading to the stairway and restrooms.

We settled down, and a waitress brought two bottles of champagne in coolers. She set them on the table at the end. Luca leaned in and spoke in her ear, and she nodded, smiled, and headed back to the bar.

He had invited two other couples to meet us at the club, figuring it wouldn't be much fun sitting in a cordoned off section with just the four of us. Alexis and Kyle were friends of his from the office. I liked Alexis a lot; she was fun-loving and a little ditzy, but I could see there were no flies on her.

Another couple, Harry and his wife, Marla, were his close friends and neighbors. They were a little loud, but after talking to them, I figured that they were mainly lacking in confidence, and that was their way of hiding it.

Conversation was a little strained between all of us at first, but once we found common ground, we all relaxed and began to have a lot of fun together.

Luca walked over to where I was sitting and looked down at me, flashing his sexy smile. "Dance with me?" It was a question rather than a demand.

I smiled back and nodded, placing my hand in his as he led me to the dance floor. He was a very smooth mover, and it felt nice to be with someone I felt I might be interested in romantically.

I hadn't slept with anyone since Alfie. After him I had mostly sworn off men. I was scared to get involved with anyone again. He'd hurt me that badly. Any guy that tried to take it a little further than second base was gone within days.

I would find flaws in their personalities, or I tried to compare them to how I felt when Alfie touched me. Zack, a lovely guy I'd met at one of Louie's clubs, was the only one who'd got a little closer, but even with his laid-back attitude, I just wasn't feeling it with him.

Now I was in the arms of a hot, beautiful, Italian man who had piqued my interest. Although, I wasn't sure our relationship was one I wanted to pursue.

Luca was very attentive toward me and appeared attuned to my every need. He was considerate and affectionate, and didn't touch me in excess just for the sake of it. He had laid hands on me at times, demonstrating his protective side. Other than that, he was respectful of my space.

When we arrived, he had placed his hand on the small of my back and guided me to where we were seated. He opened doors for me and checked if I was okay at regular intervals. His timing was just right, and it didn't feel forced or overbearing.

As we danced, his hands were placed on my body with perfection. One splayed across my back, the other resting on my hip. He didn't take liberties, and I really liked his consideration for me.

The halter-neck dress I wore had a low back. Luca placed his hand mainly over the material of my dress, except his thumb grazed back and forth over the exposed flesh as we danced. As we got lost in the music, I leaned into him, resting my head on his chest. His thumb began to form a lazy arc, back and forth across my skin.

It gave me a tingling feeling. Not a feeling as intense as what I'd felt with Alfie, but a warm feeling that I was enjoying.

Luca took a sharp intake of breath and bent his lips to my ear. "You have beautiful skin, Lily, it feels like satin and smells like paradise," he murmured.

I smiled and tilted my head back to meet his gaze. "Paradise has a smell?" I rolled my eyes, and he smirked.

"Sure, it smells like you," he teased.

"Good answer," I smirked.

He tilted his head. "May I?" His eyes flicked to my lips. As they did, my tongue wet them in anticipation of what he wanted to do. I smiled and nodded, telling myself I was ready for this.

Immediately he closed the space between our lips and pressed a gentle, soft kiss on my mouth. He drew back and smiled affectionately into my eyes.

"Mmm…I think I may need another." Both of Luca's hands moved up to cradle my face. His long fingers burrowed into my hair as he pulled me toward him.

His hot, wet lips parted mine as his tongue probed my mouth, begging for entry. I obliged, parting my lips and kissed him back. My tongue tangled with his and for the first time since Alfie, a kiss excited me and turned me on.

Luca's hands slipped to my hips. His fingertips grasped the material of my dress, pressing into my flesh through the material. Then, he pulled my body flush against his.

I heard the effect our kiss had on him as he softly groaned against my mouth, before clearing his throat when his lips left mine. We were both a little breathless when our eyes met.

I sensed he was holding himself back and was thankful for his self-control. His body leaned into mine and I knew wanted more but I Alfie was still on my mind and so long as that fact remained I couldn't give him more.

Luca flashed his sexy smile and led me back toward the seating area. Holly had been people watching and was pointing out a girl that was obviously either drunk or very extrovert.

She was dancing wildly in the center of the dance floor alone. Luca grinned and crouched in front of me. "Bathroom break for me. I'll be right back."

It was getting late, and the music had taken on a slower tempo. I slumped back in my chair, suddenly tired. A ballad by One Republic began to play, 'Stop and Stare', and I thought their band's music played nearly as much as Crakt Soundzz did these days.

The heavy black drapes, separating us from the next VIP section, moved, and my eyes were drawn to the small chink of light, which opened more until there was about a foot gap in the otherwise black wall of fabric. What I saw sent a shocking jolt of electricity straight to the center of my chest. A metallic taste formed in my mouth from its effect. I'd had the feeling once before, right before I passed out.

Alfie was sitting about twenty feet away from me in the next VIP area. My first instinct was to look away, but I couldn't. One Republic's track was blaring around me. Ryan Tedder's voice filled the room with words of a song which was so full of meaning for the both of us.

As always, it hurt to look at him and not be able to touch him. My body and soul were screaming to be in his arms again. Just once. The girl I had seen him with in magazines and on the internet appeared beside him, and I wanted to die.

He turned and looked up at her. A slow smile spread on his lips, but he didn't touch her. He didn't reach out for her. He couldn't be near me and not touch me.

She climbed on his lap and straddled him, and he leaned

back against soft white seating, his hands still resting by his sides on the chair.

Inside my head I screamed. I wanted to climb over the half partition and pull her off him. He was still smiling at her though. Then, his hands moved slowly from their resting place, to rest on her hips.

Tears burned in my throat. A wave of nausea washed over me. Struggling to swallow past the dry lump which had formed as I watched one of Alfie's hands move around to her back. He stroked it gently, affectionately, back and forth. His hips arched a little as he spoke to her and the only thought I could muster was, *that should have been me.*

I could hear her faint giggling as his other hand began to run up and down her ribs. Alfie was teasing her. I knew exactly what his hands felt like when he did what he was doing to her. He used to do that to me.

It stung because he appeared relaxed and content over there, while I felt incensed, because she made him smile. I knew I had no right to think like that, but I did anyway. I felt angry with him as well. How could he act like that with her when he'd declared his feelings again for me only a week ago?

Slouched low on the seating Alfie's legs were spread apart. I felt sick when I saw his girl wiggling her crotch against him and figured she was probably making him hard.

The whole scene made me feel desperately sad. I wanted to run away, but I didn't. Instead, I continued to watch, like some sick, crazy person. Like I wanted to punish myself for what might have been between us.

It became clear to me that his girlfriend was drunk. She flopped over his chest and rested her head on his shoulder. Then, she didn't move.

Alfie closed his eyes, as she lay against him. I studied his face. Alfie used to be great at hiding how he felt. He couldn't do that anymore. I had learned to spot his 'tells', especially when he was angry or struggling to contain his emotions.

From what I was seeing, there was so much more going on in his head. Closing his eyes couldn't shut everything out. Alfie was thinking. I could see it from the way he was chewing the inside of his cheek near his mouth. I think I would have given just about anything to know what was going on in there, and if he was thinking about me.

Sitting there staring at him, my rational side told me that it wasn't fair for me to think that way. I knew, now, exactly how Alfie felt about me. He'd told me in the dressing room. I only wished things could have been different.

Even after everything we'd been through, I still thought he was the most perfect man I'd ever seen. He mesmerized me. I only had to see him, and I was captivated. I just sat there staring at his stunning features. Fascinated. If I was honest, I'd never been able to describe him adequately.

Angry feelings almost ate me alive. It was sick of me to keep looking, like I wanted to torture myself. But had to do it. Watch him. How could I not? I was still madly in love with him.

My eyes briefly fluttered closed as I tried to imagine the smell of his scent. When I opened them again, he had tilted his head back and stared up at the ceiling.

His hand swept through his hair. It was another one of his 'tells'. Something was bothering him. Moving his head forward, he glanced down at his sleeping girl. Slowly, he moved her off him. She rolled onto the seat beside him, curling up, and placed her hands under the side of her face, in a prayer gesture.

Alfie edged away from her and slid down the seating more, his face completely passive. He stared straight ahead of him. He obviously didn't see me. If he had, I knew he would have reacted.

Des came into view and leaned in, asking him something. Alfie shook his head slowly and put a hand up, with his palm toward Des, who was holding hands with someone. I couldn't see her at first, until he strode past Alfie and out of sight again taking her with him.

I had a clear view of Alfie, from head to toe, by then. Looking at him, he still had the same effect on me as he always had. My whole body screamed with feelings of lust, love and want, hate and despair. It was like Alfie had never been gone.

I yearned to be near him. To touch him. To run my fingers through his hair. Hell, I wanted to be the one straddling him and laying across his chest, kissing him. He should be teasing me. Touching me. I hated the girl lying next to him, and I'd never even met her.

Chapter Seven

TRYING TO MAKE IT

*H*olly turned her head and smiled at me. When her eyes connected with mine, her expression changed rapidly. Frowning, she rushed to my side as her eyes narrowed. I must have looked dreadful from her response.

"Jesus, Lily, what's wrong with you?" I shook my head, and my eyes went back to the curtain. She must have followed my gaze because she sprang into action. "Oh. Shit. Restroom. Now! Suck it up, honey." Holly tugged me to my feet, and I kept my head down.

When we reached the restroom, she swept me inside. Elle was standing right in front of us, refreshing her make up in the mirror. "Lily, what the Hell are you doing here?"

Holly sneered at her. "What the Hell are you doing here? Is that any way to greet your friend, Elle?" Elle threw her a dirty look and swept past her, wrapping her arms around me. She pulled me into her in a tight hug.

"Sorry, love. I was just so surprised to see you in here." She swallowed hard. "Lily..." Holly cut her off.

"She knows. We're sitting in the next fucking area to y'all." Elle stared in horror at me then her eyes softened. I hated the look of sympathy there was in them. "How do you know that?"

Tears rolled down my face as I stared back at her. "I've just been treated to an affectionate display between Alfie and his girl, that's why. Someone disturbed the drapes and I was faced with the truth, that's all." I bobbed my head at her and Holly as a tear ran down my cheek.

"It's okay. Really. It was just a shock to be faced with the PDA of him with his girl. Although, it wasn't really in public. I was the one that shouldn't have been looking."

Elle sounded angry. "I hate that you saw them. We never go to the clubs in Miami. We were all in agreement. You shouldn't find yourself in this situation. I just never expected to see you in here. I'll get us to leave."

I didn't want that. "Don't you dare. It's life, Elle. My choice. I can't expect everyone to keep hiding and worrying about me. I hate that everyone's doing that. I just need to get on with it. Go have fun, I'm not running. We came here for a night out and Luca has gone to a lot of trouble to give me a good time."

She hugged me tight again. "You're here with a guy? Wow. Are you sure you want us to stay? Do you want me to come over and stay with you?"

I squeezed her hand. "I'm a big girl, Elle. Holly's with me, please go back to Drew. Pretend you haven't see me."

Elle gave me a concerned look. "I don't want to leave you."

I was insistent and pushed her away softly. "I'm okay, really I am. Go."

Elle left the restroom, and Holly and I headed back to Luca and Brett. I really didn't want to be there anymore. We arrived back just in time to see Elle arrive and draw the drapes together.

Luca watched me approach him. "I thought maybe I'd

scared you off, Lily." He smiled and gestured for me to sit next to him. "No more than I'd scare myself off, Luca." I smiled as I dropped down beside him, resting my head on his shoulder.

The rest of the time in the club was difficult. I tried hard to look as if I was enjoying myself, but I couldn't ignore what I knew was happening on the other side of the curtain.

Luca tried hard to get to know me better, and to be fair, I did try hard to push away my feelings. The memories of my time with Alfie swamped me and prevented me from getting involved with someone new.

He was the nearest I'd ever come to moving on with my life beyond Alfie, and it was only fair I gave Luca a chance. We danced for about an hour after my talk with Elle before we headed home.

Luca casually draped his arm over my shoulder and pulled me close to him, when we were making our way downstairs to the exit. Alfie was standing right by the glass partition at the bottom of the stairs. I almost fell over when I saw him standing there.

His girl was standing flush against him with her hands in his back pockets. He had one hand on her hip and was holding his cell phone, scrolling down the lighted screen with his thumb.

Turning my head in Luca's direction to hide it from Alfie I looked up at him. He smiled down at me and bent his head to plant a soft, chaste kiss on my lips.

I smiled at him and when I began to focus on where I was walking, Alfie's eyes met mine and widened. He stood rigid, staring at me, and his jaw muscle ticked. Call me crazy, but I felt like I was cheating on him. Another man's arms were around me. Alfie's face was scowling so badly, and his jaw ticked again. He was mad.

Eye to eye, our gaze connected. I could see how hurt he

was about our situation. Then, he surprised me by giving me a soft, slow smile. It broke my heart.

No words passed between us. We just stood, suspended in time. Our eyes locked on one another, having an unspoken moment. I looked away not able to hold his gaze any longer. When I looked back, he had turned his back to me. Walking past him felt wrong somehow, and although I had asked for this, his snub in public again almost crucified me.

I struggled not to cry as we left the building, and I could swear I could feel his eyes boring into my back as I left.

Luca didn't talk to me in the car, which felt awkward. I was going over what I saw in my head again, at first, I'd felt numb until my feelings caught up with me, then I was heart-broken all over again. Alfie was only man who truly had my heart, and now we were acting like strangers.

I didn't ask Luca upstairs, agreeing to see him the next day. We arranged to meet at Eject, where XrAid was playing.

Not surprisingly, I never slept at all. Alfie was on my mind all night long. Tossing and turning I cried until I fell asleep exhausted. Feeling like the living dead the following morning, I dragged myself over to Lennon's for a band meeting. He had sent me a text asking all of the band to be at his place by eleven.

I was the last to arrive and the guys were sitting by the pool chilling out. "Finally!" Lennon exclaimed. "Get yourself something to drink out of the cooler and come over here."

Pulling a peach-flavored ice tea out of the cooler, I wiped it down with a napkin and climbed onto the hammock beside him. We both bounced around a little until we got our balance, then I laid back and waited for him to speak.

"Okay guys, we have a decision to make today."

Cody's eyebrows were bunched. "We do?"

Lennon nodded. "Here's the deal. You remember the demo tape Lily gave to Barney?"

Shawn nodded. "For fuck's sake Lennon, spit it out."

Lennon scowled at Shawn. "I'm trying, but you fuckers keep interrupting," he huffed, looking exasperated. "Anyway, Barney thinks that we're ready to record. Thing is, Sly Record label also think we're ready. Barney's deal would offer us state-wide exposure whereas Sly can guarantee us venues and promotion all over."

Shawn got up and ran his hands over his head. "They're going to give us a fucking deal?"

Cody's beer came out his nose.

"Cody, you really shouldn't drink beer if you can't keep it in the hole you put it in," I teased.

Digs shook his head. "Too funny, Lily."

Lennon scowled at the digression. "Can you all stop fucking about? I'm trying to impart some serious shit here." He exhaled loudly.

I giggled, but stopped when I saw how ticked he was getting. "Sorry, Lennon," I mumbled, feeling sorry for him.

Lennon rubbed his knee absentmindedly, and I could see he was nervous.

"Go on, Lennon," I said, encouraging him to spit it out.

"The feedback from the festival was that Sly Record label wants to do a deal with us. It wouldn't be rocket science to know that we'd be traveling a lot with them. With Barney we'd be headliners, but in State, with Sly, we'd be a supporting band. Maybe, we'd only be a supporting band for a long time at that. However, it would get us right out there. Bigger gigs, bigger exposure. If we gamble, we may get international recognition."

We all sat numb, silent for once and stared at each other, digesting Lennon's information and what it would mean for us as a band.

Cody was the first to speak. "Sly. I want Sly. None of us have any long-term ties or responsibilities here. Sure, we have

K. L. SHANDWICK

families, but we don't have sweethearts or kids. If we're doing this, we should take the gamble for the biggest return."

Digs smirked. "I'd miss my family, but hell, I don't see why they wouldn't make time to come see me if I couldn't get home. Besides, if we were doing the state thing, it would all be by bus, and we'd be out on the road anyway."

Shawn sat stroking his goatee beard. "Lily?"

I shook my head. "Nope. You first Shawn." I didn't want to sway anyone's opinion by what I wanted. Hell, I wasn't sure what I wanted.

Shawn huffed and blew a slow breath. "Guess I'm with these guys."

Lennon turned to face me. "I guess it doesn't matter what we say, majority rules, right?"

I smiled. "I'm okay with whatever you guys want. I just want to make music." That wasn't strictly true. I was worried. Crakt Soundzz and Cobham Street were with the same label. Chances were, if there was a major gig in the future, we could find ourselves sharing a stage again.

However, I felt comforted by the fact XrAid had a way to go before we'd ever have to face supporting either one of those two bands. Lennon blew his breath out. "I wanted Sly too...just for the record."

We all sat quietly while Lennon made the call. Cody was grinning from ear to ear. Shawn threw himself into the pool backwards, and Digs stared intensely at Lennon as he spoke on the phone with the label.

I knew I'd have to smooth things over with Barney, but deep down he'd be fine that we chose the bigger label. Lennon swiped his phone closed. "Okay guys, I need to call Louie now. We have a meeting at two o'clock today, and we need to bring a lawyer with us. Louie told us that James Stein, his lawyer, was ours whenever we needed him." Lennon rang Louie and

66

grinned widely when he finished his call. "No sweat, Louie is ecstatic for us. James was with him and will meet us at the 'suits' office downtown ten minutes before our meeting."

We all squashed into Lennon's car, and he drove down near the label's office. We had lunch in a little diner, but I was too nervous to eat anything.

The feelings I had were similar to those I had the first night I ever played with XrAid. I was so choked with nerves that anything I tried to put in my mouth got stuck in my throat.

I sat sipping my diet Coke, my other hand fiddling nervously with the condiments on the table. Cody swiped the ketchup bottle away from me and set it back in the metal condiment holder. "For fuck's sake, Lily, you're making me nervous," he growled.

By the time we got into the offices, my brain was in a complete fog. Their space was very trendy, all clean lines and decorated in a minimalist way.

Huge picture windows brightened the room and the plush white leather sofas and black carpets gave it a modern feel. I couldn't help myself for thinking that the carpets would be a nightmare to keep free of lint.

The pretty Hispanic receptionist smiled and poked at a touch screen monitor. She announced our arrival and asked us to take our seats and wait for Kieron Hughes, the CEO of Sly Records.

I wandered over to where Cody was sitting, glancing up at the array of records hanging on the walls of the office.

Gold and Platinum records were displayed in glass, chrome, and gold frames with little tags underneath. Each had a small logo of the band as well as their name and the name of the record. As I looked around the room, it was filled with Crakt Soundzz and Cobham Street discs.

There was one for Crakt Soundzz that was different. "Guys, does anyone know what a Diamond Disc is for?"

Lennon smirked, and shook his head. "Ten fucking million units." I swallowed audibly. Good grief. I couldn't even begin to imagine my music being bought or downloaded; never mind that much. What made it all the more impressive was that less than two years before, they hadn't even been signed as recording artists.

At the time when Alfie told me they had been signed, I knew they would make it, but it never occurred to me what it really meant for them. Never in my wildest dreams did I ever think I would be sitting in a record label's office on the cusp of an adventure like that.

It was a surreal and scary feeling, and I felt like a fraud. There were so many people out there who were much better musicians than I was.

I knew the guys in XrAid had talent, but with me, I couldn't help but feel that luck had played a huge part in me being along for the ride. "Send them in please, Maria." The self-assured voice rang out in the office, and the pretty receptionist flashed her beautiful smile again.

"Mr. Hughes is ready for you all now. You can go in." Her head gestured toward the double oak doors with the huge brushed chrome handles.

Lennon stood and wiped his sweaty hands down the front of his jeans. Glancing over at the other guys, they were all making a nervous gesture of one kind or another. This meant everything to them.

James was pulling a small laptop out of his briefcase. He flashed a confident grin at us. "Let's do this, guys."

We all shuffled in the door behind James. Kieron and two other 'suits' were sitting at his desk. Kieron got out of his seat and came around the large glass and chrome desk to meet us. "Great to see you all. Welcome to Sly Records."

He shook all the guys' hands and hugged me. "Excellent." His voice sounding excited, and he looked pleased with himself for getting us there.

We sat through two hours of legal jargon before James was satisfied we had a good deal. I stared at the framed posters on the walls of Kieron's office as the faces of Crakt Soundzz and Cobham Street smiled down on us.

The record label wanted to offer us a two-million-dollar deal. James managed to negotiate it up to three. It was fabulous for a first album. We left in a daze, after being given a PA and an events manager. The first job we had was to do a small tour in shopping malls and other venues to get our name out there, while we were in the studio cutting our first album.

The plan being we'd cut the album in the studio on weekdays and play in two venues on Saturdays and Sundays for the next two months, starting next week.

We met our obligation to Louie that first week, but that was the end of performing at his clubs. I felt a little sad about that. Louie had been great to us and to me in particular. When we went over to see him from the record company's office, there was nothing but pride for where we were headed.

He wasn't concerned that he was losing us as a group, because he knew there would be fresh faces waiting in the wings for their moment on his stage.

He was relaxed and accepting of our success; his only comment was that we had to keep in touch and not forget our roots. "If you ever need to be told you're an asshole when everyone else is singing your praises out there in the future, I'm your man." He smirked.

I had a feeling that comment was the sign of a true friend. I could easily see how a life on the road, with people catering to our every whim, could affect us. It could make us lose touch with reality to a certain extent.

Spence stopped by once, but the main man on our project

was Kieron. He was a nice guy, but a slave driver. For two months solid, we worked our butts off, playing in shopping malls in sixteen states.

The company jet flew us between venues, and we slept when we could. As we were pretty tight with our material for recording, we were in the studio ten hours a day.

Chapter Eight
SURREAL SITUATION

*W*e spent most of our time in the studio putting the album together. We ate, breathed, and napped between. At first, each of us was taking turns, playing our individual instruments, then we worked as a band.

I felt envious of Shawn more than once as the percussions were the first sound to be laid down for each song. He seemed to have the longest periods of time to himself between and was constantly asleep on the large black leather sofa in the mixing room.

In just eight weeks, here we were, launching years of work and dedication. The mixing had been mastered, and our producers had done an amazing job.

The artwork for the cover was ready, and the marketing company was all over it. In the short time we'd been in the hands of Sly, we now had our own logo, website, Twitter, Facebook, Instagram, and official fan club.

We were involved in several photo shoots, and the image people took over everything from what we could wear to what we couldn't be seen in.

The label threw us a launch party; the venue they chose

held five thousand people and radio stations were running competitions for listeners to win tickets to see us perform at the launch.

Launching the CD was crazy. I was no longer in charge of what I wore, but I drew the line when the image designer tried to put me in some converse shoes to perform in.

I insisted on my six-inch heels and told her that was not up for negotiation. The rest of the outfit wasn't a far cry from what I would have chosen for myself anyway.

The image designer had picked a tight leather skirt and a silk, dark green sleeveless top. A white lacy bra showed through this, and my hair was styled and straightened.

Sandy, the makeup artist, told me that I was, by far, the easiest client she'd had. She hardly did anything to me except kohl, mascara, and lipstick.

She did tell me that when I traveled abroad and lost my tan, she'd have to apply a lot more makeup to me. Especially if I didn't want to look like a ghost on stage with the bright lights.

Lennon came in and stood facing the mirror, his arms across his chest. "You all set?" He smiled. Sandy pulled the heavy rubber shoulder guard that was protecting my clothes off and peeled the gown away that she'd draped over me.

"Ready as she'll ever be." She grinned.

Lennon saw my bra under the top. "Fuck," he muttered.

I chuckled. "Jeez, honey, are you getting all horny over my bra again?" I teased.

He shook his head, and I grinned at Sandy. "Private joke." I smirked.

As I headed back to the dressing room in front of Lennon, he caught up with me and tugged my hand. I turned and smiled at him. "Come here," he said, hugging me. "No matter what happens from this night on, Lily, we've all got to be there for one another."

I nodded, knowing he was worried that we'd either fuck this opportunity up, or we'd get too big for our boots and change for the worst as people. Fame could do that.

Hugging him back, I replied, "No worries from me, Lennon. You can guarantee that I won't change. My outfits will always get you hard and piss you off at the same time."

"Thing is, getting into that outfit isn't as easy as imagining what's underneath." I grinned.

He smirked and burst out laughing. "How come you always know the right thing to say to reassure me?"

I winked cheekily. "Woman's intuition, Lennon, I don't expect you to understand."

Cody got to his feet and hugged me when he saw me. "You look scrumptious."

I smiled and checked them all out. "Damn, I'm gonna be up there with four hotties tonight. Who's got my back, covering *my* mistakes?"

They all looked at each other. "I figure it's time to audition for an ugly new member for the band," Digs quipped and grinned wickedly.

Spence came in with one of the stagehands. "Ten minutes, guys." He grinned as he took in our appearances. "You all look great. This is where the magic starts to happen."

Shawn muttered, "Umm...that's my line." We all burst out laughing, and Spencer walked away grinning and shaking his head. "Get out there and enjoy your moment, we'll talk after the gig."

That night was our launch concert, and I was physically shaking with nerves. Spencer opened the dressing room door, and we all traipsed out after him.

Standing backstage, Cody's arm snaked around my waist as it had many times before when we were waiting to go out there.

"You are going to be fantastic, Lily. We've done this

hundreds of times before. Just imagine you're in D'mond. The crowd might be bigger, but remember, all those guys are out there because they love you. They don't want you to fuck up any more than you do. Just enjoy it."

A smile spread my lips. Cody was right. The fans hadn't bought tickets, because they felt sorry for us. Our fans were out there because they believed in us.

Suddenly, the lights in the auditorium went out and the emcee began introductions. I could hear the familiar tick of Shawn's drumsticks, and my heart was beating wildly in my chest. Cody's fingers linked with mine and tugged me forward onto the stage.

With the first chord, we were bathed in bright lights. The intense heat from the spotlights bore down relentlessly on us. Loud riffs from Lennon's guitar reverberated as he played the familiar intro to our first song.

Digs bass boomed out from the huge amplifiers on each side of the stage. Strange, a lot of people hate heavy bass, but I've always found the familiar vibrations comforting. It spurred me on to forget my nerves.

Cody smirked and grabbed the mic as I was pulling my guitar strap over my head. He went into his routine of greeting the fans, warming up the crowd, and thanking everyone for coming.

We ran through the set we knew so well, only this time, we were doing it to make sales as well as to entertain our audience.

About three songs into the performance, I began to feed on the buzz from the crowd.

They began to sing along to the words of songs I had helped write. For the next hour and a half, we gave our fans everything we had.

I could tell they were feeling our music, and the thought of that made me smile. Being able to move people with music was what I had aspired to when I set out to study. I never believed in a million years that it would be at this level.

After the gig ended and we'd done an encore, Kieron and Spence took to the stage. Kieron welcomed us again to the record label and told the fans that we'd be touring in the New Year. This was news to us.

After encouraging everyone to buy the album, either on CD or digitally, he echoed our sentiments of a few moments ago when we thanked people for their support.

We were buzzing when we left the stage and headed back to the dressing room. After a quick change, we were whisked off to our after-party.

We were packed into a limo and taken to a downtown hotel. I had no idea what the name of the hotel was. I'd hadn't paid attention to that part of the information pack we'd received. I had been so focused on the *playing live to the five thousand people* part that I'd not noted anything else.

The hotel foyer was beautiful, decorated in rich gold leaf painted ceiling cornices, with crystal chandeliers, and faint red-colored walls. It felt extremely opulent and reeked of 'old' money.

We were ushered into a room where there were a few hundred people waiting. It all felt like a crazy dream.

My worried eyes searched the room for someone I recognized. They almost bulged out of my head when I saw Rick Fars standing there. Rock God, Rick Fars. He was the lead singer of Cobham Street, and I couldn't believe he was actually at our launch party. He was standing there, so confidently, at the front of the crowd of people.

Well he wasn't really in front. I think my mind just magnified him. He was someone who would instantly be recognized. I was a fan after all.

It was hard to understand why he had a wide shit-eating grin on his face and was clapping with everyone else. For us.

Kieron made another short speech about XrAid, and then we were left to mingle. My head was spinning from all the praise and well wishes from everyone.

It was at least an hour before I finally grabbed a proper drink and took a seat. My feet were killing me in my heels.

Cody had stuck with me throughout until I sat down, but abandoned me to find a big busted blonde who had caught his eye. I was looking over in Shawn's direction when a warm hand touched my arm.

Turning into the direction of the touch, I tilted my head and came eye to eye with Rick Fars who was grinning down at me. "At last, you have space to breathe, huh?" He chuckled. "May I?" He gestured at the seat next to me.

I nodded, a little star struck that this man was even here, let alone making time to talk to me again. When Alfie had supported Cobham Street in London, Rick Fars, the lead singer, had come to talk with him and introduced himself to me. That was New Year's Eve a couple of years ago. I didn't expect him to remember that we'd met before.

I had embarrassed myself by waffling on about studying music in college to a guy that made millions doing just that on a weekly basis. "Well, well, I guess that college education paid off." He smirked and wagged his finger at me.

My jaw dropped. "You remember me?"

He chuckled softly. "You look like that and ask an old horn dog like me if he remembers you? I always remember the women that don't let me in their panties." He stared at me, his face utterly serious.

I sat in an awkward silence, and he belly laughed. "Don't sweat it, baby, I'm just fucking with you." He chuckled again and wiped tears of laughter from his eyes. He stared back at me again seriously, "or not." I smirked, realizing that he was being playful.

"I saw your band's gig tonight, Lily. You were fucking

great. There's a lot of talent in that little band. Plus, you look so fucking hot. I'd pay to see you for sure." He grinned and placed his hand on my shoulder.

I took a second to have another 'pinch-me moment' as I sat beside with one of the biggest stars in rock music. And he was talking about paying to see my gig. Crazy.

We talked about some of the songs we'd written. I was still a little star struck, but when I got past that, I realized he was in no hurry to move on from talking to me.

Someone I figured might be his personal assistant came up and whispered in his ear. He shook his head. "No, no more stroking egos, I'm done for the night. Lily and I have things to discuss here."

While Rick was talking, Lennon's eyes narrowed when they connected with mine, and he raised an eyebrow. I knew he was asking if I needed to be rescued.

Shaking my head discreetly I gave him a thumbs-up signal at the side of my leg. His face relaxed, and he nodded once before turning to talk to the group of people near him again.

Rick was so easy to talk to and not at all like I had judged him from the first time we met. He was very knowledgeable and understood what was needed to survive in this business. He gave great advice.

At one point, something flirty he said made me make a comment about his womanizing way and his face became serious.

"I know I've slept with a lot of women, but they've done that willingly with me. I've been clear on each and every occasion, it would only be sex. I told them, if they were looking for something more, they needed to walk away and I've known the name of every woman I've ever been with. That's not to say I would remember all of them if they came up to me again. I'm pretty ashamed of that part. Drinking makes people do stupid things and being in the music business has its excesses, you know?"

He drifted off for a second, as if contemplating his own words, before looking me in the eye again.

"I'm never gonna let one poor woman lose sleep over what I'm doing, or who I'm doing it with. When I'm ready to settle down, I won't be touring anymore. I'm not ready to find '*the one*' yet, but when I do, I believe in being faithful to the mother of my children." With those words, Rick Fars' womanizing was completely justified, as far as I was concerned.

When he finished his statement, his mouth spread into a grin. "Well, well. Don't look now, Lily, but we have company. My night just got a whole lot more interesting."

Looking over my shoulder, I almost dropped through the floor. Alfie was striding toward us looking as appealing to me as ever. My hungry eyes ran over the length of him, feasting on how good he looked. Finally, I registered the scowl on his face. Alfie was extremely pissed.

Chapter Nine

HONESTY

*R*ick got to his feet and extended his hand. "Alfie, dude, how the fuck're you doing?" He smirked waiting for his reply. Alfie's dark angry eyes flicked from me back to Rick.

"I'm good. I need to talk to Lily." His gaze flicked back to me, and I almost allowed mine to lock with his then quickly dropped my gaze to the floor before looking back at Rick.

Rick stared silently at me for a second. It was as if he was waiting for me to say something. I couldn't think of anything except how to get the fuck away from the table.

Rick exhaled, smiled at me, and in an amused voice declared, "Everyone needs to talk to Lily tonight, Dude. Right now, though? She's talking to me." He smirked, looking pleased with himself, and it was evident that he had no intention of granting Alfie's request.

Alfie shifted from one leg to another. "Dude, I want some fucking time alone with Lily." Rick scratched his chin. I could hear the bristles of his spiky unshaven skin grating over his calloused fingertips.

"Why?" Alfie's jaw ticked, and I knew that Rick was really aggravating him.

"It's personal," he huffed. I could hear the aggravation in his voice, as he ran his hand through his hair.

Rick smirked again. "Hmm, don't believe you have personal stuff when you have a girl already, Alfie. Where is Zoe anyway?" Oh, great. I suddenly felt sick. The woman I hated had a name, and Rick knew her as well.

Feeling awkward and hurt, I just wanted to run away. How mortifying for me. There was Rick, someone I barely knew, and he was defending my position to Alfie.

Incidentally, the fact that they were both world famous recording artists, made the situation even more obtuse. I mean this stuff just couldn't be made up.

I cleared my throat and both men looked in my direction. "It's okay, Rick, what do you want Alfie?"

"Alone, please?" His eyes pleaded with me. I sighed heavily and swallowed hard. My heart felt like a medicine ball sitting in my chest.

"Can we have a couple of minutes, Rick?" Alfie ran his fingers through his hair again and mouthed, "Thank you." He gave Rick a small smile while raising his brow.

Rick stood up and squeezed my shoulder. "I'm giving you five then I'm coming back for her. Is that okay with you, Lily?" I nodded, too emotional to answer.

I clasped my hands on my lap and looked down at them. Not trusting them to be anywhere else. Alfie smelled amazing when he walked past me to sit down at the table. His faint cologne was making me feel heady.

He gave me his signature slow, sexy, lopsided smile, and my heart melted. "Hey," he cooed. I tried hard to control my breathing. My heart was beating erratically, and my palms had started to sweat.

His hand reached out. He placed it over both of mine,

still clasped on my lap. "Don't," I whispered, swallowing hard again. My eyelids fluttered closed. "Please don't touch me." My voice was still barely a whisper.

He pulled his hand away. "Please, Lily, talk to me."

I met his gaze. "This isn't fair, Alfie, please. Just let me go. I don't want to talk to you. It hurts me."

Alfie's fingers ran through his hair. "Then don't talk, just listen." His voice was low and rumbly. "You are so fucking incredible, Lily. You have grown, in every way, since I first met you. I have no idea how to explain this to you. How I feel about that. About you."

My eyes flicked up and were met instantly with his, the green hue apparent in them. I knew there were feelings behind the color, feelings that I also had but refused to give in to. The lust and want his eyes were holding for me were clearer than any words he could have ever found.

"Alfie, I don't care how you feel. Our relationship is dead and buried. We love each other, but you have *a new* life now, and I have *mine*. I like my life, Alfie. How would your girl feel about you being over here? Talking to me, and telling me you don't know how to explain how you feel about me?"

His body remained still, but his head looked over his shoulder in the direction, I guessed, she must be. I didn't follow his gaze, so I couldn't be sure. He looked back at me. "I would really like to talk to you. Alone."

He gave me a sad smile that didn't reach his eyes. My face was deadpan. "And I really *wouldn't* like that," I whispered back.

"Why? It's a fair question." His eyes searched my face for a response.

I unclasped my hands and twirled a lock of my hair as I thought about how to say it. I couldn't say what I really felt. No, because I still love you, because I want to feel your arms around me. I just want to find an island and keep you there.

"I'm with someone else, Alfie." The shock and hurt on his face almost killed me.

"Who? Not the smooth guy from the club?" I nodded and smiled at Alfie's description of Luca.

"Yeah, Luca's great, I'm having fun with him. Don't come along and interfere with that...not now. I'm happy," I lied.

Alfie looked around the room. "If you're so fucking happy, where is he?" His hands went out from the sides of his body.

I smirked because there was a genuine reason that Luca wasn't here tonight. "He's in Milan right now. Unfortunately, Luca had a prior engagement he had sole responsible for, and couldn't get out of, but he's coming home in two days."

Alfie was digesting this news when Rick came back carrying two glasses of champagne with Zoe in tow. "Are we all done here?"

Alfie pushed himself up from the table. "Take care, Lily, until next time," he mumbled and strode back across the room with his hand on the small of Zoe's back. She glanced over her shoulder at me, then she turned back to look up at Alfie. He dropped his hand from her, and she was left walking behind him.

I watched as they disappeared into the crowd on the far side of the room. Rick rubbed my back. "I felt you needed rescuing, did I do the right thing?"

Giving him a sad smile, I said, "I think we're going to be good friends, Rick Fars, but you know I'll never have sex with you, right?" He laughed, throwing his head back.

"That'll be a novelty for me. A girl who's my friend? That I haven't fucked? I won't get bored of that. It guarantees we'll be close friends."

Rick punched my number into his phone and called mine. "You can call me...anytime. But I think I'll be checking in on you from time to time, if that's okay with you."

I remember how I felt when I got on the 'crazy boat'. I

was out of my depth, and there were always plenty of sharks circling the water around me.

"At least your guys are protective of you. I've seen the looks I've got tonight while we've been talking. All of them making sure I wasn't going to whisk you off and have my wicked way with you." I giggled at his shrewd assessment of my bandmates. Nothing much gets past this guy.

I excused myself to freshen up, and Rick commented, "Yeah, I suppose I should be getting back to my date." I felt really bad when he told me that. All this time, he'd been sitting with me, and some poor girl had been in the room waiting for him.

Cody caught my arm as I walked past him on the way to the restroom. "That looked cozy," he scowled.

I smirked and decided to play with him. "You have no idea, Cody. The guy wants me to take part in a threesome. I'm just going to freshen up first though."

The look on Cody's face was priceless. "Jesus, Cody, I'm teasing you. I've already told Rick he's never getting in my panties, and guess what, he's okay with that. We swapped numbers though...in the event we change our minds, of course."

I winked and walked away stifling a chuckle as Cody moaned loudly behind me. "Over my dead body."

Passing the elevators on my way to the restrooms, I turned my head and smiled at the wife of one of the executives. I'd briefly spoken to her on another occasion. My eyes were just focusing forward again when the elevator door opened.

Alfie was alone inside the car. His hand jutted out and grabbed my wrist, pulling me inside. The buzz from his touch on my bare skin distracted me, and I stared at his hand. It happened so suddenly, and it seemed like a completely opportunistic act on his part.

The doors closed and the elevator began to move upwards. Alfie had pressed the PH button. His key was still in the lock from his trip down. "Please stop this right now," I hissed. He shook his head, staring into my eyes as the car sped up the shaft and stopped at the Penthouse suite.

When the doors opened two burly security guys, with white flexed wire protruding from ear pieces, greeted us. When they saw it was Alfie, they retreated to a discreet distance. Alfie pulled me out to the hallway beside the double doors leading into the suite. "I'm not going in there with you," I said sounding determined.

"You don't have to, Lily. I don't expect you to. I saw you heading for the restrooms and took my chance. I wanted to be alone with you...so now...I am." I swallowed and licked my dry lips.

"Always the same, Alfie, aren't you?" I shook my head and stared him right in the eyes. "Can you even hear yourself? *You* wanted to be alone with me. What about what *I* want, Alfie?" I smacked my hand against my chest. His sexy smile never wavered for a second. I've always found it so seductive, so I looked away in fear of caving in to him.

"Well, you say one thing, but you forget, Lily, I know your body. It's telling me a whole different story." He smirked.

"What about Zoe? What are you doing with me...to me? You gave me the whole, "I've never been with anyone since you, Lily." You expect me to believe that now? After the little display you've been putting on for me right now? What's your girl doing while you're here with me?"

He ran his hands through his hair. "What I told you *was* true. I had never looked at anyone else but you, Lily. From the day I met you, until about thirteen months after your last call. Until Zoe, I wasn't interested in anything more." A lump formed in my throat, stunned by his admission. Until Zoe.

How could he have had all those women throw themselves at him and not take the bait?

"I've never been with anyone else since Zoe either. That's not how I work."

"So, this isn't being unfaithful to her? Lusting after me? Kidnapping me and pulling me into the elevator? How is bringing me up here is you being faithful to her?"

Alfie pushed me back against the wall and straddled his hands either side of me. I had an instant flashback to the times when he did this before, when he was relentlessly pursuing me for a sexual relationship.

The intensity in his eyes was unnerving as they locked onto mine. We connected for the briefest time until he let his head drop, his forehead resting against mine. His eyes reconnecting again. I swallowed hard and fought the pain of loving him and what we were doing to each other.

"Don't Alfie. Please. I'm begging you. Don't." I said softly, shutting my eyes and pinching my lips. I was fighting helplessly against the tears I knew were beginning to fall. I couldn't stand to be this close to him and not feel his lips on mine or his arms around me.

Standing there silently with him, the tears overflowed and rolled down my cheek. Alfie's forehead left mine, and I was about to open my eyes when soft lips brushed against my cheek, catching my tear.

I heard him swallow hard. It clicked. And he inhaled deeply through his nose. He held it and exhaled forcibly. "Fuck," he muttered. "Please...you're killing me, Lily." He followed his verbal words by mouthing another silent, "Please."

When I didn't respond, his hand banged against the wall then stabbed at the button to call the elevator. He moved away from me, and we stood silently until the elevator car arrived.

85

We reached the ground floor and the door opened, Alfie didn't move. Just let me step inside. He pushed his key in and as he was about to turn it, he glanced back at me.

"Press the PH button when you leave and send my key back." He stepped out of the elevator and didn't turn around. I stared at his back as the doors closed.

Tears pricked my eyes and flooded my face as I stood in silence, while the car sped back to the ground floor. As soon as it stopped, I knew I couldn't leave things like that.

I pushed the PH button once again and let the doors close. I was still inside the small softly lit cabin, propelling me back in the direction of the only man that would ever hold my heart.

I had no idea what I was going to say when I got there. No idea what I wanted to happen. I just knew that I couldn't leave things the way they were.

As the door opened, Alfie stood in front of me. His face tearstained. The sight of that destroyed me. The last thing I ever wanted was to hurt him.

I didn't get the chance to speak. Alfie rushed me, his arms pulling me hard against his whole body as his mouth crushed mine in a move that was epically important for the both of us. I couldn't help but kiss him back.

Goosebumps radiated across my skin and wetness trickled from my core onto my panties. When he broke the kiss, he began frantically peppering kisses all over my neck. His vise-like hold on me was leaving me struggling to breathe. I felt dizzy.

An array of emotions rushed me. I struggled with feelings of euphoria, pain, fear, and lust. These were all overridden by the feelings of love, and the pleasure of being against his body again. We just seemed to fit together like the finest set of hand-forged spoons.

I pushed him back against the wall and staggered back

against the other side. "Stop, Alfie. I came back because I knew I couldn't leave with a bad feeling. I came back to speak to you, not for that to happen." I pointed to where we had been kissing.

I sobbed. "I hate the fact that we can't even be in the same room, but I can't get involved with you again. It's not what I want. I am beginning to do something with my life, Alfie."

I tried to sound convincing. "You need to leave me alone. I can't stay strong when you're pulling this shit with me all the time. I've struggled with the decision I made about us. Please don't let it be in vain for me. You have achieved everything you set out to do. It's my turn now, Alfie."

Alfie's jaw twitched. "You don't have any idea how I feel about you, do you?"

I smirked. "Alfie, you moved on. Zoe's your life now. I bet that poor girl did what I wouldn't, and gave up everything, just to be with you. I would say she loves you more than I do after that, wouldn't you?"

Alfie ran his hand through his hair again. "Leave her out of it." I bunched my brows and scowled at his lack of consideration for the girl he was currently with.

"You're a piece of work, you know that? You'd blow this girl's life just like that, huh? Poor girl. You're so fucking selfish. I'm glad I made the choice I did, but I don't want this constant mind fuck every time we see each other."

Growling in frustration, Alfie held me by my arms. "Tell me you don't love me, and I'll walk away." I swallowed and held his stare. It was boring holes into me. The thought that he'd cheated with me on his girl, that I was responsible for making another man cheat on his girl, just like Will did with Saffy, gave me the strength to do the only decent thing I could now.

"Part of me will always love you, Alfie, but I am not *in*

love with you anymore. I just don't like to see you hurting." My face was passive.

"I'm still attracted to you, but that's not the same thing. Don't blow everything you have now with Zoe because of me. I'm never going to change my mind about you. Luca's my future now."

As soon as the words were out, I was shocked that I had been able to deliver such a bold lie with such conviction. "The reason I came back up here was because it is totally possible we are going to run into each other from time to time. We both need to be able to handle that. We'll be pleasant to each other, but apart from that, I don't want you to converse or seek me out to do this shit again. Do you understand me?"

Alfie continued to stare at me for the longest time. He finally threw his hands up. "Fine, go." He hit the elevator button again for me to leave.

He traveled down with me this time. When I stepped out, he let the door close again. Leaving me standing in the foyer alone.

Digs was coming out of the men's room and as soon as he laid eyes on me, his hand swept under my armpit, and he frog-marched me into the deserted breakfast room.

"What the Hell happened to you?"

I shook my head too choked to speak.

"It was that piece of shit, Alfie, wasn't it?"

I tried to sound calm and unaffected. "I'm okay, Digs, it was just something I had to do." I gave him a small smile and tried to sound unaffected by what had just happened. "Digs, really, it's all good, we just cleared the air, that's all."

His eyes searched my face for reassurance, and he must have convinced himself, because he nodded. "Want to go home soon?" I smiled, grateful he wasn't pushing me further.

"Yeah, it's been a big day and it's caught up with me." We

left the party at two thirty in the morning and headed back to Lennon's place.

I flopped onto his queen bed in the spare room barely registering that my head was on the pillow and crashed immediately.

Chapter Ten

EXPOSURE

*W*hen I woke during the night, there was someone lying beside me. I froze. His hand was draped over my hip all slack and relaxed, and from the faint snoring, he was sound asleep.

I reached out and found the little switch on the wire of my bedside light. With a soft click, the room was bathed in lamp light. Cody lay beside me, unconscious, wearing a pair of Calvin Klein boxer briefs. Thankfully he was face down, so I only had his backside to deal with.

"Cody, what the fuck are you doing in my bed?"

Cody peered up at me through one open eye. "Sorry, I crashed in Lennon's room, and the dude got into bed. As if it wasn't traumatic enough having a dude lying next to me, the guy sleeps like a fucking gymnast doing a floor routine. So...I kinda gave up that gig and came in here. I figured with you having the only other bed, you wouldn't mind all that much, you being used to sleeping with Jack n'all. I just needed somewhere to lay my weary ass," he mumbled.

I exhaled loudly, trying to decide what I thought about

Cody lying in the same bed as me. I had not wanted any misconceptions about why he was there.

"Hang on." The mattress dipped under my weight, before I stood and walked to open the bedroom door. Then, I got back into bed.

"If you have to touch an ass in your sleep, make sure it's your own, Cody. And, if there is any snoring you're on the tile floor with a blanket, got it?"

Cody chuckled. "You needed to open the door to tell me that?"

"Nope, I opened the door to prevent the others from thinking I was getting jiggy with you." I smirked.

I didn't mind Cody being next to me so long as we were clear. It actually felt comforting to have someone lay next to me. I slept like a contented baby. When I woke up, I was the one spooning him with my hand cupping a pectoral muscle, and my body snuggled up tight to his ass.

My eyes sprung open and as soon as I realized what I was doing, I jumped back like I'd been scalded. Cody's body shook in silent laughter. "Been lying here wondering what your reaction was going to be when you woke up to what you were doing."

He looked over his shoulder, and the shock on my face made him crack up with laughter. "You left me lying like that? You're a fucking pervert," I hissed.

As his eyes crinkled up with humor and he chuckled. "Hey, less of that. I wasn't the groper here, I was the one being groped, remember?"

Lennon walked past the room and tracked back on his heels. "Shit. No fucking way, this isn't happening." Completely freaked out at seeing both of us in bed he stalked into the room. Cody looked at me and winked.

"Lily was promised a threesome with Rick last night, and it didn't pan out, she was a little...what was the word you used again, Lily?" He left the conversation hanging in the air, and I struggled with whether I should play along or tell Lennon the truth.

Seeing Lennon's devastated face, I decided to put him out of his misery. "It isn't what it looks like, Lennon." He puffed his cheeks out, then let the breath he was holding hiss past his lips.

"It never is," he commented blandly.

I grinned. "Seriously, Lennon? It's your fault. You drove Cody into my bed."

Turning to Cody I asked, "What was it you said, something like, Lennon sleeps like a gymnast doing a floor routine?"

Lennon's wide eyes flicked between the both of us, and I reassured him again. "We did sleep together, but that's all we did."

Lennon smirked. "Gotcha! I had you going there, didn't I?"

He smirked again and turned to Cody. "Get the fuck out of her bed, Cody. Besides anyone fucks Lily... it's me. Boss' perks an' all." He winked, laughing loudly at his own joke, before walking away in the direction of the family room.

Once we got out of bed we all spent the day lazing around and resting. I was reading on my Kindle and listening to music when Luca called. He had just landed at Miami airport. It was a surprise; he'd come back a day early.

I wasn't sure how I felt about seeing him, especially after kissing Alfie and all the shit that happened between us at our launch party. Part of me already knew that Luca could never make me feel the way that Alfie did, but he deserved the chance. It was early between us, and I had a lot of baggage.

The problem was that I knew something now that I didn't when I started dating Luca. Alfie still loved me. Love just wasn't fair sometimes.

I couldn't let myself go backwards. Sometimes, I used to get mad at myself and think, fuck the music. I loved Alfie. He was everything I wanted. Then I'd fool myself into thinking that I could live without making music, that listening to him and his band could be enough.

Maybe I could write music for them, rather than playing it. If I were a music teacher or wasn't successful with XrAid, what would I be doing with my life? Most musicians aren't lucky enough to play for a living.

Then, in my more rational moments, I knew I couldn't do it. I'd end up jealous and angry at Alfie for me not being able to do the one thing I knew for sure I was good at.

Oh, but the way I craved him was like a drug. He was my addiction, and I was still learning to fight against it. Alfie and I had our chance together, and we blew it. Now, after the launch party, everything had changed.

I really needed to let him go for good. Despite how I beat myself up about kissing Alfie, the last thing I would ever want was for his girl to suffer because we had been lusting after each other. Her life would be turned upside down, and I was not going to take responsibility for breaking them up.

Luca drove directly to my apartment. And, as tentative as he had been up to that point, when he saw me he pulled me into his arms and kissed me passionately. He stirred me more than any man since Alfie, and as desperately as I tried not to compare, I did anyway.

The feelings I had weren't nearly as intense as with Alfie, but his touch was experienced and sensual. I moaned, and he responded with a grunt, leaning back to look at me. "Ciao, la mia bella regazza," he said in a husky voice. *Hello, my beautiful girl.*

I smiled, and he closed the distance between our lips again. His open hands splayed down the sides of my hips to my thighs and back, before wrapping tightly around my back, pulling me closer.

My hands pulled his shirt out of the back of his pants and began to roam over his strong back, but it was Alfie I thought about.

I raked my nails down his beautiful smooth skin and he groaned. I could feel goosebumps erupting where my hand trailed across his skin.

Suddenly he shivered and moaned loudly. "Oh, Damn," he muttered as his thighs pressed into mine motioning me back against the wall.

His hands moved up and tangled in my hair as he deepened the kiss. I moaned loudly and his mouth swallowed the sound I made.

Suddenly I remembered who I was kissing and pushed him away from me. "Stop, too fast." I stared at him breathlessly.

Luca looked worried. "Lily. I don't want to mess this up by pushing myself on you when you are not ready." I smiled and said a silent prayer of thanks.

"Luca, I'm not ready to have sex with you. It doesn't mean I don't want to touch you, or for you to touch me, but I need to slow it down."

He smiled affectionately at me, his eyes holding my gaze. "Good, because I don't think I can ask my hands to restrain themselves much longer around you. You're a very, very beautiful girl, but I'm trying to be patient."

Smiling I nodded, "You told me that already today."

He smirked. "I only speak the truth, oh, and Lily...from my perspective? You may touch me whenever you want." He winked playfully.

Luca drove me to his place, where he showered and changed after his travels. Afterwards, we went to dinner in a little Oceanside grill near his home.

The food was amazing. It would have been a very romantic evening, had I been less preoccupied.

The restaurant had a musician playing an acoustic set, and his choice of music was very easy listening until he sang a cover of The Wanted, 'All Time Low.' When I listened to the words he sang, it was as if he was daring me to ask myself the question, "How do I choose between my head and heart?"

On the way to the restaurant, I had spent time in the car talking about the previous night's gig with Luca. I even tested him a little by telling him about Cody's sleeping arrangements.

Luca wasn't put out by what had happened. "I've heard of a lot worse than two bandmates sleeping in the same bed." He chuckled and told me some tales from his time promoting music tours for bands in Europe.

The more we talked, the more I liked him. Luca had been in the music business and was still loosely connected, but not as a musician. He got me, but without us having to think about spending years apart, like Alfie and I would have if I continued to make music.

Luca and I walked the boardwalk after dinner, and he slung his arm over my shoulder. We strolled along the South beach, and although it felt balmy, there was a slight breeze. His thumb stroked up and down my upper arm absentmindedly as he talked.

If I was going to do this with Luca, then he should know about my broken heart. It wouldn't be fair for him to do this without knowing what had happened last night with Alfie.

I took a gamble by telling him, and knew it could have ruined my chance at happiness, however, honesty was important to me, especially after all the shit Alfie and I had gone through.

I liked Luca too much to start getting into this with him without honesty. This was partly why Alfie and I could never have worked. Our whole beginning had started out with Alfie not being frank about his situation.

Luca stood quietly, his face not giving away any feelings he may be having at what I was telling him about my altercation with Alfie last night.

When I was finished, I huffed out a ragged breath, trying to suppress the emotions that recounting it had stirred inside me again.

Luca tugged me into his chest and hugged me. "You told him you care about me. I can tell you mean that, Lily, by the way you've been honest with me. I don't like that he kissed you, or that you kissed him back." There was a sick feeling in the pit of my stomach. I stared into his hurt eyes, waiting for him to tell me I was too messed up. Hell, I might have agreed with him.

Luca took my shoulders in his hands and pushed me away from him, his arms stretched straight, looking me right in the eye.

"Thank you for your honesty, Lily. I'm glad you told me. I don't want there to be any secrets or lies between us. A loving relationship is built on honesty, straight talking, and consideration for the other party involved. I'm sorry he hurt you, and I get that you still love him. I can hear it in your voice when you speak about him."

He smiled his slow, sexy smile. "I'm willing to try to help you heal and maybe one day your love for him will be replaced by your love for me. It is early in this relationship for you and me. I'm very happy with how we are. I'm kind of excited actually about what the future may hold for us. So, I'm willing to give us a shot if you are."

I smiled at him feeling relieved and placed my cheek on his chest. His heartbeat was strong and steady, beating in time with mine.

Luca's hand stroked my hair, and he tilted my chin with

one hand and bent to take my lips with his. Giving me a slow, tender kiss. My hand slid under his loose-fitting shirt and stroked the warm, silky skin on his back.

I was wearing a cropped top, and he was already touching my flesh because his hand was resting on my waist.

We headed back toward the restaurant and came across a bench that was set back near a shower area. Luca took my hand from under his shirt and clasped my fingers in his. He lifted it to his mouth and brushed his lips against it.

I tilted my head, and his lips spread into a slow seductive smile. He pulled me over to straddle him, and we began making out. We briefly forgot where we were.

I was surprised at myself, and he was definitely affecting my senses. I wondered if how Luca was making me feel was the same way Alfie had felt when he met Zoe. Pushing that particular thought aside, I allowed Luca to work his magic at turning me on in a way that I had long forgotten.

I began grinding my heat against his. He was solid beneath the material. He grunted and groaned as we continued to turn each other on. The soft moans we made and the occasional rustle of material only heightened the passion between us.

We were getting carried away. I placed my hands on his chest and pushed myself off him. "Sorry," I mumbled.

"Venite qui e baciami," he murmured, pulling me toward him again. He said it with so much passion I melted.

"Oh, God," I groaned. Don't talk to me in Italian." His voice and the way he was looking at me was very seductive. "What did you say?"

He smirked, but there was passion in his eyes. "Come here and kiss me." I didn't say anything else, just moved closer again, and stared into his hooded eyes. He pulled me closer and kissed me hard.

When he broke the kiss, he began stroking my back,

allowing his fingers to run up and down the ridges of my spine. "Your skin is incredible. I love the way you feel."

He drew in a sharp breath. I smiled against his neck and lifted my face to look at his eyes. They were incredible. The color of dark chocolate, set against the whitest background. They were framed by dark thick eyelashes, and his facial features were perfect.

Luca was true to his word. We made out but, apart from his hand on my ass, it was me that almost lost control. He didn't try to take things further.

I was pleased, but frustrated at the same time. So, goodness knows how he had been feeling about that. I stayed the night with him. We even slept in the same bed, but we didn't take things any further.

Chapter Eleven

MUTUAL REWARDS

*W*hen I woke, Luca was sleeping soundly beside me. His face was peaceful. He must have been exhausted after traveling yesterday, and I did briefly feel him get up in the night, probably out of sorts with the time difference between Europe and the East coast.

Six hours was a big difference to deal with; I knew that from my experiences traveling back and forth. The fact that he was knocked out gave me a chance to study him as he slept.

His beautiful olive skin looked amazing and, from my memory of last night, it felt every bit as good as it looked. He had flawless tones and although it was dark, the hair covering his arms and torso wasn't excessive.

He had some slight hair growth on his lower abs and a trail disappearing into his boxers. Other than that, he looked quite smooth everywhere apart from the shadow of growth on his chin.

Oh, and his hands, God, his hands were incredible. Large and soft, not a hint of callouses; the pads were like silk, unlike those of the musicians I knew.

He rolled over onto his side and opened his eyes. "Were you staring at me?" he asked in his gruff morning voice with that smooth-as-chocolate panty-melting accent, added to his sex appeal.

I snickered. "What? What's funny?" he asked in an amused croaky voice.

"Just thinking how you could be a movie star with your great looks."

He chuckled. "Damn, maybe I should just move right on over to Hollywood, eh?"

I grinned. "Don't you dare." His arm swept under my neck, and he pulled me close. "Hmm, showing signs of being clingy already, I may have to watch that." He chuckled.

He leaned in to kiss me, and I pressed my mouth closed. "I have morning breath," I muttered through closed lips.

"So do I and we both ate garlic last night. I don't care. I'm not getting up to brush my teeth to kiss you, it would take too long. Besides, after a few minutes I'll have you forgetting all about that." He smirked. His mouth crushed into mine, and he was right, I never noticed after a few seconds, I was too busy coping with my hormones and fighting the feelings of climbing inside him.

Luca rolled away, his breath ragged. "Go shower, I'll make some breakfast." His voice was abrupt, but I knew he wasn't mad. He just wanted to keep himself under control.

I smiled. "I might just stay dirty today," I teased, stretching out on the bed.

"Move it, or you'll be dirty in more ways than you can imagine, belladonna," he scowled, but he was grinning. Luca shoved me to the edge of the bed. "I'm fighting for control here, so don't push it."

We had spent over five weeks getting to know one another. I had slept in his bed, and he in mine, many times since that first night, but we still hadn't gone past second base, and to be honest, it was killing both of us.

I felt sure that Luca had to be taking care of himself in some way, from the amount of self-control he was demonstrating.

We showered, dressed, and had breakfast before Luca dropped me off at home. He had business in Fort Lauderdale, and I was meeting with the girls at my apartment.

It was almost Christmas, and Mandy, Holly, Elle, and I were discussing some party nights out together. The subject of Luca came up, and I had been thinking about wanting to take things further for a couple of weeks, but the thought of hurting him held me back.

XrAid was going on tour in a couple of weeks, and the long-distance thing was going to be very difficult. Luca said he was okay with it, and that he could begin to synchronize his schedule more in line with mine as the year went on.

I had a feeling that things weren't right with Elle. The vibe she was giving off made me think she was hiding something from me.

We were preparing some dips and snacks on a tray, while Mandy and Holly were plugging in the karaoke machine, arguing over the songs they wanted to sing.

I asked Elle if she was okay, then flat-out told her to spit out what was worrying her. "Drew has asked me to marry him," she said without expression.

The way she said it told me; this was about me. She would have been ecstatic to share her news with me under normal circumstances.

I put the knife down I was using and flung my arms around her. "Congratulations, Elle," I squealed. "Why the hell didn't you tell me before?"

I knew why, and I was hurt. She felt she couldn't share

one of the most important events of her life with me. I knew she was trying to spare my feelings.

I went back to cutting the celery for the dips. "Elle, I am so happy for you both. Don't ever let what happened between Alfie and I affect what you and Drew have. I'm okay with the choices I've made. I've got Luca now."

Elle started crying and placed her head on my shoulder. "Sorry, Lily, I just didn't know what to say. I know how long you struggled with all that shit about Alfie."

Her brows bunched again. "What, Elle?" I asked, and her eyes searched my face.

"I wanted to ask you something, but I don't want you to have to say yes, if you feel uncomfortable in any way."

"Shoot!"

She swallowed and took my hand. "I want you to be my maid of honor, but Alfie is the best man. I don't want to put you on the spot. I had an argument with Drew that I'd known you first, but as soon as Drew told Alfie, he felt obliged to ask him right away. I think Drew feels the same about you guys and doesn't want to make things worse for either of you."

I hugged Elle again. "You won't get any drama from me. I can do this. No problem. You are my best friend, Elle. Well, apart from Jack, and he doesn't count this time, because he's a boy."

Elle smirked. "Oh Jeez, you don't think he'll want to be a bridesmaid, do you?" We both burst out laughing.

"Hell, with Jack, honey? You never can tell." I giggled at her wit, but with Jack, there was an outside chance that he'd want a role in the limelight.

Elle asked Mandy and Holly to be bridesmaids as well. They were amazed to be considered. Elle knew that Maddie, our friend in London, wouldn't make the trip out to the USA for the wedding.

She had a toddler to think about and was pregnant again.

Emily, our other female friend, was currently working on a production for a local theatre group, and her world revolved around musical theatre.

She wouldn't be available for the next few months, and Elle didn't want to plan her wedding to Emily's tune.

I was delighted that Mandy and Holly were going to be with me in the bridal party. Apart from them being my friends, with Alfie being the best man, it would be important for them to have my back if I needed them.

When we were talking, I knew I had to make this okay for Elle. We couldn't have any bad feeling between us. It would have created a horrible atmosphere for Drew and Elle's wedding. I would hate for that to happen.

All this stuff between Alfie and me had gone on long enough. We needed to be okay in the same room as each other, if only for their sakes.

"Does Alfie still have the same phone number?"

Elle's eyes widened. "Yeah, why? I shouldn't tell you this, but when they hit the big time, the 'suits' wanted them all to have new numbers. Alfie wouldn't change his. He didn't want to miss you if you ever wanted to call him."

My heart stuttered, then I felt sick again. It was such a sad statement, because it meant he'd been waiting to hear from me, just like sometimes I stared at my phone waiting for him to call.

I, on the other hand, did something to deal with that craving. I changed my number, not once but twice, since I had called him that last time.

"I'm going to call him. We all need to blow this thing wide open and be the adults we are. He's with someone else. I'm with someone else. You and Drew are getting married. I'm not having one of the most important people in my life cut out, because we didn't work out."

I looked at the girls and their mouths were gaping wide.

Holly stood up and walked over to me. She felt my forehead then hugged herself. "Do you have a fever, honey?"

I smirked. "I'm serious. Look, give me my cell."

Before I could back down, I called the number that was on my list of contacts. Yep, he was still in my phone, and my heart was pounding once I'd pressed the button.

The last time I had called, it was when I had ended things between us, but it ported to each new phone I'd had along with all the other numbers. I never deleted it again after he punched it in again when we got together last time.

The line connected and Alfie answered on the fifth ring. "Yeah?" It occurred to me that he didn't know who was calling him. When I heard his voice, I almost hung up.

My lips were dry, and my eyes flicked to the girls who were all sitting holding their breaths, waiting to hear what I was going to say.

I cleared my throat after holding the phone against my chest so that he couldn't hear me. "Alfie, it's me, Lily."

He sounded shocked, "Hey, it's really you?" His voice sounded gentle, melodic, and bearly hid his surprise.

Myy eyes closed as I savored the sound of his voice, but I forced myself to focus on the task at hand.

My heart was racing. A longing to see him again flooded my senses. I wasn't going to get hung up on how much I loved him, or how not being with him made me ache again.

I was acutely aware that he hadn't said my name. I wondered if he hadn't because Zoe was with him. "Can you talk?" I heard rustling and then, a click as if he'd gone outside. When I heard a lawn mower in the distance I knew he had and the wind whistled into his hanset microphone. "I can now," he cooed down the phone.

Not wanting him to think the call was about anything else, I launched straight into the reason why I was speaking to him. "I need to talk with you about Elle and Drew."

Alfie's tone was a little clipped, and I could imagine his jawline flexing. "What about them?" I exhaled and told him that I was maid of honor, and he was the best man.

I heard him chuckle, but I ignored it. "Alfie, whatever our differences, we will have to spend time together to help Elle and Drew to plan. We need to be mature about this and allow our friends the respect to have their perfect day. I know that's going to mean parties and activities leading up to the big day." He listened silently. "We all have time off over Christmas, let's organize some nights out. We need to show them we can do this. They've made their choices of the people they want to stand up for them. The rest is up to us, Alfie. We have to show them they chose well."

I was so proud of myself until Alfie's reply to my suggestion rang in my ears. It wasn't the reply I needed. "Lily, I'll do whatever it takes to spend some time with you."

Choking back a lump in my throat, I pressed on. "This isn't so that we can spend time together, Alfie. I'm doing this to make our friends feel happy at having us in the same room together for their big day."

He let out a long breath. "I'll do whatever it takes to make Drew and Elle happy," he murmured.

"Great, make sure Zoe has plenty of rest. Us girls are going to party hard from now on. Oh, and Alfie, I will make sure that Zoe feels part of the group, just make sure you do the same with Luca."

Alfie growled, "You want me to be friends with some other guy that's fucking you, Lily? Are you out of your tiny mind? You really think I can do that?"

I didn't correct him about how Luca and I were. "Not only do I expect it, but for Drew and Elle, you have to do it."

The conversation drifted, and he asked me how I was doing, and I knew the conversation was leading to something I wouldn't want to talk about, us.

Politely I told him I was with the girls, and they were waiting to eat. "I'll call you tomorrow, have a great night," he said, his voice sounded sarcastic. "Thanks," I gushed trying to sound enthusiastic and hung up, trembling inside.

Elle hugged me hard. "You don't know what this means to me," she cooed.

I nodded. "Sure, I do. That's why I'm going to pull up my big girl panties and deal with Alfie and Luca being in the same room."

She smirked. "You're definitely not the same meek little girl I sent out here to study."

Mandy turned and smiled at me. "You were meek?" She giggled, but she knew exactly what Elle meant. Holly chuckled. "Yeah, Lily was a peach until she discovered being a bad ass American rock chick was much more fun than being a holier-than-thou virgin from England."

The girls and I spent the following three hours planning some amazing nights out. Afterwards, we sang loads of crap songs on the karaoke machine.

The four jugs of margaritas we drank made our choices fun. We picked some really hick tunes to rock out to. I loved spending time with them and knew how important they were going to be for me in the future. Especially once I started to tour with XrAid.

A thought occurred to me, I was going to struggle for female company on the road. I'd be depending on Mandy, Holly, and Elle to meet with me whenever we could. These were my friends before fame, and I planned to do what was necessary to keep them.

They were the ones that would always keep me real in the future. I was lucky, as I also had my friends in London. So, I had some people on both sides of the pond.

Luca and I were getting closer by the day, and although it

wasn't love yet, he was becoming important to me. He came over in the afternoon on the first of our planned nights out.

Chapter Twelve

STOLEN GLANCES

I was just about to shower when my doorbell rang. I had begun my pampering routine to prepare for the night out. Jack and Rosie were at the beach.

I answered the door in my robe, and Luca pushed me back, playfully grabbing me by both lapels. "Non posso vivere senzate." He smiled seductively at me. "Venti qui e baciami." His lips met mine, and he dipped me, giving me a passionate kiss that left me breathless.

"Wow! Now in English, I want the full effect." I giggled.

"The first part I can't live without you. Come here and kiss me...you already know."

I smiled. "That's very romantic, Luca."

He shrugged his shoulders and laid on his thickest Italian accent. "Whata can ah saya...I'm a very romantic guy." He smirked, then chuckled, but leaned forward and kissed me again more slowly.

Luca lay on my bed making phone calls while I took my shower, and when I came back into the bedroom, his eyes were focused on my towel.

"You want me to go somewhere while you get ready?"

I smirked. "Oh, you want to run now?" I teased.

Luca scowled, "Why would I run? You're here."

Luca had been consistent and patient with me, waiting until I was ready. He hadn't judged me or pushed me to do more than I was ready for. I shook my head. "I don't mind getting dressed in front of you, but I don't want you to feel like I'm teasing you either."

Luca grinned. "Sure, I can handle you getting dressed in front of me; the fact that you're willing to do that shows me we're making progress."

I didn't dress slowly or provocatively. I was already dry, so I pulled my underwear out of the drawer before I dropped the towel.

My modestly was all but gone from dressing in front of the guys in the band, but this was a little different. None of them had seen me fully naked, although, some of my undergarments left nothing to the imagination.

Luca remained passive but didn't take his eyes off me until I was fully dressed. I was glad I had extended my boundaries today. It gave me the confidence I needed to face Alfie when we went out. I hoped dressing in front of him gave Luca the confidence to deal with him too. Luca was normally a very confident man, but I think he was a bit intimidated to be competing with a rock star.

The only time I have ever seen any self-doubt from him had been around me. I had to be sure that whatever Alfie tried tonight, Luca would be able to manage.

. Today was four days before Christmas and I was excited for tonight to come for another reason. Jack had flown in from London, and although he had Rosie with him, Elle and I were so happy to spend time with him.

I was overwhelmed Jack was spending Christmas Day with me. In all the years we had known each other, we'd never woken up on Christmas morning together.

Both his parents and mine were in New York, but then planned on coming to Florida tomorrow, the day before Christmas Eve. My dad had rented a six-bedroomed villa so that we could all stay in one place.

Jack and Rosie had a room, my parents and his parents were in two others, leaving one each for Lennon and Cody, Holly and Brett, and me. Mandy and Neil, and Digs and Shawn were spending the day at their parents' homes but coming over in the evening. It was going to be amazing.

Jack and Rosie were staying with Holly and me until tomorrow. Rosie was still struggling with Jack's relationship with me, but I think she took Mandy's warning to heart and was trying not to let his flirty ways toward me affect her.

I told him to tone it down, but Jack still felt that if Rosie couldn't handle our relationship, then she shouldn't stay with him. It made me wonder if he really loved her, because he wasn't considering her feelings that much.

I knew I didn't love Luca yet either, but I wouldn't like him to feel bad about Jack and me either. I was wondering how Luca would cope when Jack began his banter with me. I had spoken about him a lot to Luca, and I felt sure that Jack would put him to the test in the following days.

We had decided to go to D'mond for the first of our planned nights out. Mainly so that we could all touch base with Louie.

We hadn't seen him in weeks, and although the band had moved on, he was still a close friend. Being in familiar surroundings was important for me tonight too.

Being a little apprehensive, I knew I'd need my wits about me, especially socializing in the same place as Alfie.

Dressed in a short, clingy, deep wine-colored satin dress with matching shoes, I knew I looked good; I was going for a confident look not an alluring one. The weather was cold enough for me to wear silk thigh highs and they always made me feel sexy. I wore my hair down and applied a little mascara and lip gloss. When I walked into the sitting room, Jack and Luca's heads turned in my direction.

"Damn, Lily. You look so hot I might have to strip that dress off you right now to stop you from catching fire." Jack smirked, wiggling his brows.

He rose off the chair and kissed the side of my cheek. Rosie looked ticked and stared down at her lap. "Behave yourself, Jack. Everyone knows you're all talk and no action," I chided, feeling a little sorry for Rosie and Luca.

Jack's brow bunched, and I realized this was the first time I hadn't gone along with his flirty role play. When I saw what I said had hurt him, I closed the space between us and cuddled him. He kissed the top of my head.

"Sorry," I mumbled not caring what we looked like to the others.

Jack flashed a grin. "You're forgiven." He smiled down affectionately. When I broke away, I saw Luca's face. It was passive, and if the exchange between Jack and I had affected him, he masked it well. Rosie, on the other hand, got up and headed into the bedroom mumbling she'd left her purse in there.

We had hired a minibus for our night out, because we knew we'd all be drinking alcohol, and no one wanted to be the designated driver. With it being so near to Christmas, everyone wanted to have some fun.

When we walked to our ride for the night, Luca clasped his hand in mine and lifted it to his lips. "You look so elegant, Lily."

I smiled at him. "I don't believe anyone has ever said that to me before."

Luca placed his lips near my ear. "I would say a lot more, but I don't want to make you blush in front of your friends."

He smirked at me, and I saw the briefest glimpse of his perfect teeth through his lips.

Holly and Brett weren't getting a ride to D'mond but would be traveling back with us at the end of the night.

We picked up Cody, Lennon, and Digs on the way, and Cody disclosed that he'd actually invited a girl tonight.

Lennon mumbled something about having to use Digs as his wingman tonight, and how that might diminish the quality of the women he could hook up with.

We giggled at Lennon's comment, and I wasn't sure if he was being serious, so I wanted to make sure that Digs wasn't hurt by his lack of tact at the way Digs looked.

"Digs, honey, don't mind him. If you accept that you two are pairing up tonight, it would be the quality of women Lennon attracts, that *you* might be concerned about. I know I don't mix business with pleasure, but just for the record, you're my favorite." Digs flashed me a grin and winked at Lennon, who scowled and shook his head.

Jack muttered something about him getting relegated to the back benches with all these American guys demanding my attention. Luca smoothly interjected that I had been merely playing with them, and that now I'd discovered hot Italians were a much better class of man.

Smiling up at Luca he laughed his eyes twinkling as he glanced at the deadpan faces of my bandmates and my best friend.

I had hoped we would get to the club first. I was disappointed when we arrived, and I saw Alfie and Drew were sitting at a large table in the VIP area with Zoe.

Elle was standing by the bar talking to Louie, and Des was dancing with some scantily-clad woman on the dance floor.

My feet faltered when I caught sight of Alfie but I pushed myself toward the table. I must have tensed because Luca's arm tightened around my waist in an instinctive move.

Luca was amazingly smooth. He took charge of the situation, and I knew that he was anticipating how I must be feeling to have Alfie and him in the same space.

"Luca." His soft, low Italian accent cut into the quiet between songs, as his hand extended toward Alfie.

Zoe stood up and thrust her hand at Luca. "Hi, I'm Zoe, Alfie's girlfriend. You met Alfie the other day." She said nodding in my direction and mentioning him like I wouldn't have known who he was otherwise. The guy was world famous for crying out loud. Alfie stood there checking Luca out, a scowl on his face. His jaw ticked, but he said nothing.

Luca gave Zoe a warm smile and turned his full attention toward her. "Very nice to meet you, Zoe." He lifted her hand to his lips and kissed it and I felt he had some common respect for her; she was in the same position as he was, whether she knew it or not.

No matter what the circumstances. Alfie and I still had strong feelings for each other, yet the two people beside us were our new partners we were trying to build separate lives with. My heart hurt.

Not deterred by the fact that Alfie hadn't spoken, Luca turned to him. "You have a very beautiful girlfriend, Alfie." Cody interjected and asked Alfie when he thought that Andy would be arriving. I knew Cody was distracting Alfie and I used his interjection to move over to Luca. I put my hand on his chest in support. He squeezed my waist and I glanced up and smiled at him. Luca bent to kiss my forehead.

Alfie glanced at Luca's hand. His eyes darkened and glanced up to meet mine,"Fuck," he cussed and turned his upper torso away to glance at the bar behind him. My eyes followed in his direction, but Luca caught my chin with his forefinger and turned my face back and up to his. He held my eyes with his in a beautiful sensual gaze. "Venti qui e baciami." *My beautiful girl.*

Compounding the situation Luca stroked his lips back and forth against mine. "Don't worry, Lily, he'll learn to deal with it," he whispered, and I was impressed that he was being so mature about the whole situation.

Gorgon City blared out 'Ready for your love,' and the sound filled the room. Luca's sexy smile widened. "Dance with me." With that, he guided me toward the dance floor.

For a few minutes, I lost myself to the music and wound up dancing with my back against Luca's chest with my eyes closed. Luca's hand stroked my belly; skimming back and forth against the satin material of my dress as we swayed to the music, but I wasn't dancing how I usually would because I never wanted to hurt Alfie.

When music changed to the next song I opened my eyes, and it was as if Alfie's eyes were magnets for mine.

Sitting forward on a bar stool with his legs widely apart, Alfie leaned forwared, one elbow balanced on his thigh. His beer bottle sat prompted against his lips as he gave me a hard stare. As soon as we locked our gaze I was stuck. All the tight, hurt feelings I'd fought hard to suppress struck the center of my chest, until they nearly choked me, when a lump formed in my throat.

I thought I was coping well, but when my eyes connected with his in that way, any hopes I had of being free and clear of him evaporated.

Suddenly aware of a gesture he made with the neck of the bottle it took me back in time. As he stroked the tip of the bottle back and forth across his lips, his stare seemed to intensify. I knew it was a silent message. A very private one; reminding me of a time we went dancing in London

Nothing could distract me in that moment. Nothing could stop staring at him...staring at me.

I was transfixed, mesmerized. I couldn't drag my eyes

away and didn't even feel bad that I was leaning against another man—Luca.

Who was I kidding about my feelings for Alfie? The hold he had on my heart was so powerful, and at that moment I was afraid I would never be free of him.

Knowing I needed to do something to push him away from me, I turned to Luca and placed my arms around his neck.

Luca smiled seductively at me, his head bent towards mine and he wet my lips with his tongue. He placed his mouth on mine, and I closed my eyes, wanting to scream. His tongue probed deep in my mouth, and my heart cracked, because I knew my action would hurt Alfie. But I kissed Luca back with everything I had, knowing I needed to fight my feelings for Alfie. I couldn't afford to be weak about it, not after everything. Not after all this time. We couldn't go back.

Luca led me off the floor and back to the table. Zoe stood up as Elle came over to me. She smiled at Elle, but Elle's eyes flicked from me to Zoe, and I could sense something was up.

"Hi, I'm Zoe. Alfie's girlfriend. You're Elle's friend from London, right?" I struggled for what to say back. What could I say, *Alfie was mine first? Was he ever really mine?*

I forced a smile. "Yeah, Elle's friend from London," I muttered back, but wanted to say I was much more than that. She seemed like a nice person, and I was fed up about that, because I had wanted her to be a bitch. Then I could have hated her without trying.

Zoe chatted easily, and it became clear she had no idea that Alfie and I had a past and boy could the girl talk. "So, you're in a band too. I saw Alfie talking to you at the party. That must be exciting for you. I didn't see you play at your launch night. Alfie had me come direct to the after-party. I guess he was doing stuff with the management, and he didn't want me to get bored."

I wondered if that was the real reason he left her behind. Or, had it been in the event he might run into me?

Elle briefly excused herself and came back with Drew. I could see that he was hesitant about Zoe and me being at the same table as well. Jack came running over to us.

"Elle, dance with me. I've missed you, beautiful." Elle giggled, and Drew threw his eyes in the air. "Don't move, Lily. I know how jealous you get, but be patient. I'll be back to wriggle myself against your hot little body after this song." Jack smirked.

"Promise?" I pouted, and he gave me a chaste kiss on my lips. I swore I heard Alfie growl.

"Trust me, gorgeous, you're the one. These other women...I'm just sharpening my skills to give you the best of me." He winked and grabbed Elle by the arm, dragging her in the direction of the dance floor.

Zoe bunched her brows. "You're with him? I'm confused. I thought you were with the hot Italian guy."

Alfie smirked and put his bottle down. "Yeah, it's all too easy to get confused about her, Zoe. She's with everyone."

Luca scowled and stood up. I threw my hand up to stop him. "What's that supposed to mean?" Luca asked.

Alfie shrugged. "I don't know, you tell me. I can't keep up, and I've known her a while. I can see how Zoe's confused." Alfie's jaw ticked, like he was barely containing himself. Pushing himself to stand, he walked away in the direction of the bar.

Zoe's head spun in Alfie's direction then back at me. "I'm so sorry, I don't know what's got up his ass, let me go talk to him. I don't know what just went on but he should at least apologize for his behavior."

Drew put his hand on Zoe's arm. "Leave him. Let him come out of his own funk. It's not the first time he and Lily have clashed."

Drew's eyes were full of sympathy at me having to deal with Alfie and his girl, when I'd been trying to be the bigger person in all of this. Zoe looked at me puzzled.

"I guess I didn't realize you knew Alfie too, apart from the party, but I thought you were Elle's friend. I guess Elle's been around a while, so it makes sense you'd have met all the guys in the band at some point."

For the first time, I felt sorry for Zoe. I found it hard to believe she really had no idea why Alfie was behaving so irrationally toward me.

Chapter Thirteen

TELLING THE TRUTH

orcing a smile at Zoe, mainly because I felt sorry for her for being embarrassed about Alfie's behavior. I might have even liked her under different circumstances.

"Seriously, don't worry about it. I'll go talk to him, and we'll sort it out between us. I'm not going to ruin everyone's night," I replied.

Luca gave me a smile and a nod, so I began to walk away to find Alfie and divert another crisis between us.

Lennon grabbed my arm. "Think about what you're doing right now."

I frowned and shifted from one hip the other. "What the Hell does that mean?" Lennon pulled me toward him.

"You're going after him, when the guy you're trying to have a relationship with sits and watches? How long do you think Luca's going to hang around when he realizes, no matter what he does, he's going to come out a poor second?"

I knew Lennon was talking the truth but I wasn't going to admit that to him. "So, what? I allow him to talk about me like I'm some piece of community ass? Free for anyone who wants me? That's how he just described me to his fucking girlfriend."

Lennon's solid look told me he was worried. "No, Lily, he wanted to get a rise out of you, and guess what? It worked. Think about it. He walks away while you take off after him. Mission accomplished."

My rational side would have seen that and I could appreciate that Lennon was trying to stop Alfie from drawing me into a situation where he could gain the upper hand with me again, but my temper didn't want to leave things as they were.

"Thanks for the analysis Lennon, but I'm not letting this one slide. If we don't sort it out tonight, then Elle's going to have to find another maid of honor, because I'm definitely not going to see her big day ruined."

Alfie was sitting at a table on the far end of the bar surrounded by fans. He was taking tequila shots with them.

I tapped his shoulder, and he glanced over it. His eyes widened when he realized it was me. "Sorry guys, I need to spend time with my girl here."

His arm went around my waist and he pulled me close to him then led me away from the table.

"Don't, Alfie, for goodness' sake get a grip." He glanced down at where his arm was and pulled me tighter.

When I felt his hot breath close to my ear, his low voice sent vibrations through me. A shiver of pleasure ran down my spine. He made me weak. "Is this tight enough now for you, Lily?"

I pushed him back, but his lips skimmed the length of my neck before I could free myself, sending an electrical current through my whole body. I averted my gaze over his shoulder because I knew he'd see the desire in my eyes.

"So, you're going to treat me like a whore now?" Alfie dropped his hands immediately, and his palms were chest height, stretched out in front of him.

"Jesus, Lily, you know me better than that." My eyes met his and my heart immediately ached.

I scowled and exhaled heavily. "Do I? That's *exactly* how you just treated me back there." I pointed in the direction of the group. "You know, Alfie, poor Elle and Drew want nothing more than a drama-free wedding. I was willing to put the issues with us to the side, but you couldn't think about anyone but yourself."

Alfie stared intensely at me, running his hand through his hair. "No, Lily, it's not because I'm thinking about myself. It's when I'm thinking of you. Don't you know you fucking destroy me? Do you realize what it feels like to see some guy with his tongue down your throat, but more than that, when you're responding to it? I fucking remember how we both felt when we did that together."

He swallowed hard and put his hand on my arm. He stroked it slowly as his eyes pleaded with me to give in to him. Every minute I was near him I felt my resolve crumble. Turning away in preparation to leave I looked over my shoulder. "What the Hell are you doing? Your girl is sitting thirty feet away, Alfie."

He exhaled and his eyes flicked over in the direction of her again. "You know what Lily? Zoe is a great girl, I really like her. I do." I was about to say I felt the same about Luca, but he wasn't finished what he wanted to say. "She's not you though. It's always going to be you. You fucking own me. I love you more than life itself. Forever, Lily," he whispered.

I closed my eyes, feeling tears threatening again. "Stop it, Alfie."

Reaching out he grabbed my wrist, and his eyes darkened in anger. "Stop what, Lily? The feelings I have for the only woman I'll ever love? Stop loving the one person that could complete me? Tell me how the fuck I do that? Seeing you with that guy is killing me. When he lays his hands on you, I want to beat the shit out of him. You have no idea how fucking hurt it makes me feel. I'm dying a little inside each time he touches you."

Crossing my arms over my chest, I spoke softly to him. "Don't Alfie. Stop telling me. I can't change things about us." The look in Alfie's eyes was one of infinite sadness. My heart sank. I hated seeing him like this.

"Please meet me. Please talk to me. I need to see you without all this shit." His hand pointed at the dancing and crowds of people. "And, especially without all of them over there." He wagged his finger at our friends. My heart was breaking at just how much our situation was affecting him, affecting us; it just felt like an impossible situation.

Hearing his constant pleas made me feel less in control. I was determined not to go back. Not when I had come this far. My feeling was if he got me on my own, I'd cave in again, and I'd end up living a life that long term would only create bitterness for the both of us. I'd spent the past eighteen months telling myself I'd made the right choice.

"Alfie...no. I'm with Luca. You're with Zoe. My relationship with him is going great. He makes me happy."

Instantly, he scoffed in disbelief. "He makes you happy; does his touch do what mine does for you?"

"Don't do this," I pleaded, the desolate look on his face made me want to wrap my arms around him and tell him I would do anything he wanted.

"Answer me." His eyes stared intensely into mine. I swallowed hard, knowing what I was about to do would hurt him. "Yes, Alfie. Yes, it does," I lied. "What we had was great, but it has to be over. Luca's my future now."

The pain I felt saying that was excruciating. The last thing I wanted to do was to kick Alfie when he was so low. The alternative, though, would be suffocating for me.

Alfie's eyes closed, and he slumped onto an empty seat by

the bar. "It's really over, Lily? There's no way around this?" His eyes were frantically searching my face for the smallest encouragement.

I shook my head, but I was screaming inside, because I was letting him go. I tried to stay strong. "Let me go, Alfie." Alfie shrugged, looking defeated and began shaking his head. His eyes flew to mine and connected in the same intense way they always did.

"I'm sorry, Lily. For everything. I'll never be done being sorry for how we started out, how it shaped us, and our whole relationship."

Taking him by the hand, I fought myself to ignore the chain reaction of goosebumps our skin connecting gave me. My body betrayed me with the enormity of what I was about to say, and a tear rolled down my face. I dropped his hand. "We need to start living. Without each other, Alfie. I mean... really start living."

Alfie grabbed my hand again and squeezed it tightly. My insides fizzed from his touch making my body hum. His hand was trembling. I hid my reaction well; Alfie less well. He stared down at where we were connected, and his eyes shut tight.

I began moving toward our friends before he could talk me out of it anymore, and my hand slipped from his as he loosened his grip. Luca stood up and came walking toward me smiling, which became a grin, and he opened his arms. "Bellissimo." I stepped into his arms, and he cradled me in them.

"You came back," he whispered huskily, kissing the top of my head and drawing a circle with his fingers on my back.

"You didn't think I would?" Luca looked intently at me, his face showing just a hint of strain.

"I would never presume anything with you, Lily. That would be a big mistake I think." Luca had taken the time to figure me out, and his assessment was just right in relation to my feelings with Alfie.

Alfie and I stayed apart the rest of the evening, stealing glances at each other, and it was hard to try to have fun with all the hurt hanging in the air between us.

He barely touched Zoe all evening. The poor girl tried so hard to keep him interested, but he waved her off several times. Des stepped in to pick up the pieces by dancing with her and ensuring she had drinks.

Jack even asked her to dance. I think he thought, in some small way, it would make me feel better about how Alfie was treating her. And it did. Jack always read me just right.

Holly and I headed to the restroom. I didn't want to go alone, because Alfie might follow me. Everyone seemed determined to keep him from getting near me for the rest of the night.

Rosie followed us in. "Can I talk to you for a minute, Lily." I glanced at Holly, and she shrugged. "I'll be outside the door, don't be long." She drawled, eyeing Rosie up and down.

Rosie wrung her hands. "I know you're not interested in Jack now, Lily. I can't say I understand you guys, but I realize that there isn't anything sexual between you and Jack."

I smiled warmly. "I thought we'd dealt with this last time you were here, Rosie?"

She rolled her eyes and wrapped her arms around her waist. She shook her head. "You might have, but I definitely didn't. But seeing you tonight? The way you look at Alfie, you're so deeply in love with him. The way you look at Jack is different, it's love, but it's a different look altogether. Plus, I heard Alfie telling Drew you're full of bullshit, and he can feel how much you still love him." She smirked.

My jaw hung at what Rosie was saying. Was I really that transparent? I thought I'd been doing well in masking my feelings for Alfie. My plan to put us all in the same room had failed miserably. What in the Hell was I thinking?

Pulling opened the door, I saw Holly's hair swished in front of me as she turned to stare at me. "Alright?" she drawled. I gave her a worried look, and she reached out and touched my arm.

"I need to get out of here. Tell Luca to come and meet me, and I'll get a cab. Make sure Jack, Rosie, and the guys get in the minibus okay?" Holly didn't stop to question me, which I was grateful for.

I waited in the restroom with Rosie, so I took the opportunity to put her worries about Jack and me to bed.

"I love Jack, Rosie. It's a weird relationship to other people, and I don't want to hurt you. He's the nearest thing to being my brother without being my brother. That's why we can do all that flirty stuff, but that's all it is, stuff. I know that you don't want to hear this part, but I'm going to tell you anyway. Jack and I have slept in the same bed for years. Every time we got the chance. We've snuggled up to each other, spooned, and Hell I even woke up once with my hand on his dick. That was an accident. We have never crossed the line. It isn't that way for either of us at all. Jack is my platonic soul mate, and I'm his. If you can accept how he is with me, I figure you could well be his partner for life. Jack is a fiercely loyal, amazing man. He's never going to give me up. Even if I tried to shut him down, he wouldn't give us up. Trust me when I say this, Rosie, what we have is weird, but wonderful for both of us. Alfie even got it when I was with him. He once said he could never fuck with my relationship with Jack, because Jack just completely got me. Alfie hates anyone touching me, but eventually, he accepted that Jack wasn't a threat to him, even if we did walk a fine line at times."

Holly swung the door open. "Luca's at the front door talking to Louie. You should leave now; Alfie's on the dance floor." I hugged Rosie, and Holly walked out in front of me; shielding me from any of our friends.

Luca came forward and took my hand. "I hear we're going home," I stated as Louie pulled me in for a hug.

Louie signaled to one of his security men. "Take the limo and call me."

I smiled affectionately and kissed Louie's cheek. "I'll call you tomorrow."

Luca and I were ushered outside. The chauffeur opened the door for us. When we were inside, Luca exhaled and held my hand. "Tough night for you," he stated. I didn't know how to respond so I didn't.

We sat in silence, and he put his arm around my shoulder, drawing me into his side, and kissing the top of my head. I felt like crying. Luca was everything I should want, but Alfie was messing with my psyche again.

We pulled up by my building, but Luca didn't move. Henry, Louie's chauffeur, opened the door for us. Looking up at Luca, I saw his eyes were filled with sadness.

"Go, Lily. Sweet dreams," he murmured. I smiled, feeling bad for the way Alfie behaved.

"It's okay for you to come up, Luca."

Luca shook his head slowly and drew in a deep sharp breath. "No, it isn't, Lily. You're not ready for me. I like you very much," he hesitated and huffed a breath out. "Tonight, from what I witnessed, I know there too much unfinished business between you and Alfie, more than even I can deal with."

He held my gaze, looking at me affectionately. "I am a tolerant man. I could fall hard for you, Lily. But I'm walking away. This isn't for your sake, it's for *mine*. Goodnight, Bellissimo."

I stepped out of the car, and Henry closed the door, got

behind the wheel, and pulled away. This had to be the perfect ending to the shittiest day on record for me.

Such a desolate feeling washed over me. Feeling dejected, I had managed to fuck up my whole life because I met Alfie.

I barely made it to the elevator before I started crying. By the time the elevator door opened on my floor, I was a teary mess of mascara and snot.

As soon as I got home, I sent a text to Holly to tell her I was home and that I was alone. I was on my bed, still numb, an hour later, when I heard the door open. Holly had come home to see me, because Luca had dumped me.

Chapter Fourteen
FACING FACTS

*L*ying in bed with the sheet over my head I heard the door handle latch click. I knew someone had come into my room.

"I'm fine Holly, just leave me alone," I sniffed, notwanting to talk about what had happened.

The mattress dipped, and a caring hand landed on my back. I had a sudden feeling of elation, and my heartbeat raced. The touch ignited a buzz giving me feelings of a more sensual nature.

I threw the sheet back and jumped into a sitting position. Alfie was sitting at the side of my bed, his face looking gaunt.

Turmoil passed through his eyes and I felt once he was in front of me he didn't know what to say. My heart sank to my stomach because I'd spent the last year and a half trying to be clever about avoiding him and he was sitting on my bed.

"What the fuck are you doing here?" I snapped, embarrassed that I had been crying and devastated he was able to see my feelings laid bare.

"I knew you needed me." His low voice cracked with emotion as he said it. I shook my head and tried to get up.

Alfie pushed me back on my pillow and leaned over me, his hands on either side of me. We were face to face.

"Alfie, you're the last person I needed tonight. How did you get in here?" I just couldn't understand any of this.

My heart was racing from how near he was. I could smell his scent, and my body hummed with the sensation of his touch. I was still trembling from the adrenaline rush I'd had when I realized he was actually in my bedroom. All of us girls had picked this building because of its security features.

"Holly's phone was on the table in the club when your text arrived. Her keys were in her purse. I saw it was from you and read the text as it displayed when it came through. So, I took her keys. I wanted to know if you were okay."

"I was okay until I saw you again, Alfie. My life was coming together and now you're back. Here, in my bedroom, giving me the same mind fuck that you always do."

"No, Lily. I gave up that particular line of pursuit with you a long time ago. My life has been meaningless without you. I. Can't. Fucking. Live. Without. You. I don't want to," he whispered softly.

Alfie's eyes searched my face frantically, as if he needed me to understand what he was saying.

"I fucking know you love me, Lily. Don't try to deny it." His fingers dug into the flesh of my upper arms. His eyes pleaded for honesty from me.

Placing my hands on his chest I pushed him back and sat up as he moved away. His hands cupped my face, and he pulled me toward him, my face close to his.

"Say it, damn it. The truth. You need to tell me you feel the same way as I do." I was stock still. I couldn't look away. We were frozen, hypnotized by each other.

Alfie's eyes filled with tears, and one huge perfect teardrop streaked down his face and ran into the side of his lip. I couldn't allow myself to react, because I'd be done all over again if I did.

He didn't move, and he didn't blink. He just sat there continuing to stare at me with a tortured look. "Please..." he mouthed silently and swallowed hard. I heard how difficult it was for him to swallow, as another tear rolled down from sad eyes.

I couldn't let it fall this time. My forefinger touched his cheek, and his tear melted into my fingertip. His hand caught my finger, and he put it to his mouth, kissing the tear away.

When he did that, it broke my heart. I couldn't keep up the pretense. Not when he was laying himself bare to me again.

My eyes closed with the admission as it passed my lips. "Of course, I love you. There's never been anyone else to love, since you." I began to sob as my confession rolled off my tongue. I swallowed hard, but the relief I felt at being able to say it out loud was immense.

Alfie's head reeled back like I had slapped him. "Say it again!" He sat openmouthed, cupping my face again. He couldn't believe that I had uttered the words he'd been waiting to hear.

I sat expressionless. "I love you with everything I am, Alfie. It doesn't mean we're going to be together again." I shook my head slowly and held the intense look he gave me.

His eyes rolled back and closed. "No. Fuck. Lily. Don't do this. Don't throw away our last chance to be together." His voice sounded desperate, begging. "What do I have to do? Name it. I can't live without you. I'll do whatever it takes to have you in my life."

"Sure, you can do it, Alfie. You have Zoe, now. She's a lovely girl." He stood up and ran his hand through his hair, then shoved both hands in his pockets.

"I'm sad that I might hurt her, but she knows the score.

She isn't you, Lily." His head started shaking vigorously. "I can't and won't be without you again. I can't bear not seeing you. Not touching you." He paused, thinking.

"The thought of some guy touching you, Lily. Touching what's mine." He shook his head again, his closed fist banging on his chest. "Doing things *I* should be doing with you...*to* you. Please, I can't..." he whispered.

Alfie closed his eyes and began to cry again. I'd never seen a man cry before, let alone the one I loved. It felt heart wrenching. An overwhelming feeling had me wanting to hug him and tell him that it was okay, that we were okay.

Each time his eyes met mine, I could feel him drawing me in, bringing demolishing those protective walls I had built around me. None of what was happening was an act. Alfie was demonstrating the depth of his feelings and what I meant to him.

The barriers I'd worked so hard to erect were slowly falling like dominos. Alfie knelt in front of me and grabbed my hand.

Placing my palm flat over his heart he then placed his over mine. When I touched his warm, hard body it was instantly familiar, and I wanted to run my fingertips over his smooth muscles under his t-shirt.

His heart beat rapidly under his shirt. He pushed my hand back in my lap and stood up, pulling the bottom of his t-shirt from his pants.

He bent his arm over his shoulder and gripped the material behind his neck, pulling the t-shirt over his head. It was as if he'd known what I'd been thinking. "Alfie..."

He glared at me. "Shush."

He picked my hand up and knelt before me again. Placing my palm back on his warm, smooth skin over his heart again, and my head filled instantly with his familiar scent of him.

He stared intensely into my eyes. "You feel that? You feel

my skin? How warm my body is? You feel my strong heart beating inside of me?"

"I do." I had no idea what he was doing.

"My heart beats strongly, because you are in my heart. My skin is warm, because you are under it. You. Own. Me. You are my heart. If you choose not to be, everything stops. I can't go on without you. Each day without you, I die a little more."

I felt a sense of panic at what he was saying. He sounded so desperate. "Alfie, you have your life, and I have mine."

"Bullshit, Lily. I don't want my fucking life if you aren't in it. Can't I get that through your thick skull? This crap fucking stops now. Today. I am not doing this shit with you another minute." He wagged his finger no.

He pointed at me. "You're mine," then pointed to himself, "And I am yours, Lily. We're never going to be over."

Alfie was my first love. He was my only real love. I had even more feelings for him at this point than I had at our best and worst of times.

After all this time, no one else came close to the way he made me feel. At that moment, I just wanted him to have all he wanted from me, because I realized I wanted it too, but I was scared.

The difficulty was the same sticking point we would arrive at all our lives, unless one of us called a halt to it. Exactly what I was trying to do.

Alfie was making it extremely difficult for me, though. "Tell me Alfie, what do you see happening if we did this?" He frowned.

"We'd be happy for a start," he said flatly.

"Sure, we would...at first." I waited to see what else he would add to his short answer.

"We'd have fun, make music, travel, settle down, have

131

babies, and have a helluva time making those babies." He smirked.

"Yeah? Exactly how do we both make music? I'm in a band that's going in one direction, and you're going in another."

Alfie smiled. "Don't you see? It's even better than where we've been before?"

I didn't. "Enlighten me."

"You get on great with the guys in my band. They're all cool guys in your band. We'd have a blast touring together. You'd get time to spend with Elle on the road, play music, and be with me." I sat quietly thinking about what he was saying.

"Okay, so you just go to the record label and say, 'Oh by the way, XrAid is going to be the resident supporting band for Crakt Soundzz from now on?'"

Alfie smirked. "Fuck, Lily, I'm in the hottest band in the world right now, I could tell the 'suits' I'll only speak to them if they are dressed in chicken suits and pretending to peck on corn from the floor when I walk in the room, and they'd do it."

I grinned, it was too funny. Some of the executives from the label were very conventional. "Well, Alfie, you have this all figured out in your mind, don't you?"

Alfie smirked. "Don't ask, you don't get." He put on a thick southern accent and rubbed his chin.

"What about everyone else involved, Alfie? This is what you want. What about what everyone else wants?"

He scowled and rubbed his hands together. "I'm sure what's best for me is best for the band." I sighed. He could only see his side of things.

"What about XrAid, Alfie? The guys have free will. They won't want to hang with you guys all the time. It might work in the early days, but what if...what if...we get to be just as successful in our own right? We won't be supporting anymore and then there are two lots of tours to negotiate." I was on a roll now. "Are we all going to be cozy on one bus? How do we travel? How do you envision all of us taking turns with the one big room on the tour bus?"

Alfie growled, "Stop! Just fucking stop, will you? Your need to know the end of the movie frustrates the fuck out of me. What we have right here is a love song. People would sing about us until the fucking cows came home. We have a once in a lifetime thing right here. That's not enough for you to throw caution to the wind?" He threw his hands up and began ranting, "Oh no. You're going on about fucking buses and sharing bedrooms, and...and...jeez, you're fucking crazy. You ought to be certified, girl."

I stared up at him pacing my room, running his hands through his hair. I giggled nervously. I couldn't help myself.

"Now it's funny...you think this is fucking funny, Lily?" I collected myself and tried to appear as serious as I could. It wasn't funny but hysteria was setting in.

"I don't think it's funny at all, apart from the part where you abandoned your girlfriend, stole someone's keys and intruded on my privacy by breaking into my home. You came into my bedroom, and *I'm* the one that's certifiable?"

"I didn't break in, I had a key remember?" Alfie threw himself on the bed and lay on his side with his head raised up on his elbow.

"I love you, Lily Parnell. Me. Alfie Black. And. You. Love. Me. Back. I fucking know you do. We'll find a way. You need to take that stick out of your ass, and stop beating yourself with it. I'm never going to leave you alone, Lily. You need to let yourself take that leap of faith, and get by my side."

I stared at him, lying there on my bed, with his perfect mouth stretched into the most adorable smile.

In the hour since he'd arrived, I had seen him go through a range of emotions, from a broken heart to elation.

"Get off the bed, Alfie." He grinned at me cockily with an air of mischief about him. "Or? What? You'll get down here with me?"

I wasn't smiling at all. I was serious. In fact, his lack of regard for Zoe was pissing me off.

"You need to leave, Alfie. I don't want you here. You have a girlfriend, and I've made enough mistakes since I met you. What happened at our launch night should never have happened. Zoe doesn't deserve it."

He stood up and the mattress bounced as his weight left it. "You're right. I need her to go."

Shaking my head, I snickered in disbelief. "Just like that, huh?"

He spun around to face me. "You think? She knows the deal. She just doesn't know that you're the one."

My mouth hung open. "You told her you love someone else, and she's with you anyway?"

He nodded. "Things are rarely what they seem, Lily. You should know that about me by now. Zoe knows the score. I've never lied to her. Our relationship is built on sex." I stood up and walked out of the bedroom to my front door.

Grabbing the handle, I flung it so wide, it creaked loudly on its hinges. "Get out."

He folded his arms. "Why? Is it because I'm having sex with Zoe?"

"No Alfie, it's because the poor girl has fallen for your 'fuck buddy' lines, except this time, you've used me as the excuse why she shouldn't love you."

His hand reached up to his mouth, and he began pulling at his bottom lip, as he thought about what to say next. "Nope, not the same... and Zoe...she doesn't love me."

Crossing my arms to hug myself, I said, "Listen, we could do this all day, Alfie, but I'd rather not."

He smirked. "I can think of better things to do with you

instead, as well," he quipped, smiling so widely his dimple was showing.

I sighed. "Just go, Alfie." He walked over to the couch and planted himself down heavily, thrusting his hands deep into the pockets of his leather jacket and shook his head.

"Nah, I can't do that, Lily. This might be my one shot at making you see sense and getting you back." He smirked, and I could tell he wasn't about to leave.

I took a seat near him, the front door still wide open. He stared at me, and I stared right back.

We had reached a stalemate, and I didn't know what to do next. Alfie's voice broke into the silence. "You're so fucking stunning. I know you've heard me say that before, but right now? Damn it, Lily. I'm blown away by you. You get more fucking beautiful with every year that passes." I watched him talking about me, and recognized the hooded lust-filled eyes. I was turning him on just by sitting here.

He was a master manipulator. Alfie was breaking down my defenses. He was so close, and my heart ached for him. Alfie was the only man I've ever known who made me want to kiss his soft lips whenever I saw them.

My mind flew back to the first time he kissed me in the long grass on campus. My fingers automatically stroked my lips. I didn't realize I was doing it until he sat forward on the couch, drawing himself nearer to me.

"You want me to kiss you?" My eyes closed. He knew what I was thinking, and I wanted nothing more.

My eyes flicked to his lips, then to his eyes. "No." My voice was barely a whisper. I cleared my throat, but I didn't get to speak before he did.

"I want to kiss you, Lily. I want to kiss you so fucking badly. I want to kiss you everywhere. I want to feel your fabulous ass in my hands as your pubic bone grinds against me, and your heels and nails dig into my butt in your effort to draw me closer. I want to strip you bare and lay you down in front of me. Look at you until I've teased myself so much that I can't keep my hands off you. I want to taste you, devour you. I want to tease and pleasure you, until you're screaming my name and pulling my hair, while you drag those same fingernails down my back."

He swallowed hard, and his voice this time was a thick whisper, so low I could barely make it out. "Most of all, I just want to be with you and love you and for you to want to be with me and love me back."

I couldn't stay passive any longer. I pulled myself forward on the seat and stood up. For all our flaws, Alfie and I did love each other desperately. There was no doubt in my mind about that.

I knew if I touched him again I'd ignite a passion, so fierce inside of us we'd be powerless to ever extinguish it.

Chapter Fifteen
LAST CHANCE

I pushed Alfie back against the couch and straddled him. His hands skimmed up my tank top and cupped my breasts as his mouth crushed mine. "Oh. God... God," he growled, his body vibrating with want for me.

His hands dropped to the hem of my tank top, and he pulled it clean over my head, tossing it behind him, while his hands went back to give attention to my breasts.

Dipping his head he took one of them in his mouth and sucked, deeply, greedily, as he looked up into my eyes. The passion in them took my breath away.

Seeing him there, sucking on my breast and looking up at me, sent my hormones into overdrive. I was so desperate with need for him. My hips gyrated in small circles over his huge solid mass, pressing hard into my wet panties.

Turning me over in one smooth motion, pinning me on my back on the floor. The weight of his body crushed me, squeezing the breath out of me, until he took his weight on the forearms that were tightly drawn against my head.

When he gazed longingly into my eyes, I knew that whatever happened next would be something I would never be able to burn from my memory.

I had completely surrendered to the feel of him on me. I couldn't believe that I had denied myself this for so long. Once I admitted that, I knew it was impossible to live without feeling like this.

The bands, Zoe, Luca, and the complications of our love didn't matter at that moment. What mattered was us, being completely honest and belonging together. I had been in denial for years now. Not now. Not when the connection between us was so strong. We had to find a way. We'd regret it forever if we didn't.

Alfie kissed me hungrily, fervently at first, before it slowed to a less breathless pace, but just as passionate. When he broke the kiss he asked, "Do you know how much I wanted to do that to you earlier in the club? I wanted to wipe that fucking guy's taste from your mouth."

Swallowing hard I said, "Don't..." His mouth crushed mine again, and he dragged his tongue across my teeth, first the top, then the bottom.

"I hate that he's tasted what's mine."

I struggled to free myself. "Stop..."

Alfie pulled back, but his stare was just as intense. "Tell me you're mine, Lily. I need to hear it."

His face was only inches away from me. His forehead dropped to rest on mine as our eyes locked. At that particular moment, a wave of peace washed over me, settling the turmoil I'd been in for so long. I didn't want to live life without Alfie in it a moment longer. "I can't be yours until Zoe isn't."

Alfie closed his eyes and slowly bobbed his head. He took my hand and smiled slowly. "Anything, I'll tell her tomorrow." Just like that, she was surplus.

"So, what? You go home for one last fuck and tell her?"

Alfie rolled his eyes. "You might not believe me, but I told you, I haven't had sex with her since I kissed you at the launch party. I haven't even kissed her. I've been putting her off and was going to tell her I couldn't have her around anymore." My lips formed into a line on my face, taking in what he was telling me.

"You need to take care of her, Alfie."

He smirked. "I already did."

"You did?" I frowned.

Alfie tilted his head back to face me and scowled, "Don't I always face my responsibilities?"

I had to hand it to Alfie. His previous history with Kara, his deceased soldier friend's girl, was proof of that. "What does that mean for Zoe?"

He shrugged his shoulders. "She already has a place. I set her up when she decided to come on the road with me."

There was no doubt in my mind as to how unaffected he was about letting Zoe go. "She's also had a monthly allowance paid into her account, so she could walk away whenever she wanted. I don't think she's ever drawn a penny on that the whole time she's been with me. She puts her clothes and anything else she needs on my card account. Zoe worked in retail and brought in minimum wage when she met me. So, she was happy with the set-up between us. She knew it wasn't forever. This just means she can get on with her life a little quicker is all."

Concerned at how easily Alfie could discard Zoe, I knew I had to shake the feeling off because if I wanted a life with him I had to believe he never really didn't had an emotional tie to her. I pushed him to the side and sat up.

I fished around for my tank top and pulled it back on. "Time to go, Alfie; call me when your relationship issues are resolved." I pointed to the door, and Alfie stood slowly.

"You mean it? We're going to be together?

Nodding I gestured toward the door. "Zoe," I said prompting him to bring whatever they were to a conclusion.

"We'll talk tomorrow. I'm going to need a lot of convincing, but you have bought yourself a hearing," I said as I pushed him outside the apartment into the hallway and closed the door.

Restless, I couldn't sleep after Alfie's visit. My mind went over and over about me backtracking and accepting I had to be with him again. At least I didn't have sex with him. I needed some kind of reassurance the band wouldn't be affected by anything I did. I owed them that much.

I showered and changed into some yoga pants and a little red tank and sat eating cereal. I was so apprehensive, but excited, about being with Alfie again. Above all, I prayed I was doing the right thing.

I needed my sounding board, so I pulled my cell from my purse and sent a text to Jack.

Lily: you are never going to believe what I'm thinking.

It was 3:45 am, and Holly wasn't here, so I knew they were probably still at the club.

Jack : no fucking way...don't do it! I'm coming home now.

Lily: huh?

Jack : you're thinking of sleeping with Alfie...is he there? That piece of shit disappeared about an hour after you did.

Lily: I'm not sleeping with him, he's not here.

Jack: Thank God for that, but we should talk. Don't make any irrational decisions, it's men that think with their dicks, Lily, and as far as I know, you don't have one. This, I'm assuming, is your saving grace when making decisions about Alfie.

Smirking, I sat back tapping my cell on my chin. I knew

Jack would believe I was letting myself down. He had no idea how incapacitated I felt when I couldn't be with Alfie.

Every one of my friends were going to go ballistic when they heard I was going to give Alfie another shot.

At 5 am, Jack, Rosie, Holly, and Brett showed up at the apartment. I was still buzzing and couldn't wait to see what the next day brought.

Holly told me that Alfie had left, and she couldn't find her keys to the apartment. She had reported it to the front desk, and they were taking care of it, having new locks fitted tomorrow.

I couldn't tell her that Alfie had let himself in here with them. She would hold herself responsible if Alfie had got back with me, because she had left her keys unattended. Depending on how this worked out with him, I might hold it against her in the future as well.

Jack had called it just right but knew better than to talk about it in front of Holly. I knew as soon as he got me alone, I would have to give him the edited highlights of Alfie's visit here earlier.

There was an entirely new set of issues to deal with at play here. I had to somehow make it all okay with the band, get the executives to agree to let us support Crakt Soundzz, and make that okay with my XrAid band members; not a short order.

My cell buzzed.

SEXPERT : I can't wait to see you today. What time, where?

Pink Lady: Zoe?

SEXPERT : Drunk, Des has her in his apartment.

Pink Lady : Des?

SEXPERT : I sent him a text telling him she wasn't coming back to my place again.

Pink Lady : When things are resolved with Zoe, contact me.

Jack tried to force my hand. "Who are you texting with Lily?" I smirked. Jack could be a sneaky bastard sometimes.

"Another, musician, why?" I smirked.

He shook his head. "No reason, just curious." He rubbed Rosie's back, and she turned and kissed him chastely. Jack smiled at her.

"Okay Rosie, as Lily won't let me snuggle her butt when you're here, I suppose you'll have to do."

I was annoyed with him. "Jack, please, that's not funny."

I looked at Rosie apologetically. Rosie smiled at me and winked. "Well, Lily, Jack thinks he has to perform when he snuggles with me." She stared at him. "State he's in? I'm betting he's going to feel a tad pissed at himself when it's just not happening down there."

She stared at Jack's groin. "Guess he doesn't have any pressure to do that with you, huh?" I smirked at Rosie's comeback, she was learning to deal with us, and I felt sure she'd only get better at that with time.

Everyone was slightly drunk and tired and turned in for the night. Jack and Rosie went to bed in the spare room, and I went back to mine.

I was lying in the dark when the door cracked open. "You still awake, Lily?" Jack's smooth voice cut into the darkness. I sat up as Jack's silhouette stood in my doorway and started toward me, but disappeared when he closed the door.

He pulled the sheet back and climbed in beside me, placing me in the crook of his arm. "You're not done with that revolving door that Alfie has you in, Lily?"

"Jack, please...don't give me a hard time. I've been fighting this for over two years and really...I think I would be fighting it for the rest of my life...like alcoholism or something." Jack took a deep breath and held it, then kissed the top of my head before exhaling.

"Lily, I've never seen anyone fall harder for someone, like you have with Alfie, and deny themselves at least a chance with them."

I nodded, looking up at him, barely making Jack's face out in the dark. He smoothed my hair and tucked a strand behind my ear.

"If you do this Lily, you have to be sure this is what you want. I'm saying this because I love you, not because I don't, someone has to. You can't keep turning the passion on and off around Alfie. It's not fair, you're playing with some pretty heavy feelings that he has for you."

Irritation shot through me. I stiffened, and Jack squeezed me tight, and I relaxed again in response. He was talking about how Alfie felt. I had been through some rough times in the past couple of years with him.

Jack sighed. "I know what you're thinking, Lily. You can stop that right now." I moved away from him, plumped my pillow, and leaned my head against the headboard.

"You know what I'm thinking now?" Jack snickered and tried to uncross my arms from my chest to take hold one of my hands, but I resisted and pulled it away.

"Sure, I know. You're thinking I'm taking Alfie's side blah blah...but I'm not. Think about it. How many times have you got back with him and left again? It had to have made his life Hell. He's done all the running, and you've shot him down so many times, it's a wonder the poor guy can stand at all now."

I'd never seen it that way. He was definitely the one that did all the running, but at the same time, I was the one who said he didn't want to have a relationship with me.

No wonder I was so confused by him. Jack's voice broke into my thoughts. "What about his girl? What happens to her now?" He thought like me. The last thing I wanted was to see someone homeless because her boyfriend wanted to walk away.

I explained what Alfie had told me, and Jack sat still, listening to the story about their arrangement. "Well, I've heard stranger things, Lily. I still think you're gonna get a rough time from all the guys in both bands about you both trying to make this thing work again."

I could feel tears welling again, and I was done shedding them about my love for Alfie. "I'm really scared Jack." There I said it. "I can't see this having a happy ending for anyone."

Jack scooted up and leaned against the headboard next to me. He crossed his legs and slid his arm behind my neck then cupped my shoulder pulling me into his side.

He sighed heavily and sat silently for a moment. "You're scared to try because it might not work? Don't you think you're overthinking things? What happens when people date?"

Jack didn't let me answer before he went on. "Sometimes people date and get married; sometimes they date for a long time then split; sometimes they have a date they absolutely never want to repeat...I know plenty about that one."

He chuckled, and his thumb grazed up and down my bare upper arm. "Lily,, you have to take risks with love. It doesn't come around very often...not the kind you and Alfie have. Rosie and I, we have a kind of love where she affects me in here." He tapped the center of his chest with his middle finger. "We're good together, but I don't really know if we're great you know?" I didn't, but I nodded anyway.

"The question for me isn't what might happen in the future with us, Lily, it's do I feel enough to want to spend the rest of my life with her? I'm really not sure about that part."

One of the things I loved about Jack was that he had always been able to see the trees and not just the wood. Tell me what you feel, Lily. Is that what you're scared of?"

I smiled in the dark, because he had just simplified my question for me. It wasn't that I couldn't envision spending the rest of my life with Alfie, I could.

The question was whether I could be with him and play music. There was more to it as well. "I have a dilemma about taking Alfie up on his idea of us supporting his band. What happens if we were to split? If... it didn't work out. I couldn't ask the guys to change the arrangement, because I wasn't in a relationship anymore."

Jack pulled away from me. "Okay, you need a plan B in that case." I sat wondering what could possibly be a backup if things went wrong. "Hmm, you're too clever for me, Jack, but I have an idea. I don't know if I have the guts to make the call, but it might just give me a little security in all of this if I can."

Chapter Sixteen

STRIKING A DEAL

"What if...I ask Rick if he can share our band with Alfie's?" Jack chuckled and bent his leg, digging his heel into the mattress and rolling his body on its side, pulling himself further up the headboard, so that he was completely upright facing me now.

"Who's Rick?"

I smiled at Jack. He was slow on the uptake because of all the alcohol he'd consumed tonight. "Rick Fars," I said flatly.

Jack snorted. "You're just gonna call Rick Fars? Cobham Street, Rick fucking Fars?"

Grinning, I chuckled at Jack. "Sure, I have Rick's number, and he has mine. He's going to check in with me periodically to see how I'm doing. He said I could call him for anything."

I knew that this conversation between us would be relayed to David, my friend in London and an avid Cobham Street fan. He would go ape shit that I had Rick Fars' phone number.

Jack shook his head. "Don't call him, Lily. Alfie's one thing; Rick Fars would eat you for breakfast."

Annoyed with Jack's assessment of Rick. I stared him

down. He had no idea how nice of a person he was, but I didn't feel like protesting his innocence. Maybe at some point, Jack might meet him and come to that conclusion on his own.

At 6 am, Jack snuck back into his own bed. I half worried that Rosie was going to wake in the night and find that Jack had come to my room anyway.

That would have been awkward, and I wasn't all that confident we'd be able to convince her that Jack and I were just talking about my love life. After Jack left, I fell into a fitful sleep and didn't wake again until 2pm.

When I woke, I lay staring at the ceiling thinking about what Jack had said. I plucked up the courage and decided to put in a call to Rick. I was nervous to talk to him, but he had said 'anytime', so I felt that this was it.

I explained everything to Rick. He was surprised to hear I was thinking of getting back with Alfie. He did disclose he found the sexual tension radiating off us hot in itself.

Rick thought I was being smart about not wanting to make the band exclusive to Crakt Soundzz. I doubted whether the guys would go for that anyway.

He surprised me by offering us a deal, which was where his support acts shared half the tour with Alfie's support act, namely XrAid, for the next tour.

This way I'd get to spend some time with Alfie, but the band would have exposure from working with two household names. I was humbled that this big time rock star would do this for me.

Not only were we going to support Alfie's band, but I was stunned Rick had that much confidence in XrAid to invite us to support his band during their international tour.

I only had two things to achieve now. One was to get the guys to agree to the arrangement. That would be hard as soon as Alfie's name was mentioned.

The fact that I had pulled off us supporting two of the biggest bands on the planet would maybe help them see past that.

As for Alfie? I knew he was going to throw a hissy fit that we wouldn't be together all the time. This was my condition. If he wanted me to take a chance on him, he would be able to concede.

When I brought it up, he was a little indignant about the whole thing and didn't want me to work with Rick. When he realized it was this or nothing, he was more than happy to agree with the arrangement.

I called Lennon and asked him to get the guys together at his place, because I had something I needed to discuss with the group. "Am I going to be pissed about this, Lily?" I bit my lip and chewed the inside of my mouth, as I decided how I was going to answer this.

"Well, maybe, but not if you take a deep breath and consider what I'm bringing to the table." He growled down the phone at me.

"Does this have anything to do with that shifty shit, Alfie?"

I giggled. "Hmm, that's not very kind Lennon."

Lennon mumbled almost to himself, "Maybe, but it's definitely fucking apt." I finished the call, telling him I would be there by 4 pm. It was 3:10 pm now, so I had to get moving.

I showered and dressed in a pair of cut-off denim jean shorts and a little cropped t-shirt. It hung off one shoulder. I brushed my hair and wound it up into a messy bun, securing it with a clip.

I ran around with a small trundle case, throwing in my outfit to wear tonight, shoes, and some makeup.

When I went into the sitting room, Jack and Rosie were cuddled up watching TV. Jack was eating my new pack of ham.

"Great. I'm starving, are we going out to eat? There's only rabbit food in the fridge." I knew he meant healthy stuff, like peppers, lettuce, celery, and other salad items.

"I'll drop you at the diner, Jack. I have a meeting with the band right now." He glanced at me, looking annoyed that he'd hung around for me to eat.

"You should both spend the rest of day doing last minute things before our parents arrive."

I'd made reservations for dinner and booked our parents' tickets for the theatre this evening. "I'll pick you up at seven for dinner, and we'll leave my car at the place; Elle's booked a VIP section for tonight. All you have to decide is if you're coming back here tonight or going to our parents' place."

Jack gave me a look that told me that he was coming with me, without saying anything, and I nodded.

Rosie turned to Jack. "What do you want to do, baby?"

"It's all sorted." He kissed the top of her head, and I could see Rosie's brows bunch, because she had no idea how I knew what he'd decided.

I kissed Rosie and Jack goodbye, and Jack pulled me in for a hug. He started sniffing my hair. "I missed that smell."

I giggled and smirked at Rosie. "He's a pervert, isn't he?" I teased, and we laughed together as I opened the front door. Jack winked at me, and I pulled it closed it behind me.

By the time I drove to Lennon's place, Cody and Digs' rides were sitting out front. I wasn't sure if Shawn had come with one of the guys or if we'd have to wait for him to get here.

Reaching for the screen door I opened it, calling out to them in the back. "Hey, guys, it's only me."

The toilet flushed as I passed and Shawn came out of the guest bathroom. "Ah, everyone's here already." Shawn smirked.

Lennon's voice cut through the quiet. "Okay, what's up?"

Smiling, I wrung my hands. "Well, I have something I need to run past you guys."

Cody smirked and looked at Lennon. "Does this have anything to do with Alfie?" I blushed that I was so transparent.

"Now there's a sight I haven't seen in a while." Cody pointed at my face, which I knew had gone red.

"Promise to hear me out?" I looked at them, concerned this wasn't going to be as easy as it sounded when I spoke to Rick earlier.

I explained about Alfie coming to see me, and my feelings for him. I told them that even though a lot of people would view it simply, I was aware that my predecessor had left the band because of a guy.

All I wanted was to reassure them this wasn't what I wanted. I was considering the band before I made any final decisions about getting involved with him again.

Cody's eyes lit up like a Christmas tree. "You have us touring with both bands? How the fuck did you pull that off?"

I explained about Alfie's suggestion for us to be together, but my reluctance to have XrAid stuck touring with one act. So, I'd called Rick. I smirked at Cody when I remembered telling him about us exchanging numbers.

"I just wanted to run it by you all, and to tell you guys I know you're apprehensive about me becoming involved with Alfie again. But, I love him. I've been denying it, but I owe it to us to try. I've been running away from him almost since I met him. I need to know if we're supposed to be together. I think he's the love of my life, and he says he knows I'm his."

The guys all sat staring me until Digs slapped his hands on his legs and pushed up onto his feet. "You do what you have to do, darlin', but he gets one chance. He fucks with your head again; I'll make sure he never gets near you again."

I smiled. Digs was very protective of me, but was always the first person to see the good in people.

"Well, we have to do our tour first, before we do anything else." Lennon was now talking in practical terms. We had eighteen dates in twenty-one days.

So, for the first three weeks after New Year's Day we would be touring eighteen states. Alfie would be on the back-burner no matter what. The difference this time was that it was me who was going away.

My cell rang and when I saw the SEXPERT ID, my heart skipped a beat. Even before I heard his voice, he had my heart racing.

I swiped my phone, and his voice cut into my ear like a warm, velvet caress. "Hey." That one word from his lips always gave me goosebumps, but this time it also held hope.

I couldn't let him know that just yet. I had to make sure he had taken care of Zoe, and that she was able to leave Alfie behind before we could go forward.

"Zoe?" Alfie exhaled loudly. "She's gone, Lily. Des took her to the airport. She's flying back to D.C. as we speak. She has an apartment there, and she wants to go to college. I've already arranged that for her. She was lucky; she got enrolled for the January intake studying at the college of Arts and Science. She had great scores from high school but her parents didn't have a college fund, so she ended up working at a truck stop"

"Where are you?" I asked, hearing traffic.

"I'm sitting in my car outside your apartment. Can I come up?" I thought about Holly, and her likely reaction if I went back there. I explained that I wasn't at home.

"Shit, where are you; I'll come pick you up." If we were going to do this, then I knew I needed to be firm and inde-pendent from the onset.

"No, Alfie, go home. I'll see you tonight. It's only a couple of hours away."

Alfie exhaled heavily. "Lily, it's been way over a year. I can't wait another minute." I smiled, and my heart flipped over in my chest. Hearing him say that and knowing I was finally giving in to my feelings made me extremely nervous. I was determined to play it cool.

"Tonight." I chuckled. "I promise it will be worth the wait."

Alfie groaned into his cell. "You are determined to kill me, aren't you?" I giggled at his groan.

"I think you'll live, see you later." I swiped my finger on the red phone icon and closed my cell, throwing it in my bag.

I had contemplated asking him to come to dinner with Jack, me, our parents, and Rosie, but I needed time to persuade my dad to give Alfie another chance.

When I looked up, Lennon was shaking his head. "Here we go again," he grunted, crushed the beer can he was holding, and threw it at the trash can.

It missed. "Well, I hope Alfie's better at scoring tonight than you are." I smirked, and Digs high-fived me.

"There's that smart-ass mouth again. Something tells me this time with Alfie is going to be different," Digs quipped.

I smiled warmly at Digs, who seemed to have the most confidence in me. "Bet your ass it is, honey."

Digs, Shawn and I messed around in the pool before I showered and dressed at Lennon's place and once I had collected Jack and Rosie we went to have dinner with my parents. I hadn't told them about Alfie yet.

As usual, Jack did his best to make me squirm a few times but stopped short of dropping the bomb that Alfie was back on the scene.

Jack's mother secretly harbored some notion he and I

would end up together. She dropped less than subtle hints in front of Rosie a few times.

Biting back a grin I watched Jack burst her bubble about us. "Lily and I are incompatible," he stated.

His mom, Jacqueline, furrowed her brow. "Nonsense, Jack, whatever could make you think that?" Jack smirked, and I cringed as I waited to see what was going to come out of his mouth.

Jack paused for effect. "I could never sleep with my sister, and I know it's the same for her. We're not from that kind of town." He grinned.

I was relieved he'd kept it clean for once, and also relieved that he hadn't embarrassed Rosie. After dinner, our parents went back to the villa to change before the theatre. We drove to a club I had never been to before.

It was one that the Crakt Soundzz guys seemed to be favoring in Miami, since I was playing at Eject, D'mond and Blazers.

I felt both hurt and touched they had been avoiding coming around me while I wasn't with Alfie.

I'd been to the part of Miami where the club was, it was had an impressive entrance with big gold letters called 'Ziggy's Palace'.

It was every bit as flashy as Louie's clubs and filled with beautiful people. It was most likely the number four spot in Miami, because everyone knew that the clubs owned by Louie were the places to be.

Jack talked non-stop from the moment we got in the car, and I could see that Rosie was a little worn by his constant energy levels.

"So, Lily, I get first dance tonight right? I never got one last night, and I'm having withdrawal symptoms." He looked at my scowl and turned to Rosie.

"You don't mind if Lily and I dance, do you?" Rosie's jaw

dropped. She was caught off guard as she squeaked, "Not at all, Jack."

He turned and smirked at me, then winked when Rosie began rummaging in her bag for some imaginary item.

I was wearing a skintight dress, which was off-the-shoulder in a deep green color. It was a beautiful little dress. Holly and I had been shopping together, and I fell in love with it on sight.

It was understated, but with a few choice accessories, it was soon jazzed up. Jack told me I looked like a million dollars dressed in it.

Chapter Seventeen
MY GIRL

*A*rriving at the club, Alfie was hovering just inside the door with his bodyguard, waiting for me. When he saw me, he came running across and opened the cab door. The girls in the queue for the club instantly recognized him and began to scream. When we stepped out of the cab and Alfie placed his hands on my hips, the girls screamed louder.

Dipped his mouth close to my ear and whispered, "Where have you been? You look so fucking hot by the way." He smiled widely. There was a buzz of excitement coming from the line of girls waiting to get into the club, and they continued to scream for Alfie's attention.

They began making catcalls to him, offering themselves in one way or another, from one calling that she would show him the "best night of his life," to choruses of, "We love you, Alfie."

One voice rose above the rest. "Hey, Alfie, when is it my turn to be grabbed." Alfie smirked and turned to address the crowd of girls. "Sorry girls, I only have two hands, and they don't like touching anyone except my girl here."

The girls let out a collective groan. "Lucky bitch," one called out.

I smirked and looked up at Alfie. "They all want you. What does it feel like to be able to have any girl you want?" He scowled at me and shook his head.

"I didn't know until tonight, because I have only wanted one girl for so long. She didn't want me until recently. So, it's a new concept for me."

"Good answer," I replied.

He grinned widely and had a glint of mischief in his eyes. "Now that I have her, my heart is bursting with joy, and I have an excruciating ache with the wood in my pants." He chuckled.

I looked over at the girls that were still making loud comments, and Alfie's finger hooked under my chin. He turned my face back toward him. "They may think they want me, but I know not a single one of them could ever come between us."

He pulled me closer and looked at the girls again. "Well..." One of them shouted. Alfie looked at me, "Guess they are waiting for me to kiss you now."

The lustful way he looked at me with a serious sensual stare made me shiver, and I was instantly wet. My body vibrated slightly in anticipation of his next move.

He brushed a strand of hair behind my ear, and slowly his sexy, lopsided grin appeared. It widened until his dimple was on show." Do you mind?" he asked, staring at my lips, as his tongue brushed along his in preparation.

I almost had to pinch myself, to reassure me this wasn't a dream. I had dreamed about being in his arms for so long, and now I was actually here. Alfie dipped his head and licked his lips, making them shine. He dropped his forehead onto mine, his eyes heavy with passion.

Grinning down at me with so much tenderness in his

voice, Alfie softly said, "This will be our first official kiss as a couple, Lily. I'm nervous, are you?" I swallowed audibly thinking, hell yeah, but just nodded, speechless.

Alfie's lips brushed lightly across mine. He stroked his nose over my face inhaling the scent on my skin. The noise from the queue of girls was deafening, but then they seemed to disappear, and there was only us in the moment.

His scent was the one thing, out of everything, that always did it for me. As soon as I inhaled him, I always wanted to crawl inside of him. Something about it just turned me on and drove me wild, but I had to remember we were in front of everyone.

He tilted his head when he found my mouth. His soft, moist lips melded with mine, while his tongue probed for entry. My lips parted, and the feel of his hot, wet tongue tangling with mine was electric. A rash of goose bumps extended from my scalp to my toes.

His hand swept up the side of my body until his fingers fanned through my hair. He wound it around his fingers and pressed the back of my head toward him to deepen the kiss. The sensation between our connection and the tingling in my scalp was almost enough to send me over the edge.

Alfie placed his hand on my lower back and pushed our bodies flush against each other. I could feel his need for me as the bulge in his pants grew harder when he made a subtle friction movement between us.

In that moment, I heard nothing but the soft, low moan of want escaping his throat and the feel of it entering my mouth as it vibrated. Breaking away from the kiss, we both stood breathless. Our eyes transfixed on each other. "Wow." One of the girls shouted, "Oh. My, God! That was so fucking hot," another screeched.

Alfie smirked and chuckled softly, but his eyes were still

fixed on mine. Slowly he broke his gaze and turned to the group, still smiling.

"Damned straight it was," he shouted, as he pulled me tightly to him and squeezed my ass.

I giggled and bowed my head into his chest, still trying to cope with the aftermath of what just happened. Our kiss had the same effect on me as being drunk.

He slid his hand around my waist again, and we began to walk into the club. I could feel Alfie still trembling, buzzed from our connection, when he held me tightly to his side. Jack had been standing by silently.

"Thank God you stopped. For a moment there, I thought I was going to have to do my boy-scout-thing and erect a tent for privacy. I would have called out for you to get a room, but I doubt you would have heard anything with what was happening between you."

I swiped his arm, feeling a little embarrassed. "It wasn't that bad, Jack." I made eye contact with Rosie hoping for some reassurance, but she looked a little red and flustered, so I thought to myself, yeah, hell, maybe it was.

Alfie smirked and leaned into my ear. "How long do we have to stay here?" His voice was raw and husky. "I need to get you alone, babe."

I frowned, knowing that he was going to be upset with me. "After that display, we're definitely not going to be alone, not just yet. We still have a lot of things to hash out between us."

As I predicted, Alfie looked really annoyed with my rejection. "Lily, you're not being fair here."

I smirked, but stood resolute on my decision. "Alfie, just trust me. If we're doing this, we need to give this our best shot. I'm not rushing that, because this is our now-or-never moment, a chance to make things work out between us."

Alfie stared at me, the strain suddenly leaving his face.

"You're really serious about being with me this time, aren't you?" He laced his fingers in mine and brought our hands to his lips.

"You have no idea how happy you are making me feel right now. I've agonized about the last time I left you, because I should never have gone. I wanted to put you first... always, Lily. I am desperately in love with you, and I'm desperate to show you how much. But if you need me to wait a little longer, I'll try." He looked sincere, his handsome face with his solemn expression gave weight to his words. They meant more to me now than ever.

I placed my hands on the sides of his head and pulled his face to me. He stood silently, while I kissed his eyes and peppered little kisses over his face, until his tongue ran along my lips, and our mouths melded into one another again.

The effect of his sensual kiss with our soft moans drove me crazy and made me desperate for him to be inside me, to be part of me.

My panties were soaking, and I was in danger of going back on my decision and have him make love to me right now.

"Are you going to suck faces all night or is the big shot rock star going to put his hand in his pocket and buy us all a drink?"

Jack had decided I needed help with my self-control, and to be honest, I was glad he was capable of making decisions, because my judgment was becoming less rational by the minute with Alfie around.

This night was a complete contrast to last night with our friends. Although we had a VIP section in our group, there were five guys not currently dating. They all danced on the main dance floor, and at one point we commandeered a table near the bar in one of the main rooms.

This was mainly due to it being easier for the guys to keep

drinking and dancing with some of the hot girls. Some were especially eager, mainly when they recognized Des and Andy. Cody and Lennon were beginning to get recognized too, but Cody had brought the girl from last night, Angela.

Surprise of the evening was when a very pretty dark-haired girl with a gorgeous smile was introduced to us by Digs. "This is Freya." Digs looked completely smitten, and she seemed shy, and a little star struck, at meeting everyone.

Elle and I made her feel welcome, then she went to sit at Elle and Holly's table with Digs, Brett, and Drew. Elle later told me that Digs had told her that he'd been seeing her for two months, but didn't want to say too much, because it was still fairly new, and XrAid was going on tour.

I guessed he didn't think it was new anymore, as he'd just taken things to another level, by bringing her to meet us.

My chest felt so light, the constant ache to be with Alfie now gone. Letting my love for him out had taken care of that.

Judging from Alfie's playful banter, he was having the time of his life. He never left my side, but seemed really relaxed and carefree. After a while, I realized no one had even asked me to dance. Maybe they all knew. We just needed time without any interruptions. Even Jack didn't dance with me, but gave me several knowing smiles.

I also wondered if the reason no one else had asked me to dance was because they'd witnessed my dancing with Alfie. The sexual tension between us was ridiculously hot.

I caught up with Elle in the restrooms. She was so excited I'd given Alfie another chance and told me when she first moved in with Drew, she'd hated Alfie. However, she got to know him better on the tour bus. The more time she spent with him, the more she realized how much he loved me, and how much our break up had affected him. She commented she'd never known anyone that loved a girl as much as he appeared to love me.

She told me that I was all he ever talked about, but that he didn't use my name. Zoe was well aware that I was 'the love of his life', and he had told her he had no heart, he'd given it up before he met her. My heart ached that I had put him through all of that, but it was reassuring that Elle could confirm a lot of what Alfie had said when he'd come to see me.

She explained that she would have told me all of this before, but she'd kept her word not to talk about Alfie to me, or me to Alfie. I really hadn't been fair to ask that of her. I had put Elle in the same position as Mandy. They had become friends with Alfie but couldn't support him when it came to talking about the one issue he felt he had needed it with...me.

Elle hugged me when I told her that we would be touring with Crakt Soundzz, squealing loudly. She began jumping up and down, and I could see she was already picturing us getting up to all sorts while the guys had rehearsals and sound checks to do.

We made our way back to our guys at the table. Alfie was surrounded by lots of hot looking girls. I stood back and watched him, interested to see how he behaved when he thought I wasn't around. He was polite and charming, the 'stage version' of Alfie, but he didn't off a vibe of being interested in anything, except talking about the band and his music.

The thing I noticed most was women wanted to touch him a lot. One ran her hand through his hair. Alfie flicked his head away from her, and his hand came up grabbing her wrist, before he gently but firmly pushed her arm gently back in her direction.

Henry, one of Alfie's security guys, seemed to gauge it just right and moved in as the advances on Alfie got more personal.

Sliding between Alfie and the girl, Henry used his interception to create a barrier between them. Engaging her in pleasant conversation, Alfie's body guard stepped in her direction forcing her to step back to create a safer distance between them.

One girl tried to sit on Alfie's lap, and he moved slightly, so that she just missed achieving this. His head tilted as he looked in the direction I had disappeared in, and I knew he was waiting for me.

I stepped in front of him, and he pulled me onto him. "Sorry, ladies. I only have eyes for my girl, and if you don't mind, we'd like a little privacy now," he cooed.

They mainly dispersed after that, but if others came up and began to annoy him by ignoring me and hitting on him, he would kiss me and pretend like they didn't exist.

"Are we going to be subjected to this all the time on tour?" Lennon's voice was sharp. I wasn't sure whether Lennon meant the women hanging around Alfie or us kissing. Alfie took it as him commenting on us as a couple.

Lennon was scowling, and Alfie grinned at him. "You don't have to watch, Lenny. Get a girl of your own, and I'll teach you what to do." Alfie grinned at Lennon's confused face, as he digested what he said, then chuckled.

"Don't worry, man. You're not even going to be on the same bus as us. I don't want my girl's ass being gawped at when she gets out of the shower. Drew and I are sharing a bus with Elle and Lily, and all you sweaty guys can fuck as many groupies as you can get your hands on."

Cody slung his arm around Lennon's neck and pulled him close, hitting on the opportunity to tease Lennon further. "Don't worry, Lennon, you can be Shawn's wingman. I'll scout the girls for you both. You'll only have to drop your pants."

Shawn looked at me and smirked. "Hmm, guess my mass-produced junk is going to see some action in the near future." I chuckled as Shawn waited for my reply.

I wrinkled my nose in mock disgust. "I'd definitely use glitter sprinkles on it, Shawn. Just to up your chances, an' all." I winked. The XrAid guys and Jack cracked up laughing. Alfie looked puzzled, and Shawn shook his head at Alfie's expression.

"Dude, you just had to be there, I guess," Shawn commented, walking away belly laughing wickedly.

Alfie squeezed my arm. "What was that about?"

I smirked. "Later. It's a longstanding joke from my first ever gig, and it would take too long to explain tonight."

At the end of the night, Alfie tried to persuade me to go back with him. I wouldn't even let him come back with us, because I knew I would end up in bed with him.

We left after we made final arrangements to meet for our Christmas Eve bash, and I had already promised him a couple of hours of my time during the day. The highlight of our night, apart from his kisses, was when I invited him to spend Christmas Day with my parents and everyone else.

His surprised reaction was incredible. "You mean it? I get to spend Christmas with you, all day and night?"

"What about your sister and your aunt though, what are they doing?"

"Yeah, I'm supposed to see them on Christmas morning." He looked dejected.

I'd never met his family before. "Would they come to us? Spend the day with all of us?"

Alfie's eyes went wide. "Seriously?"

I nodded. "Sure. The more the merrier."

Alfie smiled. "Henry can bring them and take them home."

I nodded and squealed when he swept me off my feet and planted a wet kiss on my cheek. "Damn, Father Christmas just gave me my present early," he cooed.

Chapter Eighteen

MAKING PLANS

*A*lfie's text was waiting for me when I got out of the shower this morning.

SEXPERT: On my way <3

It was Christmas Eve, and I had agreed to spend some time with Alfie today, but we were discussing the details of how we would manage to spend enough quality time together with us both having busy schedules.

Apart from that, we'd be traveling to different places, often spending long hours cooped up with Drew and Elle on a tour bus, and had to work out how to have a proper relationship, while living in close proximity to all of our respective bandmates.

We'd have pressures from the tour itself, and the added pressure of accepting time apart, while XrAid went off to support Rick's band.

We needed to set some boundaries first. We needed to try to work out days off in sync, so that we could allow ourselves to grow a lasting bond with each other, which would rise above the fucked-up-ness of being in the music business.

Although, there was only a little interest in XrAid as a

band from the media, Crakt Soundzz was a completely different story.

Alfie was regularly hounded by the media for any morsel of information. I knew this would be a constant headache for me, because it was one of the things that had put me off being with him in the past. I hadn't thought I could handle it.

I was younger then, and less self-assured. I knew for certain I'd be a little less likely to accept everything I saw in the papers, online or anywhere else, without giving the person involved the opportunity to explain it to me.

However, I'd be lying if I said I wasn't nervous about the fans targeting me about being his girl, but also about being in a band myself. People just couldn't approach me on stage.

When we signed, we were also given some security detail for when we were on the road. If I was with Alfie, then I had his. Alfie wanted to discuss getting someone to be with me permanently, now that we were back together, so I guessed that would all have to be finalized when we talked.

My apartment intercom buzzed and the doorman told me that Alfie was waiting downstairs. He'd arrived in an old Jeep I hadn't seen before. His Mustang was his usual ride.

He looked totally awesome in his old faded cargo shorts, which hung low on his waist, and a black tank top. I really loved when he was dressed way down like this.

I knew that sounded stupid, when his band attire revolved around jeans and t-shirts, or if he was at a function, he was really smart. But like this, it was just Alfie, my Alfie, the private man. No bells or whistles necessary.

For a rock star, he looked far too healthy, with his shiny hair and flawless skin, bright sparkly eyes and great physique, but Alfie did take care of himself. He didn't do drugs, smoke, or eat excessively.

His muscular arms and torso were displayed perfectly by

his attire. His hair was still wet, and he smelled like heaven when he bent in to kiss me.

As soon as he touched the skin on my shoulder, my skin reacted. The magnetic pull we had to each other was ridiculous. I found myself having to squirm out of his arms before he squirmed his way into my panties.

He chuckled and rubbed his hand on my lower back. "Hey," he cooed.

I smiled and checked out his attire. "So, we're not going anywhere fancy to talk?"

Alfie checked me out in my little bronze-colored sundress. "You going to go naked on the beach or do you still have a bikini in the trunk of your car?"

He'd remembered that in my early days of being in Florida, I seemed to constantly struggle with what to wear for the weather.

In the beginning, I wasn't used to having an ocean with a beach on tap all the time. When it was cloudy, I would over-dress in my air-conditioned apartment and melt as soon as my feet hit the pavement, because I was dressed in too many clothes.

By way of dealing with this I kept extra light clothing and beachwear in my car, just in case the opportunity arose to use them.

Today, my forward thinking was paying off. Either that, or Alfie's was with the thought of seeing me in my bikini.

Alfie drove us down toward The Keys, pulling alongside a little beachside café. He told me that this was one of his favorite places. He had fond memories of playing on the small beach as a child.

He was usually a closed book about his family, yet this morning he told me about how his sister Layla and he had spent hours building the best sandcastles, while his mom and dad sat at one of the restaurant's tiki tables and chatted happily about their lives.

"They were always planning something." Alfie was staring out at the ocean, obviously reflecting upon the happy times he spent here.

His face looked tinged with sadness, but when he turned to face me, his eyes fixed on mine and seemed to come alive when he smiled.

"I just figured that this was a great place to bring you, so that we could do our planning here too. They were an amazing couple, Lily. They were so smart, loving, funny, supportive; until my mom got sick."

I nodded that I understood he missed them, especially on anniversaries such as Christmas, and leaned over to hug him. He kissed my cheek and signaled for the waiter to come over.

We didn't agree on everything that we wanted as we ironed out our differences on how this was going to work, and I knew most people didn't ever plan how to start dating, but we weren't under normal circumstances.

We would probably get about ten weeks a year altogether, without commitments, where we could actually be in the same place at the same time without the bands. Even during this, we would have to schedule some rehearsal time with our bands. I was also conscious that the other band members might have commitments of their own, which would further complicate our situation.

Alfie begged me not to overthink us. This was usually the point when I told him we couldn't do this.

Suddenly I realized for the first time, how much I had hurt him by struggling with my conflicting feelings. "Lily, when you truly love someone, you take what you can get. Nothing else matters," he cooed.

I wished I could see it in the simplest of terms like Alfie did, but my brain didn't function that way. It made me consider I could be making him feel insecure by my constant striving to find reasons why we couldn't be together instead of ways we possibly could.

Part of me wondered if Alfie was questioning just how much I loved him, when I was meeting to decide how much time I could spend with him, and if it was really worth it.

I was the one constantly placing conditions on us now. In the beginning he wouldn't commit, but since he had, the only thing that he'd done that was difficult for me was to go to work.

How many other women live with their husband's traveling? There were many occupations where one partner often had to leave the other.

I felt ashamed, when I thought about military families, where the added pressure for them was affording to live and bring up families, and each time they parted could be the last time they saw their loved one.

Instantly I knew what I had to do. Taking Alfie's hand, I knew I had to meet him half way. "You know what, Alfie?"

His eyes searched mine, and I could see a fleeting glimmer of insecurity before he answered. "Yeah?"

I smiled slowly. "It doesn't matter, none of the planning, the traveling, the bands, the fans. We just have to do this. You told me you were desperately in love with me. I want to show you that I'm just as desperately in love with you. Apart from you being faithful and loving to me, I have no conditions on us."

Alfie rose slowly from his seat and walked around the little tiki table. He came up behind me and bent over, wrapping his arms around me in a hug. As I went to close my eyes, he scooped me up and ran full pelt into the ocean with me.

I shouted for him to let me go but he was also telling everyone around us my declaration. "She loves me," he called out, attracting the attention of everyone on the beach, and those inside the restaurants were now straining at the windows to see what all the commotion was about.

He didn't stop until we were fully submerged. I struggled for air as I broke up through the waves. He was already standing waiting. He grinned and pulled me tightly to him.

Forgetting everything I went with the moment and wrapped my legs around his waist as he bent to kiss me. We could hear cheering from a few of the sunbathers on the beach.

When we walked back to the shoreline, I heard an older woman tell her husband, "You need to get that Alfie's number. He really knows how to show his girl he loves her, maybe you can get some tips from him." I briefly wondered how she knew him, before I remembered everyone knew who Alfie Black was.

Alfie and I made our way back to my apartment. He was begging the whole time to come upstairs. I still wanted us to take things a little at a time, but reminded him that he would be staying with me tomorrow night. And I was secretly hoping that I could hold off that long as well.

He dropped me off and reluctantly went home. Jack, true to form, was eating a massive bag of tortilla chips he'd gotten from Walmart.

"That shop is crazy. It has just about anything I need. In fact, I could probably go on a vacation to Walmart, pitch a tent in there, and spend a week sightseeing." He glanced up at me and did a double take, "Jeez, Lily, did you fall in the ocean or were you pushed?"

I smirked at Jack's question. "I was romantically thrown in the ocean." I pretended to swoon.

Jack's brows furrowed. "That's like saying I was romantically thrown under a bus. You could have died either way." I giggled at Jack's analogy and swatted his arm.

"Alfie was happy. He demonstrated it. What can I say?"

Jack glanced at Rosie who snickered then looked back at me. "Well best not piss him off in that case beautiful, that's all I can say".

I rose above Jack's comments. "I'm going to take a shower."

"Okay, give me five to send Rosie to the store, and I'll join you." I shook my head and smirked.

"You're crazy, Jack." He never could let me have the last word so he called out, "I know that's code for you want monkey sex with me, right?"

Rosie giggled, and I felt relieved that she was beginning to get that Jack and I were really not interested in each other sexually, and it was our strange way.

I stepped in the shower and washed the ocean out of my hair. By the time I'd finished, I no longer smelled like a fisherman's boat.

My cell began to vibrate on my nightstand, and the 'Crakt Soundzz' ringtone for 'Listen' rang out. I smiled when I saw the ID SEXPERT.

I pulled on some fresh lace panties and swiped the phone to answer. "How the Hell did you manage that?"

Alfie sounded confused. "Huh?"

I raised my brow even though he couldn't see me. "The ringtone?"

I heard him chuckle. "Well…I figured that if you heard our song, you wouldn't be able to ignore your phone."

A smile spread on my lips but I pretended to be annoyed with him. "No, Alfie I meant how did you get my phone and change the ringtone for your number."

There was a pause, and I could hear the humor in his voice. "I did it when you went to put your bikini top on at the restaurant. You left your phone on the table, so I figured there was nothing you didn't want me to see. Oh, and by the way, you're bound to find out, but I deleted that tool Luca's number for you too...I saved you a job, right?"

Normally, things like that would have made me so furious, but Alfie was right, I had no need for anyone else's phone number any more.

"Thank you," I said. I could hear him exhale heavily. He must have known that his action could have gone either way.

Alfie cleared his throat. "So, shall we start the call again?"

I giggled at him. "Sure." Alfie hummed some of the introduction from 'Listen'.

I played along. "Hello?" Alfie's voice sounded seductive as he cooed, "Hey." The fresh underwear I had put on was now soaked, and I knew that I had to start carrying some in my bag in reserve those for times when Alfie turned me on.

Hell, I would need a trundle suitcase to haul around most times, the way he affected me.

"I love you, baby."

Smiling I replied, "I love you too. Why did you call me?"

I could hear the smile in his voice. "Because."

Silently I waited, thinking there would be more to his answer, and pulled on some new panties, "Are you still there?"

His end was completely silent until he spoke. "Uh, huh."

I smiled again. "Okay, you were telling me why you called."

He chuckled. "I did."

I shook my head, even though he couldn't see me. "Nope, you didn't."

"Seriously, Lily? I did. I told you I called because."

"You've lost me, Alfie. I have no idea what you're talking about."

"You need me to expand?"

I giggled at him. "Expand what?"

He huffed a breath pretending he was the one annoyed. "I called you because...because I can do that now. Because I love you. Because I wanted to hear your sweet voice, with that sexy accent. Because I know you'll have just got out of the shower and could possibly be naked. I called you, because I can't wait for tonight. Because I love you; I said that already, right? I also called because I can't wait for tomorrow night to hold you in my arms. So, you see, Lily, I called you 'because'."

"Wow," I said breathlessly. "Alfie, I think I just fell in love with you a little more after that." His seductive voice had already won me over. For someone who didn't do hearts and flowers relationships, his thoughtful ways and choice of words left me breathless.

"Did you know that because is a 'wow' word?" I smiled, waiting for him to answer.

"Why?" he asked. I could hear he was puzzled.

"Because, anything that's said after because is what makes the sentence have reason. I love you Alfie, and wow, I've finally realized you are my 'because'."

Chapter Nineteen

SEXIEST MAN

*S*pending Christmas Eve at Eject. Louie was there, and it felt like one big private party. The club had a big VIP section, and there were people here from different disciplines within the arts, all getting to mingle together.

There were a few movie stars, musicians, and other celebrities; some I didn't recognize and others who were only famous for being famous.

We had a fantastic time. It was lovely to relax without someone hitting on Alfie, or trying to get a piece of him. A couple of young actresses were very flirty, but Alfie was oblivious.

Holly was the one stars struck tonight. She spent ten minutes hanging on the arm of Baz Hartley, who had just been voted Sexiest Man of all time.

Garbage! - My man was number one in my eyes. Holly was grinning from ear to ear, and Brett was pissed at her.

Alexia Rainy, a starlet from the latest Tom Cruise movie, had walked up to Brett and dragged him onto the dance floor. He hesitated, but when Holly was still drooling over Baz, he put his hand low on her back and winked at me, before going with her.

I knew Brett couldn't see past Holly—they were perfect together—and I knew what he was doing. I casually walked over and whispered in Holly's ear that she'd better take care of her man or someone else would.

Taking one look at Brett and Alexia, she left Baz in mid conversation to claim what was hers. She abandoned me beside him. Baz flashed me a smile which told me I could possibly be his next victim. I smiled back, trying to figure out how to get away from him without being rude or embarrassing myself. I worried for nothing because Alfie's hand slid around my waist from behind, and he pulled me flush to him. There was a growing bulge in his pants.

"Damn, why did you turn your back, I couldn't resist that sexy little ass of yours," he cooed in my ear, sending shivers down my spine.

I didn't know if Alfie had realized it or not, but his little perversion had saved me from a possible awkward situation.

During the night, we had gone from fun loving to just plain loving. We danced so closely wrapped in one another's arms, not interested in who was around us or what else was going on.

It was the most peaceful I had felt since before I ever met him. If I had to experience everything I had again, just to be at this point with him, I wouldn't hesitate to do so.

"Are you ready to go home?"

I was. I smiled slowly. "I am. Are you?"

His voice almost cracked. "I am. Let's get out of here."

Henry had Alfie's car brought around. We climbed inside, and he put his arm around me, pulling me tightly to him, kissing me slowly, sensually, and full of passion. "Mmm...I can't wait until tomorrow. Spending Christmas with you is something I've dreamed about. I never thought it would ever happen."

He appeared very happy, and I knew then I couldn't send him home alone. I didn't want us to wake up on Christmas morning without each other.

I had arranged for him to come over in the morning, but I wanted to wake up with him. I didn't want to wait a year again before we could spend Christmas morning with each other.

"Henry, can we go to Alfie's first?" Alfie's brow lifted in a quizzical look. Before he got the wrong idea, I quickly explained what I was thinking.

He looked ecstatic. "Seriously? You've changed your mind, I can stay with you?" I couldn't believe how easy it was to make him happy.

Seeing his gorgeous face grinning, I couldn't help but feel guilty at how I had treated him. Our journey to get this far together hadn't been a straightforward one.

I waited in the car while Alfie went inside to gather up his things. There was no way he was getting me behind closed doors, because as strong as I had been, I was definitely not strong enough to be alone with him without anyone to interrupt us.

He appeared again after ten minutes, carrying a suit carrier and an oversized bag with wheels. "Jesus, Alfie, I haven't asked you to move in with me. It's one night." He chuckled and glanced at the bag.

"It's Christmas," he stated. "I had a list drawn up and got my PA to shop for me today. I wasn't shirking my responsibilities. It's just that I didn't want to spend time shopping instead of spending it with you."

Slipping his hand into mine he faced me after clipping his seatbelt on. "I did take the time to shop for your present though. I didn't want anyone else to do that." He smirked and kissed my hand. My man was turning out to be the best boyfriend in the world, this time around.

My dad was surprised when I turned up with Alfie and wanted to know where he was sleeping. At twenty-three years old, I figured it was time my dad realized I wasn't a virgin, no matter what he'd been telling himself.

He was the most important man in my formative years, but Alfie was the one I wanted to spend my life with. I knew he'd want me to be happy no matter what.

It wasn't that I was disrespecting my parents. I just wanted to be honest and not sneak around pretending we wouldn't be having sex. I felt it would be more disrespectful to try to dupe them like that, but I wouldn't be rubbing it in their faces either. I had a chat with my parents while Alfie kept Jack's parents entertained with anecdotes from his tour.

Finally, after some reservations, my dad resigned himself to the situation. He hugged me and was able to see my point of view about being honest.

My mom was more concerned over whether Alfie had brought drugs with him. She was of the opinion all rock stars did drugs. I pointed out that I was in a band and didn't do them either, and the same was true of Lennon, Cody, Digs, and Shawn as well.

I could see from my mother's face that she hadn't thought of me in the same vein as other rock musicians. As far as sleeping with Alfie, she was quite liberal in her thoughts.

She inadvertently gave me a rite of passage, when she dropped Dad in it by telling me about the time Dad had stayed the night at her parents' house but almost got caught.

He'd sprained his ankle when he went to jump out of her bedroom window and slipped when my granddad opened my mom's bedroom door as he was leaving.

My dad gave my mom an, *are you fucking serious telling her this* look and smiled at me kind of sheepishly. I had to keep myself from bursting out laughing.

Jack's mom and mine did a great job of decorating the villa. They must have bought most of JC Penney's Christmas displays.

Everything looked great, and I could smell turkey cooking. My mom always insisted on putting it in early and cooking it overnight to let it rest before cutting it.

When she told Alfie this, he looked confused, "If the turkey is dead, why does it need to rest?" He was serious and I smiled at my rare glimpse of his innocence.

We sat drinking wine, chatting, and my dad and Alfie got along well. I was so pleased, I would have hated to end up picking someone to be with that my dad didn't like.

We were all getting ready to call it a night, when Jack burst through the door. "Merry Christmas." He was wasted and hanging onto Rosie.

When he saw Alfie, he scratched his chin. "Hmm, that's not going to work." He shook his head while everyone stared at him with smiles on their faces waiting for what he was going to say next.

He glanced at Rosie and back at Alfie. "Okay, that'll work...you can sleep with Rosie. Lily's ass is mine."

Alfie's jaw ticked, and I grinned at him; he was jealous. He ran his hand through his hair before looking back at Jack.

"Sorry, Dude, but horny, inebriated Jack isn't getting anywhere near my girl's ass tonight, best friend or no best friend."

Jack pretended to pout. "What does Lily say?"

I smiled, trying to be careful about everyone's feelings, remembering how Jack was when he was drunk in bed.

"Jack, you know how much I love when you're drunk and drooling in my hair right? Tomorrow is Christmas morning, and I promised our moms that I'd help get lunch ready. If I have to wash the drool out, it doesn't give me a lot of time to help them now, does it?" I'd kept it clean and saved Jack the embarrassment of pretend rejection in front of everyone.

I hugged him and told him that we'd still snuggle on the couch tomorrow as we watched a classic movie the networks usually showed on TV during the festive holiday.

This seemed to placate Jack, and he grabbed Rosie's waist and pulled her to him. "Smile, baby, you do realize you just got lucky, don't you?" Our dads started chuckling, and Rosie smiled and rolled her eyes. I could see she had definitely started to become a keeper.

There was an awkward moment when I said we were going to bed. Alfie seemed fine, but I felt the attention on me magnify when I told everyone that I was going to head over to my room.

I half ran, half walked to get out of the main sitting area and into the hallway leading to my bedroom. Alfie walked slowly behind me, completely unaffected by the fact we were going to be in the same bed, but then again, it wasn't his parents, and he wasn't someone's little girl.

As soon as the door closed, Alfie smiled. "Your family and friends are amazing, Lily. I can't believe I'm here with you."

Staring, I pulled my lip as I thought about my resolve. I wanted him, more than anything, but I was determined not to sleep with him tonight.

"I'm not having sex with you tonight, Alfie, remember that." His face was serious, and he nodded his head. His voice was husky when he spoke. "Whatever you want, Lily. I'm just glad to be here."

I showered and brushed my teeth, then swapped places with him in the bathroom. I noticed that his gaze lingered on my bath towel, knowing that it was the only thing keeping him from seeing me naked.

When he went to shower, I opened my little case that I'd

dropped there earlier and pulled out some boxer briefs and a t-shirt. I quickly pulled these on and then slid between the sheets.

I was so nervous; my heart raced and I could imagine my face was flushed. My heartbeat pulsed in my mouth. I prayed that I perspire because I'd have wanted another shower.

When I switched off the bedside light I felt less self-conscious, and lay in the dark, trying to calm myself, but I was excited for him to be in my bed me at the same time.

It had been almost over a year since the last time we had shared a bed. Memories of that night flooded my brain, and I could feel myself becoming moist between my legs.

I groaned silently at just the thought of him lying beside me. It was going to take all my resolve not to climb on top of him and go wild.

The door of the bathroom cracked open and Alfie padded out, the light giving a soft glow behind him.

He had his clothes in his arms, and a white towel wrapped around his hips. I swallowed hard and wondered if I'd had a period of temporary insanity in the car when I said he could stay over tonight.

Alfie placed his clothes over the ottoman at the bottom of the bed and went back to turn the light out. I lay there anticipating him getting into bed, so when nothing happened, I wondered what was wrong.

"Alfie, what's the matter?"

Swallowing with difficulty he cleared his throat and eyed me cautiously. "Not too sure I can get in there with you, Lily." It was my turn to swallow. I knew exactly how he was feeling.

"Come sit on the bed." Alfie didn't move. He just stood there in the dark, and it worried me. He seemed to be having a difficult time with this. The old Alfie would have been in my bed before I'd showered.

The sexual tension was intense between us, so I tried to inject humor as a way of helping Alfie to relax.

"Maybe I should have let Jack in here after all."

Alfie growled, "Not fucking funny, Lily. I like him, but I hate that he's rubbed his dick on your ass when he's laid beside you in bed."

"It isn't like that, Alfie."

"It *wasn't* like that, Alfie," he corrected me. "That bastard is never touching you again, understand? I can just about tolerate the sexual flirting and shit, but not that." The pain in his voice told me how much our behavior had hurt him, and I thought about how I would feel if the tables were turned.

To be honest, part of me had wanted to hurt Alfie when he was in London but not now. "Alfie, I haven't allowed Jack to sleep in my bed since he's been with Rosie. He's learning that it seemed harmless fun when we were kids and weren't in relationships, but as adults, it definitely isn't acceptable. He was joking tonight. I'll speak to him though. It isn't fair to you or to Rosie." I smiled in the dark. I figured I'd distracted him.

"Okay, Alfie, are you ready to get into bed now? I'm tired, and I really do have to help with lunch tomorrow." He didn't move. I pushed the sheets off and crept off the bed to stand beside him.

He was wearing his boxer shorts now. "Come on, you can do this. I promise you it will be nice. We owe it to us to take this slowly, just for one more day. Actually, less than that, it's about three am now."

When I led him to the bed, he crawled over to the side I'd been lying on. He inhaled deeply. "The pillow smells like your hair." I could hear the smile in his voice.

We lay there in a tense silence until his shallow, ragged breathing slowed. I thought he had fallen asleep until his hand found mine, and he squeezed it tightly. "I love you, my little Lily. Merry Christmas."

I squeezed his hand back. "Alfie, I've never stopped loving you. Tonight, this moment... it's all my Christmas wishes coming true at the same time."

There was a strained silence as we both lay, not trusting ourselves to touch anything except our hands, and we both managed to stay strong until we fell asleep.

Chapter Twenty

SURPRISES ALL ROUND

A calloused thumb drew lazy circles on my belly as I gradually woke up, and I briefly forgot where I was. The décor of the room we were in was so different from the one at my apartment.

It had a white wicker headboard with a fancy design around the top with loosely woven thick wicker but with a solid bit in the middle. It seemed to creak at times without anyone touching it.

Calloused fingertips moving over my belly was a sign Alfie was awake, but he wasn't touching me anywhere else, just that spot with one hand.

I could feel his hot breath on my back, but he was laying still, those fingertips gently strumming on my lower belly. What he was doing felt safe, but it was pleasantly teasing at the same time.

The act in itself wasn't supposed to be sexual. Yet, my skin had reacted with an eruption of goosebumps as the charge of electricity we seemed to create between us was ever present.

His body was strategically placed away from mine.

Reaching down, I laced my fingers in his before rolling over to face him. "Hey," he cooed sleepily.

"Morning," I croaked, my voice still struggling with the concept that it was time to wake up. "Merry Christmas," I squeaked.

His eyes darted back and forth over my face. He wasn't smiling back, but his eyes lit up. "Fuck." The word came out in a rush.

When I into his gorgeous eyes and saw raw, pained emotion. I struggled to swallow, watching Alfie go through what seemed like an emotional moment before he spoke.

"Do you have any idea what it feels like for me to wake up with you?" He swallowed audibly. "I never believed I'd ever get to do this again." There was a reverent pause before he continued. "You know the saying 'all my Christmases have come at once?'" he whispered, pulling my head gently toward him and kissing my forehead.

I smiled widely at him, thinking he was being cheesy. "Seriously, Lily, I'm never going to let you down again." Staring intensely his attention became fixed on him, my smile slowly retracted as I gazed back entranced.

He leaned in to place a kiss on my closed mouth. "I love you so fucking much, it hurts," he mumbled against my lips and squeezed my hand hard. If it was possible to 'touch' the concept of love, I would have sworn we were holding it between our palms right then.

He inhaled deeply and pulled his hand out of mine. "We need to get out of bed," he stated sharply, inhaling hard and rolling away from me.

Frowning, I shook my head. "It's still really early, Alfie." He snickered and slid out of bed, the mattress bouncing with the loss of weight from him standing.

His boxer shorts were tented, and he glanced down at

them briefly. "My dick doesn't know the concept of timing, day or night. I'm always hard when I'm with you."

I smirked. I seemed to have the same problem, my lady parts acted like a radar whenever he was near me, just the sight of him dampened my panties.

Alfie was different and I was glad he hadn't just tried to have sex with me like he would have back in the day. He showed restraint and I took his consideration as a welcomed sign he wanted me for more than just my body.

"Do you want to shower first?" I offered. Alfie nodded and glanced down at his boxers again. "This is kind of painful, and I've been struggling with it for most of the night. I'm sorry, but I need to take care of it or I'm not going to get through the day without someone commenting."

I laughed, but I knew he was being honest. Nodding my head toward the bathroom door, I smirked and dropped my eyes to his boxers again. "Have fun." I would have gone and helped him out with that, but I figured I would have caved once I saw him naked.

Alfie had obviously thought the same thing, because he came out in a pair of Bermuda shorts. He wouldn't have thought twice before about walking around naked. His muscular chest was still bare. The sight of him freshly showered was stunning, a mini Christmas feast in itself.

His skin was so perfect, smooth and silky, making me have crazy thoughts about what I wanted to do to him when I got him alone.

By the time he'd come back, I had laid out my attire for the day. I had chosen a mid-thigh length dress in a soft, ruby red velvet with a sweetheart neckline and a low back.

Alfie groaned when he saw it. "Fuck," he hissed, rubbing the material between his thumb and forefinger. He shook his head, knowing he had to wait to see me in it. I still had plenty of time to wear my little black bikini with a black and white silk sarong beforehand. The weather was warm enough for us to lay by the pool in the sunshine.

Fighting the urge to run my fingers down the trail of fine hair that started at his belly button and disappeared into his shorts, my eyes feasted on his abs. Sexual tension was high between us, but I was impressed with Alfie's self-control so far.

Already, I had a sense it was going to be an early night for the both of us; I was just hoping I could wait that long.

He left the room, and I showered, taking my time to make sure I shaved in all the right places. Treating my skin to a soufflé that my mom had picked up from a spa she visited in New York, I knew I smelled great as I headed out to find him.

Alfie was sitting alone by the pool. The look on his face proved my effort had been worth it. He grabbed my hand as I passed by. "C'mere, I need you right beside me, babe," he cooed. We gazed at each other, and I instantly felt our connection.

Alfie's eyes were mainly green, and I could see that he was turned on just by looking at me. His pupils were dark rimmed and dilated, and his eyes shone but were heavy with lust.

He scooted over and pulled me beside him on the lounger. His face burrowed into my neck. "Damn, you smell good enough to eat. Are you trying to fucking kill me?" I giggled when he squeezed my ribs at both sides, tickling me.

When he stopped, I stared seriously into his eyes. "Alfie, if anything were to happen to you, I would die. A little teasing never killed anyone, did it?" I giggled, but this was swallowed by him when his hungry mouth crushed mine in a passionate, tongue-probing kiss. Growling deeply, he broke the kiss and inhaled shakily.

"You are going to be ruined tonight, you know that, right?" he murmured into my ear, in a low seductive voice. It made me shiver. His eyes flicked up, sparkling brightly, and he glanced over my shoulder to make sure no one was listening. I grinned wickedly and raised my eyebrow.

"Oh, Alfie, I hope so." He chuckled and lay back. Turning to see what I was snickering at, he followed my gaze to his shorts. They were tenting again. "Damn." He smirked and rolled over onto his side.

Everyone gradually surfaced, and my parents dished out Buck's Fizz. We had smoked salmon and eggs benedict for breakfast. Lennon and Cody sang their own version of a couple of Christmas carols and had us all in stitches from laughing at them.

They had done a version of the 'Twelve days of Christmas' and had kind of captured the essence of my parents and our friends in it.

Alfie's sister Layla and his aunt Connie arrived. They were surprised to have had the invite. Alfie was so happy. He just welled up, his eyes brimming with tears as he hugged them. I had been a little nervous to meet them, but we hit it off right away, and my parents and his aunt seemed to find plenty to talk about.

We decided to do presents before lunch, because my mom was worried most of the boys would be too drunk to do this sensibly afterwards, with all the wine and beer that was flowing already. Plus, there would be the alcohol and liquors after lunch too.

There was a screech from the kitchen when my mom discovered that Jack had eaten about seven of the pigs in blankets.

She'd painstakingly rolling bacon around the linked sausages to make them, ensuring we had plenty for the lunch, and Jack had tucked into them fresh from the oven. After freaking out at him, Jack was banned from the kitchen until lunch was served.

When we sat around giving presents, everyone seemed excited, and it dawned on me that Lennon and Alfie hadn't had a proper Christmas in years.

Cody was from out of state, and his parents were on a cruise, so he'd had the choice to meet them in St. Martin, or come to us. With the XrAid concert tour starting in the New Year, he'd opted to spend it with us.

My parents, being the primary hosts, started the proceedings. My dad handed out presents to everyone, and they all got busy opening them.

Lennon freaked out. "You got me a weekend rental of a fucking Ferrari? Seriously? You're not fucking kidding me?"

My parents were getting used to the F word. The guys injected it into everything. My dad chuckled at Lennon's reaction when he gave him his gift.

Dad passed Lennon an envelope. Lennon looked overwhelmed to have two gifts. "You're getting helicopter lessons right here in Miami when you've finished your tour. When you complete them, I'll let you come and fly my helicopter with me over London."

Alfie squeezed my hand when he saw Lennon choke with emotion. I gave Alfie a smile that said, 'I know my dad is amazing'. Lennon had never known a dad's love, so this coming from my dad, after only meeting him a couple of times, meant everything to him. Lennon hugged my dad without embarrassment, and even Jack had a tear in his eye.

Cody was up next. Dad had gotten him a pilot navigator's course up at Indian River County. He also chartered him a yacht for a weekend. Cody was stunned with his gifts. He loved sailing.

My dad told him that he couldn't be a rock star when he

was seventy, so he wanted these guys to have a career after they got fed up with being mauled by girls every night.

The presents continued like this, and when my dad had gone around everyone, Alfie was the only one who didn't have a gift from him.

My dad turned to Alfie and told him that he didn't know he was coming, but he'd been keeping a gift for him for the longest time. Alfie looked puzzled then my dad took my hand. "This girl is the most precious gift God has ever given me. This will be my gift to you, when you can demonstrate to me you deserve her. Meanwhile, you will have to be content with a week in Hawaii, when you both have time on your calendars."

Everyone in the room sat staring, first at my dad, then at Alfie. Eventually, they were looking at me, waiting for one of us to say something.

Alfie looked like he was in shock. Suddenly, he seemed to collect himself, and ran his fingers through his hair, before clearing his throat. "You have no idea what you just did for me. You have given me the best reason in the world to be a better man."

His gaze turned to me, and he spoke to my dad but looked into my eyes. "I want to be everything that Lily could ever need and want in life. I will work every single day to make sure that I achieve that. We have both struggled long and hard to get to where we are now, to finally commit to our relationship, and we have an idea there isn't a clear path to our final destination as a couple yet. I believe we can achieve everything and 'us', somewhere down the line."

My dad stood up, and Alfie followed; they shook hands, and I stood and hugged my dad. "Thank you, Dad," I whispered, wiping a tear from my eye and burying myself into his chest.

I turned to look over at my mom. She was a blubbering

mess, so I tried to lighten the mood. "It's okay Mom, you don't have to worry. Alfie knows the present is from both of you. Fabulous as he is, Alfie doesn't think Dad produced me on his own."

My comment to my mom broke the seriousness of the moment, and all our guests went back to enjoying the present sharing.

When everyone had given their gifts out, Alfie had something for every person there. I was amazed he knew exactly who was going to be there.

For the girls, he had pamper-packs and had arranged for Jack's and my mother, Holly, Mandy, Elle, Rosie, and me to go to a weekend spa in an exclusive resort at Lake Tahoe.

This was to take place before Elle's wedding. He had also included Elle's mom in this gift, even though he'd never even met her.

For the XrAid guys, and his own band members, Brett, Neil and Jack, he had arranged a snowboarding weekend at the same time, telling us he'd rented cabins for everyone present, including Layla and Connie.

For my dad and Jack's dad, Alfie had arranged helicopter flights over Lake Tahoe and up into the Colorado Mountains.

He then handed out small gifts, which were mainly humorous. When he got to Jack, he presented him with a small dark-haired blow up doll and a bottle of Jack Daniel's with the comment, "for when Rosie's not around and you can't sleep alone."

Jack took it in good humor and chuckled at Alfie's ingenuity of getting his point across; that he wasn't sleeping beside me anymore.

When it came to me, his gift left me breathless. He gave me a box containing a tablet. When I opened it, I gave him a puzzled look. He knew I already had one. He turned it on and opened the gallery icon. I scrolled the gallery, and it began to play a slideshow.

He had transferred all the pictures from his tablet to mine on a micro card. What was there made my heart crack. If I ever needed evidence of how much he missed me, it was right here in my lap.

Alfie had made a photographic account to memorize all the places he had been during his international tour. He was standing by the Trevi Fountain in Rome, the Eiffel Tower in Paris, Buckingham Palace in London, The Opera House in Sydney, and Times Square in New York, among many others.

He posed as a lone figure in all the shots, looking miserable. He had adopted the same pose in all of the pictures, standing by the landmark with one arm stretched out at his side.

"Lily, I couldn't take you with me on that journey, and I understood why, but every moment was a moment I only wanted to share with you. Without you, it was just another tourist attraction. So, with that in mind, I filled my days when we weren't traveling by taking pictures of the places we passed through to catalogue all the sights that weren't that memorable, because you weren't with me. Next time we'll go together. Maybe, we can replace these pictures one by one with pictures containing the both of us, because I really want us to build happy memories for when we're old and grey. Look, see my arm? It was out waiting for you to join me. Next time, it will be cradling you, and I'll be smiling, because you are with me, and you love me as much as I love you."

Again, the room was silent, and I sat scrolling through the pictures, speechless that he'd thought of me every day he wasn't with me.

Eventually, I touched his face and kissed his cheek. "I can't wait to see those places with you and replace these pictures, because I really do love you." He grinned and hugged me tightly, before placing a soft kiss against my closed lips.

Alfie nearly fell over when I gave him a gift certificate to a music memorabilia site. It was for a guitar that once belonged to Ronnie Wood of the Rolling Stones. Alfie was over-whelmed. Alfie thought Ronnie was the world's best guitarist ever, and he was a major influence on Alfie as a musician.

Guitar players were a debate we frequently had, because I thought no one beat Brian May's playing. At least he was rooting for a British guitarist, so I couldn't be that hard on him.

Alfie leaned over and whispered, "I'm saving the rest for when we're alone, if that's okay."

I smiled and raised my eyebrow because we were on the same wavelength. "Me too," I replied and winked.

Alfie widened his eyes in surprise at my comment, and the sexual innuendo of it wasn't lost on me. I immediately knew it was going to be a long day.

Chapter Twenty-One

CHEEKINIS

W e ate lunch, and Jack's and my parents were the perfect hosts. They somehow managed to make everyone feel special during the day. Even Connie commented that she felt part of the family.

Dad and Alfie sat out on the patio for a while, deep in conversation. My dad looked serious, and Alfie was nodding. I really hoped Dad wasn't giving Alfie a hard time because of the stuff we went through before. My dad didn't know the whole story, just that I was seeing him and then we broke up.

Holly and Brett arrived, then Mandy and Neil, so we had a very full house. We played a silly game of charades, and Jack was especially funny when the card he picked to mime was *National Lampoon's Christmas Vacation*. I'm glad he had that one to mime and not me, because I wouldn't have had a clue what to do with that.

Screaming with laughter, my eyes scanned the room; everyone was having fun. It dawned on me this was the first time I'd seen Lennon carefree and happy in all the time we'd worked together.

Mandy rigged up the karaoke machine from our place,

and the neighbors next door came over and joined us. Their two teenage boys couldn't believe their luck when their dad came around to complain, and we'd invited them in. They nearly fainted when they saw Alfie. They were massive Crakt Soundzz fans.

My dad had never heard Alfie and knew nothing of their band, but when Alfie sang a ballad, my dad came over and placed his hand on my knee. "I can see why he's famous. If I was thirty and competing in the world with that, I might have had to kill him." I grinned at him and gave him a hug.

"No competition, Dad. Besides I've seen Alfie drive, he barely gets from A to B, never mind flying a helicopter for a living. So, I guess he had to be good at something else," I cooed but was doing a happy dance inside that my dad was becoming a fan of Alfie.

Jack's mom and mine did their version of The Three Degrees, 'When Will I See You Again.' It contained the line, 'When will we share precious moments?'

It was pretty apt considering us all being together, and the fun we were having. The last time Alfie and I did karaoke, Alfie sang to me, putting his feelings out there, in front of a whole bar full of people. I felt it was only fitting that I sing something to him, by way of returning his PDA toward me.

I had heard the perfect song on the radio the other day, and I felt it was significant in our situation. I began to sing 'Ordinary Love' by U2. Alfie listened, and a slow smile spread across his face. When I sang the line, 'are we tough enough for ordinary love', Alfie nodded slowly, held my gaze, and mouthed, "You bet we are, baby."

On the last word, Alfie was out of his chair stalking across the room before anyone could draw a breath. He scooped me into his arms and kissed me slowly; it was an intense moment between us.

Jack interrupted, "Is this where I run for the tent?" Alfie

snickered against my mouth, and we broke the kiss. There were lots of puzzled faces in the room apart from Rosie. Alfie and I snickered at Jack's comment, but we didn't elaborate on it for any of them.

Stomachs were on the verge of bursting, buckets full of champagne and wine consumed, and we'd played everything from board games to PS3's latest offerings. Christmas day was as near to perfect as it could be for all of us, barring absent loved ones. Surrounded by all my important people, apart from Elle, I'd never had such a wonderful day.

We said goodnight to Layla and Connie. Henry took them home, and as we closed the front door, my nerves began to fray. Today had given me the time to realize, for sure, that I wanted to be with Alfie. As if he knew what I was thinking, Alfie appeared by my side.

Sliding his arm around my waist, he pulled me toward him and kissed my hair. "I really want to be alone with you now."

I licked my lips and nodded slowly. "I think I'd like that, too." Turning my head, I saw everyone either deep in conversation or eating again.

Some were out by the patio, some in the family room. "I think now would be a good time to sneak off unnoticed," I whispered. Alfie grinned and led me by the hand in the direction of our room.

Grabbing a bottle of champagne on the way past, he tucked it under his arm. "In case we need lubrication." He winked then wiggled his eyebrows wickedly at me.

My core pulsed and I grinned as I scooted inside the bedroom door so that he could follow me inside and thought once the door was closed, unless there was a fire, no one would disturb us...not if they valued their lives, that was.

Alfie closed the door and leaned against it. The palms of his hands were flat against the door behind his back, the bottle of champagne still under his arm.

He took a sharp breath. I heard it catch in his throat. "Damn, now that we're here, I want someone to kick me in the balls, so that I can check this isn't yet another dream."

I snickered. "Another one?"

I raised my eyebrows and waited for his reply.

"Lily, the times I've dreamed about holding you in my arms, sure it was real, only to wake up and feel a deep despair at the fact we weren't together..."

I chewed my lip, feeling horrible. Listening to the effect I'd had on Alfie made me feel so full of remorse. It had been as agonizing for him to be away from me as it was for me to be away from him.

I sat on the bed, but Alfie remained standing by the door. "Are you going to come over here?" I asked, slightly giggling at him still pressed against the door.

"Not sure."

My smile slowly dissipated. My heart fell from my chest to my stomach. "You're not sure? What aren't you sure about Alfie. Us?"

Tight squeezing in my chest alerted me to the fact that my heart had stopped beating, and I was holding my breath. I was confused and filled with panic. Alfie didn't think this was a good idea any more. Struggling with the feeling of possible rejection after finally letting him in, I was in danger of losing control.

Alfie exhaled raggedly. "Yes and no."

My heart stuttered with shock then beat rapidly trying to make up for the lost beats. I jumped to my feet as panic set in and I paced the floor, hugging myself.

"You're not sure you want to do this again?" Immediately the words hit the air between us; Alfie's eyes locked onto mine, and I felt our connection.

"Oh, I want to do it all right. I want nothing more in the

world. I'm just not sure that if I do, and you change your mind again, I'll ever recover from this."

What he said devastated me. To think I had inflicted as much pain on Alfie as he had on me was crucifying me. "I really want this to work, Alfie. That's why I took things slowly these past couple of days. Remember you did that before. I was the one lacking in self-restraint."

Walking over to the door, I pulled the champagne bottle out of his arm and placed it on the wicker nightstand. Turning back at him, I could see that he was having an internal struggle about what was happening between us.

Reaching around him, I took his hands and placed them in mine. I tilted my head and smiled gently up at him. "Alfie, I really want to be with you. I love you with everything that I am. I need you to believe that. It isn't going to be easy with our careers. I am oh, so, willing to do this, because there is no one in the whole of this planet who makes me feel the way you do." I stretched up on tiptoes and brushed my lips with his slowly.

His arms wrapped around me, and he pulled me hard against him. I felt the desperation in his movement. "Lily, I love you with every fucking bone in my body. You make me tremble when I'm near you. Just the sight of you fills my heart with so much love, I sometimes wonder if it will burst. You are my sun and my rain, light and shade, pleasure and pain. If we do this, promise me you won't just bolt at the first hint that something isn't right."

I stared into his eyes and could see how distressed he was feeling. "I promise I'll speak to you. I promise that I will hear what you tell me, so long as you can promise me honesty, Alfie. I promise to let you grow, but you need to do the same for me. I don't want either of us to stifle the growth of the other."

I laid my head on his chest and swallowed hard. This

wasn't as simple as picking up where we left off before. This time we had to learn to trust and rely on each other.

Alfie's beautiful face lit up when he smiled affectionately, and he shook his head. "I'm sorry if I'm being a pussy." I smirked, but I really understood where he was coming from.

"Are you showering first, or am I?" I wanted to move forward, because the night was becoming somber, and I worried that we would end up in a long-assed debate about some aspect of relationship analytics.

Alfie frowned. "Doesn't the shower fit the both of us?"

I smirked and instantly the mood changed again. "Well, I have still to give you your Christmas gifts. So, I was going to fix things here for that while you showered."

Alfie went off to shower but was back in less than five minutes with a towel around his waist. This was a change as well, Alfie never usually thought twice about walking around naked.

He looked so alluring, with his shiny, just showered skin and smelling so fresh and clean. Not to mention damp. Self-control was difficult, I had to fight not to whip that towel away from him like he was the biggest gift under the tree. That one thing I'd wanted at the top of my Christmas list.

"Your turn," he cooed. My shower lasted even less than his, I think. I had a small beach wrap, and I pulled that on instead of a towel. It had been hanging behind the door in the bathroom. I figured this would be easier to move around in, without inadvertently falling out of it, like I could in a towel.

My eyes honed in on Alfie as he lay on his back on the bed, his hands behind his head. He was watching MTV with the remote in his hand. When he saw me, he flicked to a radio station, playing easy listening music.

"C'mere, I have something for you." Wandering over I sat on the bed beside him, and bounced the mattress. It sagged a little as he adjusted himself upright and handed me a small gift box. "Do you know how hard it is to buy something for a girl who has it all?"

"Alfie, the gift you gave me was amazing."

He smirked. "Good, then you won't mind this lot." He chuckled nodding at the small pile between us.

Tearing the first package, I found a small red velvet box inside. I swallowed hard. Alfie snickered when he saw that my face was in conflict about what could be inside. "Don't worry, it isn't an engagement ring." My eyes glanced at his and I felt relieved.

I cracked the box lid and there were two platinum plec-trums inside. One with the letter L and one with an A engraved on it.

"I know it's cheesy, but we like cheese now and again, right? When we're apart, and we're playing on stage, having these in our hands will keep us thinking about each other. The A is for you, the L is mine."

He pushed another box at me. "This one is next." I opened the box and saw a private jet voucher. "This is for when you're missing me too much. You call the private airline company, and they will bring you to me, even if it's only for a few hours. I bought one of those for me too. I know we have the record label jet, but this way it's extra security that we're never that far from each other."

Alfie pushed an envelope at me. "This is the second to last one, I really didn't have much time to put a lot of thought into this, forty-eight hours is a lot of pressure to get this just right."

Cupping the side of his face in my hand, I smiled affec-tionately. "I think you're doing pretty fantastic up to now." He nodded at the envelope, and my fingers trembled as I opened it. The effect of him sitting near me was making my body hum, and I had to fight with myself to concentrate.

I slipped my finger under the end of the envelope and

tore it open. My eyes flicking between him and the envelope as I gradually teased it open. There were two tickets for the cinema. I waved them in the air at him. "Cool, we can use these over the holidays." He looked serious for a second before he snickered and took my hand.

"Lily, these tickets may just be cinema tickets to you, but for me, they are a reminder of the one night we spent just trying to be friends at my house."

The way he stared at me was piercing. "Do you remember when you came over to watch movies with me? I couldn't believe you came that night, I thought it was my second chance with you. Being able to watch you after you fell asleep in my arms made me feel incredible, Lily. All I wanted was to hug you so tightly and never let you go. I had never seen anyone so beautiful."

I nodded, of course I remembered it. "I have a vivid memory of that night."

Alfie held my gaze, his eyes widening. "You do?"

I swallowed hard and prepared myself to confess. "Yeah, I woke up on your couch, and you'd gone to bed. I went to find you, and you were laying naked, face down, the wrong way up on your bed."

"Ha," he huffed and snickered. "Yeah, I tossed and turned after leaving you alone on the couch. Trying to sleep when I knew you down there was painful. It took all my reserves not to carry you to my bed. I struggled to keep my hands off you that night."

Alfie sniffed pretending to be cocky. "I knew I should have just claimed you and not walked away from you on that couch. You wanted me too, huh?"

I smirked again still staring into his eyes. I could see the humor in his. "Actually, I did, more than you know, but there was no way I wanted to be with a manwhore who couldn't care less about me."

I was referring to the woman I had seen Alfie with long before he explained his job as a male escort. Before our conversation deteriorated, Alfie pushed another box at me.

"These are really for me, but you can open it and borrow it any time you like." He winked. I pulled the wrapping off the last package. When I opened this box, it made me giggle.

Inside was a pair of panties from Victoria's Secret. They were red satin Cheekinis, panties that were kind of like boy shorts, but fancy with mesh panels at the back and three red, satin bows.

"Holiday panties!" He smirked. "Just in case we get lucky." He winked and grinned devilishly.

I chuckled softly, standing up. "Okay, you use them...if you want to get lucky I mean. You told me they were for you. I can't decide whether I see anything I like or not, until you do."

Alfie took them from the box by scissoring his index and middle fingers and lifted them delicately, high above his head to inspect them. He stretched the elastic at the top of the panties, placing both splayed hands down either side. Just as if there were hips inside.

He rotated the panties so that the gusset was next to his mouth, his eyes darted in my direction then he smirked. Next, his tongue flicked lightly over the gusset, small flicks, before his mouth closed over it. All the time his eyes were on mine, watching me, watching him, and damn if it wasn't turning me on.

I heard him making sucking sounds, then his head lifted slightly and he teased one side of the gusset aside. He then made his way to the waistline and began to remove the panties from his hands with his teeth. I was breathless watching him.

Once he had the panties between his teeth, he took them in his right hand and held them to his nose, inhaling deeply.

While doing this, he got off the bed and moved over to where his jeans were laying.

He picked them up and stuffed the panties in the back pocket. Turning his attention back to me, he smirked. "So, did you like what you saw?" I gasped out the breath I'd been holding. Never in my wildest thoughts did I think a woman's panties could ever turn me on like that.

Chapter Twenty-Two

SLOW DANCE

I giggled at Alfie's panties demonstration, but the air was thick with anticipation between us. I reached over and grabbed the bag I had hidden carefully for Alfie.

"It's your turn for gifts." Alfie smiled and took the little square box I had carefully wrapped for him in shiny silver paper. He opened it slowly, his eyes darting between me and the package.

He laughed loudly when he saw what was inside. He was now the proud owner of backstage passes to all our XrAid's gigs for the upcoming tour and a copy of our CD for him to listen to when he was in rental cars.

Alfie was really disorganized with adapters and wires, and although he had every gadget existing to play music, I thought that an old-fashioned CD would be something 'physical' he could connect with, and the best way to be close to me.

"I didn't want you to wait in line if you wanted to come and see me, baby," I cooed, snickering at the pleasure I got from giving my bigshot rock star passes to *my* gig.

"This means more to me than anything else, you know that, Lily?" I thought he meant the backstage pass, but he was waving the CD. He tapped the hard, plastic case against the palm of his hand. "It makes me feel so fucking proud you did this, Lily," he whispered huskily, his voice cracking a little with emotion.

He stood and tugged me up off of the bed, holding my hips as he gave me a sensual smile. "Most women in your position would have just gone with the fame and their guy."

He shook his head. "Not you. You stuck to your guns, wanting to make music, and chasing your own dreams. I fucking hated it, hated you at times, but at the same time, loved you all the more for it. I can take the fact we've spent that time apart. All the heartache and lonely nights, knowing now, it wasn't in vain. This..." he tapped the plastic CD holder again, "makes me realize how different you are from any other girl. You're one of a kind, baby. Unique."

Placing my hand on his chest, I began to stroke his skin. The buzz from our contact was instantaneous. Leaning in, my lips peppered soft kisses over his pectorals and down his abdominal muscles.

Alfie shivered and his towel was becoming misshapen at the front as he struggled to keep his desire hidden from me. He looked down and grinned. "Fuck it," he commented as he pulled the towel away and spread his legs slightly as he pulled me in tighter.

"Stop. I have one more gift for you." Alfie was kissing down my neck and the effect it was electric on my aching, wet core. I'd never forgotten what being with him had felt like, the sensation of having his mouth on one part of my body, and its ability to wreak havoc on just about any other.

Alfie's body was trembling as his fingers skimmed across my skin, and my body hummed in response to his touch. My last gift to him was all but forgotten in that moment.

Our body language was exclusive. Alfie told me no one had ever made him feel this way, and in my experience, I could say without a doubt it was the same for me.

His fingers hooked over the towel as he inched it down my body until my breasts were exposed. He looked up, his eyes instantly gazing into mine. The sensual look he gave me almost ended me. His mouth engulfed the nipple of my left breast, and a low growl tore up from his chest while his hand teased and stretched the nipple of my right.

Between my legs, the hot, sticky juice overflowed and was trickling onto my thigh. It took me everything I had not to try to speed up his movements, because I was going out of my mind with lust for him.

Drawing my towel wrap down my body to my ankles, I stepped out of it, and Alfie threw it aside. He took a sharp breath as his eyes climbed up my body, and he made his way back to standing, devouring every inch of me as he did this.

Teasingly, a finger began to trace my spine lightly and continued over my shoulder blade and back to the center. His hot, ragged breath was on my face as his mouth was only inches from mine.

I stared into his beautiful lust-filled eyes. He brushed my hair behind my shoulders, so gently, like I was fragile. There was another reverent silence between us before he drew a deep breath to speak.

"Hey," he cooed. His eyes sparkled with love when his smile widened, and he shook his head. "I can't believe you're finally mine." His finger tenderly traced the outline of my face, and his thumb dragged across my lips. Bending to kiss me, I felt his ragged breathing as the tension between us seemed palpable.

He walked me slowly backwards to the bed and gently pushed me down. "How did we go from being the way we were to this?" His voice was sounded slightly scared.

I knew what he meant, the old Alfie was kind of fearless and fun in bed. "We'll be even better than we were before, Alfie." We were afraid to do anything, as if one wrong move was going to stop what was happening between us. We were both fragile and desperate for this to work. I smiled in reassurance, wanting him to know that I was committed to making this work this time.

Lying down beside me, Alfie stroked his finger from my collarbone, through the valley of my breasts, and down to my pubic bone. The effect was electrifying. I could swear my flesh was fizzing just under my skin in its wake. I lay completely still, knowing he may need a minute just to explore me and remember how my body felt.

It had been well over a year since the last time we'd made love. And I felt, for the first time ever, that Alfie seemed tentative. I felt he needed help with this.

Before he could hesitate, I quickly maneuvered and straddled him. His lips curled into his sexy smile as he ran his fingers up my body and raked his fingernails gently down my front. The fire he was igniting in me was mind-blowing, especially when he lazily raked his fingernails over my skin.

I bent to kiss him, but he was still tentative about touching me. Remembering another gift I had bought for him, an idea came to me.

"Wait here." I bounced my way off the bed and bent to pick up the electric blue colored square box. "Before you open this, I need to tell you the gift inside is purely practical...work attire."

Alfie grinned. "Hmm, work attire? It doesn't look like a pair of skinny jeans so it must be a classic t-shirt, correct?"

I smirked and thought the gift was lame, but perfect for what I knew I had in mind for it. "Nope, open it and see." Alfie opened the box and grinned.

"You got me scarfs?" He asked with a questioning look. I'd

bought him two silk scarfs, one in a slate, gray color with a guitar printed on it, and the other was a lighter gray, with a dark skull on one side.

"Rocker chic, but they will protect your voice from the cold and keep you warm when my arms can't be around your neck."

A smile played on his lips, but his brow was furrowed at me. "You interrupted sitting on me, naked, to give me scarfs?" I giggled and silently hugged myself that my idea was beginning to take shape.

I took one of the scarfs and carefully folded it. I grasped Alfie's wrist and began wrapping it around it. Alfie's eyes lusted instantly and his cock twitched, as it grew from semi hard to a full erection. "Fuck," he replied and gave me a low growl.

Taking the scarf I wound it around the top section of the wicker headboard. "Hope you have good restraint and don't try to wriggle too much Alfie, this isn't the strongest of head-boards." I giggled.

Alfie laughed heartily and it was music to my ears. "Damn, Lily, you are just full of surprises." He let out a guttural groan, and his voice was an octave lower, so I could tell how turned on he was by what I was doing. I focused my attention on doing the same to the other one.

Once I knew his wrists were secure, he tested the restraint, and I knew this was going to drive him crazy. When I had completed my knots, and satisfied myself that he was secure, I got off the bed. I bent over in his sight, with my legs straight, to take the panties he'd bought, out of his jeans pocket.

Alfie groaned loudly, "Jeez, you're killing me." He pushed his hips into the bed, and his cock bobbed and twitched in response to the movement.

I bent over and very slowly pulled the panties on and

wiggled my ass into them. This gave him a view of the crack of my ass through the mesh panels.

Winging it, I tried to figure out what to do next, but I could feel the walls breaking down between us. I turned the music on the TV up a little. The stars seemed to be aligning for us, because I could hear the introduction to 'Kiss' by Prince. I was a little self-conscious, but damn, Alfie deserved this at the very least from me.

I climbed back on the bed and spread my legs, just out of Alfie's reach at the bottom of the bed, and began to undulate and gyrate my hips. "Damn it, Lily," he snapped then groaned again.

It wasn't easy to dance, because the mattress kept dipping, and I needed all my concentration to keep my balance. Thinking about the lessons Zack tried to give me on the surfboard to correct my center of gravity helped me to remain upright at least.

Spreading my legs wider and rocking my hips back and forth, I crouched down bringing my ass almost onto the mattress. I had still been facing him at that point, but then turned and did the same with my ass in full view of him. "Fuck," he spat and tried to sit up. I glanced over my shoulder and saw him first smirk, then bunch his brows. His legs waved in the air as he tried to gain traction with his ass to push himself up.

When that didn't work, he tried to reach with his feet. "Definitely no hands this time, Mr. Black," I teased, giggling and reminding him of an incident where he showed some ingenuity. "Do you want me, Mr. Black?" I spoke in a seductive tone and smirked when I saw his cock was twitching more often as I continued to dance.

Alfie was showing signs of struggling, and tried to free one of his wrists at one point, but the scarfs held him in place. He protested to be let loose. I shook my head and smiled at him. He licked his lips. "Fuck, what I'm going to do to you." He threatened and groaned in a pained, thick-with-lust filled voice.

I gave him my best seductive smile and raised an eyebrow, "No, Alfie...what *I'm* going to do to you. I believe I'm kind of in charge right now." I smirked, and he let out a loud guttural sound. I quickly shushed him, reminding him my parents were somewhere outside the door.

Rubbing my hands over my ass and up the sides of my body, I turned and did the same at the front. As my hands travelled down from my breasts and down my belly I let them slide inside the band of the panties.

Alfie's head jerked as did his cock. He groaned and muttered, "Oh, God...Fuck." I smirked again, commenting, "Good to see your two heads in coordination for once." His smile at that was adorable. Making me want to stop all the nonsense and just kiss those inviting lips of his. Stoically, though, I stuck to my plan.

As the song was almost finished I straddled over his hips and spread my legs again. I repeated the bended-knee-ass-wiggle thing, except this time, I allowed my panties...or Alfie's, to brush against his cock briefly.

"Fuck, enough," he mumbled, growling low and long, as he struggled with his arms, to reach out for me, then raised his hips trying to gain contact with me, again. The scarfs were doing their job. He was stuck fast to the headboard, and I felt completely empowered.

When the song was over, I continued to tease him with the panties. I sat on his cock and rocked back and forth, raking my fingernails down his body, and sending shivers all over him.

Standing again, I placed my feet on either side of his head. He was looking up at me, so I briefly pulled the crotch of the panties to the side so he could watch me touching myself.

Alfie licked his lips and moaned with a pleading look in his eyes, then raised his head and stuck his tongue out, trying to reach me. That made my smile widen, and I giggled.

His legs were bent up in an effort to reach me, and he was so turned on his belly glistened with the pre-cum that was oozing from him. His eyes were fixed on mine now, and I was trying to make this memorable for the nights he was out on the road without me.

Popping the cork on the champagne, I poured some down his chest. He flinched then groaned, "Jesus," before he took a sharp breath. I began sucking and licking it from his torso as he hissed loudly, before he twisted trying to turn his quivering body to the side.

"This is too fucking much, Lily, let me touch you," he commanded.

"It's okay, baby, you can touch me later," I cooed sweetly, and he moaned again, a pained look of frustration on his face, especially when my tongue began to trace his V muscles, right beside one of his main erogenous zones.

I briefly stroked his cock, and he seemed to relax a little, but just when he thought things were progressing, I straddled and walked up the length of him to the headboard.

With my back to the wall, and my legs parted, Alfie could see the wet patch on the fabric between my legs. I crouched all the way down to kiss him, and his hand managed to brush against my bare thigh.

When he did this, I broke the kiss, and he groaned again. "Enough, my turn," he muttered before letting out guttural growl as I began lowering my crotch to his face.

When I reached Alfie's face, he sucked and nibbled at the cloth and licked at the fabric. He was groaning with pleasure and tried to hook the crotch to one side with his teeth.

I gyrated my hips creating friction against his mouth, and Alfie's ridged cock twitched and bounced on his belly. I fell forward to my knees on either side of him, my body flush with his.

Reaching out, I took his cock in my mouth, flicking his apa with my tongue. He hissed and groaned into my core, and the vibration sent another rash of goosebumps rushing over my skin. I was so turned on, riding his mouth, but I didn't want to come that way.

Desperate to feel Alfie inside me, I stood up and slowly slid the panties down my legs. Alfie's eyes were once again fixed on mine. When I had the panties in my hands, I brought them back to Alfie's face, and he inhaled them deeply, his cock twitching again, before I left the bed. I tucked them back in his jeans pocket and took out the condom I knew would be waiting there.

Creeping back over his body to straddle him, I ripped the condom packet with my teeth, setting it down near me by his leg. I sat squarely across Alfie's hips and rubbed my wet folds around his groin and over his now way-past-hard cock.

Alfie's face and neck were flushed red. I'd never seen that happen to him before. His irises were almost completely swallowed up by his dark, widely-dilated pupils. He was definitely enjoying what was happening.

Shuffling down his body, I scooped my hair into a makeshift ponytail, taking Alfie's cock in my mouth again and feeling the silky, smooth skin of his length and the cool metal of his apa.

Wrapping my fingers around him, I stroked him with one hand and sucked him gently. He'd had several leaks of pre-cum before I'd even touched him, and the sticky, salty taste spurred me on.

I sat upright, my weight bearing down again on his length, as I rocked and rubbed myself against him. His head was flailing from side to side; I was driving him crazy. "What do you want, Alfie...tell me."

Alfie hissed, "Inside."

Creasing my brow, I teased him by pretending not to hear him. "What did you say?"

Growling he thrust up toward at me, his eyes dark. "Inside. Fuck. Please, Lily." I smiled and reached for the condom, taking it from the now open foil packet. I had been using birth control since my scare with him previously. Even though I hadn't been in a relationship, I wasn't ready to let Alfie go bareback.

Taking his thick, veiny, smooth, hard cock in my hands, I rolled the thin latex over his shaft and poised it at my entrance. "You're sure now?" I teased, but also wanting to quash any doubts he was having earlier.

"Certain. Never been fucking more so," he husked.

Painstakingly slowly, I glided down his length, letting him penetrate me. Alfie pushed up with his hips at the same time, spreading me until I was down to his root.

A long moan tore from both of our mouths simultaneously. "Ahh. Oh, God." I gasped, then stilled, before leaning forward to kiss him. Alfie moaned loudly into my mouth, the vibration buzzing against my lips. Rising, I freed myself of him again.

Growling he bobbed his head and dropped it to the pillow, "Do that again and I'll come," he scowled at me. I pushed him back inside and stilled again, before I started to rock against him.

He met me with a need that was off the charts, and when I leaned forward and freed the movement in his hips, he thrust up into me from below like he was shaking off demons. "So fucking amazing," he growled.

My release came quickly, and my voice screeched his name. "Alfie."

Alfie was only three hard thrusts behind me, hissing, "Oh, Lily. Fuck, I'm coming, babe." As I felt his hot, pulsating length pump his release into the condom inside of me, his body jerked, and his eyes closed in his moment of ecstasy.

Panting loudly, beads of sweat had erupted over his nose and top lip. He had never looked more appealing. "Fuck. I'm sorry. You turned me on too much." I chuckled, still breathless myself, and kissed his nose.

"Alfie, you can never be too turned on." I untied his wrists and kissed them, gently rubbing the circulation back in his arms. He wrapped them around me and pulled me in tightly to him.

Reaching down, I carefully removed the condom and tied it off before dropping it on the floor. There was no way he was getting away from me at that moment.

We lay in a quiet peaceful silence for a few minutes, until Alfie's smooth voice cut into the night. "I love you, so fucking much, Lily, and what you just did there...I like it better when you wear the panties, you can keep them. My panties never tasted anything like they did when you wore them."

We laughed again as Alfie squeezed me tight in his arms. Holding each other close, we made out with slow lazy kisses and stared silently at each other. We were mentally and physically exhausted after the past two days, and when we finally fell asleep, we slept like the dead.

Chapter Twenty-Three

PREPARATION

*J*ack and Lennon were talking loudly in the hallway when I woke up. Alfie was lying on his stomach with his hair tousled around his brow, and his lips were glossy and a gorgeous dark, pink color.

Staring at Alfie's luscious mouth I figured all I wanted to do was kiss him for hours. He cracked an eye open. "Hey," he cooed. A smile slowly spread across his lips making them even more kissable, if that was at all possible.

I just couldn't wait until I brushed my teeth, so I scooted down until my face was an inch from his and licked his lips. Moving swiftly he rolled me over and pinned me under him then gave me a sexy smile.

"I think it's my turn to be in charge today." He grinned and brought one of his hands up to brush the strands of hair away from my face. He brought his forehead to mine and stared into my eyes. We stayed like this for several minutes, with him still on the outside, even though inside my hormones were on overtime, producing sticky, moist liquid between my legs and a whole range of reactions throughout my body.

Alfie dropped his head, and his lips pressed into mine. If I thought that we could stop the world and just stay like this forever, I'd have done it. The connection we had in that moment was epic.

His hot, wet tongue licked my lips, parting them softly as he began exploring my mouth. Ever. So. Slowly. Tongue to tongue. We exchanged hormones sending messages throughout our bodies that we wouldn't be satisfied with just this, preparing us for a more intimate connection.

When we made love this morning, it was intense. Once Alfie had the condom on, he laced his fingers in mine and lifted them high above my head. He gripped my hands tightly, squeezing and relaxing his fingers with every slow thrust. He slid inside me, staring into my eyes. We worshipped each other with our bodies and connected in mind and body and soul.

It was a spiritual experience as much as a physical and emotional one. Until the last few minutes, every stroke, every thrust, kiss, and touch was done with our foreheads touching and our eyes fixed, entranced by each other. I didn't really have words to explain what it was like between us.

Alfie and I showered together. I got a little embarrassed when I stepped out into the hallway, and Jack snuck up behind me whispering, "I know what you've been doing." I blushed and wanted the ground to open so I drew Jack a dagger of a look that made him wince.

Everyone ate breakfast at different times, but apart from Cody and Lennon, everyone else had left. My dad and Lennon were sitting with their tablets connected to the same site talking helicopters, and Cody looked like he was struggling with a massive hangover.

He was managing to text someone and have a conversation. Every few seconds there was a beep-beep to let him know another text had arrived. I was so glad I could spend time with my friends and family yesterday.

It was the perfect Christmas, especially with Alfie here. I never believed a week ago that Alfie would be back in my life again.

The following days leading up to New Year's Eve were hectic. My parents, Jack's parents, Rosie, and Jack all went back to the UK, and we had rehearsals for our upcoming tour.

Alfie was rehearsing as well, because Crakt Soundzz was playing on New Year's Eve in Los Angeles. I wanted to go to L.A. with him but, as we were leaving on January 2nd for our tour, it was impossible.

I kept telling myself that we were going to work this time, and we could stand to be away from each other for a few weeks. Alfie only had this one gig, and he'd be back on the East Coast. At least we'd see each other from time to time during XrAid's tour, which was only three weeks long.

On the day before New Year's Eve, Alfie came by the apartment on his way to L.A. Thinking it would be better to say goodbye at my own place, I had asked him to drop by because I knew I'd cry. "I'll call you when we get there, and tomorrow night after midnight," he cooed. "Next year is going to be great baby. I can't wait until we spend time together. We'll make it work, you'll see."

He kissed me tenderly and smoothed my hair behind my ears, gazing into my eyes like he always did when we shared these tender moments. "I'm just going for a few days. I'll be back before you know it. I'm not saying goodbye, I'm saying I can't wait to see you again, okay?"

I nodded and buried my face in his t-shirt, inhaling his scent deeply, and twisting his shirt in my hand. "I can't wait to see you too. You will come and find me, won't you?"

Alfie smirked. "South Carolina on the third, right? I have

this cool, hot, rock chick who has given me backstage passes to see her band. You have no idea how relieved I was to get them, because I didn't fancy giving the security guy a blow job to get backstage. Wonder if I'll get lucky when I see her." He chuckled and made me laugh softy.

He smiled down at me, and I'd been doing great up until that point. But the tears started flowing, and my heart was heavy at having to let him go, when we'd just found each other again.

Holly came in and interrupted our moment, so Alfie left before it became even more difficult. I tried to keep myself busy after he left. Thinking about not being able to share New Year's Eve was hard, and knowing he'd be at a New Year's Eve party without me was horrible.

Life wasn't fair sometimes, but it had been my choice to do my own thing, so I had to suck it up and get on with it.

Every time I had a lull in my schedule I thought about Alfie. I felt so miserable without him. I kept telling myself he'd had two other New Year's Eves without me, and I had survived those. So, I could do it again, because this time I knew he was coming home to me. I was going to make sure we made it this time.

I practiced with the band for most of New Year's Eve, and we went to D'mond for one last night of fun before the hard work started for our tour. I tried to enjoy myself, but the whole time my mind was on Alfie.

When the midnight celebrations started, I briefly hugged and kissed everyone around me before making my way outside to wait for Alfie's call. I stood in the cold for half an hour, but there was nothing.

I checked my cell to make sure I had a signal, and I did. Wondering if he was having problems with his signal, I headed back inside. It was freezing cold, and I couldn't help

but feel pretty hurt and let down so soon into our relationship again.

Checking my phone for the tenth time, I sent him a text
telling him I was at Louie's but going home. I texted Jack
next. I wanted to tell everyone else in the UK Happy
New Year.

By the time I arrived home there was still nothing. I could
just have called him, but I didn't want to appear clingy.
Worrying and wondering why he hadn't done what he'd
promised to was getting me nowhere.

Getting prepared for bed, I kept rushing back to my cell
just in case there was a message from him. The more time
that passed, the angrier I was becoming. It was almost three
in the morning, and he hadn't called or texted me. Grabbing
my cell from the counter, I sent him a text.

Pink Lady: Happy New Year x

I didn't trust myself to send anything else. I was getting
frustrated and didn't want to say anything that would affect
the next time we saw each other.

At almost four o' clock, my cell rang. SEXPERT ID
flashed on the screen. I was beyond pissed at him now, when
I knew he was okay and was calling me. "Hey," he cooed.
Usually when Alfie said this, it made all negative thoughts
about him disappear. Tonight, it made me madder.

"Hey?" I had been out of my mind about what had
stopped him from calling me for the past couple of hours and
all I'd got was hey? "That's it?"

He exhaled heavily. "Hey, I'm in love with you and I miss
you like crazy?" Well, it was better but still didn't make me
less mad.

"You said you would call me after midnight."

He snickered down the line. "It is after midnight." His
voice sounded like he didn't know there was a problem.

"Where have you been?" And there I was, sounding like a clingy girlfriend.

"Sorry, we got caught up with the fans afterwards."

I couldn't help myself. "That would have been almost four hours ago now, Alfie."

He exhaled heavily again. "Yeah, well they kind of hung around for New Year, since there was only about ten minutes left of the old year. Actually, Lily, it's nearly one o'clock here. You forgot about the time difference; we haven't been off stage for two hours yet."

Oh, God, the time difference. How could I have forgotten? Feeling stupid, I smoothed things over, and we talked about when he thought he'd arrive in South Carolina. Alfie loved me. Trusting him was imperative if we were going to make it.

Dropping into bed, I didn't even remember going to sleep, but my cell pulled me out of my slumber when Lennon called. We spent the day sorting out all the stuff for our tour with the technical guys.

I didn't speak with Alfie again before we left for South Carolina as we didn't have the same breaks in our schedules. When we arrived at the parking lot to pick up the bus for the tour, it was a turning point for us as a band.

Cody and Digs were the most overly excited about the whole deal. The bus seemed a bit like a UK trailer, but upscale with padded leather seating in the dining table area, and a small kitchen area as we walked in the door.

There was a massive U-shaped seating area with a huge square black wooden coffee table in the center. Opposite the seating there was a sound system and a seventy-inch satellite-ready TV affixed to the wall.

Past this, there was a smaller sectioned off game-room with recliner chairs, again in leather. On the opposite side was a shower and toilet.

The bus was a double-decker and upstairs again there was a small seating area, toilet with shower, and five sets of bunk beds, each with a curtain.

Kieron and his personal assistant, Jerry, would be traveling with us, and the rest of the support were traveling separately. I picked the set of bunk beds right at the end of the bus, because I felt this would give me the greatest privacy.

No one would have to walk past me. Lennon and Cody took the row next to mine. Digs and Shawn had the next. This left two rows, one for Kieron and Jerry, and one for the drivers.

We had two drivers and a lot of miles to cover. They would swap out after a week and two new ones would come in for safety reasons.

As the only girl living in such close proximity to the guys, Lennon was overly protective, and I knew without a doubt that whatever happened during the tour, I could rely on all my bandmates.

Lennon delegated me the bed above mine as well. "Lily has more shit and high heels than anyone else, so she needs the space, and Alfie can stay there when he comes to see her," he informed the others in the band.

We settled and looked around, before going back downstairs to see Kieron and Jerry coming on board. Jerry handed us some packets with important information. It was mainly numbers we needed and we were advised to key them into our phones.

We got passes as well. We might have been recognizable to our fans, but some of the security would still have difficulty separating us from the fans and groupies.

It was 4pm, and we were headed for South Carolina. Hopefully tonight we'd spend the night in a hotel. Apart from this one, we'd only have three nights in a hotel for the next three weeks.

I tried to call Alfie and left a voicemail; he was traveling home from L.A. I just wanted to call to hear his voice on the voicemail. I missed hearing it.

I had to focus on the band now. Although Alfie and I were going to do everything possible to be together now, I had a responsibility to the guys in the band. Lennon nudged me. "Lily, we're on tour!" I giggled at his playfulness and smiled. The tour had to be a success, especially for these four fantastic men that had brought me this far.

Chapter Twenty-Four

ON TOUR

We arrived at the hotel around midnight and tried to get some sleep. I was too excited, though, and as this was another pivotal moment in my life, my mind went over everything that had happened to me since coming to Florida.

There had been some tough times in the past, especially with how I'd dealt with finding my sexual identity, and I'd made a few pretty stupid decisions, even the one including Alfie.

Accepting that a lot of what happened had helped me to grow, I still felt that I should have been able to say no. I often reflected on why I was so weak willed back then and think it might have been because I had no one around that truly knew me. No one I completely trusted, like Jack, who I could have talked to at the time.

The strength I'd gained as a person had made me more confident and assertive, which in turn had made my decision making much clearer. I did the things I wanted to do, not because of pressure from other people.

Alfie had been a constant thorn in all of my planning.

He'd been the curveball I just never saw coming. I never expected to fall in love with anyone for a while, and I didn't know how powerful or debilitating loving someone could be until I loved him.

Sometimes I wondered if he hadn't told me not to fall in love with him, if I would have. Then again, I'd be lying to myself. Falling in love with Alfie was a foregone conclusion for me from that first kiss.

After breakfast, we headed over to the venue in Columbia and did our sound checks, then ran through a few of the numbers in full, just to hear the acoustics as a band.

I was nervous. Those excited, 'on the brink', feelings I'd felt yesterday were now replaced by the nervous feelings I felt whenever I sat in the dentist's chair. I now had a bad case of nerves.

The venue in South Carolina was one of the biggest we were performing at, holding five thousand people. Panic threatened to grip me when I thought about walking out there and seeing only three people in one row and five in another.

I envisioned someone handing flyers out stating, 'free concert', telling anyone in the street to come and fill some of the seats, so that it wouldn't look as empty.

It wasn't a sell- out, but it wasn't empty either. Kieron reckoned there were almost four thousand tickets sold already. Stupid, really, but I was focusing on the thousand that hadn't, which was still a lot of space to fill. I calculated twenty percent unsold.

Kieron explained the ticket sales were going well for the other venues, and we were sold out in all but five states. "Extremely promising," for a band such as ours, with the little exposure we'd had so far.

By the time we were going on stage I thought I was going to puke. I hadn't been able to eat anything that day. My choice of outfit was meant to make me seem super confident and sexy, just in case I needed that distraction on stage if my playing sucked.

Lennon looked incredible, the image consultant had dressed him in black leather pants and a fitted white t-shirt, with a leather sleeveless vest over it, and biker boots. She had told him not to shave, so he had that sexy stubble thing going on, and they had put kohl on his eyes and product in his hair.

It was the hottest I'd ever seen Lennon look. I'd always thought Lennon was a hot, yet understated guy, but the way they had tweaked him, he was going to have some serious female fans when they got a look at him.

Cody was his usual cocky self, and I had to admit he had every right to be. He looked incredibly attractive in blue jeans, a grey t-shirt, and a red button-down suit vest, the back of which was red satin. He'd been letting his hair grow out, and it suited him. He was a gorgeous looking man.

Digs was left kind of grungy, in jeans and a red biker t-shirt. Once I had learned to look past all the ink, it was apparent he was a pretty good-looking guy. I think I was just intimidated by all the tattoos on my first impression.

I didn't really think anyone had to do anything in particular to Digs' appearance. With such an individual look, it would have been kind of stupid to try to enhance what was already unique.

Shawn's look was the other pleasant surprise for me. His hair was a buzz cut, but he'd had XrAid shaved into the buzz and dyed black, white, and silver like our logo. It was very cute.

Like Digs, Shawn didn't need to wear anything except short pants and a vest top. Watching him go out to work on his drum kit was like watching a track athletic training. He was so fit with huge biceps. This was reflected in his ability to play complex percussions and maintain the strength to do it at the same time for hours on end.

Lennon didn't give me shit about my outfit either. I had chosen to wear the same outfit as I did the very first time we ever performed. I used it at times when I wanted that little extra bit of confidence to go out there.

Once we were all ready, we were talking and psyching ourselves up, when there was a knock on the door. Kieron's head peered in. "Someone to see you, Lily."

Kieron extended the door open, and Alfie was standing there grinning widely, that sexy dimple of his showing. He was wearing dark denim jeans with the belt that had my favorite buckle, and his brown leather jacket; his hands were stuffed deep into his pockets.

Alfie took my breath away as usual, and my heart almost burst out of my chest. He always looked so stunning. It was hard for me not to pass out this time.

Next thing I knew, he was striding toward me, his hands appearing from his pockets. I was sitting at the dressing table, and he squatted down to my height. I smelled his scent as he disturbed the air beside me and inhaled deeply.

"Hey," he said in a soft calming voice. He gave me a peck on the lips, then scooped me out of the chair, sat down, and placed me back in his lap. I let out the breath I hadn't realized I was holding, and my heartbeat was a little more under control, but the effect he had on me, just seeing him, was electric.

"Miss me?" he whispered, his hot breath tickled my neck. A colony of butterflies took flight all at once at his words.

All the anguish I had been fighting for the past few days about him being somewhere else without me dissolved and was replaced with a feeling of completeness, like he was the one thing that was missing in all of this.

His hand ran up my neck and into my hair. "C'mere," he

murmured as he wetted his lips. "I need to kiss you." He bent his head to my forehead and husked, "Fuck, I missed you so much."

I swear that I had some cavewoman tendencies right then, but I fought to stay in control. I let him give me a small kiss but pulled away after that, conscious there were four other horny guys in the room. I wasn't about to give them a peep show.

I distracted him, because if I didn't, I was going to have to change my panties. He had already turned me on just by touching my skin and saying that stupid, "Hey," thing he did all the time. "So, Alfie, tell me, which was it, the backstage pass or the blowjob?"

Cody snickered and stared at Alfie. He didn't know what I was talking about, but he was not going anywhere until Alfie answered either. Alfie burst out laughing and raised an eyebrow at me.

"Hmm...did I tell you there are females on the security detail out there?"

I swatted his arm. "There are?"

Alfie then stood and wrapped his arms around me. "Who do you think frisks all the female fans?" He chuckled. "Trust me, seeing them, and looking at you...backstage pass, no competition." He winked. I smiled, it was a good answer.

We got the call and headed toward the stage. My nerves as I stood in the dark, waiting for the cue to take to the stage, were making me crazy. They were beginning to freak me out. Cody put his arm around me and began speaking softly into my ear.

I thought I heard Alfie growl, but Cody just raised his head slightly, before refocusing on me again. This was a routine that Cody did to help me take that first step out on stage. To be honest, I needed him more than I needed Alfie in that moment. This was strictly work and had nothing to do with anything else.

The anticipation of going out on stage, without the security of the small familiar venue and captive audience in the clubbers we had at Louie's places, made me freak. This time we were facing people who had paid a lot of money to see us, and this raised the bar for their expectations of us.

Knowing this gave me a great sense of responsibility to ensure that they had a great time out there. Being in a rock band might seem glamorous, but in reality everyone had to be pleased with your performance, both on stage and off.

I was a wreck when the emcee gave his greeting to the crowd and announced our imminent arrival on stage. The crowd roared and whistled their appreciation and then a hush fell over the auditorium as the lights dimmed and the stage went black. I glanced to the side and saw Alfie wink at me. "You'll be fabulous," he mouthed.

Cody laced his fingers in mine. "Come on, babe, show 'em what you've got." He pulled me by my hand and led me out to the front of the stage. Someone handed me my guitar, and I pulled the strap over my head.

I was still facing backwards when we were suddenly bathed in light, and we began the intro to our first song. Turning to the audience I heard the erupting screams of the fans and a sea of hands, raised above their heads clapping and cheering.

The volume of noise at a concert and the atmosphere always invigorated me. Being on stage was so much more exciting than looking on--as I had when I saw Alfie play-- from the side of the stage that first time.

We gave our fans everything we had. Playing like our lives depended on their pleasure. Lennon was on fire with his solos, and Shawn was drenched in sweat by the time we finished. We must have been doing something right, because the fans demanded an encore.

When we came off stage, Alfie dipped his knees and grabbed me by my hips, lifting me so that I was looking down at him. "Fuck me. You were fucking awesome, baby," he growled and buried his face in my neck, making me shiver with his sensual act.

Lennon was at my side when Alfie placed me back on the ground. I turned and hugged him tightly. "Good job. You were amazing, Lennon." I smiled up at him, and he bent his head to kiss my forehead.

"Ditto." He smirked.

Cody came up and lifted me off the ground and twirled me around, growling, "Damn, sexy girl. You were on fire out there." He chuckled. Alfie chewed his lip watching Cody intensely. I hesitated about Cody's behavior, but he was only letting off some steam after the gig, and it felt good to get feedback from my bandmates.

Cody was still hugging me when Digs placed his hand on his shoulder. "Dude, do you mind. You're encroaching on my hugging time." Cody smirked and let me go as Digs swooped in for a hug. "Excellent gig, baby girl." He patted my hair down and away from my face. Digs was always looking after me.

That first gig we played was an incredible buzz. I'll never forget the feeling of walking out there to a massive crowd. Our own fans. I still couldn't believe I was doing all of this, and I had the four guys in the band to thank for letting me be part of it.

Alfie stood with his arms folded, looking like he might punch Cody or Digs, but I was secretly pleased that he wasn't immune to the fact that guys could hit on me just as women were doing with him all the time.

If he needed further evidence of that, it was to come after

the show. We had been fortunate these past couple of weeks when we went out. There hadn't been that much opportunity for his fans to interfere with our private lives, apart from a few times at the club, but we'd dealt with that.

As usual we met with some of the fans backstage. There were a few that had won contests via a local radio station, and there were some that had been selected from our newly formed fan club.

My camp of fans seemed to be split into two groups; the high school or first year college kids on one hand and some very muscular guys about my age on the other.

The fans were mainly polite and wanted to talk about our music, but two of the older guys passed me CDs to sign. Both had written notes with their telephone numbers on them. When I opened one of them to sign the paper inside, he had put a naked picture of him inside and winked at me when I looked up at him.

Unnerved, I politely signed the CD paper and drew pants on the photo before handing it back. When he saw me do this and hand it back he said in a low voice, "You don't know what you're missing, baby."

Smiling sweetly, I nodded for him to take it back saying, "Yeah, I do, I've seen you now remember? And from what I saw, I'm not missing much. Sorry but I prefer a bit of mystery in my men. Maybe you shouldn't have been so...out there with the picture."

Lennon's sixth sense kicked in, and he appeared at my side. "Sorry, Lily, we need to move it along a little." Ever the diplomat, he'd come to my rescue. When we talked about it later, they all shrieked with laughter at what I'd done. Even Alfie thought it was funny, after a few minutes of cussing about the naked-picture-cd guy.

Chapter Twenty-Five

CUBBIE

*A*lfie travelled on the bus with us to Virginia, and he had booked us into a hotel. We didn't arrive there until 5am, but we weren't needed at the venue until 3pm.

I would have been happy sleeping on the bus, because it was still a novelty for me. Alfie was much less enthusiastic about doing that due to his years of traveling like this.

"It's bad enough when I *have* to do this. Plus, I haven't seen you in a week. I'm not getting laid in a bunk bed our first night together again. I'd definitely pull a muscle, and it's fucking impossible to change position in those things. What if I wanted to stand?" He asked.

I stared back at him completely deadpan. "Who said anything about getting laid? Is that why you made the effort?"

Alfie chuckled. "I knew I should have taken that blow job from that butch looking security chick."

I snickered. "I meant that it would have been you who would have giving the blow job to security had I not given you the backstage pass."

I bunched my brows at him, and he looked straight at me. "Ah, but that was you assuming that it would be a dude I'd have to get past. She actually looked disappointed that I had a pass because she definitely wanted to blow me, being famous an' all." My jaw dropped. Alfie was way too quick for me.

Settling into bed, it felt amazing to be in Alfie's arms again. We were exhausted by the time we finally got off the bus but still managed two rounds of lovemaking.

We had this intensively intimate but awkward moment when Alfie was lying on top of me. We were getting carried away, and he rolled completely over me, settling between my legs and taking his weight on his forearms.

He leaned back to look at me and dropped his head onto my forehead again, just like he had so many times before. "I just want you to love me for the rest of my life." I smiled, and we continued to stare into each other's souls.

The tip of his cock was lined up with my wet, swollen folds. I ached for him to be inside. He nudged me there several times, teasing me, almost entering me. It felt amazing, his hard, bulbous head with the smooth, silky skin, and the metal of his apa, almost breaching me.

My legs instinctively widened, and he nudged forward just a little more. The head of his cock was being hugged by my entrance. "Fuck. That feels so fucking perfect. You're so ready for me," he said huskily, his voice soft and thick with sexual tension.

"I just want to slide myself so deep inside you right now, Lily. All it would take is one little push of my hips, and I'd be balls deep, filling your sweet pussy." He swallowed hard, staring at me.

I knew what he was asking. He wanted permission not to use the condom. He wanted to be with me, skin to skin, but I had no idea if he had been protecting himself with Zoe. Apart from that, the last time this happened, I'd had a pregnancy scare. So I shook my head. "Don't. Get the condom,

Alfie." He breathed deeply, closed his eyes and nodded, not stopping to argue. I was worried that rejecting his request was going to ruin the moment, but it didn't.

The pleasure we gave each other was incredible, and we were so in tune with each other, it took me to new heights. He told me that no other woman had ever made him feel how he did when he was with me. This made me feel so lucky, because it was the same for me.

After he put the condom on, there was much less restraint. He was more like the Alfie I knew in the beginning, but I guess it was the first time we'd been able to have sex without someone else within earshot. Obviously, any people next door in a hotel room didn't count for that purpose.

Playful and adventurous in his lovemaking, it turned me on so much to have my sexy, sensual, drop-dead gorgeous Alfie back. I had never forgotten what it felt like when Alfie touched me. The chemistry between us was always electric and when he was inside me, I couldn't describe what he did to me.

Sometimes the sex between us bordered on both ecstasy and agony. For me anyway, it was the ecstasy of the release and the agony of the tease leading up to it. His strength and stamina made me delirious at times.

It used to terrify me that I would never have the connection we had with anyone else. When I said this to Alfie, his feelings were the same.

It was the reason he had never dated anyone since me, until he met Zoe. I couldn't stop myself from asking when he said that. I had to know, but I wasn't sure that I wanted the answer either.

"So, you felt the same chemistry as we had with Zoe?" I was lying with my head on Alfie's chest, drawing lazily on his torso with my index finger and trying to pretend I was being casual about my question.

"Hell, no, Lily, I told you, I never even came close to the feelings I have for you with anyone else." He adjusted my head in the crook of his arm so that he could look at me. "Are we being honest here?" I nodded.

"I wouldn't have asked. But I'm curious," I squeaked. Inside my heart was beating two beats for one, not wanting him to tell me about some of his conquests, which I was sure was coming next.

"Every fucking night women threw themselves at me. Some did crazy things with no shame, just to try to get my attention. I hated it, because all it did was make me miss you more."

"Then there was Zoe," I pointed out, expecting a proclamation of how she made him feel. Alfie had a high sex drive, but I sensed with her it was more than just sex; it wasn't just a physical thing like he'd said. Smiling at me, he took my hand, lacing our fingers together, looking at them when he did it. When he glanced back at me, he exhaled.

"Zoe...she came into my life at a low point. Until her, I hadn't had sex with anyone else since you. Almost fifteen months I waited, thinking you would find me again, Lily."

My jaw gaped, and I moved my head up lying eye to eye with him. He really did feel the same as me back then. Even, in the beginning, when he was denying his own feelings.

I bunched my brows thinking that all the while I had expected Alfie to be out there lapping up the fame and excess, he was miserable inside because of me and my dreams.

Staring straight at me, I waited for him to continue. "Zoe was working in a truck stop we were having breakfast in one morning. It was quiet, and we were the only people around. She poured herself a coffee and, without being invited, sat beside us saying she was "bored shitless here." She knew who I was but wasn't impressed by fame."

He snickered at the memory. "She has a good heart, and

she needed to be rescued from that place. Before I knew what I was doing, I told her to come along with us for the ride. She took off her apron and climbed on the bus. She took a chance, that's how desperate she was for change. She just hung out with us guys, and we developed a friendship."

I rubbed my hand lazily over the smooth skin on his hard chest, and traced over the ink on his arm, continuing to listen. "I was drinking a little too much after that, and one night I told her all about you. Not your name. I didn't want her using your name when she spoke to me about you. It just didn't seem right for some reason. She listened and gradually, I began to put the pieces of my life back together."

He swallowed audibly. "It was after Mandy sent me the video of you... it set me back. When I saw you play in the club, I thought I'd lost you forever."

Alfie snickered. "She wasn't stupid, and I was honest from the start with Zoe." I sat listening to him talk and remembered he'd behaved the same way with me, telling me that he couldn't get involved with me.

"We both knew that what we were doing wouldn't last, that's why I insisted on setting her up with her own place and gave her some money. That way she could walk when she got 'bored shitless' with us." He chuckled.

He cleared his throat. "Anyway, she listened, and I think I would have gone into freefall if she hadn't been there for me at the time.

"Gradually, I began to put the pieces of my life back together, and that's when my relationship with Zoe became physical." I found it hard to swallow when he voiced that.

"Neither one of us made a play for each other, we were just drunk one night, and it happened. She was a temporary substitute for you, Lily."

As Alfie had been honest, I wanted to be honest with him

as well. "It makes me insanely jealous that she had you, even for a short time," I whispered.

"She never had me, Lily. We had sex, but I think my heart has belonged to you since the day I met you, even if I didn't know it at the time." He smiled.

"Luca..." I began, but his body tensed, and he cut me off. "I don't want you to tell me about him, Lily. I could see that feelings were involved." Alfie's jaw muscle ticked.

"What Zoe and I had was just friendship and sex. I had nothing to offer her. With you and that guy...like you said, you didn't want to be with someone just for the physical side of a relationship. You're with me now, and whatever shit happened between you in the past is done, right?" I nodded and raised myself onto my elbow to see his face.

"You are all I've ever truly wanted, Alfie." I smiled at him and gazed lovingly into his eyes.

"Yeah. Me and music," he corrected. I lay back and placed my forearm over my head, ignoring his blunt comment.

"We'll make it this time, Alfie. Look at us, we're talking about what really matters. Maybe we'd have been together for a short while before, but now, we're going into this wiser, and I'm ready now. We know what we have to do."

He turned his body to face me. "C'mere." I turned my body inwards to meet his. Sliding one arm under my neck, his other pulling me flush against his warm, hard body. His scent and his warm arms were around me, his hand splayed on my back, holding me tightly to him. It felt perfect.

Alfie's breath disturbed the air over my face. "No one and nothing is taking you away from me again." He swallowed noisily. "Nothing."

Another watershed. Here we were, able to talk openly and get our feelings out there. We were both desperate for things to work out with us this time, and it was great that we were both still able to follow our dreams. We lay in bed for as long as we could, wrapped up in each other, fully content to just be together.

After Alfie had gone, Will came to see me when we were in Ohio. I was thrilled that he made the effort and it was great to catch up on all his news. I was so pleased for him when he told me he was in a relationship. He deserved happiness; he really was a fantastic person.

I didn't make further arrangements to see him again. I figured we'd just keep in touch like we had been doing. Besides, if I had, I doubt whether Alfie would have been too keen on Will and me making plans. He'd made his position about Will very clear in the past. Alfie saw Will as a threat despite my constant reassurances. He had nothing to worry about on that score.

Alfie came to see me a couple more times during the last week of the tour. Once we did have to sleep on the bus and Alfie was right about the 'bunk bed sex'. It was an experience. A hot, sweaty, claustrophobic one and we thought we had been quiet until Shawn's frustrated voice bellowed from two beds down.

"Are you all done back there now? I put my headphones on, but the side of the fucking bus was shaking, so you were both a bit hard to ignore down there, and I need to get some sleep."

Alfie chuckled and winked, calling out, "Yeah, Lennon, put that dirty magazine down, we're all trying to sleep here, Dude."

I was mortified, but I knew I would have to learn to accept that this way of life meant that there were very few secrets between us - either that or everyone's sex lives were going to be severely curtailed. Anyway, I think that Shawn was just jealous. This was the first night in a week he hadn't dragged some groupie on the bus with him.

The rest of the XrAid tour went brilliantly. Each concert

performance was better than the last, and we couldn't believe the following we were beginning to have. We met hundreds of fans, and Kieron was impressed with the numbers.

He began bringing in extra security as we were becoming recognizable. This made me nervous, but I was dating one of the most popular guys on the planet, so either way, I wasn't going to be allowed to fade into the background much longer.

By the time we arrived home in Miami, Alfie was in meetings arranging Crakt Soundzz's upcoming tour. Alfie's band had just recorded a new album before we got back together, and their tour dates had been arranged months ahead of that.

Supporting for Crakt Soundzz and Cobham Street was a daunting prospect, and we had twenty-two dates over a four-week period. At least I was going along with Alfie this time, and we'd get to spend every day together when XrAid was supporting them for some of the tour anyway.

Alfie and I would wake up together at the very least. We were both on a natural high about this and about spending time with Elle and Drew as well. This was beyond anything I could ever have imagined. Best of all, traveling by bus, we'd have nothing else to do but be together.

XrAid had a ten-day hiatus before we went on tour again, so I used the time to catch up with my 'non band' friends. I saw my bandmates for rehearsals, but we didn't socialize.

Three weeks on a bus on the road, and we were sick of the sight of each other. We needed to recharge and regroup before we began living and breathing life on the road again together.

Cody had turned into a bit of a drunken manwhore during the three weeks away. He was like a horny teenager with some of the women that threw themselves at him.

Most shocking from the tour was when I opened the dressing room door and felt like I'd stumbled onto a porn set. Three naked girls were getting down with Shawn.

One had her ass in the air, folded over the sink. Shawn was giving her a vaginal examination with his tongue. Another was rubbing her breasts near his face, and his junk was in the mouth of a third. When he'd heard the door open, he lifted his head, looked me in the eye, and smirked. Just smirked. Before turning his attention back on with what he was doing, like it was nothing. Guess Shawn must have taken my advice on the glitter.

After that display, I really didn't worry that he may occasionally hear Alfie and me. We were in a normal relationship, unlike the less-than-natural stuff that seemed be going on in his sex life.

We all worked on our tans by sitting by the pool to catch some last-minute sunshine. Being the middle of February and freezing in Europe, we were stocking up on vitamin D to carry us through the rest of the winter.

Tour demands meant we had to stay fit and healthy. That, and we had to be image conscious for the pictures that would be taken of us during the next month.

Chapter Twenty-Six

BAREBACK

Cobham Street's tour had started three days ago.
XrAid was performing twelve dates with Crakt
Soundzz and ten afterwards with Cobham Street. Their
support act, Bubble Card, was to join Alfie's band when we
swapped over in Hamburg.

Alfie's band was due to finish the tour a few days before
Cobham Street, and we'd planned to meet up in London to
see my parents.

XrAid, apart from me, were so excited to be going to
Europe and acted like a bunch of kids. On stage, it was a
completely different matter, their dedication as musicians was
never in question. Apart from their musical ability, all of
them had shown me brotherly love and provided protection
ever since I've known them.

When the day came for us to board the jet, Digs was
quiet. I knew that he was going to miss his family; they were
close. We'd had a long chat one night when we were in
Chicago, and the last tour was the longest they had ever
spent apart. Digs had gone to the same college as me, but

dropped out when he was offered the chance to play with XrAid.

We were flying on the label's jet to begin the tour, and I was surprised to discover that none of the guys from XrAid held a passport. They explained that they had never flown outside of the USA, so only needed their identity cards.

They didn't understand why we didn't have those in the UK. Lennon was like a child with his and worried he'd lose it. He was excited, because he was going to London and excited to see my dad who had promised the guys a tour of London in his helicopter.

The label limo picked us up one at a time, and by the time they collected me, all the guys were sitting in the back. My place was nearest the airport. I could feel the excitement radiating from them, and wondered if it would still be there by the time they had spent eight hours in the air.

Both bands were flying together. The Global 8000 record label jet had nineteen seats. There were nine of us in the two bands, plus Elle, Kieron, Jerry, and two Crakt Soundzz management guys. We also had an official photographer, reporter/blogger, and a publicity guy. We were a full house once the two cabin crew were included.

Alfie was already aboard when I arrived; his band was high profile so they were driven directly onto the tarmac. We cleared customs the minion way. He had already taken the two seats near the back of the plane and pulled me into his arms as soon as I reached him.

"Hey," he cooed. "Excited?" Well, I'd been doing just great until I saw him, but my heartbeat was now racing and I just wanted to crawl inside him, so yeah, excited.

"Mmmhmm, yeah, a little." I smirked. He hooked his fingers through my belt loops and tugged me closer, his mouth closing in on mine. The sudden electrical sensation, and the skill of his tongue on my body, sent my erogenous zones into overdrive.

Kissing Alfie was definitely a multisensory experience; he smelled incredible, he tasted of spearmint chewing gum, and I couldn't begin to tell you what the exchange of bodily fluids in my mouth was doing, except to say it was wreaking havoc between my thighs. He drove me crazy with want and left me breathless.

"More excited now?" he teased.

"Uh huh, that'll about do it," I muttered smiling against his mouth, swooning, and still trying to catch my breath. He chuckled and pulled me down on his lap.

"Ask me," he commanded.

I creased my brow. "Ask you what?"

He snickered. "Ask me if I'm excited." I smirked at him, he was being playful.

"Okay, Alfie. Are you excited, honey?" He nodded, and his mouth breathed into my ear. He whispered, "Today, finally, I get to be a rock star and join the mile high club." I looked around at all the people sitting around us.

"Um, no. No, you don't," I hissed quietly, with my eyes flicking between the seats to see who heard him.

He nodded. "I'll win, you'll see." He winked wickedly.

Alfie let me sit by the window so I settled in the seat. Cabin crew were super serious, taking us through all the usual life jacket... emergency door stuff, while I sat wondering for the thousandth time as I have during all the other flights, what use was a life jacket if you fell from 33,000 feet.

I've tried to jump twenty-five feet from the diving platform in the public pool and hurt myself, so I doubted I would be alive by the time I hit the water.

I looked at Alfie who was paying no attention at all and glanced at Lennon who might have been either writing a song or taking notes.

The flight took off, and everyone began to relax. We'd been given drinks and pretzels, and afterwards I fell asleep. I did it all the time when I got on a plane, something about the waiting to get airborne tired me out. When I woke up, Alfie was kissing my neck, and his hand was under my sweater, cupping my breast.

Cracking my blurry eye open I muttered, "Did you lose something? My eyes darted past Alfie quickly to look at Cody's row, across from us, to see if anyone was watching.

"Relax," he cooed. "No one can see us," he whispered. The way he whispered excited me, sending shivers down my spine, and my nipples pebbled under his touch. Alfie moved to the side so that his back was shielding us, and he licked up my neck.

"I so want to suck this," he whispered slowly, sexily, as his thumb brushed across my right nipple. "Fuck," he husked. By then, my panties were soaking wet; I was so turned on by how horny he was.

My fingers curled round his hand and pulled it from under my sweater. "They're bringing food, Alfie, stop it."

He chuckled and dipped his head to my ear. "I have very particular tastes." He winked, grinning devilishly at me.

As plane food goes it was excellent, a really tasty pasta with a fancy Italian name, which had been prepared by a famous chef. As usual with plane food, there didn't seem to be enough of it.

The little chocolate dessert was to die for, and I ate Cody's and Elle's too. Alfie didn't eat his but wouldn't give it to me either. I started to think maybe he thought I was getting fat, but he assured me that my figure was perfect to him.

Once we had all eaten, the atmosphere on the plane changed and the cabin lights were dimmed. There were reading lights for everyone, but only Elle's kindle and the PA's tablet at the front of the plane glowed, as well as the blue pathway lighting on the floor.

Everyone else seemed to want to sleep, but I was wide awake due to my nap before dinner. Alfie's hand swept over to find me, and he laced his fingers with mine. Smiling at me, he dipped his forehead to mine. "I love you, Lily Parnell." I smirked. Playful Alfie was fun. This was my favorite Alfie mood.

He leaned forward and licked my lips. "Mmm, I can still taste chocolate," he murmured next to my mouth.

My tongue swept over his lips. "It was so good, Alfie," I whispered sensually.

Taking out the little cup he'd stuck in his pocket, he peeled the silver foil off the top. He dipped his index finger in and scooped a little onto it.

"Want some?" he teased. I smirked and opened my mouth as his chocolate-loaded finger poked into it. "Suck." The way he said it, almost as he exhaled, the word barely there, was such a fucking turn on. I closed my lips around his finger and sucked it hard.

Grabbing my hand, he placed it over the bulge in his pants. "Feel what you're doing to me with your mouth. Fuck," he growled quietly, leaning forward and stuck his tongue in my ear. Damn, he was rock solid. I licked and sucked his finger, and he pulled it out. It made a small popping sound, which made our eyes dart around to see if we'd been heard, as we chuckled quietly together.

Alfie scooped more of the dessert and smeared it across my lips, then scooped some into his mouth. He bent his head and began kissing me. I giggled, it was sticky, and I would bet my shirt that there was chocolate over half my face by now.

"Stop it." I giggled.

He chuckled again and continued with his wet, sticky kisses. "I want this on your other lips."

My eyes flew wide. "Absolutely. Fucking. Not." My mouth was in a silent O, and he chuckled harder.

"Uh, huh." He grinned.

I shook my head. "You're fucking nuts, if you think that's going to happen here."

Alfie looked down the cabin, his sneaky peeks adding to the intimacy of the moment. No one was moving. He stood and quickly unclipped my seatbelt. "Move, no one is looking." He pulled me into the toilet right behind our seats, the little concertina door was struggling with both of us in the tiny toilet.

He had a wide grin on his face at his achievement. "Now then, where were we?"

I frowned, "We were figuring out how to explain that both of us were in the toilet together, Alfie." I half giggled but felt embarrassed as well.

He scratched his chin as if he was trying to figure out an excuse. "Well they'll all think we're doing it now if they were watching, so we may as well." He chuckled.

He was right, if anyone saw us, no matter what we did now, they would think we were going at it in the tiny toilet. We were standing hard up against with each other, and the look of joy on Alfie's face was priceless.

He lifted me onto the little sink and began to pop the button on my jeans. The look in his eyes as they flicked between me and my zipper was all I needed to know. We were definitely doing it, no matter what.

When my jeans were open, he lifted me down again, and shucked them down my hips, dragging my panties with them. It was a real job to get them down to my ankles, but when he did, he bent me forward and turned me until my ass was in the air, and my shoulders were resting on the toilet seat.

His head was between my legs, which were draped over his shoulders, but still confined by my jeans. He smirked down at me. "So..." He pulled out the half empty chocolate dessert and put his finger in. "Where were we?"

I couldn't believe how ingenious he was. He had me right where he wanted me, but at that moment, I was very glad his creative talent wasn't just confined to music.

He dipped his head and licked me. "I need to taste you first, then the chocolate. Don't worry I'll leave some for you as well." He winked, and that was the last funny comment he made.

After that he was all about giving me pleasure. He was sucking in little pulses on my clit with his very talented mouth, sucking hard and soft, licking firmly and feather light, until I came so hard I thought I was going to pass out in that position. I was seeing stars and could feel the blood rushing to my head.

I was trying to catch my breath when he smeared the chocolate over my labia and inner folds and began the task of pleasuring me again. This time his moans drove me wild, the vibrations and soft lapping and slurping noises of his tongue flicking over me were heightened, and I shuddered with almost all of my body when I came.

He growled and kept licking me, until I told him that I needed to be upright because I was beginning to get pins and needles in my legs from the lack of circulation.

Alfie somehow righted me and slipped his fingers inside. "Are you going to come again for me?" he asked as his fingers made come-to-me motions toward my G-spot, and I was a melted mess in front of him. My knees buckled, but I didn't fall because I had nowhere to go.

He turned me to face the mirror. "Look, you're so fucking beautiful right now." I was staring at myself in the mirror, and my hair looked like I'd been in a fight. I had chocolate still smeared over part of my lip, a bit on my chin, and some on my nose. My face was still flushed from being practically upside down, and I was seriously questioning Alfie's perception of beauty at that moment.

He shuffled me around again and sat me down on the toilet. I jumped with the shock of the cold plastic toilet seat under my ass and looked up at him. "Fuck, you're amazing, baby" he whispered softly.

"Now for your reward." He pulled his jeans down just enough to expose his rock hard cock and handed me the cup of chocolate. "Knock yourself out." He chuckled.

I giggled and took it, smearing it over his length and around his balls, then set to work. Alfie was moaning and hissing, his head rolled back, and he was leaning on the far wall. His hands splayed wide against both walls of the toilet. Licking slowly from base to tip, my tongue fluttered over his apa. Intermittently, I sucked the tip then took him deep.

"Fuck...goddammit, just like that," he hissed and growled. His head was moving from side to side. I looked up at him, and he shook his head.

"Good girl. This feels so fucking good. You do that so fucking perfectly," he muttered and bit his bottom lip. Right before he came, he pushed my head away.

"Here." He stood me and turned me so that he was sitting on the toilet seat now, his jeans at his ankles. He licked his fingers and began to tease my clit. My back was to him. I was still drenched with my juices and Alfie was turning me on all the time.

He started to draw me back into his lap, his cock nudging at my entrance. "Please, Lily," he pleaded. I knew what he wanted and had no hesitation this time. My body relaxed, and he eased himself inside me. It felt incredible, tight and hard, but slippery, at the same time.

"Fuck...damn...this feeling's like nothing on earth, you feel so fucking good," he growled. It was a low guttural sound into my hair. He moved my hair to the side, and I began rocking on him. All the time he was whispering how much he loved me, what he wanted to do to me, while he kissed my neck, nibbling and giving me small sucks.

After a few minutes, he raised me slightly and started to move faster under me until he was eventually pounding into me, and I felt tingles that told me that I was not going to be able to hold my release back. "I'm coming."

Those words from me seemed to be all the encouragement Alfie needed. "Do it!" he commanded, and I did, with him beginning to shudder under me as he chuckled softly into my neck. "Welcome to the mile high club, baby," he cooed breathlessly.

Tidying up nearly took as much energy from us. working in the small space we had, but luckily, we had face and hand tissues and a mirror. So, when we did eventually get out of the toilet, our appearances looked normal.

Alfie smirked. "Do you want to go out first?" Did I? If I opened the door and someone was watching us, I thought I would drop dead on the spot. Okay, maybe that was bit dramatic, but I knew I'd be mortified. "Well?" Alfie was staring at me, and I knew I just had to do it.

"I'll go first." He smiled and kissed my nose. "Atta girl," he said, pulling me back for one last kiss. He clicked the latch, switching the toilet from engaged to vacant, and launched me back into the cabin. Weaving my way back to my seat I thought we were free and clear but as we clicked on our seatbelts the guys burst into a round of applause. Alfie turned and cradled my head to his chest and smiled, "I guess we weren't as quiet as we thought," he said, leaned back and smirked. Covering my face with my hands I could feel the heat in my cheeks because they'd heard what we'd done, but Alfie flipped them the bird and their laughing quickly died down.

Chapter Twenty-Seven

PLAYING WITH THE BIG BOYS

*I*t was early morning when the plane arrived in Warsaw. The tour was working from East to West, top to bottom, of each country, and we had a lot of traveling to do.

Thick, compacted snow lay on the ground, crunching under our feet when we ran from the tarmac runway, through the wiring fencing, and into the SUVs that took us to the hotel. Freezing clouds puffed out of our mouths as the hot air from our lungs hit the coldness.

I had a few layers of clothing on, but when I looked at the XrAid guys, they weren't prepared at all for it being this cold. After being transferred and settled in, my bandmates headed for the spa to sit in the hot tubs; they were chilled to the bone.

The accommodations were good as some countries went. After being in India during my gap year, a shower that wasn't reliant on cold water pouring from holes in a gasoline water holder was luxury to me.

Some of the tour was by airplane and the rest by bus, depending on the distances involved. Alfie was delighted about our bus having two double beds. I couldn't wait for that part of the tour; us just spending time together without other demands.

We spent the evening eating, and discussing what we needed to do because tomorrow we'd all got a long day with sound checks, various interviews, and the 'Meet and Greets' that were planned.

This was in addition to the concert itself. I was incredibly nervous, because I'd seen Crakt Soundzz play several times now, and I hoped that we wouldn't let them down. Alfie told me that even if I wasn't his girlfriend, he'd have XrAid supporting them on tour.

Alfie had just gotten out of the shower and was walking around, his semi hard erection wagging back and forth. I was drying my hair with a towel when he saddled up behind me.

I turned to look at him. "Hey," he cooed. I smiled and sighed, that word from him always made my heart melt. "Hey, you." I grinned back.

He smirked, but it stretched into a grin, his dimple showing. I always fell in love a little more each time I saw that. "So…"

I smiled. "So…"

Alfie scooped me up and tossed me gently on the bed. "Poland," he said deadpan. I nodded. "We need to get memories, I have my camera. We need to get up tomorrow morning early." Two images needed to be replaced, one of him in the Old Town, and another at Lazienki Palace.

It had slipped my mind about Alfie's vow to replace the pictures of the places he'd been alone with one of me by his side. Smiling affectionately, I felt bad. Touching his face, I said, "I'm so sorry I wasted all that time without you, Alfie."

Giving me a dark look he shook his head. "It definitely wasn't time wasted Lily, look at you. Painful as it was, I would do it again, just to see you where you are today with your music." Hearing the pride and heartfelt support for my choice to study made me even more confident we'd make it together.

Alfie started chuckling heartily about what we'd done on the plane. We thought no one had noticed what we did, but the both of us admitted how hot it had been to do something so sneaky.

He grabbed my jawline and kissed me roughly. The following hour was of fun in bed, and I had no doubt that Alfie loved my body. We fell asleep still tangled up in each other, belly to belly, so close together. He was hugging me so tightly, like he was afraid to let me go. The last thing I remembered was him kissing my hair and sighing deeply.

I woke to intermittent buzzing noises filling the room. Alfie's alarm on his phone was cutting into the dark and silent room.

It was just after seven in the morning and still dark outside. Alfie leaned across me, and his arm brushed over my breasts as he grabbed his cell. "Damn, that's painful." He winced.

I raised my head thinking he was hurt. "What is?"

He chuckled. "The morning," he grunted and snuggled under the covers, grabbing me and pulling me tightly to him.

We showered and dressed, then made our way to the foyer. Alfie had arranged a car with a driver to take us to the spots he wanted to take pictures of.

Warsaw was fascinating. The history of the city was tragic but the people seemed very intelligent and progressive. There were a few things I had learned about Alfie that surprised me, mainly his closet country music genre preferences and his talent for photography. Once he'd fiddled with the settings and situated the camera on the tripod, we ran to pose for the shot.

He ran back and checked the digital display. He took

about twenty pictures from all different angles, and when I started to get cold from standing, I commented it was the landmark that the shot was about, not what angle we were standing at.

Back at the hotel it was breakfast time. The bands and crew had already eaten and were getting ready to ship out to the venue. Alfie and I grabbed some toast, coffee, and orange juice and headed back to the room to pack.

We went our separate ways at that point, because his band had a radio interview, and mine was doing our soundcheck first.

By the time we were about to go on, I was ready for bed, but adrenaline kicked in and I was soon wired and buzzing with excitement. My nerves started to build, and to be frank I was shitting myself, because there were 18,000 people out there.

To think I had been worried about 4,000 just a few weeks ago. Alfie came into our dressing room and led me to a quiet space in the hallway outside. He pressed me gently against the wall by his hips and straddled his hands on either side of my head on the wall.

His forehead dipped, landing softly on mine, and instantly it was just us. If anyone else was around, we were oblivious. "You're going to be great, Lily, just have fun. I love you." He kissed me so tenderly, and I sighed into his mouth.

He chuckled. "Okay, now that you're relaxed, I'm done here. See you on the other side." He winked and spanked my ass as I turned to go back to the guys.

Pushing the dressing room door open, I went back to the guys. No sooner had the door closed we got our ten-minute warning. Cody was super confident. Digs was quiet. Shawn started slapping a beat on his thighs, and Lennon was warming his vocals, singing into a towel.

Cody and I had done our warm-up just before Alfie

turned up. Lennon looked up. "Okay, let's fucking do this," he growled. It was the most pumped and aggressive I'd ever seen Lennon.

We entered stage right and our sound wiring was fed into our clothing. It was mainly wireless technology. This was the fail safe. Cody glanced at me, and smiled.

"C'mere," he said, holding his arms out for me to walk into. Giving me the speech he usually did about how amazing I was going to be, and I wished at that moment I had the confidence levels he and Alfie had for going out on stage and belting out rock tunes.

I didn't get time to think about it too hard because within a few seconds of him finishing his pep talk we were on stage, getting the job done.

I couldn't see much because the lighting was so strong. Only the first few rows, which were mainly women, and I was sure that was due to Alfie and Crakt Soundzz being the main act. I knew these women had probably paid extra money for the most exclusive seats, just in case Alfie took a shine to them.

Sorry, ladies, but Alfie wasn't looking for shiny things because he was mine. We put in a great performance and were carried by the crowd. They were really generous to us, but we were there to warm them up, and the fact that they liked our music made us feel great.

We finished our set and left a roaring, screaming crowd behind. I hoped it was because we were an awesome supporting band for Crakt Soundzz, and not just because we were finished, meaning that Alfie's band would soon be on. Alfie was heading toward me as we began to walk back.

"Damn, girl, you rocked." He grabbed me by my top and pulled me to him. His tongue was in my mouth before I could draw breath. It was hot and wet and fucking with my hormones that were already wreaking havoc on me.

"If I didn't have a job to do I'd fuck you right here and now," Alfie whispered to me. I smirked. "Yeah, and you think I'd let you do that?"

He grabbed my waist tighter. "By the look on your face right now, I'd say it was a done deal." He smirked, pecked my lips again, and let me go. "Love you," he cooed as he walked out into the dark for his band's entrance. There was no intermission at this gig.

Standing at the side, watching him in action, I could see all the things that made me fall so hard for him before he was famous. He was just so fucking sexy. The way he moved and his charismatic manner, not to mention his self-confidence on stage. It was his music that drew me in before I even saw what he looked like though. He was a master musician with a voice that would melt the panties off a nun.

Alfie was a world-famous rock artist. By the way people bowed and scraped to him, he should have had an inflated ego, full of diva demands and bat-shit crazy bad habits, but he didn't. I think maybe that was why he was so popular, because he didn't live life to excess.

When I thought of anyone else that came up to where Alfie was at, I could only think about Rick Fars in the same vein, and although his reputation preceded him, I was surprised at how normal he was as well.

Seeing Alfie jumping across the stage, he exuded that confidence and charisma, and I just couldn't stop staring. He was incredibly fascinating to look at when he performed; it mesmerized me.

I began to wonder what he was doing with me, when he could have practically any woman in the world at that moment. He began to sing 'Listen', our song, and turned his head to me. He knew I was there. He smiled and kept looking back at me all through the song.

When he replaced the mic, he smiled and blew me a kiss,

before Drew rocked out the intro on his guitar for the next hit on their set list.

I left after that and went to spend time with my guys. I couldn't let them think I didn't want to share what we did tonight with them. When I went into the dressing room, Shawn was in a towel as usual.

"Damn, Lily, I didn't think you were coming back or else I would have waited for you." He flicked his eyes to the towel, and I knew he was teasing that I had missed catching him naked. "There's always tomorrow." I smirked and raised an eyebrow. "Besides, Shawn, the number of times you've wagged that little thing in my face, I think I could draw it from memory now."

They all burst out laughing, and Lennon jumped up to hug me. I apologized for not coming straight down with them, but they told me they understood.

It had been a long time since I had seen Alfie play live, the last time being New Year's Eve over two years ago in London, before they were signed.

At the end of the set we went up to the side of the stage to watch the encore then Alfie and the rest of the guys piled off, covered in sweat and buzzing with the high of their performance.

Alfie scooped me up and wrapped my legs around his waist carrying me toward a dark, quiet area. He pushed me up against a wall and this time, I could feel the hard, hot bulge in his tight jeans. It was pressed against me, letting me feel how turned on he was from the whole experience out there.

He was kissing me passionately, and it left me breathless. My panties were drenched. His hand slipped under the skater dress I was wearing and around to the globes of my ass. His right hand continued its journey under my ass and into the crotch of my panties.

"Fuck," he hissed, dropping me to my feet. "With me.

Now!" he demanded and began to stalk down the hallway in the direction of XrAid's dressing room with me in tow. He knew all the guys were up at the stage. When we got inside, he swung me around and banged the door shut.

Covered in sweat, Alfie's raw sex drive took over. He crouched down and pushed my thigh length dress up around my waist in a hurry. He knocked my legs apart with his hand and pushed his face straight up into my crotch, sucking my lace panties hard.

I lifted my leg and placed it on the arm of the leather sofa, my head lolling to one side. "Fuck," he growled before turning me around and bending me over the arm of the sofa.

"I fucking need you right now, Lily. You were driving me insane standing there, just out of reach, when I was on stage."

Conscious that he hadn't locked the door, I glanced in its direction until he buried his fingers deep in my folds from behind. He rubbed my clit, making me wet and massaging my sensitive spot with his finger as his tongue delved deep into me.

Breaking away from me, Alfie unfastened his buckle, tugging hurriedly, and unbuttoned his jeans, before freeing himself and sliding his thick, hard cock into me.

No condom, skin on skin. He gasped, "Fuck." I moaned loudly. "Fuck, those little sounds...you drive me insane. They make me so fucking horny." He began to rock into me. "Are you okay?"

As soon as I nodded, his movements increased from a fast, steady rocking to hard fucking; it was intense, hot, and animalistic. Alfie sensed me tighten, and I came almost immediately, as Alfie growled, "Damn, do it." I clenched around him, squeezing him tightly. "Oh my God, Lily. Soooo... tight. Sooo fucking good...shit."

Slowing his pace as I continued to spasm through my climax, Alfie's eyes studied me, looking for signs I was beginning to relax. When he saw them, he increased the intensity again, pushing me over the edge into another orgasm, right before he followed. "Goddammit, you're here. This was a fucking wish, and it came true," he husked raggedly into the back of my neck.

We were both covered in sweat, and Alfie quickly wet a towel, which we wiped ourselves down with, then I went to fix myself up quickly. As we made our way back to our respective bands, Alfie looked guilty and squeezed my hand. "Sorry, I know that was really bad, but I just needed to have you so fucking much."

He squeezed my hand again in support as our bandmates came into sight. "You know we're gonna get shit, right?" He smirked. There was no doubt what we'd been doing. We couldn't hide it this time.

I was flustered, fumbling my way through the 'Meet and Greet' with sly looks from Cody and Shawn. When we were making our way back to the dressing room, Cody whispered, "You know that dude Alfie? He's one lucky son of a..." He shook his head and dragged his hand behind his neck. I was embarrassed, but smiled. I wasn't going to let Cody get the better of me.

Walking past the area that was set out for Crakt Soundzz, I looked up and saw Drew first. He smiled and winked at me, then turned back to listen to the guy that was talking to him.

I caught sight of Alfie, and as I did, a tall redhead flung her arms around him and planted a kiss on his lips. When he held her by her arms, I paused to watch what he did next. He brought her arms down and nodded twice. Henry, his security guy, stepped between them and, with the same motion as I had seen him make at the club, made distance between them.

Alfie looked across as if he sensed me and signaled for me to approach by waving two fingers in a, 'come here', motion. I walked through the room where various groupies and fans were hanging out, and he stepped around a few to reach me.

Taking my hand, he pulled me back to where he'd been sitting. A couple of the women eyed me up and down, one sneering right at me.

Alfie placed a hand on my neck and moved my face to his. "Hey," he cooed. A smile curved on my lips as he whispered in my ear, "These people are no one I want to know, understand me?" I nodded, and he kissed me so tenderly, not caring that we were in a room full of people.

When he released me, he held on to my hand. "Please stay with me," he pleaded. I squeezed his hand, and he rewarded me with a gorgeous dimpled smile and another soft kiss.

We chatted with the lingering fans and some paid compliments to XrAid by telling me that they would buy the album. By the time we left the venue it was almost eleven thirty. I was exhausted and so was Alfie. We only had one night in Poland, but we were staying in the hotel again. Tomorrow, at six in the morning, we were flying to Athens.

Sitting in silence on the way to the hotel, we just cuddled and held hands. Holding hands was amazing. I didn't really remember even getting into bed.

Alfie was in the shower because he didn't get time after the gig. I was asleep by the time he was finished. I never even felt him getting into bed with me. I'd been on my feet for about 15 hours, which might not seem harsh to most, but the adrenaline I expended today had left me no stronger than an ass wipe.

Chapter Twenty-Eight
M&M'S

*L*oud pounding on the hotel room door startled us awake. "Get your asses out of bed. The plane won't wait, and the coach is here to transfer us to the airport." Drew's voice invaded my warm, fuzzy slumber. Trying to focus my blurry eyes on my phone, I saw it was only five thirty am.

I groaned and nudged Alfie. His legs were tangled in mine, and he was sound asleep. When I tried to move, his arm reached out seeking me under the covers, and he snaked it around my waist, drawing me close to his warm body. "C'mere," he coaxed.

I tried again. "Drew says the bus is waiting Alfie, come on." He cleared his throat. "Tell him we'll get the next one," he muttered, snuggling his face into my neck. It tickled, and I knew I was going to have to get him out of bed, or I'd be flat on my back, doing something a lot more pleasurable than sitting on a bus at the butt crack of dawn.

Giggling, I nudged him. "Come on rock star, you need to shake your ass out of this bed, we have a job to do." He grumbled and stretched, his arms going up under the pillow as he pulled it into his face, squashing his cheek.

I slipped out from under the comforter and dragged it away with me, taking the sheet as well. Alfie was lying naked, face down on the bed. I sighed, and he peeked up at me with one eye. "I don't think I'll ever get tired of that." I winked.

Alfie smirked, still lying on his stomach in the same position. "Damn, you're objectifying me again."

I smirked, "Of course I am. I have to have some perks."

He chuckled. "So...I'm a treat?"

I leaned over and spanked his ass playfully. "Of course you are, you're right up there with M&M's...the peanut ones."

He sat up and raised his eyebrows. "M&M's, huh?"

I nodded. "Yep, I'm serious about my treats." Alfie shuffled across the mattress and stood up next to me, taking the comforter and sheet from my hands.

"It's the nuts... the common factor, between me and candy?" he asked wiggling his finger. "Or, is it that once you've had a taste you just have to keep going back for more? I mean, can anyone only eat like five peanut M&M's?"

Alfie smirked and walked past me, turning back to drop to his knees and sink his teeth playfully into my ass cheek. "Get your pretty ass covered up, we've got a bus to catch." He smacked it playfully and ran into the bathroom.

Loud knocking interrupted us as we were dressing. "Come on, the fuck guys. We're all sitting waiting for y'all." Drew was screaming from the other side of the door again. Alfie walked over and pulled the door open.

"Dude, we're up. I had to see to Lily's nut fetish before we could get out of here, but you're good to go now, right?" My mouth gaped at Alfie, then I twisted my lips, making my way over to the door.

I pushed past him. My hand briefly patted his chest, and Drew stood aside to make room for me to step into the hallway. Carrying my large leather tote and oversized purse, I turned and sneered at Alfie, then flicked my gaze over to Drew. "In his dreams, Drew. The guy is a fantasist, what can I say."

I heard them both chuckling and Alfie explained, "Dude, you can totally see why I'm so into her, can't you? She's got a sassy, smart mouth, but I'll keep you posted on the nut fetish, she's only let that one slip this morning, and I didn't have time to explore it more."

They both chuckled as I shook my head at them and smirked as I entered the elevator. Alfie dropped his rucksack) and took mine out of my hands and handed them to Drew. "Here Drew, make yourself useful."

Alfie slipped his hands from my stomach to my back, his fingers probing the back pockets of my jeans and pulling me flush against his hips. "That's better, I'm definitely awake now."

He smiled and dropped his mouth to my neck, his hot breath soothing me until the elevator stopped on the ground floor. Inhaling deeply he straightened up, kissed me chastely on the lips, then bent down and picked up his bag. He scooped me into his side, and we headed for the bus.

There were cheers as we stepped on to the bus. One of the PAs was sitting with Styrofoam cups of coffee in one of those cardboard cup holders. Alfie took one and offered it to me. I shook my head.

Des was annoyed and shouted at Alfie, "Did you have to leave us sitting on the fucking bus while you got your rocks off, Dude?" Alfie turned and smirked, cocking an eyebrow at him. "Des, dude, it's been ten fucking minutes since Drew woke us, does Lily look like someone I could only spend ten minutes on?"

Both Des and Alfie glanced at me together, and I was mortified. Alfie turned his attention back to Des. "So...to answer your question numb nuts, I wasn't getting laid, but I hope to remedy that later when we get to where we're going, Buddy."

Alfie gestured me into a window seat on the coach, then settled himself beside me, chuckling quietly at the dazed face that Des was sporting.

Alfie's hand fell to rest on my thigh, and he squeezed it a little. "Sorry, he pisses me off complaining all the time." In the time I'd been around all of the guys in the two bands, I had grown a thick skin and was now able to keep my feelings to myself no matter how embarrassed I felt at what they said.

"You need something to drink?" Alfie gestured the coffee at me again. I shook my head. "Nah, I'm good," I said searching into my oversized bag. "What're you looking for?" I smirked and pulled out a half-eaten family pack of peanut M&M's. "I'm just doing a spot of research." I winked and popped some in my mouth.

Alfie smirked and whispered, "No matter how many of them you pop into your mouth, Lily, they'll never satisfy you like my nuts can."

We both chuckled, and Elle piped up, "What has you two giggling at this time of the morning?" Alfie smiled over at her. "Lily's love of M&M's, Elle." He replied, and winked.

Once we were settled on the plane and in the air, it was like we'd all been shot with tranquilizer darts. Everyone slept like they'd been drugged, and I woke with a crick in my neck and Alfie slumped against me. Our fingers were interlaced and aching. I slipped my hand out of his and sat up straight.

I couldn't help laughing at the sight of everyone else around me, especially Elle, who was wearing an eye mask that had slipped and was half across her cheek, one eye visible. Her hair looked a tangled mess, and she was hanging off the side of the chair with her head on her lap like a rag doll.

One of the cabin crew members brought me some orange

juice and a hot flannel to freshen up. It was bliss. She mouthed that she was turning the cabin lights on in ten minutes. I sat watching Alfie sleep, thinking that I would never get enough of just being able to look at his face.

This beautiful man was one of the world's greats. A special person who rose above others in what he did, yet he was amazingly unaffected by the crazy world he lived in. That fact alone made me love him even more, if that was at all possible.

We had started our relationship in a bad way, and it had taken us both quite a journey to where we were now, but it made me treasure it even more for all we'd been through.

The rest of the journey and the transfer went smoothly, and we had another night in a hotel. Having experienced sleeping on a bus by then, it was luxury. I was still looking forward to the time we'd spend on the bus though, because that would be special time with just Drew, Elle, Alfie, and me.

Athens was a truly historical city, full of landmarks I'd been taught about in school. The venue wasn't as big as the one in Poland, holding only about twelve thousand, but the crowd was just as rowdy.

I couldn't get past the fact that Alfie's band was known worldwide, and even somewhere like Greece, with all its ancient culture, had fans of the music Crakt Soundzz played.

The fans were polite, which was great for Alfie. It meant that he could at least have a sense of normalcy and wander around the streets.

He commented that just being able to sit in a small road-side café with me, gave him so much pleasure now. It was the simple things he struggled to do now, without someone needing to speak to him or being disrespectful to me by hitting on him.

The gig went very well and was fairly uneventful, apart from when one of my strings broke and caught in my hair briefly. Luckily, the guitar tech had my reserve guitar to me in seconds, and Lennon helped me get loose of the string before I stopped the flow of the music.

Even the 'Meet and Greet' was short. The event organizers and promoters were all polite and the after-show food and drinks finished at a decent hour. We were in bed by 1am, and even though we were tired, Alfie still made good on his comment to Des from this morning about taking his time with me.

It felt like deja vu when we woke to the sound of knocking. It was room service. Alfie padded into the bathroom and pulled a towel around him before going to answer.

A small stocky woman, dressed in a crisp, powder-blue uniform with black, braided hair and olive skin, wheeled a tray over to the balcony. She pulled the stainless steel lids off the plates of meat, cheese, bread, and bowls of fruit and bowed her head as she started to leave.

Alfie dug into his jeans and pulled out some Euros, handing them to her. Her dark brown eyes lit up. It must have been a lot, and she thanked him profusely, bowing and walking backwards until he closed the door behind her. "Sheesh, Alfie, competition for me?" I grumbled in mock disappointment.

When we had eaten breakfast, Alfie arranged for us to take an early sightseeing bus trip. The driver stopped at the Parthenon and The Acropolis, where once again, Alfie set up his camera and took pictures to replace the ones in my album. "God, Lily, you have no idea how happy I am right now," he exclaimed, kissing me sloppily on the cheek.

He dipped his head to look at me and whispered, "I love you," as he tucked my hair back behind my ears and kissed me slowly. An elderly English woman who was getting back on the bus cleared her throat.

"Oh, my, you both look so in love, you could probably get a job modeling for the tourist board here," she swooned.

Alfie chuckled. "Thanks for the vote of confidence ma'am, if my regular employers get fed up with me I'll keep it in mind."

We headed back to the hotel and once again, we were on the road. We flew to Italy, and had two venues to play there: Milan and Rome. We were playing two nights in Rome then we were heading to Milan by bus overnight.

In Rome, we'd been to the Coliseum and to The Vatican for Alfie to collect memories of us during the day, and my heart was bursting with happiness having all this time together. The gigs were amazing, and the Italian crowds lived up to their hot, passionate reputations.

I was so excited when I saw the bus we were staying on when we moved our stuff from the hotel the last day in Rome. I could barely contain myself. Just like Alfie said, there were two double beds on the bus. It was more like a large motor home really, but seemed to be coach-size. Alfie and I took the room at the back of the bus, and Elle and Drew had the one in the middle, which was slightly smaller.

Our large cases had been moved onto the bus for us, so we unpacked then settled ourselves in with some cheese and wine we found in the fridge. Elle was like a big kid, running around opening doors and squealing with what new surprises she found.

We had another nine days on this bus, before we swapped with the other band, which was currently with Cobham Street.

I was beginning to get pangs of regret that we wouldn't be with Crakt Soundzz for the whole tour by then, but it was the right decision for the band. It wouldn't have been fair to commit them indefinitely because of my personal feelings.

Shaking my depressing thoughts aside, I was determined not to think about leaving. I was happy to spend more time with Alfie without any demands on us for the first time, while we were on the bus anyway.

There was a shower between the two rooms, and after I unpacked I went to freshen up while Alfie did some vocal stuff and rehearsed a little on his guitar. Stepping back in the room, I opened my towel to dry myself and screamed loudly when a truck driver pulled alongside the large window at the side of the bus.

I dove down the furthest side of the bed naked, and Alfie's body folded over with laughter. "They can't see you Lily, it's one-way glass." He leaned over and pulled me up and across him. The guy in the truck stared at the bus, and I squirmed trying to hide my body again.

"I know, but still...are you sure, he's definitely studying something about our window. Maybe it's flawed, and he can see me. I'm definitely not putting the light on in here when it gets dark."

Alfie smirked. "Oh, no lights, eh? So, we're having blind sex tonight?"

I exhaled loudly. "Only you would turn my concerns to your advantage, Alfie." I giggled, but it was going to take some coaxing for me to be comfortable with that big ass window right at the side of the bed. Already, I had decided to claim the other side of the bed for sure.

Once Alfie started kissing me and stroking his fingers lazily down my back, I was much less worried about people seeing me, and much more interested in what he was going to do next.

We had our first tryst on the bus within an hour of being on there. Honestly, we were like bunnies since we'd gotten some space to be alone.

Every chance we had was mostly spent in bed. If we weren't having sex, we were planning. People kept telling me that once the novelty wore off, couples tended not to have as much sex in their relationships.

As much as I tried to imagine that, I couldn't see it ever being the case with us. We both seemed to be sexually compatible, and there had never been a problem with the physical side of our relationship.

Alfie rolled me over and lifted my arms above my head. "My favorite position for you."

I smirked. "It is? Why is that?"

Alfie grinned. "You're completely submissive." I shook my head and lifted my head forward, lightly nipping his neck.

He gasped, "Jesus." His voice immediately sounded thick.

"Yeah, I'm submissive, Alfie. In your dreams, honey."

Chapter Twenty-Nine

BUSES

The following nine days flew by. Alfie and I had settled into a great little lifestyle cocooned on the bus. Our own little bubble and it was an incredible feeling. We just got in deeper and deeper during that time. I couldn't help thinking that we should have been like this from the start. It was the first real chance we had to really learn more about each other.

Alfie still took me to the special spots he'd visited and gradually replaced most of the pictures in my album with ones of the both of us. He kept telling me every day how much he loved me, and even when fans recognized him and wanted to intrude in our special time, Alfie balanced it just right.

I wasn't neglected. I was in awe of his humble approach, and his love for me. We couldn't have been happier. The hours we spent on the bus together were the probably the happiest I've ever had in my life. Just cuddling up with each other and spending time with Elle and Drew felt special.

We all made plans for vacations together in the future-- the trip to Hawaii was going to be the first, and we shared stuff about our pasts that we didn't know about each other. I learned so much about Alfie and Drew and just how much they had been through together.

Drew had helped Alfie with Layla when his mom was dying. She was still in high school and didn't have a car. Alfie told us how Drew took on the task of ensuring that she got to and from school and even helped her with homework, while Alfie drove his dad back and forth to the hospital to see his mom.

Hearing how Drew had supported Alfie just confirmed my initial feelings about Drew. What a great guy and I was really happy for Elle. She had someone special, and she deserved the best.

Elle and Drew made a lot of wedding plans during the tour, and because Alfie and I were playing key roles in the wedding, it was good that we got to do everything face to face instead of trying to arrange stuff by phone.

The wedding was due to take place three weeks after both Cobham Street and Crakt Soundzz tours' finished, so things were still to be done, and there were a lot of last minute arrangements to do when we got home to London.

They decided on London for their wedding, because Elle had tons of relatives. The guys from XrAid were excited about it too, because they were getting to spend a lot of time in my hometown.

I knew my dad was making plans to do a lot with them and had taken some time off from his business to devote to them. I was excited to keep Alfie with me in London for a while as well. We needed a do-over there to make new memories, since his last time in London had ended on such a sour note.

Traveling up through Italy into Switzerland, and then on to Germany, was incredible. Between gigs and fancy restaurants, we got to experience the mundane, normal things that couples did. We watched YouTube clips, laughing at some crazy people, and I even shared my Kindle with Alfie when he wanted to read some of an erotic book I had been halfway through when we got on the plane back in Florida.

By the time we reached Paris, I was feeling really sad the days had gone so quickly, and I would have to leave after Paris. This was the only city where we had two consecutive days off, and Alfie wanted to make the most of it.

A tour bus took us on a whirlwind tour of all cultural highlights such as the Champs Elysees and the Arc de Triomphe. Alfie wore a beanie hat and a trench coat, which made me giggle a lot. Personally, I thought he was more noticeable in his disguise, but then I'd have noticed him anywhere.

Camera shutter noise clicked incessantly as Alfie took pictures of us at all the sights. Then we ate lunch near the Eiffel Tower, before heading to the top. It was an amazing couple of days, but what made it more awesome was that we did it together.

"Perfection." Alfie was staring through the lens of his camera as I stood with Paris as my backdrop. "Did I ever mention how hot you are, Lily?" He smirked. I could only just see his mouth, the rest of him covered by his obscenely large lens.

"You're not so bad yourself," I teased.

"Oh, I know," he teased back, as he dropped the camera to his side and tugged me quickly into his chest, crushing his lips to mine. As he broke the kiss, he smiled. "You are the love of my life, you do know that, right?" he said, squeezing me. I smiled, still feeling breathless from our kiss.

"I do know, Alfie. And you are mine," I stated matter-of-factly.

"I am," he confirmed. We both knew it was our last day together. Alfie had booked us into a hotel for the night and instead of eating in the restaurant, he had a selection of foods brought to the suite.

After we had made love slowly, twice, I lay with my head on his stomach. Alfie picked up my hand and laced our fingers together. A lump formed in my throat, and I was choked. I felt sick that we weren't going to be together after today. "You're really quiet, Lily. You okay?" I swallowed audibly with a loud click, trying not to cry. I didn't want to ruin the precious time we had together.

"Mmm, yeah I'm fine." Alfie scooted down and turned me in the crook of his arm to face him.

"Nope, Lily. I know you. Come on, what's up?"

I exhaled shakily, still trying not to cry. "I've just had such an amazing time with you, and I don't want it to end."

Alfie smiled affectionately and stroked my hair. "Having second thoughts about the Cobham Street tour?"

I nodded and closed my eyes, still struggling with my emotions. "Yeah, but it's the right thing to do for XrAid."

Alfie leaned in and kissed my forehead before exhaling raggedly. "It's only two weeks, Lily. We can do that, right? It'll go faster than you think. Plus, we've got FaceTime and our phones. We'll be okay." I felt a little hurt that he didn't seem as devastated as I was, that we weren't going to be together.

I shrugged off the bad vibe I had, but it was in the back of my mind and kind of marred the rest of the night. It had become difficult to look at him at times today, because leaving him behind was going to hurt so badly.

Sometimes, I wondered what he was thinking because one minute he would be laughing and joking around, and the next, he was kind of withdrawn. I caught him watching me when he thought I wasn't looking, a sad look in his eyes.

That last night together I lay awake listening to Alfie's even breathing. His warm body cocooned mine in a tight, possessive embrace. I didn't want daylight to come. I had no idea how I was going to be able to leave him and get on the other bus with my band. I eventually fell asleep, but not before my eyes stung with silent tears, and my head hurt.

When I woke up, Alfie had already gone to rehearse over at the concert venue. Our buses were in a cordoned off area at the back of the stadium, with tight security.

My heart sunk to my stomach when I reached out and found his side of the bed cold and empty. Dragging myself out of bed, I tried to find the motivation to face what was going to be a very difficult day for me.

Elle sat on the bed talking to me as I packed my trunk to transfer to the other bus that I would be sharing with my bandmates. I could see that she was feeling pretty much like I was about us and our time together ending.

"Don't worry, Lily, it's only a couple of weeks then we get set loose in London."

I nodded, but the tears flowed down my cheeks anyway. "I don't want to cry in front of Alfie, Elle. I need to be strong about this. It was my choice after all."

Elle stared at me and shook her head. "You need to stop with this bullshit, Lily."

I scowled at her, surprised that she was ragging on me. "What in the Hell does that mean?"

Elle walked over to me and sat me down on the bed, the mattress sagging as she sat back down close to me. She stared at her hands, rubbing them together then smoothed the front of her top down.

"Lily, you can't be with Alfie because of the music, and when you get a solution to that, you can't be with him because of the band. You're the one that keeps placing obstacles in the way. Alfie's already told you that you can tour permanently with him."

She pursed her lips and looked seriously at me. "Listen, I used to feel really bad for you, but knowing Alfie, and seeing how he feels about you, it's him that I'm starting to worry about. Alfie's just happy to be with you. I've never seen him so happy and content since you've been around."

She stood up and crossed her arms across her chest. "You know I love you, Lily, and I want you to be happy." She breathed out heavily. "To be honest you're the one putting conditions on your relationship."

Elle talking to me this way stung. She was the one who always had my back. I couldn't believe she was judging me after everything I had gone through. "You might be happy to give up everything for Drew, but why should I do that? I've worked hard to get where I am now." As soon as I said it, I wished I could have taken my words back.

"Are you really going to pull that shit on me, Lily? You're telling me my training was less valuable than what you're doing? My career and all the pain I went through, fifteen years of dance class, yoga, and endurance training, to get on that West End stage wasn't as hard as what you've achieved?"

She was really ticked at me now. "You went to one audition, Lily. You hit the fucking jackpot with XrAid. I went to twenty-seven auditions, all the time knowing that I was good enough, but wondering if it would be my day, every time." She swallowed hard, looking more agitated.

"You have no idea what that feels like. The constant rejections. Apart from that, half the time the girls being chosen had already been on the casting couch, and I never stood a chance before I even put myself out there. The only *real* difference between you and me, Lily, is that I love Drew more than I love dancing." She wagged her finger between us to emphasize her point.

Elle looked down at her hands and began pulling her fingers. "I'm not going to lie, Lily. It was a hell of an adjustment for me, but one I'd do again, because Drew means that much to me. The real question you have to ask yourself is exactly how much does Alfie mean to you?" My jaw dropped, Elle and I had never had a cross word before, and here she was tearing me a new one.

"You don't get it, Elle. Alfie means everything to me." She cocked one eyebrow at me. "Yeah, keep telling yourself that, Lily. If that's so, why are you putting distance between you?"

I became fed up with her making remarks. "Listen, Elle, I'd appreciate it if you would just take your opinions somewhere else and let me finish up here."

Elle stood up and squeezed my shoulder. "Someone's got to make you see sense, Lily. A guy like Alfie won't stick around forever, while you pick and choose which parts of a relationship you're willing to give him." She walked out of the room and closed the door quietly behind her.

By the time I'd finished packing, Alfie still wasn't back from the soundcheck. I was hoping to spend some time with him before our bus left.

Lennon appeared at the door. "We're almost done, Lily; we need to get on the road in fifteen minutes." I twisted my lips, thinking that the time had come for me to say goodbye to Alfie. It had been the one thing in all of this I was dreading, and I was wishing I didn't have to do it now.

We were leaving for Munich and had a hard five days ahead of us before we had another day off. Sound checks and rehearsals awaited us as soon as we arrived. Running out the bus door, I headed over to the venue to find Alfie.

The guys weren't on stage or in the dressing rooms, and I was all out of places to look. My heart was sinking to the pit of my stomach. I was going to have to leave without seeing him. I had missed him this morning, and he hadn't come back to see me.

I doubled back and checked again, asking the crew that were around if they had seen where they had gone, but no one knew anything. I felt sick that I was leaving, and I knew that when I went back to the bus, I would have run out of time.

Hell, I already had. We should have been on the road about ten minutes ago. Cody was coming in the stage door just as I was about to cross into the area where our buses were parked.

"There you are, we need to get going, Lily. We've got a lot to do when we get there."

I nodded. "Yeah, sorry Cody, I know, but I can't find Alfie to say goodbye."

Cody pulled me to him. "I saw the band head out in one of the limos about an hour ago. I guess they must have an interview of some kind." I swallowed hard and burst into tears, my heart cracking open. He was gone.

Alfie hadn't come back, and I never got that last precious hug or kiss from him. I stiffened up and wiped my tears on my jacket sleeve. "Okay, let me get my jacket, and we're out of here."

I ran back to the bus, and Elle was sitting on sofa in the lounge area using her tablet. She looked up at me. "See you in London, Lily. Good luck with Cobham Street." She looked back at her tablet and didn't get up, and I knew her well enough to know that this wasn't just about the argument we'd had earlier in the morning.

"You knew, didn't you, Elle? Alfie wasn't coming back this morning to see me."

She shrugged. "I'm not getting involved, Lily. I was just... trying to be your friend, that's all."

Elle didn't get up or look at me again, and Cody appeared at the door banging on the side of the bus. "Lily, ass in the bus right now. We're leaving." I turned and jumped down to the ground and looked back. Elle still hadn't moved. I closed the door and made my way to our bus with a heavy heart.

How could Alfie do this to me? We'd had the time of our

lives and now it was ending on a sour note. I tried to text him.

Pink Lady: Where are you? Can I come and see you before we leave?

Alfie didn't reply, and I had to close the bus door. We pulled out of the compound, and Cody pulled me into his arms while I buried my face in his shirt. "You'll be okay, sweetheart. We'll keep an eye on you. I know we're not Alfie, but we love you too, Lily." Cody rubbed my back as I let the tears flow.

Chapter Thirty

ALICE

*D*inner on the bus was strained. I was very poor company afterwards. Digs and Cody had cooked for us. I made a big deal of being tired and crawled into my bed to try to get some privacy.

There was still no word from Alfie. I texted him three times and left a voicemail about how sad I was to be leaving. I knew that he'd be on stage now and wouldn't be sending me anything any time soon. I broke down and cried myself to sleep.

When I woke the cubby was hot and stuffy. My head ached, and I had the most nauseous feeling. The bus engine hummed and the bed felt claustrophobic. I edged my way down to the end and off the bunk, walking unsteadily to the toilet. This little space was also stuffy and seemed to magnify the waves of nausea that were hitting me.

I spun around quickly and spewed the contents of my stomach into the bowl. The vomit just kept coming in copious amounts, until there was nothing left, and it turned into dry heaving. Sweat drenched me, making my tank and shorts stick to my clammy body.

Eventually, it felt safe enough to leave the toilet without being sick. Lennon was sitting with one leg balanced across the other knee, and he was holding his ankle. As soon as he saw me he stood and placed his hands on either side of my arms. "Jeez, Lily, are you okay?"

My breathing sounded shaky. "Not really. I feel like shit. It must be food poisoning." Lennon called Kieron, who had flown ahead to Germany. It was only five am, but he felt I'd needed some treatment, especially as I still had a further six hours to travel by bus to Munich for the gig.

The motion of the bus wasn't helping. At times, I wasn't sure whether the sickness I was feeling was due to the movement of the bus, or the food I'd eaten.

Kieron had a medic meet us at a service station. The doctor gave me a big jab in my butt for the nausea and some horrible salty tasting powders to rebalance my electrolytes. It made me feel better. Lennon was a brilliant help and was the type of person everyone would want in an emergency.

If I was ever in doubt about how Lennon felt about me, I wasn't now. He held my hair back, wiped my brow, and summoned help. He encouraged me to keep drinking fluids, and when he'd done all of that, he just sat holding me and stroking my hair.

I slept the rest of the journey and by the time we arrived in Munich I felt a bit better but was still feeling depressed about the way that Alfie had dealt with me leaving yesterday. I checked my cell, and there was still no contact from him.

I kept staring at it. Willing it to beep with a message. Anything to make me feel better. I couldn't bring myself to contact Elle for information now either, because I doubted she'd feel like helping me after I'd shouted at her the way I had. I showered, dressed, and after a couple of glasses of honey and lemon, I began to feel like I'd get through the day.

When we saw the stadium we were playing at, my mouth

went dry. The place was gigantic, and I had a sudden attack of nerves.

We made our way into the cavernous tunnel and out into the massive space. When we neared the stage I could hear Rick's voice shouting to the lighting guys.

I was stage right and stood hugging myself, waiting patiently for him to finish so that I could check what time the production team wanted us to be out there. Rick spoke to the girl with the clipboard and turned back to speak with someone on my side of the stage.

His face broke into a wide grin when he saw me. "Lily," he shouted, loudly. "Hello, sweetheart. Great to see you. Alice liked hot, but jeez girl, you leave her in the shade. All set to do your thing here tonight?" I smiled and wondered who the Hell Alice was but tried to look confident and covered my nerves.

"I can't wait." What I really meant was I couldn't wait for the next two weeks to be done so that I could get back to my life, but Rick couldn't know that.

"Who's Alice?" I asked; he'd piqued my interest by comparing me to her.

"Lead singer with Bubble Card." This was the band replacing us to support Crakt Soundzz. How the fuck did I not know that they had a female lead singer? It would be fun to swap stories with her about her experiences, because I hadn't come across any other females in rock bands to date.

Rick and I chatted easily, catching up with what had happened with both our gigs to date, until he left to go lie down. I giggled when he told me he needed to do that.

Women threw themselves at Rick Fars. He was regarded as a stud and hell-raiser, and here he was sneaking off after his sound check to take a nap. It just didn't fit at all with his image. He kissed the top of my head as he was leaving.

"Has that Alfie not made an honest woman of you yet,

Lily?" He smirked and raised his eyebrows at me. "I might have to do that, if he isn't going to make a move on you soon." I smiled at him, but it was frozen on my face. He waved behind him as he headed back to his bus. "See you later."

Alfie and I had never really talked about us long term, apart from me being 'the love of his life'. Since he hadn't been in touch, I'd been feeling like I made a mistake. We still haven't even spoken about what happened when I left. It had been almost forty-eight hours since we last spoke, if I counted when he fell asleep in bed beside me.

Anxiety set in. He hadn't answered my texts or even attempted to call me. What did he expect from me? And I wondered how in the Hell we were supposed to make it, when he was stumbling at the first hurdle?

It was quite a difficult thing to deal with. Not knowing where I stood would have to be put to the side. I knew I had to maintain focus on what XrAid had to do tonight, and being unwell last night meant I was now drawing on my reserves to help me through.

By the time we went on stage, Kieron had brought us up to speed on everything that was expected of us. The production team had been clever with our setup, and Lennon was uncharacteristically animated in his account of having an early dinner with Cobham Street.

I was absolutely delighted about everything that was happening for Lennon; if anyone was a professional musician it was him. He deserved this chance, and I had no doubt about his level of commitment to making the most of this opportunity.

Cody was a brilliant support to me, as usual, just before we went on stage; Digs was as well. Shawn, being Shawn, loved to get a rise out of me with some of his naked jokes which helped me control my nerves. I ached from laughing at him; he was a great distraction. As well as the usual anticipation and nervous energy of stepping out on stage, tonight we were playing to our biggest crowd.

The thought of standing out there and making a mistake in front of sixty thousand people was almost paralyzing, but like Cody said, they were there "because they wanted us to do well, not to see us fuck up on stage." I really loved Cody's eternal optimism about things.

Alfie was right. It was easier to play to a larger crowd than a small one. I couldn't really see many of them, so it was easier not to focus on the crowd and just enjoy playing in an amazing space. The fans were fantastic, and the constant roaring between songs was like an injection of adrenaline spurring us on.

After the gig, Rick's band's runner came to our dressing room. Rick wanted to have drinks with us after the 'Meet and Greet'. This was my least favorite part of the day. I found the after-parties the most difficult thing about doing live performances.

We were expected to do an hour to an hour and a half, which was really strenuous set, then continue with another three to four hours of socializing. The expectation of us to meet fans, that part I could understand, but the constant networking with music execs and promoters, radio DJs and reporters was something I could really do without.

I leaned into my purse and pulled out my cell to check if there was any word from Alfie. Again, there was nothing at all. I threw my cell back in my bag and saw Shawn smirking at me. "Still nothing?" I felt that if he made some crass joke at that point, there would be a high chance I would have decked him.

"He hasn't answered *any* of my texts or calls, happy, Shawn?" He stood and walked over to me. "You want me to call him, Lily? I could just see that he was okay for you, at the very least." I swallowed hard. Shawn was concerned, and that took the wind out of my sails.

I had been ready to take all my pent-up frustrations out on him, but he was being really sweet and offering me genuine support. I shrugged at him. "I guess he doesn't like me being on tour with Cobham Street." It was all I could think of in reply.

Cody came over and slung his arm around me. "I already called him. I told him what he was doing to you wasn't cool." I shrugged again and let out a large breath that I hadn't remembered taking.

"Okay guys, listen up, I'm only going to say this once. Don't call Alfie on my behalf. I'm not calling him from now on. We've got a job to do here, and I'm going to make sure that Rick and the guys in Cobham Street are happy with us supporting them. Whatever Alfie's deal is can wait until our gigs have finished."

Lennon looked relieved, and Digs came over and fist bumped me. "Always said you had balls, Lily." He nodded once and left the room to go meet with the fans.

I had no idea how I got through the night, but I smiled and made all the right noises until finally we were done and had settled in Rick's bus for drinks.

Rick was really kind to us. I couldn't believe how accommodating he was and how he took me under his wing. He was almost as protective of me as the guys were.

"We're having dinner on Friday, Lily." It wasn't a request, more of a statement. Thursday would be the last of five straight nights, and we had the next day off.

I couldn't wait to have the luxury of a bathroom and a great bed to stretch out in. Cody stared at me when he overheard Rick. I smirked at Cody. I knew he thought that Rick would try to seduce me. Maybe a few years ago he would have. I was young, naïve, and weak-willed then, but definitely not these days.

Exhausted, I couldn't think about anything when I got back to the bus and collapsed into my bed. I didn't remember anything from that night.

The following three nights followed the same pattern, including rehearsing and then doing the show. I lay around mainly watching TV or eating. I could see how easy it would be to get out of shape doing this.

No wonder our management team was giving us the hard sell on yoga and Pilates classes. Cody's six pack abs could turn into a beer belly in no time if he was left to his own devices.

By Thursday night I was furious with Alfie. Apart from Cody's reassurance on Monday that he'd spoken to Alfie, I had heard nothing. I didn't text him again and decided that I couldn't afford to dwell on his behavior or the fact that he had been so off with me.

My mind kept flitting back to our last night together. There was nothing out of the ordinary between us, and we had both told each other how much we'd miss being together. Yet, he'd put up a wall of silence.

We managed to get away from the management by 1am on Friday morning, and I was first back on the bus. I decided to take another shower and had already decided that I was going to send Alfie a letter via Jerry, who was flying to London. Crakt Soundzz were going to be in London on Sunday, and he could hand deliver it.

I was feeling much better after I decided to do something proactive and almost resigned myself that if there was no reply to this, I was done with Alfie.

No matter how I felt about him, there was no way I could live with this hot-and-cold behavior. My head hurt from crying buckets of tears during the past few days, and I was sick of feeling like I was less of a person because I had a career.

I turned the shower off and pulled on my shorts and tank that I was sleeping in. As soon as I opened the door I could hear a whispered, heated discussion going on between Lennon and Cody. It didn't really register with me until I got near the kitchen where they were sitting.

Cody whispered, "Well it's all kinds of wrong, Lenny, she needs to know." Lennon made a growling noise at Cody. "Keep the fuck out of it, we don't know for sure," he finished. Cody banged his hand on the table. "Who the fuck are we being loyal to here Lennon, Lily or Alfie?"

As soon as I heard my name, I realized whatever Lennon didn't want to deal with involved me. I pushed myself into view. "So...are you going to tell me whatever you think I need to know about, Cody, or are you happy to leave me ignorant about it, Lennon?"

Lennon's narrowed eyes flicked to Cody, and he scowled at him. His face was ashen, and his jaw ticked. I could see whatever it was, it wasn't going to be good news.

Cody scratched the back of his head and stood up. "Come over here, sweetheart." He pulled me down beside him at the table and pulled his laptop open. It was on a blog page the official reporter was running about the Crakt Soundzz tour.

As my eyes fell on the webpage I realized instantly what Lennon was at pains to hide from me. Alfie was sitting smiling surrounded by the band. He looked very relaxed and happy. He didn't appear to be missing me at all.

There was a pretty, tall blond in a black, skimpy dress sitting on his lap, holding a glass of wine. It looked like her other hand was tangled in the back of his hair. Alfie's hand was resting on her hip, near her ass, and they looked really cozy together.

Chapter Thirty-One

TESTOSTERONE

*S*taring at the pictures, I could see that there were about forty new ones posted since we'd left the tour. There was a common theme in them though. All of the ones of Alfie contained Alice.

She was either in the background, or he was sitting with her. This one Cody showed me was by far the most damning. Alfie looked like he was having the time of his life. Elle was sitting smiling in one of them as well, and I felt completely betrayed by her.

When I started reading some of the blurb the reporter had written, judging by this guy's account, the tour had livened up since we'd left and Bubble Card had taken over. Alice was a hit with the reporter apparently, he had mentioned her in almost every article, either by way of being in Alfie's presence or from some antic she had pulled on stage.

My heart was thumping in my chest, and I felt sick. No wonder he wasn't contacting me, he looked like he had his hands full. Glancing up at Cody with tears brimming, the look of sympathy on his face was almost too much. He squatted beside me, pulling me tight to his chest. "Sorry, babe." It wasn't so much what he said, as the way he said it, and the look of pity when he let me go made me feel like a fool.

Swallowing hard, my spit stuck in my throat. I stood up and pushed Cody away, suddenly feeling like I couldn't breathe. I was feeling panicked. Stricken by how comfortable she seemed on his lap and that Alfie was happy for her to be there in the first place. It came as a massive shock to me. I was so dumbstruck by the whole thing by then. Alfie and I had been great until the night before I left, and then everything seemed to go to shit.

My eyes widened as panic gripped me, and I stood up to find my phone. "The letter," I stated. Lennon looked confused.

"The letter?" he repeated. I started to pull out my cell, and Cody swiped it away from me. "Don't, Lily. Think about this."

Sniffing and staring back at Cody, I commented, "I'm not calling him again, Cody. I want my fucking letter back. I gave it to Jerry to take to London. I don't want him to have it now."

Cody gave me back my cell, and I called Jerry, Kieron's PA, and asked him to shred the letter instead of passing it on. Still talking, I walked back in the direction of my bed and climbed in.

Overwhelmed with grief, I knew I wouldn't be able to function, so I felt I needed space. How could he treat me like this after everything we'd been through?

Cody pulled my curtain back and started to squeeze into my cubby beside me. "What the fuck, Cody?" I sniffed, blowing my nose on a sock I'd left on my bed, because I had no tissue.

"You need a hug," he stated. He shuffled up alongside me,

and scooped me into his strong arms. He smelled of his expensive body wash, coffee, and caramel. I melded into his chest and cried harder. Cody was a great support just lying beside me kissing my head and rubbing my back, allowing me to let all my pent-up feelings loose. He was right, I had needed a hug.

Lennon called out, "Cody where in the Hell did you go?"

Cody's arms tensed, and he relaxed. "I'm in here with Lily, Dude."

Lennon pulled my curtain aside. "Get the fuck out." Lennon was angry.

Cody tensed again and he exhaled loudly, "What the fuck is your problem, Lenny? Can't you see the girl's upset?"

Lennon smacked Cody's foot. "Out here, now, before I drag you out." I started to sit up, worried about Lennon's rapidly escalating temper.

Cody pulled me back into his arms. "Lennon thinks I have designs on you, Lily. He thinks he's the only one of us who's allowed to comfort you when you're not happy."

I scooted down the bed under the sheet and dropped off the end, standing directly in front of him. "He wasn't doing anything wrong," I said quietly.

Cody had made his way out and straightened the leg of his sweat pants that had ridden up. "You know what, Lennon, I've been around Lily for over a year now and I've never touched her. Or made her feel uncomfortable, have I Lily?"

We must have had the same thought about the time he slept in my bed after a drunken night out when we all ended up at Lennon's place. He smirked. "Okay, once, but that was only because of your sleeping habits, Dude." He chuckled to himself, then squared up to Lennon and tried to get his point across again.

"What I'm saying is, maybe I should make a play for Lily. I'd make her much happier than the fucker in those pictures, letting women drape themselves all over him." I almost defended Alfie. He wasn't someone that did that, but the evidence seemed clear from the pictures that he'd changed his stance on that.

Lennon crossed his arms in front of his chest. "Yeah, Cody, and I'd beat your ass if you tried. She doesn't need any more complications to add to what she's already trying to deal with." I stood and listened to the guys talk about me as if I wasn't even there.

I had begun to understand the concept, 'Everyone wanting a piece of you'. Alfie had wanted me with him, Lennon wanted me for the band, and Cody, according to Lennon, wanted me in another way too.

It made me sick to think that everyone had their own agenda for being with me. I had never really thought about it before, but no one seemed to want me just for being me, apart from Alfie, and I figured it was too late to think about that.

"You know guys, when this tour is done... I'm taking some time off on my own. As soon as we've had Elle and Drew's wedding, I'm taking a month off. Sorry if that doesn't fit with the plans for the band, but I need to deal with some personal stuff before I can go forward."

Lennon turned and punched Cody on the arm. "I fucking warned you this would happen," he spat, shoulder barging past him and headed back down the stairs.

Cody looked hurt. "I wasn't making a play for you, Lily, I wouldn't, but he pisses me off, making decisions for me as to whom I'm allowed to talk to. What matters to me, Lily, is that you know there was no hidden reason for why I came to comfort you, other than I knew you were hurting, okay?"

I nodded. I knew that. So, I stepped in and wrapped my arms around his waist. "I felt that, Cody. I'm sorry Lennon can't see that you always offer me support without expecting anything in return."

Cody smiled with affection. "That's okay, Lily, it doesn't matter to me as long as you have the right idea about why I do it." I pushed myself up on tiptoe and kissed Cody's cheek.

"Thanks, Cody, you have always supported me. There are times when I wouldn't have been able to do this if it wasn't for you. I can't tell you how much your words have meant to me, every time we've waited to get out there on stage. Keep doing what you do for me. If I don't like it, I'll tell you to stop, not Lennon. Don't worry about him by the way. I'm going to talk to him about all of this."

Cody squeezed my shoulder and crawled into his cubby, pulling the curtain closed. I went downstairs to seek Lennon out. "I need a word, Lennon." Turning my back on him, I walked to the small private space in the bus.

Digs was playing 'Call of Duty' on the gaming box. He looked at me and smiled, and his face froze when he saw I'd been crying. "Shit, Lily, what's wrong?"

I smiled in reassurance. "I'm fine, Digs, but would you mind if I had a private word with Lennon in here. Shawn and some of the support guys are sitting out front, and I don't want anyone eavesdropping on my conversation."

Digs hit pause on the game and kissed my cheek before he stepped out, leaving us alone. "You need to stop doing this, Lennon. It's really not fair to Cody."

Lennon's eyes flicked up to mine. "I'm tired of the way that Cody eye-fucks you, but acts all innocent."

I sighed in frustration. "Lennon, Cody has always supported me. You've usually been too wound up before a gig to notice that's all. Did you know that every time we go on stage, Cody holds my hand and gives me words of encouragement that help get me out there?" Lennon looked surprised but said nothing. "I thought not."

Exhaling heavily, I explained further, "You need to cut him some slack. It isn't fair to put that on him. I'm not with any of you guys. You are all like brothers to me, but you need to stop fighting like this. Especially, when I'm the problem. You are proving Digs right, maybe there shouldn't be a girl in the band."

I sat down beside Lennon and took his face in my hands. "This stops now, Lennon. I want you to apologize to Cody, and no more comments about his feelings about me."

Lennon shrugged his shoulders. "Okay, Lily. Have it your way."

My cell buzzed for the first time in five days, and my attention was immediately diverted to it. I walked away from Lennon to get some space. My heart was pounding in my chest as I expected to see a text from Alfie, but it was from Rick.

Rick Fars: Ready for dinner? B ready in ten, limo is out front.

Shit! I'd forgotten all about dinner. I wasn't ready at all. Running up to my trunk, I pulled out a silver-gray dress that was a godsend. It was my pull-on-and-run dress made of that magic material I didn't need to iron and it never crushed. The only thing was, it was figure hugging and not forgiving, but with my slender frame it fit perfectly on me.

Spraying my hair with product, I scrunched up my curls. My hair looked wild but then again, it hung just right. So, with a little mascara and lip gloss, some moisturizer, and a little dab of perfume, I headed out.

Lennon scowled at me. I couldn't blame him really. One minute they were all fighting over me, the next I was running out the door to meet a rock star for dinner and leaving them behind to fester.

Rick smelled freshly showered and was wearing expensive aftershave when I stepped into the limo. "Hey, Lily, it's great to see you." He smiled and took my hand, guiding me to the seat next to him.

Being so well-known, Rick's PA had arranged for us to have dinner at a restaurant he'd been to every time he was in Strasburg that offered discreet dining for celebrities. We'd been back in France for two days again, and I felt like I'd been going around in circles, having been here only five days earlier with Crakt Soundzz.

The restaurant was opulent looking. Dark, ruby-red flocked wallpaper walls, oversized gilt mirrors, and crystal chandeliers were everywhere. The ceilings were high with intricate plaster borders and ceiling molds, decorated with gold leaf paint. The heavy period features made the place reek of 'old money'.'

"I fancied fondue, is that okay for you?" Rick asked, explaining his choice of restaurant.

I loved fondue. "Of course it'll be a treat after the past few days of pizza, pasta, and fried chicken on the bus."

I smiled at Rick and felt a little nervous, then unfolded the crisp white napkin and flicked it across my left knee. Rick was more than impressed when I ordered in French. I had studied it in school and spent a term at a Swiss finishing school, where all our lessons were conducted in French.

"Is there anything you can't do?" Rick smirked and drew his forefinger across my cheek. I blushed, feeling a little uncomfortable at his familiarity. He noticed my flush and grinned. "Damn, you're far too innocent for me, Lily." I didn't know how to respond. So, I sat still saying nothing. "So...tell me how you think the tour is going, Lily."

I smiled widely, this was a safe subject. "Well, I think we're doing okay. The fans seemed to have accepted us. It's hard when we have to get out there and play to a bunch of people that aren't really there to hear us, but I think we're holding our own." He was nodding while I was talking, and his lips were curved into a slight smile.

"We're impressed with you guys. You're much more polished than Bubble Card." He pursed his lips like he was thinking. "I'd definitely have you guys as our support next time." He was looking at me like he meant it as well.

"Anyway, Lily, what's wrong? I have a feeling that something isn't right with you." Rick was perceptive as well as smart. I wasn't sure that I could share what was actually wrong with me because he was my boss on the tour.

"Oh, it's just stuff," I said, trying to sound kind of carefree.

"Nah, I don't want bullshit, it's that fucker Alfie isn't it?" I shrugged, because I couldn't avoid talking to him about it after that.

"I'm just really confused about him."

Rick leaned over and placed his hand on top of mine. "Tell me what's been going on." He sat quietly while I recounted the past couple of weeks with Alfie, my leaving to join Cobham Street, and Cody finding the pictures on the blog.

Rick sat back in his chair and stared intensely at me. "I don't think you have anything to worry about." I closed my eyes, not wanting him to see the hurt I was feeling. This was one notoriously sex driven rock star telling me that another rock star wasn't playing away on me.

"Seriously, Lily, I've spoken to Alfie every day since you've been here. The guy is crazy about you." Hearing Rick tell me this should have been music to my ears, but it only made me even angrier about Alfie's behavior.

"You call him?"

Rick smirked and took a swig of the Stella Artois beer the waiter had set down for him. "The Hell I do. He calls every afternoon, like he wants an update on you. How you're playing. How the boys in your band are treating you. Is anyone hitting on you?"

He chuckled. "He always adds, 'touch her and I'll break your fucking legs...right after I cut your dick off'.'" He gave me a half-smile, his eyes softening. "I think he's pussy whipped. In fact, I keep listening to hear the crack of the whip, but then again, you're here with me right now." He laughed softly.

Rick chuckled again. "Man, that totally pisses him off." I hugged my arms not sure what to think about what Rick was telling me. "He hasn't called me since I left." I bit my lip, worried just thinking about that.

"Yeah, he can't bring himself to call you, in case he comes after you. It would mean leaving his band in the lurch. To be honest Lily, I think y'all are as bad as one another."

"What do you tell him about me when he asks, Rick?" He smiled and took another swig of his beer eyeing me appreciatively. "I tell him that you're doing great, enjoying the buzz, and were born to do this." I smiled at Rick, because he'd just given me the validation that I was looking for, he really did rate XrAid.

Chapter Thirty-Two

ELECTRICITY

inner was really relaxing with Rick, and I thought he'd be a friend for life after spending time with him. He was easy to talk to, and he paid me the biggest compliment I could ever have had when he told me that he knew I'd be special to him when he met me at the 02.

I couldn't believe when he told me that one way or another, he knew I'd be in and out of his life from that point on. I never figured him for an old hippy, but he was changing my mind fast. He told me that from what he could see of Alfie, he'd never let me go.

When we were eating, Rick told me I shouldn't waste my time worrying about Alice, because she was batting for the other team, so any pictures I saw should be taken with a grain of salt.

He reminded me of the quote, "There's no such thing as bad publicity," and suggested maybe we should mock-up some pictures of our own to keep the media chins wagging. I smiled but didn't feel one hundred percent sure, because Alfie was just about sexy enough to turn someone straight.

When Rick told me a few things about himself, I wasn't

surprised about how he had lived life to excess, after hearing some of the stories about his deprived upbringing in a poor area of New York City.

Amazing he was so normal, really, considering the life he had come from, and his contrasting success as a superstar.

I was touched when he said, "I'd give anything to have what Alfie has with you, Lily, but the poor guy doesn't know what to do with it. Equally, I don't think you do either. Something's got to give, though, because I don't see either one of you giving yourselves to anyone else if it doesn't get ironed out."

He smiled and leaned over, holding my hand across the table. A camera flash almost blinded us and a short, dark-haired, balding guy weaved his way out of the restaurant at high speed.

"Fucker." Rick chuckled. "Sorry, doll, goes with the territory. Don't worry, I'll deal with Alfie. You never know, might do you two some good."

He noticed my worried look and took a deep breath "Listen, sweetheart, one of you will come to your senses over this. You're not the first couple to both have successful careers. Most celebrity marriages never work out, but I have hope for you guys. I'd hate for you two to be casualties, because this fucked-up crazy life doesn't last forever. It means having close relationships with people who love you becomes even more important when the ride stops."

Understanding his stance, I said, "I agree, but right now, we seem a million miles from that." I dropped my head and stared at my lap. Rick put his index finger under my chin and lifted it so my eyes would meet his.

"You just have to believe this is what you want, Lily. Anything's possible. You just have to want it enough." He smirked. "Or is it that you're not sure that's really what you want? Alfie, I mean."

I swallowed hard and met his gaze. "He's everything I want. I just didn't realize how much until he cut contact with me and let me go on my own last week."

Leaving the restaurant, all eyes were on us. I knew people reacted with curiosity. I probably would have too, if I were in their shoes. However, it would be nice sometimes, if guys like Rick and Alfie could just enjoy a quiet dinner now and again. Without having to smile, nod, and put on a show when someone spoke to them, because they didn't want to offend their fans.

More than once I've wanted to say, well he may be famous but I'd like to eat my dinner in peace if you don't mind. If we were getting more recognizable I was going to have to invest in wigs and glasses, because I valued time out on my own now and again.

The limo brought us back to our buses, and I declined Rick's invite to go back to his band bus for drinks. I was living with enough smelly boys not to want to go drinking with more of them.

When I got inside, no one was home. Barry, one of the drivers, was the only one there. He told me the guys had gone to a club and offered to drop me off. Happy to have some quiet time, I declined. I showered and crawled into my bunk feeling better about Alfie after what Rick had said to me.

I was still asleep, but became vaguely aware of some very inebriated bandmates arriving home and I heard them cussing a storm as they tried to squeeze themselves into their bunks.

There were more than a few thumps as they tried to undress in semi darkness, and several stage-loud 'shushes', that thing drunken people did when they were trying to be quiet. It brought a smile to my lips as I turned over, they had obviously sorted out their differences in my absence.

Lennon pinched my toe waking me up hours later. "Lily,

get your ass downstairs there's something you might want to see." I cricked my neck from one side to the other and tried to sit up.

When I went into the kitchen area, Lennon and Digs were sitting at the table and I deduced Shawn and Cody the culprits of the drunken interlude last night because they were still sleeping off the ale.

""Well? What is it?" Lennon gestured at the internet sites where there were pictures of Rick and I everywhere. We looked very cozy. The photographer had done a really good job of making us look very 'together'. From the angle he'd taken the picture from, Rick looked completely smitten, and I appeared to stare adoringly into his eyes.

"No publicity is bad publicity, right?" I echoed Rick's comment from last night, and tried to look unfazed, but I was worried what Alfie would think when he saw it. I struggled with why it should matter because he obviously hadn't given a shit about how I felt when he let Alice sit all over his lap, whether she was 'batting for the other team', or not.

The tagline was what made me cringe though. 'Alfie Black and Lily Parnell move on'. The piece went on to ask some questions. "*What exactly does Rick Fars have that Alfie Black doesn't? Alice Bridge is a pretty girl, but is she in Lily's league?*'

The article went on, *The couple had chosen the discreet venue, but the eagle-eyed photographer captured the intimate image of the pair gazing longingly at each other. Rick and Lily were seen leaving the restaurant shortly after in the same luxury transport, and entering the band compound both Cobham Street and XrAid are currently sharing. We have to ask ourselves, what exactly was going through Alfie's mind, when he saw the intimate pictures of the couple dining in an exclusive, romantic, discreet French restaurant. Alfie, allegedly, snatched the photographs out of the reporter's hand and stared hard at them. He then slammed it back to the reporter's chest with the* comment, "Lily's a big girl. She's strong willed and independent, I'm not her keeper."

Fuck. That comment was almost as good a comment as, 'she'll fuck anything that isn't moving'. How dare he? After ignoring me for almost a week he had flaunted a woman in his lap at me, even if she was gay.

Suddenly my cell blew up. Text after text message, one from Elle, Jack, Will, Holly, and Mandy. Everybody wanted to know what I was doing with Rick.

Me? What was I doing? There had been pictures all over the internet of Alfie and his 'support act', and yet everyone questioned my behavior? Anyone would think I couldn't be faithful to him. Well given my track record in the beginning, that might have been true, but technically— we weren't together then.

"You know what, Lennon? Everyone can go to hell. I don't care what the papers say. Rick and I know what happened, and if I tell you nothing happened and it wasn't like that, would you believe me anyway?"

"Yes, without a doubt I do. I just wanted to see how you reacted and how we should play it off, is all," he said quietly.

Just when I needed someone to take this whole shitty mess out on, Lennon became the voice of reason. "I'm going to shower. Rick is probably over there rehearsing now. He said he would take care of it today. So, I'm not going to give it any more of my time. You know the press. They're like sharks in the water, always circling."

I left the guys and collected my outfit and wash bag from the cubby above me and headed to the shower.

When I was dressed, I grabbed my cell, and we all headed over to the stadium. Shit, this place was colossal, holding seventy thousand people, and we were completely unknown here.

I swallowed but there wasn't even enough spit in my

mouth to warrant it. I glanced at the time on my phone before I put it in my pocket, and there it was. The long-awaited text from Alfie, right on cue.

SEXPERT: we need to talk.

*Now he wants to talk??*I could have called him, and ranted on about the many texts and voicemails I had sent him that he'd ignored, but I didn't. I took a deep breath and punched out a short text before stuffing my cell back in my pocket.

Pink Lady: We do? Since when? No, don't answer that. I would only have to look at my cell again, and I'm too busy today. So...save it.

Maybe I appeared childish, but he'd left me for days without talking to me. He didn't even call me to reassure me about the woman who sat on his lap. *Well, fuck you, Alfie, you can stew for a while.*

We rehearsed and rested then got ourselves ready for the show of our lives. Looking out at the vast crowd, I thought I was going to hyperventilate at the side of the stage as we waited to go on. This was the first gig we'd played at that was completely uncovered outside, including the stage, since we were at the 'On the Verge of Fame' festival before we got signed.

It was a nighttime gig, and although there was some flood lighting in the stadium, by the time we were due to go on it was pitch black.

Apart from the screams and catcalls, it felt quite eerie. I took my place on the stage after my usual pep talk from Cody. He'd kissed me on the lips tonight, right before he dragged me out here, but I put it down to the adrenaline and him not really thinking about it too much.

We stood there anticipating the emcee's announcement and when it came, there was a massive uproar from the crowd. Shawn counted us in like usual, and the next thing Lennon's incredible guitar introduction brought the stage to life. Cody began his usual showmanship banter, and myself and Digs joined in playing our instruments.

I was playing rhythm guitar for this first number, and Cody sang this alone. We'd changed the set order to include a couple of covers for this gig, because of the number of people, and also with us being relatively unknown.

We were only finishing the first number when the skies opened and a heavy rainstorm beat down on us. An automatic cover was mechanically making its way over us, and we were instructed to keep playing.

We managed another two numbers, but the canopy didn't cover the stage completely. The stage was soaked in parts, and it was still raining hard. Cody signaled that we'd do one more number, and if it wasn't getting any better, we'd stop.

I had been singing with my electric acoustic guitar and was exchanging this for my Gibson. I slipped it over my shoulder, and Shawn counted us in for the next song. As soon as I strummed with my plectrum on the string, I vaguely heard a loud bang.

Instantly a sharp, intense pain shot up my arm. It struck and squeezed my chest, like a bolt of lightning had it. My mouth tingled and everything went black.

The first thing I remember after that was I heard voices echoing in the distance, and I wondered who it was. People spoke in low murmurs. I strained to listen, frustrated the voices weren't loud enough, but I couldn't make out what they were saying.

I felt utterly exhausted. So, so, tired. My eyelids felt so heavy, and I was in pain. I just couldn't pinpoint where. My head hurt as well, a sharp pain nestled in my temple. It was the pain in my body I struggled to pinpoint.

I tried to open my eyes but I was so tired, and the tiredness was pulling me further back, until I couldn't hear anything, and it went black again. I kept slipping in and out of consciousness.

The next time I was conscious I heard, "It's your own fucking fault, Dude. You think you can mess with someone like her?" I heard the voices again. I knew the voice but couldn't place it. I couldn't understand why I was so tired. Then the voices faded again.

I kept fading in and out until once again, I heard them. "I couldn't deal with her being with you guys, and not me, it fucking hurt." I remember wondering, *whose voice was that?* Then thought, *Oh, God, Alfie!*

"Of course I love her. She's my fucking world, Rick." *Alfie's here? Why is he here? Where am I? Who does he love?* I still couldn't understand why I couldn't open my eyes or where I was.

Alfie took my left hand. I knew it was him. I would have known his hands and his touch anywhere. Even though I couldn't do anything I felt the slight 'hum' of electricity—it was always there when we touched. "I love you, Lily. I'm sorry. Shit we've wasted so much time, please wake up." Was talking to me. *Am I asleep?* I felt him drop my hand back against cool soft material and realized I was in a bed. *Why? What had happened?*

Gently he began brushing my hair back, placing his hand against my cheek then he took my hand again, and I felt his warm touch. Suddenly my heart began to beat too fast. Then there was a fast, high-pitched noise.

Something bleeped then got faster, and there was a two-tone noise. *An alarm?* All It wanted was for someone to turn it off. I tried to open my eyes. I tried to squeeze Alfie's hand, but there was nothing. I couldn't move. I was paralyzed.

I remember I felt anxious. My heartbeat was too quick,

and I had pain in the center of my chest. *Someone turn off the noise.* People came into the room, their voices sounded urgent. "You need to wait outside," I heard a distressed voice say.

"I'm not leaving her," Alfie stated.

"Come on, Dude, you need to let them help her." I recognized Rick's voice. Both Rick and Alfie were in the room. *What is Rick doing here?* I wondered why I couldn't open my eyes? I needed to breathe, my heart but flip-flopped. And my chest got tighter. I began to drift toward the blackness again, at least the noise had stopped, I thought.

Chapter Thirty-Three

EAVESDROPPING

You stole my heart, right at the start, that one glance, had my heart in a trance. You spun me a line, and it's suspended in time in our song.

If I've missed my chance with you, I don't know what to do, there's no reason to live, when I only exist to be near you. Come home to me.

From that moment on, it's been a terrible crime, I wanted to claim you, for you to be mine. To make you my own, for me to be yours cuz you own me.

If I've missed my chance with you I don't know what to do, there's no reason to live when I only exist to be near you. So come on home to me.

The next time I was semi-conscious I heard Alfie singing and strumming his guitar. It was a new song. I'd never heard it before. It had the sweetest music, but the saddest melody I've ever heard. It was an ingenious attempt at a love song. Not really the kind of lyrics he was used to writing.

"I'm a patient man, Lily. Take your time. I'm gonna be right here when you wake up, and I'm gonna love you even more than I do right now," Alfie told me when he'd finished singing. He sounded tired. He squeezed my hand, and exhaling deeply. I tried to squeeze his back, but nothing happened.

Alfie started talking to me again. "There are so many things I've still got to share with you. I need you to know what you mean to me, Lily, and I'm sorry if I haven't been able to do that in the right way so far. I guess I should have just given in to my feelings in the beginning and dated you like any normal guy would have." He sniffed like he was crying.

"Seeing you lying here, so fucking beautiful, but kind of lifeless, is killing me. I need to see those big, beautiful, eyes of yours again. I need to hear that fucking cute giggle you have, and most of all, I need to feel your warm body snuggled up close, next to mine.

"It doesn't matter where you've gone...in that little locked down world you're in, as long as I can feel your warm hand in mine and hear your strong heartbeat on that monitor over there, it lets me know you're very much alive. It gives me hope." He sighed heavily. "I'll wait here my whole fucking life if I have to as long as there's hope."

His voice cracked, and he cleared his throat. "I won't go on without you by my side, I fucking refuse to. Lily, when you finally come back to me, I'm gonna be everything you need, anything you want. Just come back to me. Whenever you're ready. I love you so much."

He snickered. "Fuck I'll even buy you flowers. I may as well, cuz you already own my heart. Maybe I am the heart and flowers kind after all, I must have just been waiting on you to realize that."

I heard Alfie tap something into his cell. "Get me Calla Lilies. I don't know how many, hundreds; I want this room full of flowers when Lily wakes up. Yeah, today, as soon as they can get them here." Something bounced softly on the bed, and I thought at the time it was Alfie's cell. He picked my hand up and placed it in his again.

"Damn, Lily, I've just admitted I'm a pussy, you better make it worth my while and wake the fuck up, girl." I thought I had smiled. Alfie didn't react. So, I figured it must have been in my head. I became exhausted again, and I had no fight; everything went black again. Alfie had put the radio on and 'Best Thing', by Anthem Lights was playing softly.

"God, she looks so fucking frail lying there." *Jack! Jack's here?* There was an overpowering smell of lilies. "If anything happened to her, I don't know what I'd do. I was in Japan covering a story when I got your call. Fuck, Alfie, has it been a week, already?"

Jack sounded choked, and Alfie's voice sounded tired, although when he spoke to me he sounded positive all the time. I knew I had to try harder to wake up. I needed to stop their worry and let them know I was okay. I could hear Jack crying. *No Jack don't cry, I'm okay. I'm just really, really tired.* I had thought shouted at him, but it was still in my head.

The noise I'd come to recognize as a heart monitor, started to bleep faster. Sounding like a crazy-assed metronome and it kept time with my heart. I remembered thinking, *Is that how fast my heart is beating?*

"Fuck, Jack, stop crying, something's happening, I don't think she likes what you're doing," Alfie told Jack in an alarmed voice.

I felt Alfie squeeze my hand, and he began to talk softly, soothingly to me. His thumb grazed the back of it as he spoke. "Okay, Lily, don't worry. Jack's just a bit overwhelmed at seeing you for the first time."

I squeezed his hand back. "Did you see that? Did you fucking see that? She squeezed my hand. Lily, do it again, squeeze my hand sweetheart, let me know you can hear me," he prompted in an excited tone.

I put everything I had into my hand and squeezed. "Sweet Jesus, thank you. Quick! Get someone, Jack. I think she's waking up." I heard the door bang, and Jack's voice shouting in the distance.

Alfie spoke calmly again. "Take your time, baby. Come back to me when you're ready. I'll be right here, whenever you want, I'm right here." He kissed my hand, and I heard Jack come back into the room with a woman.

"Well, that's a very good sign. She's starting to wake up. You must have the magic touch. Keep talking to her. She likes the sound of your voice. Keep it light and positive." I heard the door close again.

"Don't overanalyze it, Alfie. I've been in her life for most of it," Jack said.

Alfie squeezed my hand when he spoke back. "Yeah, kinda says a lot though, when I've been sitting here for a week doing all kinds of shit, trying to reach her, and you've been here five minutes and her heart goes bat-shit crazy."

Alfie was so wrong, I just couldn't cope with Jack crying. I enjoyed hearing what Alfie was thinking. I had never known for sure exactly what he was thinking from time to time, and this had been my chance to hear all the things that were in his heart.

I squeezed Alfie's hand again, and I tried my hardest to open my eyes. A crack of blurry light appeared then I managed to focus. Alfie sat on the chair to my left, and Jack stood by the window. And I had never seen so many flowers in one room in all my life.

I wanted to see them. I wanted to see Alfie and Jack but I couldn't keep my eyes open, it was too tiring. "Did you see that? She looked straight at me," Alfie exclaimed. "Lily? Can you hear me? Open your eyes for me, sweetheart." I forced my eyes open, and Alfie's smile melted my heart. I fell in love all over again when his eyes met mine.

"Hey," he cooed. "Hi, sleepyhead, don't be afraid, you're okay. God, I've missed you, welcome back. Don't panic, Lily, I got you. You're in the hospital, but you're going to be just fine."

Jack came bounding across the room and almost grabbed me out of the bed. "Thank you, God!" He kissed my face tenderly. "Don't you ever do this to me again," he scowled. His face was full of concern.

Alfie's voice cut in. "You've been asleep for a week, Lily. One night after a concert, you told me you could sleep for a week because you were so tired. I never expected you to demonstrate it to me." He chuckled.

Alfie had pressed the buzzer and a redheaded woman in a nurse's uniform came through the door. As soon as she began to talk, I knew she'd been around a lot. I'd heard her talking to Alfie in the past, and today, to Jack, just before I woke up.

Glancing around the room I thought it looked like a funeral parlor. There were so many lilies on every surface. There were some in vases, some in baskets, and a few in that cellophane wrap.

The flowers were beautiful, but the smell was overpowering. I wouldn't have complained, because Alfie had put them there. "So... I thought you weren't the hearts-and-flowers kind of guy? What's happened to you, Alfie?" I croaked.

Relief made his shoulders sag as he ran his hand through his hair, and even though he was tired, his eyes shined when he smiled back at me. "You're not allowed to mention this after you leave this room. I won't have my hard-hearted reputation tainted just because I love you. Better get your cell out and snap a few pictures because the only other time I'd ever buy flowers would be for a wedding."

I suddenly remembered that Elle and Drew were getting married and tried to sit up. "Shit!" The pain I felt in my right arm was excruciating and I cried out. "What's wrong with my arm?" I looked down, and saw it was heavily bandaged from my hand to my elbow.

"Do you remember what happened, Lily?"

"No. What happened? The last thing I remember I was on stage in a stadium and it was raining, then nothing after that."

"You were electrocuted. You're lucky to be alive. You have a contact burn on your right hand and forearm. It happened when you started to play your guitar. One of the cables had a break in it and wasn't fully insulated. The rain conducted the electricity when you played with the plectrum. An electrical surge entered your body on that side.

"I saw the whole thing, and it's a sight I still see, every time I close my eyes."

I bunched my brows, confused at how he could have seen me when he was supposed to be in London.

"You're wondering why I was there, aren't you? I used my Christmas present from you to come and see you that night. I couldn't stay away any longer. Sometimes things happen for a reason, and I guess I was supposed to be there.

"You were very lucky the stadium has its own medical team and defibrillator, so they were able to restart your heart quickly."

I could hardly believe what he was saying. I didn't really remember that much about it.

"You're not going to be playing your guitar for a while. The doctors said there should be a minimal amount of scarring, but you're going to need intensive physical therapy on your arm, because the muscles and nerves were affected by the surge."

I suddenly remembered about the XrAid guys. "Where are Lennon, Cody and the others?" I realized that I never heard their voices before I woke up. Alfie smiled and rubbed my hand.

"They're playing alone, Lily. I've been keeping them updated on your progress, but they have a contract with Cobham Street, and they needed to finish the commitment they made to the tour."

I felt awful that they had to go on without me, especially after seeing what had happened to me, but Alfie was right, the show must go on

There was one thing that was still gnawing at me. Alice. "I saw the pictures of you and Alice, Alfie." He smirked and exhaled in a kind of snicker. "Yeah, that. You know she's gay, right?" I stared at him wondering why he let her sit on his lap, and he must have known how that would have affected me. As if he read my mind, he started to explain.

"She was on my lap as a message, Lily. No woman could come near me, she was protecting your position from the groupies and fans. I figured Rick would tell you about her so that you wouldn't worry." So, Rick was right after all.

My parents arrived, and my dad hugged me tightly. "Hello sweetheart, you had us all scared for a while. Guess you were waiting for Jack to show before you woke up." Dad smiled his tender smile, full of love, and I could see the relief on his face.

"The doctor says that there are a few tests to make sure there are no gaps in your memory bank, and then we can take you home in a couple of days."

As if the doctor had heard my dad, Dr. Scott came into the room. "Can everyone give us a few minutes? I want to ask Lily some questions, and she is going to need to rest again afterwards. We don't want her getting tired out." He was right. I was drained and feeling a little overwhelmed at everything I'd learned since opening my eyes.

Alfie didn't want to leave the room, insisting he could stay with me, but the doctor was firm, telling him that I would perform better without any distractions.

Seeing the torn look on Alfie's face between wanting me to perform well and having to leave me here alone was painful. I shook my head. "Please, can he stay? I want him here." The doctor hesitated, but when he saw I was becoming tearful, he agreed that Alfie could stay in the room, but had to stay out of my field of vision.

Alfie sat on a small leather couch that was over by the window, and the doctor then gave me the third degree about my memories - both since I was a child and what happened immediately before the accident.

He was satisfied that my memory was intact and smiled at me. "We'll just run one more MRI tomorrow, and hopefully we'll be able to give you the all clear to go home."

Alfie stood and walked over to me. He smiled warmly. "So," he said, and the wicked glint in his eye told me he was making mischief. "You remember when you agreed to marry me the other day." It wasn't a question, more of statement.

I must have looked confused because he continued, "You're not going to tell me you don't remember? Maybe I should call the doctor back and tell him that you're having gaps. He might need to keep you here a bit longer."

He tried to look serious, but there was a hint of a smirk playing on his lips and I knew he was teasing me. "You did. I do remember, and I believe I said no." I decided if he thought me well enough to play games with me there was nothing in the rules that said I couldn't play them back.

He looked annoyed, because his little ruse had backfired. I waited to see what he'd say next. "You did, but then we talked, and you confessed you could never live without me and agreed to be my bride." It was my turn to smirk now. He recovered well from that one.

"Well I did agree, but only if you wore one of my thongs under your tuxedo." Alfie's eyes widened in surprise, and I could see the humor waiting to burst out of him, but he bit back his grin.

"I remember, and I agreed, but only if it was the black satin ones with the side bows and frilly mesh at the edges." Alfie sat completely stern-faced, daring me to defy what he'd just told me. I wanted to giggle so badly, but I was tired again.

"We need to pick this up again later, I'm exhausted, and I think I need to nap again." A worried look crept over Alfie's face. "What's wrong, Alfie?"

He looked a little unsure of himself, and I saw he was nervous. Alfie rarely got nervous. In fact, the only time I'd ever really seen him nervous was the first time we stayed together at Christmas after all our time apart.

He touched my cheek and gazed adoringly into my eyes. "I'm frightened, Lily."

I bunched my brows. "What are you frightened about?"

Alfie stared at me and there was so much love and hurt in his eyes. I was confused as to why. I was fine. "I'm worried if you go to sleep you won't wake up again."

Lifting my good arm, I patted the bed, motioning Alfie to get in beside me. He didn't need to be told twice and climbed on, snuggling into my side. He placed his arm across my waist and stilled.

A silent moment passed between us then he inhaled deeply. "God, I've missed this." His gruff voice was loaded with emotion, and he sounded as if he might cry; his vocal range changed several times as he tried to keep his emotions in check.

"Just lie with me, listen to my heartbeat, and hold my hand. "He did, and he must have been exhausted too, because he drifted off to sleep before I did.

Chapter Thirty-Four

WEDDING PLANS

*A*lfie moving away from me woke me. "Hey," he cooed, and bent to press his soft lips against my forehead. "I didn't mean to wake you, but I'm kind of relieved to see that you are." His smile was wide, and he looked so disheveled.

I felt terrible for everything I had put him through. It was my fault I was the one who wanted to tour with Cobham Street, and so it was on me that I was in the hospital. If I had just stayed with him, none of this past week would have happened.

Jack arrived and I persuaded Alfie to go home and take a shower. He almost had a full beard, and he must have felt drained after being here for the past eight days.

Of course, Alfie protested like crazy, but when I told him I'd make him stay in a hotel in London instead of with me if he didn't take care of himself, he reluctantly agreed that he could use a good bath, something to eat, and maybe a nap.

Jack pulled him into a man-hug, and I saw Alfie's body physically sag into Jack's. "Take care of her until I get back."

His voice was raw with emotion. I wished I could have videoed the scene and kept it to show my kids in the future. "With my life," Jack replied.

My honest-to-god rock star hugged my best friend from my childhood, and my heart warmed to Alfie even more.

Who could have known that those two guys would become firm friends? Alfie got what Jack and I were to each other, and that Jack would never come between us unless Alfie wasn't treating me right.

Alfie dipped his head and kissed my lips softly. His tongue barely grazed along my lips. "I'll be back in a couple of hours." Kissing the end of my nose, he laid his forehead against mine, and gazed longingly into my eyes. Eventually, he inhaled sharply and pulled away.

"I love you so much, Lily," he murmured.

"I love you too." We smiled affectionately at each other, and Alfie backed away until his back hit the door.

Turning, he pulled the handle to make his way out, then turned back and winked before walking out, letting the door swing closed after him.

"Ack! Jesus, I'd have told you two to get a room, but you were already in one. That's sick, honey, staring all hot and sensual at each other, even when you've just come out of a coma."

I swatted Jack's arm. "Shut the fuck up, Jack."

He chuckled. "Uh huh, damn, you're defending him with his lusty, I-could-fuck-you-right-here-never-mind-you've-been-in- a-coma-for-a-week eyes? I giggled at Jack, who almost ran out of breath when he said it.

"Seriously, Lily, I am so relieved you're okay. I couldn't live without you, you know that, right? I nodded, because I felt the same way about Jack. He leaned in and hugged me, pouring all the love he had for me into it.

After persuading Jack to leave, I slept again. When I woke, the oversized clock on the wall displayed 3:20am. Alfie was sitting on the chair to my left, his head resting on his arm on my bed. I hadn't heard him come back, but felt bad that I was lying on the bed, and he was crouched over like that.

Running my fingers through his silky hair, I was rewarded when a soft moan escaped his throat. His head turned to the side so that I could see his beautiful face. Stroking his cheek produced a soft groan. Alfie's eyes fluttered open, and a slow, sleepy smile spread across his lips when his eyes met mine.

"Hey," he cooed, as he sat up, stretching his back as he ran his fingers through his hair.

"You want to come over here beside me, since you wouldn't stay at home?" I smirked.

Alfie pulled his hoodie over his head, took his shoes off, and gently placed himself beside me then scooted down a bit, taking me in the crook of his arm, and snuggling me against him.

He inhaled deeply and kissed me softly on my head. "God, Lily, I desperately wanted to do this again with you, but I was beginning to waver a little, on my faith, that he'd give me another chance, to have this closeness with you."

Pulling my head back my heart ached at the serious expression on his face. The sadness in his eyes almost tore me in two. If I had ever had any doubts that Alfie truly loved me, they were demolished when I saw how tormented he was at the thought he would never be able to hold me again.

Daylight streaming through the window woke me. Alfie was still beside me sound asleep, his arm firmly tucked around my waist. I could hear giggling and looked over in the direction of the door. There were some student nurses staring at us through the glass, as we lay together in my bed.

I heard one of the students say, "Damn, what I'd give to

be in her shoes. I couldn't imagine what it would feel like to have someone like that drool over me and sit patiently waiting for me while I was in a coma. Most rock stars would have seen it as an ideal opportunity to get laid somewhere else and blame her for being unconscious at the time."

Smiling, I glanced back down at my sexy-as-all-hell boyfriend. The girl was right. Most rock stars had problems being faithful, just from the temptation of what was offered night after night backstage.

After hearing tons of stories about guys that Alfie was in contact with, and some of the stuff I had seen with the groupies throwing themselves at guys like him, and even the guys in XrAid, I was lucky Alfie wasn't like that.

He'd even told me that there had been a few times where some of the women had found their way into his hotel suite or show, one even managed to hide in the trunk of a limo one time.

After all we'd been through, and all we were to each other, I couldn't believe that I was Alfie Black's girl, or that he was finally mine. I swore to myself that I would do anything to keep it that way.

Stretching, I turned my butt to relieve the pain of lying in one position. Alfie's grip immediately tightened on me. "Hey, are you okay?"

I smiled down at him. "Don't look now but you've got an audience.

His body tensed. "In a fucking hospital?" I nodded a small smile on my lips as our faces almost touched. Our voices were almost a whisper.

He relaxed and smiled slowly. "Well, baby, you know me, always the showman. He took his hand from around my waist and brushed some hair away from my forehead, tucking it behind my ear.

Moving to kiss me, I said, "Wait. I need to brush my teeth."

Alfie smirked. "Lily, with the stuff we've done in the past you think a little morning breath is going to stop me from kissing you?" He didn't let me answer, just pushed his lips and pressed them firmly against mine. His tongue swept out, asking for entrance, then demanding it.

My lips parted, and his tongue brushed against mine. He groaned and exhaled raggedly. I moaned, and he pulled away. "Fuck, what time do I get you home?" he muttered into my neck.

I giggled and the girls at the door were still there, but were standing silently. We heard them sigh in unison. "Damn, how hot is that?"

We heard a commotion and the voice of the nurse from yesterday telling them to get away from the door. She was scolding and shooing them, and I could hear murmurs of apology.

The nurse, whose name I now knew as Angela, came into the room and walked over to us. "You need to get off the bed, Alfie. Dr. Scott is coming to discharge Lily after reviewing the latest MRI results.

"Let's get you up and showered before he gets here." Alfie smiled at me and turned to Angela, "Okay, Angela. I'll shower her, there's really no need for you to stay as well."

Angela's eyes flicked to me then back to him. "Actually, Alfie, the way you were looking at Lily when I came through that door tells me I absolutely have to stay. Otherwise, Dr. Scott might be reviewing something he definitely won't be expecting to." She smirked at me, and I felt myself blush for the first time in a while.

Alfie chuckled. "Damn, what is it with you females? Anyone would think we can't care for our women without sex coming into the equation." Alfie was met with silence and the deadpan faces of Angela and me.

He smirked but it turned into a chuckle as he threw his hands up in submission. "You can't blame a guy for trying, can you?"

I giggled and blushed again. "Maybe you should go find some breakfast and come back in half an hour, Alfie." He nodded, stretched out, placed a chaste kiss on the end of my nose, and made his way out of the room.

Angela shook her head and sighed. "You have no idea what I'd give for one night with a man like Alfie," she swooned, looking wistfully at the door long after he'd gone.

I cleared my throat, and she smirked then looked sheepishly at me. "God, I said it out loud, didn't I?" Her face registering the shock she'd given herself. I giggled, and she relaxed. "Come on let's get you clean so that we can throw you out of here and give this bed to someone who needs it."

When I was clean and looking fairly normal, I realized that my skin had lost a lot of its color, and I was looking slightly yellow instead of the healthy glow I had built up over the past few years.

My arm still ached and was weak. There was no way I could have played my guitar. I couldn't even hold a plastic beaker of water at this time.

Dr. Scott seemed pleased with me though. He told me that I might feel a bit tired for another week or so, but to listen to my body and just rest when I felt I needed to.

I wondered how I was going to rest when there was so much left to do for Elle's wedding. This gave me the thought that maybe she'd changed her mind and didn't want me there now. I hadn't seen or heard from her since, but I'd worry about that when I got home.

Alfie had a car waiting for us when I left the hospital, and there were a lot of reporters. Alfie told me on the way down about the media frenzy there had been around what had happened. He told me that it wasn't as bad as it would have been if it had happened in London or the USA.

We were still relatively unknown here in France. I kept forgetting that, because we were in a private US hospital. Alfie was big news, and the fact that my accident happened in a French stadium, and I was still in France made me news-worthy apparently.

As soon as he wheeled me outside and stepped out of the hospital into the fresh air, there were hundreds of flashbulbs going off. Photographers all fought for the best pictures of us to sell to the newspapers.

Alfie shielded me by pulling my face tightly into his chest, while Henry and Carl pushed them aside and helped us into the limo. I was worried for the photographers as they ran alongside the car, still flashing through the blacked-out windows beside us.

We drove to a private airstrip where a charter plane was waiting, courtesy of Rick, and within about twenty minutes of being on board we were in the air and on our way home to London. Alfie stated, "I guess I need to get us one of these."

I was exhausted and fell asleep as soon as we took off, and the next thing I knew, Alfie was stroking my cheek and smil-ing. Stretching, I was suddenly reminded my arm was still sore, and flinched when I had extended it so much I jolted my damaged nerves. Alfie lifted my fingers and kissed them. "We'll get you settled in the car, and I'll find your pain relief pills for you."

The look on my parents' faces when they opened the door was difficult for me. I had caused them so much worry during the past week.

I sunk into the large leather couch, and Alfie was immedi-ately by my side. He settled himself down, and snuggled me into his chest.

"Thank God you're okay, Lily. Everything is going to be better from now on. We're just going to be guided by you. When you need to rest do it, you promise me?" I nodded, I felt as weak as a ten-day-old kitten right now anyway, so I was not going to protest about taking it easy.

I fell asleep again, and when I woke, Alfie's voice was vibrating in his chest, and I felt so comforted to be in his arms. Waking and listening to Alfie sounding so relaxed, talking to my dad, was a lovely feeling. I just lay with my eyes closed and listened to two of my favorite men getting along. It was music to my ears.

"Absolutely. I'll love this girl forever. If she wasn't with me, nothing else would matter. Lily is the other half of me I didn't know was missing, until she wasn't around."

I felt like I was eavesdropping, and that wasn't fair to Alfie, so I shifted and opened my eyes. I couldn't pretend to be sleep while he poured his heart out about me to my dad. I stretched out a little and when I stirred he looked down at me. "Hey," he said, smiling..

"You think you can stay awake a bit longer, so that you can eat something?"

I smiled. "That depends what I'm eating," I said, not sure that I had much of an appetite. Alfie's eyes lit up, and I realized what he thought and blushed. My dad was sitting right there for goodness sake, as if I would make a comment that was in any way insinuating performing a sexual act on him for crying out loud.

So, I quickly added, "I mean if it isn't something too heavy. I'm not that hungry right now," I mumbled flicking my eyes quickly in my dad's direction. My dad was reading something on his tablet thank goodness and had missed the exchange.

Glancing back at Alfie, I shook my head, widening my eyes in my dad's direction. Alfie's eyes flicked over to my dad and back to me. He smirked and kissed the top of my head, snuggling me tighter into his chest.

"Don't eat too much at once then, just keep a little appetite for dessert in case you fancy it later." He pinched his lips, and I could see a smile play on his face. The guy got away with far too much sometimes.

Chapter Thirty-Five

EMOTIONAL DAY

*D*inner was good. My mom made a very light cheese soufflé and some smoked salmon. It was the perfect dinner. I hadn't eaten much for the past week, and my stomach was delicate. She ran a bath and helped me in to soak. Alfie looked a bit miffed that he wasn't getting to sit with me in the bathroom, but respected my mom's position, and let her help me.

I had no choice but to let my mom help me bathe and slip into some sweatpants and a tank top before we went back to the sitting room. Alfie was on the phone and held it out to me. "Elle wants to talk to you." He informed me with an encouraging smile and gently gestured the cell for me to take it.

Swallowing audibly, I took the cell, but I wasn't sure what she was going to say to me after our spat before my accident. "Hi, Elle," I squeaked, my voice sounded slightly weak and pathetic.

"Hiya, Lily. I'm so glad you're okay, and you're home. Would it be okay for me to come see you tomorrow?" It was so good to hear her voice, and it had no trace of malice in it.

"Yeah, I'd like that, Elle." I smiled and felt better about our friendship as soon as I heard her tone, I felt we were going to be okay. I should have known better, we'd been friends for a long time.

"How's the wedding going?" I asked and heard the excitement in her voice as soon as she spoke. "There's still a lot to organize and that's kind of why I was coming to see you tomorrow. I only have twelve days left and still don't have a dress, and I need to pick colors for the bridesmaid's dresses and tables...I'm still not one hundred percent on those."

My jaw gaped. This girl was so laid back, she was horizontal. "You have no dress yet?" She snickered into the phone.

"Well, I wasn't prepared to pick my dress out without the help of my maid of honor. So, I had to wait for her to get home to come with me. I'll come over tomorrow and show you the choices I have for the linens, menu, flowers, and table decorations, and you can finalize them with me.

"Mandy's friend, Leanne, from fashion school is making the bridesmaid's dresses for you, Mandy, Holly, and Rosie. Don't worry she has all the help she needs so it won't take more than a day or two," she gushed, anticipating my panic that the dresses were still to be made from scratch.

"My little cousins, Molly and Jasmine, are flower girls, and their dresses are already done. They are lilac and will go with whatever color we choose. I have pink, cerise, deep purple, and a pale rose-colored material."

Elle spoke so confidently about everything that still had to be done; if it were my wedding and all this stuff still had to be done, I'd be in a blind panic. I didn't have to worry about any of that yet. Alfie might have joked that he asked me to get married when we were in the hospital, but I doubted he was at the point of committing to me forever, despite his words telling me I was his always.

Elle and I finished our call, and I was tired again. I could see that Alfie was exhausted too. "Sorry, guys but I am really done for the day, I need to go to bed. I had been hoping to have more energy, but with the flight and all the emotion of leaving the hospital, I am wiped out." Everyone agreed that I should just go and get settled in bed.

Alfie was on his feet, trying to look like he was doing this for me, when I knew that deep down, all he wanted was to be in bed beside me without the wires or monitors and a twin mattress. Not to mention the steady stream of people coming in to check on us.

When we got in my bedroom, I stripped out of my sweat-pants and Alfie's eyes fell to my groin. His eyes immediately darkened, because I hadn't put panties on after my bath. I asked him to help me take the tank top off, the spaghetti straps made it difficult to pull it above my breasts with just one hand.

Alfie walked over slowly and smiled at me. "You're going to use that hand to torture me with stuff like this for weeks now, aren't you?" His voice was low and seductive.

"I might...if you're good that is." I smirked. He slowly peeled the top up my body and over my head, taking special care to avoid my sore arm.

When he discarded the tank top by throwing it onto the chair, his gaze fell back to my naked frame. His hands auto-matically cupped my breasts. A sexy smile played on his lips, and the look he gave me was both flirty and dirty.

"Hmm...yeah." I answered, nodded, and swallowed hard. I snickered at him. "What does that mean?".

"My dick twitched in appreciation when I got you naked, I was just agreeing with him." He smirked.

Chuckling, I shook my head. "Not fair, Alfie, you have me at a disadvantage."

He raised his eyebrow. "How so?" He smiled playfully at me, trying not to let it form into proper grin.

"I've given you a lap dance, and as I'm kind of laid up at the moment, I think it's your turn to do something for me."

"Seriously? You want me to strip for you?"

I giggled. "Are you telling me you've never done that before, and you're a famous rock star an' all?" My voice mimicked that of Holly's Texan drawl, and Alfie and I both giggled at my effort with that. "Well, maybe not today, but I'll want you to surprise me with that sometime, okay?"

Alfiee chuckled. "Sure, and I can choose when it happens and the music, right? That means you'll be left in suspense until I decide to put you out of your misery with that one."

I could see his mind working already, but I knew it might be a while before he'd spring it on me. I hoped he didn't leave it too long, but long enough for me to be well enough to do something about it.

Alfie shucked out of his clothes and threw my duvet back, laying me on the bed. He turned the bedside light on and the overhead light off. The soft, creamy lighting in the room changed our mood instantly. Alfie smiled as he slipped in beside me.

"Let me just look at you," he said in an affectionate tone. He lay staring into my eyes, his irises disappearing as his pupils dilated, because Alfie liked what he saw before him. He inhaled sharply. "You really have no idea what you do to me, Lily. I am so grateful that I'm right here with you." He lay still, saying nothing for what seemed like an age again. I was taking him in as well. This perfectly formed, gorgeous man, who had risen above most of his peers in the music world, was everything to me.

"I love you, Alfie."

He swallowed hard. "You know, that just doesn't do it for me."

His words were a punch to my heart. Adrenaline instantly sent my body racing. "You don't think I love you?" Fear must have registered on my face, because he was immediately reassuring me.

"God, no. I mean, I love you doesn't begin to explain what I feel for you. I know I was a shitty person in the beginning to you, and there isn't a day that goes by that I don't wish I could have had a do-over with you for that. What I want to say is..." Alfie tried to collect his thoughts and pour out what was in his heart.

"Lily, this isn't how I wanted to do this, but right in this moment, I feel it's the perfect time." He had me confused. I didn't know what he was trying to do, so I waited until he felt able to tell me what he wanted to say.

"You are the only girl I have ever known that stirs every feeling in me that I both want to feel and never want to feel again. I have thought about that long and hard, and I've come to realize it's because when I met you, my heart ceased to be mine and became ours." He swallowed, and his eyes searched my face, before he continued, "It means that you have the ability to convey your feelings from your heart to mine, so that both of our hearts connect and communicate with our bodies without a single word being spoken."

"So." He smiled nervously, his eyes shining, but with a hint of uncertainty there. He took my hand and held it over his heart. "Can you feel it beating?"

I nodded. He'd rendered me speechless as I tried to choke the tears away at the romantic way he was telling me what I meant to him. He exhaled a breath he'd been holding in. "So...Lily, my sweet, beautiful, perfect, forever girl, will you marry me?"

I burst into tears and sobbed, and Alfie quickly tried to appease me. "Okay, I wasn't sure if you would agree, because I know you worry about how you can have a career and be with me, but I wasn't quite expecting this. Please don't cry, Lily. I'm sorry, it was stupid to do this now, especially when you've just come home from the hospital, and it's an emotional time anyway..."

I put my fingers to his lips. "Shush." I sniffed through my tears. I kept hitching my breath because I had been crying, trying to get my breath back on an even keel.

The desolate look on Alfie's face broke my heart. "Alfie, what you just told me...I have been waiting to hear for the past two years. I love you with all my heart. There has never been another man for me since I realized how I felt about you." I felt embarrassed at the other men I'd slept with since I'd known him.

I wasn't sorry about that, because it taught me that Alfie really was the one for me, no matter how I'd thought I had felt about Max, Will, and although I never slept with him, Luca. Alfie was everything I ever wanted in a man, and without them I probably wouldn't have realized just how deep my feelings for Alfie really went.

I cupped Alfie's face, and he stared with a serious look in his eyes and a worried look on his face. "You don't need to worry, Alfie, I would never turn you down, because my heart is completely operating with yours. I feel like you have one half and I have the other, so I know exactly how you feel. I don't know how we'll work it out, but now that we've started, we need to keep moving forward. A life without you is no life, music or no music."

I smiled and kissed his lips softly, and his hands cupped both sides of my head. We were lying naked, facing each other, snug under the duvet in the bedroom I had grown up in. Personally, I couldn't think of a more perfect place for him to propose to me. It was simple, honest, and from the heart.

"Alfie Black, I most definitely and absolutely will marry you...on one condition."

Alfie's brows furrowed. "Anything." I smiled at his eagerness to do what I asked.

"Never leave me without talking to me again, and if we're apart, you're never to ignore me I can't stand it, it tore me apart." Alfie smirked.

"Well, technically that's two conditions, but you don't need to worry, Lily, I can tell you right this second that it's never going to happen again, because we are never going to be apart again." He wiggled his finger between us when he said it.

"So...I'm going to ask you the question again, because I think my answer got lost in all the discussions that followed it, and I need to be absolutely clear. Lily, my sweet, beautiful little rock chick, will you marry me?"

I grinned and pushed my head forward, kissing him gently on his closed mouth. I left my lips there, not trying for anything more. When I drew my head back my gaze met his in a smoldering connection. "Alfie, nothing would give me greater pleasure in this life than to be your wife, so yes, of course I'll marry you."

Alfie grinned and exhaled loudly before he growled and scooped me into his arms. He breathed heavily into my hair. "Thank you, Lily, you won't regret it. I am going to do everything in my power to make you the happiest wife in the world. Apart from all the bullshit, we're a perfect match." He gave me his sexy, lopsided smile. "So, I look forward to waking up to you every day for the rest of my life, because you are mine, and I am the luckiest fucking man in the world."

Alfie sat up and turned the light out, crawled back under the duvet, and scooped me back into his arms. "Okay, I turned the light off because I want you to concentrate on this kiss. It's the first one as my fiancée."

I started to giggle, but it died on my lips as soon as his found mine. He poured all his love into my mouth, in his kiss. It was everything from soft, slow, and tender, sensual and passionate, to hungry and devouring. When he broke the kiss, we were both speechless and breathless.

My heart was beating rapidly, and I was so turned on but emotional, that a tear ran down my cheek. He placed my hand over his heart and then placed his over mine. His heart was beating strongly and in time with mine. "At one point I told you I didn't do emotions, but when we feel this way about each other, there is no denying it."

Alfie gave me a little squeeze. "Sleep now, baby. I'm not making love to you until you're strong enough, because I won't be able to restrain myself, and right now, I'd probably finish you off, instead of watch you recover from your ordeal."

I laughed softly as he hugged me tighter in his arms, then spun me to face away from him and spooned against me closely. His hand weaved around my belly and rested on my hip, while his other lay gently on the shoulder of my sore arm.

"Good night darlin', hope you're feeling better tomorrow." He kissed the back of my neck. I was already starting to drift, still not strong enough to fight the fatigue, but I managed to murmur, "I don't think I'll ever feel better than I do right at this second."

Alfie squeezed my hip and tugged me tighter and I let sleep claim me with his soft, even breaths soothing me as they blew over my neck. For all the emotional turmoil we'd been through, it was probably our most emotional day yet.

Chapter Thirty-Six

DRESSES

I woke up to Alfie strumming my left nipple back and forth. "I take it you're awake, Alfie, and not writing a new song on my nipple there," I muttered and stretched out.

My arm ached, and I tried to sit up. Alfie shot up to a sitting position and propped the pillows, adjusting me to sit up a little. He leaned forward and kissed me. "Elle will be over soon. She woke me when she sent a text to tell us she was on her way."

Alfie helped me shower, and he was a true gentleman. When he was helping me dress, his eyes locked with mine. "Can I ask you something?"

I smiled. "Sure."

He put his hands on the sides of my arms. "You were really serious about marrying me last night?"

Stunned he still couldn't believe I would agree to marry him. I put my good arm around his neck and snaked my hand up into his hair. "I was."

He grinned widely. "You really want to marry me?"

I smiled wider, his eyes lighting up. I felt a little flushed, suddenly a tad shy. "I do." He bent and kissed me gently, then pulled away.

"Okay, well, I have stuff to do today with Drew, so we'll pick this up again later." He smirked, smacked my ass lightly, and sexily sashayed out of the bathroom.

I was trying to put on some socks when Elle came into my bedroom. "So, you're not having sex again yet, then? Alfie's out there looking full of pent up energy," she commented nonchalantly.

I smirked at her assessment of Alfie's manner. "Actually, Elle, I think that's got more to do with the conversation we had last night and this morning."

She raised her brow at me. "Go on..."

I wasn't sure whether I should tell her or wait for Alfie and me to do it together, but Hell I couldn't wait. "Alfie asked me to marry him."

Elle's jaw dropped. "Aww, Lily, and you said yes, right?" I nodded and giggled nervously. Elle climbed on my bed and started jumping up and down. "It's about fucking time." She laughed loudly.

"Shush! My parents haven't even been told yet." I laughed, and we did this little happy dance together as best as I could with my arm hurting so badly.

Elle and I spent the morning working out all the material and colors for her wedding. I couldn't believe how lacking in confidence and indecisive she was. I half wondered if it was my taste or hers that was coming to the fore, but she eventually settled on stuff we both agreed would work well.

Delicate, pink-colored satin with this gorgeous chiffon overlay was the choice for the bridesmaids. It was perfect. In fact, it's something I would have liked for my own wedding, but if I couldn't have it, at least I'd be wearing it in Elle's.

She spoke to Leanne on the phone, and they started to

cut the fabric from the measurements we'd all had taken the day before I left the Crakt Soundzz tour.

The menu was easy, because we both had the same taste in food, and the chicken in Parma ham was delicious. We'd tasted that when it was sent to us in Paris. We achieved a lot before I got tired and had to nap again.

Elle had an appointment for that afternoon at the bridal store, where she had narrowed her dress down to four different ones and just wanted my opinion for the final say.

After napping for an hour, my mom made us lunch. Alfie had Henry take us to the store in the limo. He didn't feel I should really be out, but knew how important it was to get this part done.

Poor Elle had waited for me to help her choose, and she must have been getting more nervous with every passing day that she didn't have a dress to wear to her own wedding.

The four dresses Elle had shortlisted were incredible. Elle looked stunning in all the dresses. The first one she tried was a bit fussy, and I told her so. She wasn't sure whether she wanted a full ball gown type or a figure hugging one. The one I liked the most was cut in a flattering empire line style with an organza underlay and beautiful georgette silk material.

It was a strapless dress. The bodice was heart shaped with soft pleating that narrowed at the waist and drew my eyes down the length of the dress. There were silk and lace sleeves that came from the bodice that were finished like the petals of a flower at the wrists.

The silk material was formed into graduated organza with graduated waterfall ruffles at the front falling away from the center at each side, and it had a very small train at the back. Under the bodice there was a simple band of crystals and some handmade crystal flowers. I fell in love with it on sight. It was the perfect wedding dress. When I saw it on Elle, I wasn't so sure though.

We narrowed it down to two choices, and both were amazing dresses, any bride would have loved them. Elle was torn between an empire line and a traditional style dress with a twist. It was vintage inspired, but very elegant and modern.

With the second dress, I loved the romantic feathered skirt that was draped over the bodice. The bodice was silk but had straps, with soft bows and delicate crystal flowers on the top of each strap. It looked perfect on her and suited her frame more than the one that was my favorite.

I explained to Elle my reasons for thinking the feathered one was more suited to her. With her tall, slender frame, and smaller bust, it was much more flattering, but she couldn't make up her mind.

She even asked me to try them on since she wanted to see them on someone else, to see the movement of the dress from the back, and how they flowed without being in them.

I humored her by doing this. Wearing them confirmed to me even more that the dress for her was the romantic, feathered one. I had tried this one on first, and pointed out how it clung tightly and would have been wrong for someone with my body type. I had too much in the boob department to carry this one off.

When I put my favorite dress on, it suited my body type more than hers because of my fuller bust. Elle could see from how the dresses hung that she wanted to go with the romantically styled one. Secretly, I was pleased, because when I got married, I'd probably love a dress like this one, and I wouldn't have wanted to copy her.

Henry dropped me home and took Elle back to her parent's place. Alfie was home with my parents when I arrived. I walked into the kitchen and Alfie was instantly by my side hugging me. "Hey," he cooed, and pulled a chair out, sitting me down, while my dad poured me some tea.

I tried to tell Alfie about the dresses, but he was so disinterested and changed the subject twice so I let it drop. I supposed it wasn't really of interest to men.

My dad went to help my mom load some research papers into her car; she was doing some kind of medical trial that she tried to explain to me, but the concept just made my head hurt.

Alfie saw the tired look on my face. "You need to lie down, baby, you're wiped out." I was, so I let him guide me to my bedroom and lay on the bed.

Alfie unbuckled his belt, pulling the belt through the loops, and tugged his sweater off. He climbed on the bed beside me, scooping me in his arms and kissing my lips softly. He murmured against my mouth, "I missed you every single second today." His words instantly reassured me, and a small smile formed on my lips.

"Me too...you, I mean."

He chuckled. "Go to sleep." He kissed my temple and stroked my hair. I really felt that no matter what, Alfie and I would spend the rest of our lives together, but we had a lot to iron out before that happened.

In the following two weeks, Elle and I put the finishing touches on her wedding, and we had met several times with the wedding planner to finish the seating plans with Drew and Alfie, as well as ensure that we had our practice run for our makeup and hairdos.

Elle wanted all her bridesmaids' hair to be left down, curled and with flowers in it. I preferred this as well. For me that just meant natural, with the exception of the flowers.

Seeing my bandmates again was fabulous. Lennon and Cody stayed in London and were spending time with my dad. Digs and Shawn made a quick trip home before arriving back a day before the wedding.

I had been attending intensive physical therapy, and my arm was getting stronger by the day. I was still weak, though, and couldn't play my guitar for more than a few minutes without a sharp persistent pain in my wrist and bicep. The doctors assured me that my arm would gain its original strength, so long as I kept doing the exercises, and slowly building up my playing time.

When we went to the wedding rehearsal it was quite comical, as both Elle and Drew were nervous and kept going to the toilet. As it was a civil service, the registrar was only able to spend an hour to help them prepare for the ceremony itself.

So, when Elle went to the toilet, I had to step in with Drew, while she ran through the proceedings with him, and Alfie did the same with Elle, when Drew was almost taken short. The registrar was very patient with them all things considered.

We were conscious we hadn't even given Elle a bachelorette party, but she'd refused to have one without me. By the time I'd got home there just hadn't been the opportunity to go to the spa Alfie had arranged. Drew surprised us by giving us a pamper session at The Sanctuary Spa in Covent Garden. He'd hired the entire spa, and it was closed to everyone except the wedding party. Layla and Connie came over as well. At first I was surprised, but I supposed that Layla was as important as Alfie in Drew's eyes.

All the band guys' moms from Crakt Soundzz and XrAid came along as well. So, by the time we added the immediate wedding party, and Elle's, mine, and Jack's mom, there was enough of us to make our presence felt.

We kept the beauty therapists on their toes with the various treatments we all had. All of us were preened within an inch of our lives by the time we left and more than a little tipsy when we got back to the huge suite in the Dorchester, which was a wedding present to Elle from the guys of Crakt Soundzz.

We sat up quite a lot of the night, drinking champagne, and talking about Elle's life to date. I shared more than a few funny anecdotes about her. We eventually decided we'd better get some sleep, or else Elle was going to look exhausted on her big day.

Fortunately for us, Elle didn't protest. I think she was becoming overwhelmed. I kept catching her looking at me, and I wondered if she was thinking about all the times we'd shared as young girls. I was full of admiration for her as well, wondering if I would be half as calm as she was the night before my wedding.

As she was settling down, my cell rang, SEXPERT ID flashed. I smiled and swiped to answer. "Hey," he cooed. "How did your night go?"

I smiled at the sound of his voice. "Apart from missing you, I had a good time."

"You missed me?" I could hear the smile in his voice.

"Sure, I did, I hate being apart from you." I sincerely meant it too. After everything that had happened, I couldn't stand to think of being away from him ever again. Yet we still had to work out what we'd do about playing in our bands.

"Okay, you can stop that right now." I didn't realize I'd stopped talking and was thinking. Alfie had broken into my thoughts.

"Huh?"

Alfie snickered down the line at me. "I could practically hear you thinking, 'if we're together, how can we both be in our bands'."

I swallowed hard. "Yeah, I was," I replied honestly, because it was something that we really needed to discuss and make decisions about.

I heard Alfie exhale, and I imagined he was making himself comfortable on his bed. "Well, what about this...we both stay in our bands. I respect that you still want to make your own music."

I nodded, even though he couldn't see me. "Yeah," I mumbled, wondering how we would work that part out.

"It isn't as hard as it first appears, Lily. Both bands are with the same record company. We're only going to tour for a maximum of three months a year now. Drew's getting married, and we're going to at some point, right?"

I nodded still not really believing I was really going to marry Alfie. "So, we will want time to be with our wives and to spend quality time with them." I smiled at that thought.

"Now, XrAid and Crakt Soundzz can either tour together, or at separate times of the year. That way I can tour with you, and you can come with me. We'll get the label to schedule studio time at the same time, in the same place, so apart from the occasional promotions, we'd spend all our time together. What do you think?"

He had really thought about this. He was a huge rock star, so could actually dictate his own terms now, and although we didn't have as much clout, he could use his to influence our schedules too.

"Alfie, if you could work that out, I'd marry you tomorrow." I giggled, feeling that there was a distinct possibility that I could really have everything I wanted with him.

"Okay, now it's time to get your beauty sleep, if I'm going to be seen with you at a wedding. I mean you have some serious competition tomorrow, I look completely hot in my tuxedo and pink cummerbund and tie."

The mental image he gave me made my heart speed up. "Oh great, now I have to try and sleep with that image of you looking all masterful like that," I mumbled.

Alfie chuckled, and we started to say good night, with several 'I love you' declarations between us, until Elle crossed the room and swiped my phone from me.

"Alfie, it's almost midnight, you need to let her sleep now so that she can focus tomorrow. Look after my hot man for me... and make sure you're both there on time tomorrow."

Elle smirked and touched the red 'end' button on my cell throwing it back at me. "Bed, Lily, or we'll both look like shit tomorrow."

She grinned wickedly at me as we crawled into bed, and after about ten minutes of Holly singing with Mandy, we all settled down and eventually fell asleep.

Chapter Thirty-Seven

OKAY I'M IMPRESSED

*W*hy didn't someone remind me not to share the bed with Elle? I spent the night being flicked by her leg, her elbows digging into me, and at one point she had her hands on my back pushing me toward the edge of the bed.

Elle must have been dreaming that she was dancing in one of her shows from the way she was rolling around in the bed. Drew must really love her. I struggled lying beside her for one night, and he'd have to do that for the rest of his life.

"Morning," Elle croaked, one eye peering vacantly at me. "What time is it?"

It was still dark outside but someone had gone to the bathroom in the night and left the light on, so we could see each other. "Five forty-five," I whispered. All the others were still asleep. Elle slipped out of bed and gestured to me to come in the direction of the bathroom. There was a huge Jacuzzi bath, a hot tub, and a sauna in it.

Elle began filling the hot tub and Jacuzzi bath and disappeared back into the bedroom. She returned with a bowl of fruit, chocolate strawberries, and a bottle of Krystal.

I raised my eyebrow. "It's not even six am Elle..." I was whispering, but she cut me off, "And it's not every day a girl gets married either, Lily."

I smirked. "True, but I don't want to be drunk and let you down in my duties."

She gave me a sly glance. "Nothing you did would ever truly disappoint me, Lily. Just don't fall over and rip the dress, and it'll all be good."

Elle grinned. "Who'd have thought this time last year we'd be sitting here with me, the blushing bride, and you, my maid of honor." She giggled. "Am I going to be your maid of honor, Lily?"

I smiled widely. "Sure, but I you might have to share that honor with Jack." Elle laughed loudly, nodding. "He'd be completely up for that too."

Elle's easygoing manner and relaxed tone left me in awe. It was her wedding day, yet there were no nerves. I was only going to be the maid of honor, and I felt nervous.

Settling ourselves in the hot tub we lay back chatting about memories from our past, and what had happened in the last few years. Elle was ecstatic that we'd be living near each other again, once the dust had settled from her wedding.

She told me she'd chosen, 'A Thousand Years' by Christina Perri as their first dance song, and for her, it was the perfect choice, because it was playing the first time she danced with Drew.

"What would you choose?" I didn't hesitate. 'Insatiable.' She smiled. "Alfie was writing it the day I met him, and I gave him the line, 'Music is the sound of feelings and she listened to what he felt', and it's about making love, and how fiercely the guy felt about the girl he was making love to."

Elle was smiling wistfully. "Yeah, why did I even need to ask that question?" She smiled, then leaned over and hugged me. "We're going to a wedding today, Lily," Elle exclaimed, wiggling her legs and splashing in the hot tub.

After about forty-five minutes, we crawled out of the hot tub looking like prunes, leaving the rest of the girls, who were now awake and had joined us, soaking in it.

Room service arrived with breakfast, but we didn't eat much. After that the room slowly filled with people, as a makeup girl and hair stylists arrived to make us look pretty.

Elle had treated everyone to some French lingerie and silk stockings; she'd thought about everything. Mine was made of white satin and delicate lace and all very sexy.

Bridesmaid dresses were all lined up hanging in huge carriers, with name labels on the front. Once our hair and makeup was done, Elle unveiled the dresses to us girls. Each was designed slightly different in the same material. Leanne had been doing a great job when I'd seen it at the one fitting I'd had, so I was excited to see what it looked like now it was finished.

Elle was in charge, pulling each dress off the hangers one by one, after calling the name on the label. She looked visibly distressed when mine was missing. Her eyes met mine, and they flitted away in the direction of her mom. In hushed tones, Elle and her mom discussed my missing dress. Maggie, Elle's mom, left the room to track down the missing garment.

Concentrating on Elle, I helped her into the beautiful wedding gown. It took my mind off my missing dress. I was careful not to show my concern, because I didn't want anything to spoil the day for her.

Gasping at the visual effect of Elle in her dress and makeup, I hugged her tightly and fought back my tears. I was speechless and had a huge lump in my throat. Elle was a beautiful, elegant-looking woman, but dressed in her gown, with her hair like that, she looked stunning. I didn't think I'd ever seen a more beautiful bride.

Holly and Mandy came over, because I had dressed Elle behind a screen. They were full of wonderful compliments, and Elle had a permanent smile and looked radiantly happy.

Rosie headed out to make sure the flowers had arrived and they were set up outside the wedding suite, ready for everyone to pick up. This should have been my job, but as I was still semi-naked, she had volunteered to do this for me.

Elle's mom and mine pushed into the room, both carrying the missing garment bag. The way they were carrying it between them, anyone would have thought it weighed a ton.

Elle smirked at me. "Come here, Lily, I want a little chat with you while we're both still single." I giggled and went over to the bedroom area, which was separated from the living area for our little moment together.

"Nervous?" I searched Elle's face for signs, but she looked completely happy and relaxed. "Nope. Not at all. Not with my best friend with me all the way." I was really touched by her comment and felt privileged to have a friend like her. She'd always been so confident and encouraging to me.

"There's something I have to give you, and you need to have it now." She took a deep breath, and it was the first sign of nerves I had seen in her all day. I knew it was traditional to have a small gift from the bride. I was glad she was giving it to me privately, because it was an emotional moment, and I felt close to tears.

Elle handed me an envelope, and I could see the apprehension on her face. Her nerves were definitely getting to her.

Tentatively, I tore the envelope open, and there were a bunch of papers inside. My eyes flicked up at hers in confusion, and back to the papers I'd been unfolding while looking at her.

I saw the record label heading, and read what it said. It

was a contract from the CEO, saying exactly what Alfie had told me he could make happen.

He'd organized for our future together, and I was ecstatic about it. I wondered what Elle was doing with it, and why she was giving it to me right before her wedding

Elle had a wide grin on her face as she handed me a small gold colored envelope. "Now, this one." I recognized Alfie's writing as soon as I saw it. When I peeled it open, some small rose petals fell to the floor as I pulled out a rich, vanilla-colored card.

Okay Lily, I kept my part of the bargain from our talk last night, it's time for you, my beautiful girl, to make good on yours. Last night you told me you would marry me tomorrow, if I could arrange what you just read in the contract. So...come downstairs and meet me, the future Mrs. Black. I'm waiting for my beautiful bride so that we can write our own contract, and be signed to the most important label for the both of us. The 'Black' Label.

"I can't marry him today, not like this. I'm not hijacking your wedding, Elle. I have no dress or anything, apart from that..." Elle wagged her fingers at our moms to bring the carrier over. "Now before you go jumping off the deep end, Lily, we planned the wedding together. We chose everything together. You just didn't know we were planning it for the both of us."

My mother unzipped the carrier, and the dress I'd fallen in love with when I went to Elle's fitting was being pulled out in front of me. "Leanne made the final adjustments to it from the measurements she had."

Speechless and shaking, I swallowed audibly as I choked back my tears. "Are you serious? Mom, you and Dad knew about this?"

My mother nodded sheepishly. "We were worried that you wouldn't be ready today. Your dad and I had doubts about

Alfie in the beginning, but we can see how much he loves you, and we know you couldn't be in better hands."

Still shaking from the shock, I stared at Elle, and my mother came to help me into my dress. The soft cast supporting my arm was hidden once the silk and lace sleeve was slipped past it.

Elle had tears in her eyes when she looked at me. "I couldn't have asked for a more perfect person to share this day with, Lily. We've done nearly everything else together, so it made sense for us to kill two birds with one stone. This way we'll be able to celebrate our anniversaries together for the rest of our lives."

My dad and Elle's dad arrived, and Elle explained that Holly was going to be maid of honor for me, and Mandy had agreed to be hers. My dad looked at me, his eyes glistening with tears, only a hint of concern in them. "You're happy about this?"

I was. The whole thing was an incredible surprise. Alfie, along with my friends and family, had arranged everything behind my back, and I couldn't be happier.

The past few days began to make sense from trying on the dress to everything that was going on during the wedding rehearsals. We were rehearsing, too, just without my knowledge.

Rosie arrived back in the room with the wedding planner, Jenny, to let us know everyone was seated. Our moms and Rosie headed to the wedding suite to wait for us, after lots of fighting back tears, kisses, and hugs.

On my dad's arm as he walked me to Alfie, he dipped his head to my ear. "Lily, you are the most beautiful daughter any dad could possibly have. I am so proud of you, darling. Alfie asked me at Christmas if he could ask you to be his bride. I was worried about you living that life with a rock star, but after watching you together, I gave him my blessing." I was surprised they'd even had such a conversation.

My eyes brimmed with tears when I saw Jack dressed like my dad, standing just outside the door. I turned to my dad, and he grinned.

"Jack asked if he could come with me to give you away. I felt it was fitting. He's going to need some closure on your relationship as it was. You do know how two you are is way beyond weird, right? You can't behave that way after you're married," he scolded, but there was humor in his voice.

Jack smirked. "Well except for the times when Alfie isn't looking, Lily." He winked. I giggled. No matter what, Jack would always be important to me.

Music began to filter out from within the wedding suite. 'Love You Forever' by Ryan Huston. Softly and silently the doors to the suite began to open.

Elle leaned over at me. "Both boys picked this song because some of the lyrics fit with you guys and some with mine and Drew's past together." It was perfect.

Alfie's eyes connected with mine as soon as I entered the room. As far as I was concerned we were alone. Making my way to the front, I was mesmerized by his gorgeous smile and his beautiful features. He looked incredible in his smart, sexy suit. He was smiling widely, and his eyes held my gaze until I was standing next to him.

My dad and Jack both put my hand in Alfie's palm, and I heard the registrar ask, "Who gives this woman to be married to this man." My dad and Jack in unison said, "We do," before smiling and stepping back. As they did, Alfie's fingers closed around mine, and he squeezed gently. "Hey," he cooed.

Staring at his handsome face, I was having difficulty taking all of this in. I hadn't had time to write out any personalized vows, but as I barely managed to squeak out what the registrar asked me to repeat, I was glad I hadn't spent hours on that. Alfie wouldn't have embarrassed me by having a set of his own vows when I didn't either. Besides, we could do that on our honeymoon and recite them to each other in privacy.

I began to relax at the wedding dinner, and our reception went off like a dream. I insisted that Elle and Drew had the first dance. After all, Alfie and I had kind of butted in on their wedding. Elle had invited Will and his new girlfriend, Amy, and Alfie tolerated it because he knew I was his for life.

We were booked into another suite in the hotel for the night, but our honeymoon was postponed for two weeks until after my physical therapy was finished. He knew how important playing music was to me and my keeping to the recovery program.

When we danced to 'Listen,' for our first dance, Alfie sang the words into my ear. It was absolutely perfect. Elle and I did the bouquet-throwing-cake-cutting thing together, then kissed tons of relatives. It became a bit blurry about who was who, because of all the people involved.

Feeling eyes on me when I was chatting to one of Drew's relatives, I turned to see Alfie giving me a dark stare. I'd have recognized what was in his eyes anywhere. It was only ten in the evening, but Alfie smoothly made excuses about not tiring me out, and we left the reception before Elle and Drew.

Arriving at the door to the suite, Alfie dipped his legs and scooped me up into his arms. "Okay, Mrs. Black. Are you ready for the long haul with me?" he asked, looking tenderly into my eyes, his glinting with mischief. I smirked and nodded, before burying my face in his neck.

Alfie swiped his card and opened the door. Pale pink rose petals were scattered everywhere. Red roses and white gypsum filled the room, and I realized we were in the penthouse. We had a perfect view of Wellington Arch at Hyde Park Corner just down the road.

Placing me back on my feet, Alfie bent and cupped my face in his hands. "Lily Black, I am so lucky to be right here with you. Thank you for picking me. You know you've always been my favorite." He smirked.

He dipped his head to kiss me softly, as his hand swept from the side of my face to the back of my head. He pressed my head gently toward him, deepening the kiss. I moaned deeply into his mouth. It was a kiss full of love and passion, and I had no doubt that Alfie truly loved me.

When we broke the kiss, we were both breathless. "Can you undo my dress for me, Alfie?"

He grinned wickedly and growled. "With pleasure, I've been waiting to peel this away since you walked into the room today."

Slowly unzipping my dress, it slipped away and fell to the floor. Hungry, hooded eyes lit up and slowly appreciated the lingerie, and my body inside of it. Alfie inhaled deeply.

"Fuck. God, I shouldn't swear, but you're just...perfect." He swallowed audibly with a click. His eyes had the green hue that told me that I was turning him on, and his pupils were huge now.

"Come here. Sit," he commanded. Sitting me on the chair, he went into his bag and pulled out his tablet. Scrolling through the screen, he tapped something with his finger and set it on the table.

'You Can Leave Your Hat On' by Joe Cocker began to play. Alfie rummaged in his bag again and pulled out a baseball cap, pulling it on backwards. A sexy smirk spread on his lips.

"Now then, where were we?" he cooed as he began gyrating his hips, making small circles with them, and moving them from side to side. This was my surprise striptease.

Sliding his jacket down over his shoulders, he pulled the material tight. Turning, he wiggled and twerked his ass at me, grinning over his shoulder. It was so damn cute, and it made me laugh. He let the jacket slip to his hands before swinging it above his head. Alfie's ass had always gotten my attention. "I hope you don't mind but I skipped on the satin thong today." He winked.

Continuing with his sexy dance, he started peeling the layers of clothing away, taking his tie off and looping it over my head, sliding it gently back and forth on my neck before discarding it to the pile he was fast accumulating on the floor.

When I saw his naked, hard body, and strong, pectoral muscles flex, I was digging my nails in my palms trying to control my urge to speed things up for him. I understood what Alfie meant now about it being torture to watch. Except, no one had tied my hands.

Alfie kissed me briefly, then turned back and began wiggling his ass closer to my face. I was tempted to bite it, but he turned and wiggled his bulge and started undulating his hips. His hand moved to the button of his pants and he popped it open, placing his hand on the zipper. I lifted my gaze, and his eyes locked in with mine.

All of a sudden, neither of us were smiling any more. "We've done it, Lily," Alfie cooed. "Nothing else matters, except that we're together. I'm gonna love you my whole life, Lily Black, and you're never going to doubt what you want again." Alfie's mouth covered mine again in a slow tender kiss.

Seeing the look of love on his face today as I had made my way toward him, I had no doubts that whatever challenges we faced, Alfie would work hard to help me figure it all out.

Music would always be an important part of my life, but my accident changed my mind about a few things. I could have died, but I didn't. It put everything into perspective for me. It put Alfie into perspective for me.

If you ask me the question today, whether I still feel as strongly about my music? I don't feel as strongly now as I did. My priorities have changed. I still want to stay in my band, but I don't feel compelled to make music like I did before. I don't want my music if it doesn't include Alfie.

"C'mere," my sexy husband coos. Turning, I meet his smoldering gaze. Alfie is lying on the luxurious, gold silk bedding. He's naked, sprawling out lazily, and his head is propped up on one elbow. He's wagging his finger in a 'come here' motion at me, and giving me his sexy, lopsided smile. He's absolutely stunning, and he's really mine. I am the luckiest girl in the world. Not because I married Alfie Black, the rock star, but because Alfie Black, the man, loves me.

THE END.

OTHER TITLES BY K.L. SHANDWICK

THE EVERYTHING TRILOGY

Enough Isn't Everything

Everything She Needs

Everything I Want

Love With Every Beat

just Jack

Everything Is Yours

Rick Fars' own story is coming December 2017

LAST SCORE SERIES

Gibson's Legacy

Trusting Gibson

Gibson's Melody

READY FOR FLYNN SERIES

Ready For Flynn, Part 1

Ready For Flynn, Part 2

Ready For Flynn, Part 3

OTHER NOVELS

ABOUT THE AUTHOR

K. L. Shandwick lives on the outskirts of York, UK. She started writing after a challenge by a friend when she commented on a book she read. The result of this was 'The Everything Trilogy'. Her background has been mainly in the health and social care sector in the U.K. Her books tend to focus on the relationships of the main characters. Writing is a form of escapism for her and she is just as excited to find out where her characters take her as she is when she reads another author's work.

FIND K. L. SHANDWICK ON SOCIAL MEDIA

- **KLShandwick.com**
- **Twitter**
- **Facebook**
- **Bookbub**
- **AllAuthor**
- **Instagram**
- **Amazon**
- **KL's Hangout Group**
- **KL's Newsletter**